Hailing from Sioux Falls, South Dakota, Megan DeVos is twenty-six years old and works as a Registered Nurse in the operating room. Her debut Anarchy series amassed over 30 million reads on Wattpad, winning the Watty Award in 2014.

THE ANARCHY SERIES

Anarchy

Loyalty

Revolution

Annihilation

Loyalty

MEGAN DEVOS

ORION

First published in Great Britain in 2018 by Orion Books,
an imprint of The Orion Publishing Group Ltd
Carmelite House, 50 Victoria Embankment
London EC4Y 0DZ

An Hachette UK Company

1 3 5 7 9 10 8 6 4 2

A CIP catalogue record for this book
is available from the British Library.

ISBN 978 1 4091 8386 0

Typeset by Input Data Services Ltd, Somerset

Printed and bound in Great Britain by Clays Ltd, Elcograf S.p.A.

www.orionbooks.co.uk

For Michael, my own Herc.

Chapter 1 – Reliance
GRACE

I blew out a deep breath as I squeezed my eyes shut in an attempt to block out the pain radiating from my ribcage. Every tiny bump we hit was like a sledgehammer to my side, no matter how carefully Hayden drove. I kept my face buried in my arms to hide my grimace; there was nothing Hayden could do about it and I didn't want him to feel bad for something he had no control over.

The truck hit a divot in the road and I felt the sharp pang vibrate through my ribs again, forcing air through my clenched teeth. My hand on Hayden's shoulder gripped the fabric of his shirt tightly in my fist as I tried to ward off the pain, and I felt the truck slow a little as he tried to be more careful.

I hadn't noticed the pain until after I'd climbed into the truck, the adrenaline from the fight and Hayden's words masking the injury. Now, however, it was impossible to ignore as red-hot pain seared through my ribs. I felt the sticky, warm wetness of blood plastering my shirt to my stomach, but the ache from my ribs seemed to be causing the most discomfort.

A shaky breath ripped from my lungs as I felt the truck manoeuvring through the trees, telling me we were finally nearly back to Blackwing. I jumped when a hand landed on my back, the movement causing pain to shoot through my nerves once again.

'Are you all right?' Malin asked from beside me, her voice equal parts concerned and confused. No one seemed to have realised I was injured at first, just as I hadn't. No, that was wrong – Hayden had noticed.

'Mmhmm,' was all I managed to reply, nodding slowly while I kept my face pressed into my arm that leaned against the back of Hayden's seat. Hayden seemed jittery beneath my touch; my hand on his shoulder was the only thing keeping me grounded as I tried not to let the pain take over.

'She's not all right,' Hayden snapped, his voice laced with anger. He mumbled something else I couldn't quite hear over the roar of the engine. My heart thumped once at his concern for me, even if it was hidden beneath his angry tone. I couldn't find the strength to reply, though, as yet another bump in the road sent a jolt through my body.

After a few more agonising minutes, Hayden finally pulled the truck to a stop. I hardly managed to lift my head from my arms when I heard my door fly open. Blood rushed to my head and I felt woozy as I turned to where he stood in the doorway. He took one look at me, his eyes darting to the red stain in my side, before stepping forward and looping his arms beneath my knees and back. He pulled me from the back of the truck easily.

'Hayden, I'm fine,' I lied, blinking once to try and clear my head. His arms held me securely to his chest as he started walking, and my arms looped automatically around his neck despite my protests.

'No, you're not,' he argued gently. The truck still hummed in the background with the engine running and presumably filled with the rest of our raid crew. Hayden hadn't said a word to any of them before pulling me from the back and carrying me away.

'No—'

'Grace, dammit, you're not fine,' he said firmly. I could practically see the frown on his face even though my head had fallen to his shoulder. The pain was making me dizzy. I felt pathetically weak that I had to be carried off like this; I'd endured worse pain and had made it through alone. I could take care of myself.

Or so I tried to believe as I let Hayden carry me further. I could feel the warmth of his body through his clothes and the way his heart hammered as I rested my head on his shoulder. I was relatively useless as I felt Hayden push a door open, cutting off the sunlight beating down on us.

'Docc!' he called sharply, making me jump and sending another shot of pain through my body. Hayden noticed the wince I failed to suppress. 'Shit, sorry.'

''S fine,' I mumbled in reply, squeezing my eyes tightly closed once again. I felt his thumb stroke lightly over my shoulder as he walked, the gentle touch soothing a little bit of the ache I was feeling.

'What happened?' Docc soothed as he appeared beside us.

'She tried to fight three Brutes at once,' Hayden explained quickly.

'Oh Grace,' Docc said quietly, partly disapproving and partly impressed. 'Set her on the bed, Hayden.'

'I'm going to put you down, all right?' Hayden said quietly. He sounded very close, which I found to be true when I opened my eyes. His face was only inches from my own, and concern was etched clearly across his features. His bright green eyes were locked on mine, and his brows were pulled low over them as he watched me.

'All right,' I responded weakly. I hated how shaky my voice was and I hated him seeing me like this – weak, vulnerable, everything I hated and tried so much not to be. As a girl it was already difficult enough to be taken seriously, worse was being an injured girl who had to be carried into the infirmary. There was no hint of pity in Hayden's gaze, however, as he gently set me down on the bed. His arms stayed around me until he was sure I was settled, and he only withdrew after I gave him a small nod.

'Where are you hurt?' Docc asked calmly as his deep brown eyes settled on me. I found it difficult to look at him, however, as Hayden's gaze burned intensely into my own. The moment seemed to linger on for far too long, and Docc had to repeat his question before I was finally able to look at him.

'Where are you hurt, girl?' he repeated patiently. My eyes flicked to meet his.

'My ribs, left side,' I said, grimacing as I tried to point at the area. The area was soaked through with blood by now, something he surely noticed as he leaned closer to inspect.

'I'll have to cut away your shirt to get you cleaned up. Hayden, if you'd kindly step out—'

'No!' I blurted quickly. Too quickly. I swallowed harshly before continuing. 'Hayden can stay.'

Docc studied me for a moment with a hint of a knowing glint in his eye before he nodded slowly. 'All right, girl.'

He turned and walked away for a few moments to retrieve whatever he needed, and my gaze quickly returned to Hayden. He leaned forward onto the bed, his hands splayed wide over the thin mattress only a few inches away from my own hand. It occurred to me that he might not want to stay even though I had just told Docc he could.

'You, um, you don't have to—'

4

'Shut up, Grace. I'm staying,' he said quietly, shaking his head slowly. My breath caught as his hand shifted to cover mine, his fingers winding between the spaces created by my own as he picked it up gently. My heart fluttered at his insistence, and the pain suddenly didn't seem quite so bad. Our moment was interrupted as Docc reappeared. His eyes flitted to our joined hands; he said nothing.

'Here, take this,' Docc instructed, holding out a pill and a bottle of water. 'For the pain.'

I did as he said and swallowed the pill. I felt the cool metal of scissors Docc had procured as he cut along the hem of my shirt, causing the fabric to quickly fall away. I was left in just my bra and shorts. Docc was very professional, and Hayden had already seen me like this, or even more intimately, countless times.

I winced as Docc probed gently around my ribs and resisted the urge to look. Past experience with wounds told me that looking only served to make the pain worse; it was better not to see the damage and let it impair your judgement. My gaze stayed fixed on Hayden's, whose eyes didn't waver from my own. His thumb trailed lightly across the back of mine, and he squeezed my hand encouragingly.

'Is it the cut that hurts?' Docc asked. I could feel him wiping away some of the blood with some kind of gauze, and the sharp sting of alcohol used to cleanse the cut.

'No,' I said honestly. The cut hurt, but it was just a flesh wound similar to the many I'd endured before. This pain I was feeling now was deep and achy, much different from the pain of a cut.

'Hmm,' Docc hummed quietly. He continued to study my ribs and I couldn't stop myself from looking down. I sucked in a gasp when my eyes landed on the damaged area, which only served to send another rocket of pain shooting through

5

my ribs. A long, jagged gash ripped diagonally down my side, starting on the front of my ribcage just below my chest and trailing four or five inches, and producing more blood than I had been expecting. It wasn't particularly deep, but the length of it made it look scarier than it was.

Much more serious, though, was the dark purple bruise that had already formed over my ribcage. Such instant bruising couldn't be a good thing, and I already knew what I feared before.

'Broken rib,' I muttered quietly, assessing along with Docc. The pain seemed to increase just as I knew it would now that I'd seen it.

'I'm afraid so,' Docc said calmly. His fingers put a light pressure on both sides of my ribcage that caused me to wince again and suck in a harsh breath.

'Don't!' Hayden said quickly. Docc's eyes left my injury to study Hayden curiously.

'You're hurting her,' Hayden added quietly, holding Docc's gaze.

I squeezed his hand lightly as I returned my gaze to him. He was looking at Docc with a deep frown before he felt me watching him and turned to look at me.

'It's all right,' I said. Concern flickered across his features again as he blew out a deep breath.

'Maybe you should step outside, son,' Docc suggested gently. I knew he would have to do more that would cause me pain, just as he knew Hayden wouldn't want to see it.

'No,' Hayden said firmly. 'I'm staying.'

'All right,' Docc sighed. 'Just know, she'll have to endure a bit more pain, so you be there for her instead of telling me to stop.' Hayden frowned but nodded.

'Good. Now Grace, I'm going to have to feel around a bit, so you tell me where it hurts the most.'

'Okay,' I said before taking a deep breath to ready myself. Hayden's hand was gripped tightly in mine as I nodded that I was ready.

Docc's hand slid gently over my ribcage, feeling cautiously for any protruding fragments of bone. The pressure hurt, but not unbearably as he tried each bone. He made it three or four times around before his fingers ran over one site that caused me to gasp in pain.

'There,' I wheezed breathlessly. My body shook as pain radiated through me.

Hayden let out a heavy huff next to me, and I felt his other hand land lightly on my shoulder. His thumb ran over my skin slowly, his touch distracting me just the slightest from the pain.

'All right,' Docc said evenly, noting the area before moving on. 'Tell me if it happens again.'

I nodded but didn't respond as I tried to block out the discomfort. I felt his fingers tickle along my ribs, but the sharp, stabbing pain I'd just felt didn't reappear. He finished assessing my bones and removed his hands, allowing me to open my eyes once more. They flitted to Hayden's, still watching me, before looking to Docc.

'Well?' I asked, afraid to hear him confirm what I had guessed.

'I think you're lucky,' he said slowly, gathering up supplies to stitch up my cut. 'It's hard to say without X-raying, but I suspect you've just broken the one. It seems to be a clean break and should heal well, but you'll have some pretty bad pain for a few days before it starts to get better.'

I blew out a deep breath of relief. One broken rib wasn't too bad, especially if it was broken cleanly. Shattered or fragmented ribs became much more dangerous as they tended to damage internal organs, so I was lucky to have avoided that.

'Unfortunately you can't splint a rib, so you'll just have to take it easy for a few weeks until it starts to heal,' Docc continued. He poured what I identified as disinfectant over my cut without warning, causing me to hiss in pain. Hayden's hand tightened around my own, as if it had hurt him, too.

'I guess that's good news,' I said through gritted teeth. He had started to poke around the cut, preparing to suture it. I already knew there wasn't anything to do for broken ribs, so this wasn't really news to me.

'So she'll be all right?' Hayden asked, speaking for the first time since Docc told him off.

'Oh yes,' Docc said, nodding slowly as he focused on my ribs once more. 'Ready for the stitches?'

I nodded and clamped my jaw shut, preparing for the familiar sting of the needle. I knew how rare anaesthetic was, so I didn't even consider asking for any. I wasn't from Blackwing and I didn't want to take away what was theirs.

I turned to look at Hayden. He shot me a tight grimace and leaned closer, his hand sliding up the side of my neck before landing on the side of my face. I could feel his fingers tangle into the back of my hair while his thumb lightly stroked my cheek.

'Just look at me,' he said quietly. 'It'll be over before you know it.'

I nodded and tried to keep my breathing even. I focused on how it made me feel to have Hayden there with me, by my side, when he didn't have to be. As much as I wanted to be strong and independent, I had to admit it felt good to know someone else cared for me enough to help. It was such a strange thing – to have someone clearly care for you – because I was used to handling things on my own.

Even back in Greystone, the only person I'd ever really leaned on was my father. Celt was always there for me when

8

he could be, but his position made his time limited and thus made it difficult to really use him as a support system.

My brother had always been too brutal, too brash to really be of much support outside of physical backup, and I couldn't remember ever having a conversation with him that didn't revolve around some type of violence.

Leutie had been my best friend, but she'd been too fragile to count on. I had always been the one to support her, for her to lean on, not the other way around. She probably would have been there for me if I'd ever needed her to be, but the fact was that I never had.

But now, as the needle ripped through my flesh to stitch me back together, I needed Hayden. I needed his hand on my face, his other hand in mine, and his steady gaze to hold me together. I needed the reassurance and the strong support, even though I was scared to accept it. As much as I didn't want to admit it, as much as I knew I shouldn't, I needed him.

My eyes never wavered from his as I tried to block out the pain, and his gentle touch never stopped as it brushed along my cheek. I found myself transfixed by his gaze, the intensity taking over my thought process so much that I could hardly feel the pain anymore. The blood that had dried on his face remained ignored, and I felt the urge to clean him up despite the fact that I was in the process of getting stitches. He was potentially hurt as well, but his every action so far had been to fix me.

'Almost done,' Docc said, breaking into the spell I'd fallen under. Hayden's brows jumped up once as he shot me a reassuring look.

'You're doing so well, Grace,' Hayden murmured, his voice low and soft. My lower lip bit into my mouth as a particularly sharp jab of the needle shot up my nerves. I blew out yet another shaky breath as I refocused on Hayden and his gentle touches. My heart hammered, although I suspected it didn't have anything to do with my injury.

With one final stitch through my skin, Docc cut the suture and placed a thin bandage over the area. My shoulders drooped with relief, the tension I hadn't been aware I was holding releasing now that he was finished.

'All done,' Docc announced. He gathered up his materials and straightened back up. Hayden surprised me by leaning forward and pressing his lips into my forehead lightly before pulling back again.

'Good job,' he whispered. His thumb ran across my cheek one last time before his hand fell away and he straightened up.

I could feel Docc's eyes on us, but again he remained silent, choosing not to comment on the obvious affection between Hayden and me.

'I'll get you something for the pain and then you're free to go,' Docc said as he moved toward his storage cabinet.

'Oh, no, that's fine,' I said quickly. I didn't want to take more of their supplies.

'Hush, child. You got half of this stuff for me so it's the least I can do.'

I sighed and accepted this, feeling selfish for not arguing further because it really did hurt. The sting of the cut would subside in a few hours, but the severe ache of the broken rib would linger for days, if not weeks.

'Here, take one of these every six hours, two if the pain is really severe,' Docc said, handing me a bottle.

'What is it?' I asked, squinting at the label that had worn off slightly.

'Hydrocodone,' he said evenly. I nodded as the familiar name registered and he pressed two different pill bottles into my hands. 'After roughly a week, switch to the Acet-aminophen. You can take that every four hours as you need it.'

'Thank you, Docc.'

It seemed like lame appreciation for all he'd done for me since I'd arrived here, but I didn't know how else to say it.

'Of course. Now get some rest, the both of you. Hayden, get yourself cleaned up as well. I don't want to see you in here with an infection,' he said sternly, his gaze flitting back and forth between us both.

'Will do,' Hayden said before refocusing on me. His eyes glanced down my body quickly before he seemed to realise I was still in just my bra. His hand reached automatically behind his head to grip his T-shirt. He pulled roughly, whipping the fabric over his head before sliding it off his arms and handing it to me.

'Here,' he said quietly. I accepted the shirt with a soft smile.

'Thank you.'

I managed to lift the shirt over my head with my arm that wasn't on my injured side, but ran into a few problems as I found it difficult to lift my other arm. Without a word, Hayden's hands landed on my wrists to help guide me into the shirt before he released me to pull it down fully. I tried not to blush, feeling ridiculously helpless already.

'Thanks,' I mumbled again. He nodded gently before speaking once more.

'Want me to carry you?'

'No, I'll be fine,' I said, waving away his offer. I leaned forward slowly and focused on keeping my face blank as I swung my legs to the side of the bed. Hayden hovered close by, clearly not believing me.

'No, here, let me—'

'Hayden, seriously,' I insisted. 'Just . . . give me your arm. You don't have to carry me.'

He sighed in frustration before extending his elbow to me so I could loop my arm through it and hoist myself up. A jolt of pain shot through my ribs again but I ignored it as I took a shaky step forward, leaning on Hayden for support.

'You two take care of each other, you hear me?' Docc called from behind us. I couldn't help the tiniest hint of a smile that pulled at my lips, liking the way that sounded.

'Of course,' I replied when Hayden didn't. He appeared too focused on getting me safely out the door. A low chuckle was all I heard from Docc as we finally made it to the door, which Hayden held open for both of us. The sun had started to go down now, setting Blackwing in a soft, golden glow.

I was surprised to see Dax waiting outside the infirmary as he leaned against the wall. The truck was gone, assumedly returned to its place and the supplies we'd gathered put away as well. As soon as he saw us, Dax pushed himself off the wall and came to join us. It was only when he was a few feet in front of us did I notice he had the photo album I'd retrieved for Hayden in his hands. He took in Hayden's lack of shirt before he realised I was wearing it.

'Hey,' he said, his voice sounding the most serious I'd ever heard. 'Are you all right?'

I couldn't tell whom his question was directed at, but Hayden remained silent so I answered.

'Yeah, I'm fine.'

'She's got a broken rib,' Hayden said after a heavy sigh. Clearly our definitions of 'fine' were somewhat different.

'Ooh, ouch,' Dax hissed, grimacing sympathetically as he glanced at me. 'Those Brutes will getcha.'

'I'll heal just fine,' I said stubbornly. Dax let out a low chuckle while he shook his head slowly.

12

'I'm sure you will. But hey, I, um, I found this in the front seat and . . .' he trailed off and glanced down at the photo album in his hand. Hayden's gaze landed on it before he reached forward to take it.

'It's mine,' he said flatly. Dax watched him curiously.

'Where'd it come from?'

'My house.' Hayden's voice was stony and firm, as if he didn't want to discuss this right now.

'Did you finally go in?' Dax asked in awe, his eyes widening slightly. It was clear he knew, to some degree, that Hayden had difficulty going to that place. Hayden sighed heavily and shook his head.

'How do you think she got hurt?' he said, flicking his head towards me.

Dax's gaze flitted to me, a mixture of awe and surprise written across his features. 'You got this for him?'

I could feel my brows pulled low over my eyes as I returned his loaded gaze. 'Yes.'

He looked impressed. 'Wow.'

Everyone was quiet as Dax seemed to figure it out: not only did it mean Hayden had told me that was his house, but he knew that I'd risked my own safety to get something for him. The weight of this was not lost on Dax as he took in our linked arms and the heavy expression on Hayden's face.

'You two . . . you're like . . . *together*, aren't you?' he said. It was a statement more than a question. In all honesty, what we were remained indefinable. I wasn't sure of much besides the fact that I had feelings for Hayden. Strong, strong feelings.

'We have to go, Dax,' I said finally when Hayden declined to speak once more. He seemed too focused on getting me back to his hut to be bothered with talking to Dax right now.

13

He frowned at me as we took a step forward and ignored Dax's statement. I didn't mind that Hayden didn't answer. We made it a few yards away before Dax spoke again.

'I'm still okay with it,' he called, his voice loud enough for us to hear but not for anyone else who might have been around.

'Bye, Dax,' Hayden called deeply, disregarding his declaration once again as we moved down the path. I couldn't help but chuckle, liking the united front against Dax's attempts to clarify things.

Our steps were slow and steady to cause the least amount of pain possible, so it took a while to finally reach Hayden's hut. I felt myself falling into a weirdly pensive mood as Hayden led me to sit on the edge of the bed. The pain didn't seem so bad anymore, and I suspected the pill Docc had given me was finally starting to kick in.

'Are you really okay?' Hayden asked quietly. I resisted the urge to roll my eyes, finding his concern sweet, but embarrassing.

'Yes, Hayden. I swear.'

He knelt down in front of me so his face was level with mine now. His hands landed on my knees, and I felt his thumbs trail lightly over my skin, making sure I was telling the truth. Without really thinking, my hand reached forward to land lightly on his jaw. He sucked in a breath when my thumb traced along his lower lip, feeling the cut there that had dried with blood.

'Let's get you cleaned up, yeah?' I said quietly, my urge to take care of him kicking in once again now that I was, for the most part, taken care of. He sighed heavily, fighting his instincts to make me rest.

'Please, Herc?' I asked quietly. I wanted to wash the

damage away, clean him, fix him. I wanted to be there for him like he'd been there for me. Slowly, gently, he leaned his cheek into my palm as he blew out a sigh of defeat.

'All right, Bear.'

Chapter Two – Expunge
GRACE

'All right, Bear.'

Despite the still aching pain in my side, I felt my heart flutter at Hayden's use of his nickname for me. It was such a strange, unfamiliar thing to feel – like a *girl*. These stirrings of emotion and urges to take care of him were things I'd never felt before nor even imagined I ever would feel. The unsteady beat of my heart and flipping of my stomach made me feel warm, and I couldn't deny I liked it.

I could feel the warmth of his skin beneath my touch as my hand remained on his jaw. His gaze held a certain vulnerability I never thought I would see, but it was hard to miss as he watched me closely while kneeling in front of me. Blood still caked his face, and my urge to get it off him surged once more.

'Come on,' I said quietly, running my thumb along his jaw once more before dropping my hand to his where it rested lightly on my knee. I picked it up gently, noting for the first time that it, too, was stained with blood and heavily cut. After taking a deep breath, I lifted myself from the bed and focused on keeping my face even to mask the pain. Hayden didn't like seeing it, and I didn't want to hurt him any more than he'd already been.

His hand closed around mine cautiously as I led him

toward the bathroom, sending a spark up my arm. It occurred to me that his was the only hand I'd ever held besides my parents' when I was really little. Such a gentle touch seemed so intimate now as I felt his thumb slide over the back of my own, like the silent connection between us was linked by the innocent contact.

Hayden didn't speak as I pulled him to the small basin that sat in the bathroom and positioned him so he could lean against the wall next to it. I collected a small towel and sunk it into the basin. The temperature was cold and not at all what I would have liked, but it would have to do.

I felt my pulse quicken as I finally turned back to Hayden and met his gaze. He was leaning against the wall where I'd put him, his arms were folded loosely over his chest. I took a tentative step forward, the rag clutched in my hand, before stopping about two feet away.

'Are you sure you're all right?' I asked, noting the thin trickle of blood that had dried as it trailed from his lip down his chin. A few flecks of blood had dried across his cheek, though it was hard to tell if it was his own or not. He sighed and uncrossed his arms before reaching forward to place his hand on my hip and tug me closer to him.

'Yes, Grace,' he said quietly. 'I've had far worse.'

The memory of his jagged, marred back flashed through my mind as he spoke, the many scars proving his words to be true. He'd sustained countless injuries far worse than a cut lip and torn up knuckles, but the fact remained that I didn't like seeing him injured at all.

His hand remained on my hip as I nodded slowly and reached upward with my damp rag. I hesitated right before touching it to his lips.

'Sit still,' I said quietly. A hint of a smirk flashed across his face.

17

'Yes, ma'am,' he said lightly.

I took in a few more seconds of his intense eye contact before dropping my gaze to his lips to examine the cut. It was hard to focus as I felt the heat of his hand searing into my hip, but I tried. The cut seemed to have stopped bleeding a while ago and wasn't too deep, though his lower lip had swollen slightly because of it. My free hand reached up slowly to rest my fingers along his jaw, holding him steady as I pressed the rag down to the cut and started to clean away the dried blood.

He didn't flinch at all as I cleaned his skin, and his gaze remained ever unwavering as it was locked on my face despite me not returning it. I could feel it on every inch of my skin as he studied me silently, and I resisted the urge to ask what he was thinking.

He felt warm beneath my touch as I slowly dragged the rag over his chin, clearing away the last of the dried blood before running a clean part over his lip one last time. The green of his eyes seemed to be blazing and I could see a thousand and one thoughts racing behind them, though each and every one remained a complete mystery to me. It was like I was momentarily paralysed, unable to move or break the connection.

It was so unexpected and surreal, but standing in front of Hayden, someone who was once my enemy and captor, felt normal. It felt like I was supposed to be the one to clean him up after he was injured, like I was supposed to be the one he could lean on during times of vulnerability. I was certain that he had never allowed anyone to see him like this before, just as I hadn't, and it made me feel like I'd won something I didn't deserve.

Hayden's thumb circled lightly over my hip bone once. I blinked and drew in a shaky breath before bringing the rag to his cheek to remove the rest of the blood. There was no source, so I concluded it was evidence of what he'd done in the city.

'I usually do this myself,' Hayden said quietly, his gaze still focused on me. My eyes flitted to meet his momentarily before returning to my work.

'I thought you might,' I replied, washing away the last of the blood from his face. 'Not anymore.'

He was quiet as I leaned back to inspect him better and was pleased to see all that remained to be cleaned were his knuckles. I dropped my rag into the basin and reached down to grab his hand once more.

'Come here,' I instructed quietly, pulling him off the wall and closer to the basin. Slowly, I lowered his damaged hand into the cold water with mine. Almost immediately, the clear water was tinged with swirls of pink. I ran my thumb cautiously over his knuckles to brush away the blood. They were already an angry red in colour with a few nicks and cuts; by this time tomorrow they'd be dark purple in hue.

He continued to watch me with the same intense expression while I washed away the dirt and cleaned his hand, focusing mostly on not hurting him even though he would never say if I did. I was at a loss for anything to say, but I had a feeling that he wasn't in a talkative mood. He was oddly pensive as he watched me, as if thinking too many things at once to focus on speaking.

'Okay,' I said finally, brushing my fingers over his skin one last time. 'I think I've got it.'

I pulled our hands from the water and dried them off gently with a towel perched nearby. I felt a wave of relief wash through me as I examined him now, cleared of any blood though still slightly bruised. At least he was clean.

'Thank you,' he said softly. My hand still held his despite

having cleaned and dried it. Slowly, I brought it to my lips and pressed them into the knuckles gently in an attempt to draw out the ache he was surely feeling. He watched me closely, brows pulled low over his blazing green eyes as he took in my gentle action. My heart beat wildly in my chest.

'You're welcome,' I replied. I was surprised when he reached to grab another small rag and got it wet.

'Now you,' he said evenly. He didn't hesitate before stepping closer to me. His free hand tucked beneath my chin to tilt it upward towards him, and I felt the cool dampness of the rag run along my temple where I suspected I'd been bleeding.

Now it was my turn to watch him as he focused on me. Concern was still clearly etched across his face, and it was impossible to miss the hard set to his jaw as he worked to clean me up. His touch was gentle and soft, such a sharp contrast from the way he did nearly everything else. I could tell he was afraid to hurt me as he dabbed the rag over my skin, but his careful touch caused no pain.

I couldn't tear my eyes from his face as he carried on, swiping the rag once last time over my brow before pulling back to inspect his work. Finally, he must have been satisfied because he returned his gaze to mine and raised his brows once before tossing the rag back into the basin.

'Beautiful,' he commented simply.

'Thank you, Hayden,' I said, the volume mysteriously stolen from my voice. The tension that lingered around us seemed to be pressing in on me, taking over my ability to speak normally.

'Sure. Now come on, you need to rest.'

He ran his thumb lightly over my chin before dropping it and turning to leave. He moved smoothly out into the main room, where I followed him. Light flickered to life as he lit a candle and set it on the table next to his bed. I was about to collapse into the bed, which looked awfully inviting and comfortable, when he stopped me.

'Wait, here . . .' he trailed off before turning to his dresser. He pulled open a drawer and retrieved a shirt before turning to toss it to me. 'That one's covered in blood.'

I blinked and glanced down. I hadn't even been aware of it, but he was right. The shirt I was wearing, his from before, was stained with dried blood that must have come from the Brute he'd hit.

'Oh,' I murmured, stashing the new shirt between my thighs momentarily before reaching to tug the shirt off. I got the hem a few inches up my stomach before a bolt of pain shot through me and forced me to lower my arms once more. The grimace that crossed my face was too much to hide, and Hayden saw it easily.

'Here, let me,' he said quietly, stepping forward quickly to stop me from trying again. I let out a shaky breath as I tried to marshal the renewed pain and blinked slowly before nodding.

He reached to grip my shirt in his fingers. Slowly, carefully, he pulled it upward, until all of my stomach and chest were revealed. He managed to work my arm on my uninjured side out of the sleeve before he pulled it the rest of the way off my body.

I stood before him in just my bra once more, feeling vulnerable and comfortable all at once. Hayden's gaze, which had been fixed on mine up until this point, dropped down my body before it landed on my rib. A flash of hurt crossed his features as he took in the deep purple bruise that had settled over my entire side, the bandage over the jagged cut covering only a small portion of it.

'Jesus, Grace . . .' he murmured, frowning. He surprised

me by lowering himself so he was eye level with the wound, and I felt his cautious fingers drift feathery light over my bruised skin. His touch was different than Docc's had felt; Docc's had been clinical and purposeful, while Hayden's was meant to soothe and heal. The rough pads of his fingers traced the outline of the bruise lightly, sending chills up my spine before I watched him lean forward slowly.

My breath caught in my throat once again as he pressed his lips lightly over my ribcage, kissing the skin and letting it linger. Again and again, he kissed my skin softly until he'd covered most of the bruised area. My heart felt like it was going to burst out of my chest as he pressed one last kiss into my side before drawing back and returning to his full height.

'Please rest, Grace. I need you to get better,' he said quietly.

These gentle words and actions were too much for me to handle, and it was making my entire body feel hazy. All I managed to do was nod weakly as he pulled the new shirt from between my thighs where I'd stashed it momentarily. He worked the arm on my injured side through first before repeating his process backwards, and I felt the soft fabric fall over me as he put it over my torso.

'Rest,' he repeated quietly, ticking his head toward the bed.

'Okay, okay,' I said, giving him a weak smile. It felt like we'd been so serious for so long, and I didn't want him to feel so heavy. I could see how this weighed on him, and it made me feel guilty for putting him in this mood.

The bed sagged slightly under my weight as I crawled in and pulled the covers over me, lying on my uninjured side to keep pressure off my broken rib. I waited patiently for Hayden to join me but was surprised when he moved to the dresser and pulled out another shirt. He tugged it roughly over his head before I spoke.

'What are you doing?' I asked in confusion. He pushed his hair out of his face once before glancing at me.

'I'm supposed to go check on the tower tonight,' he explained.

'Oh, well—' I started to sit up before he shook his head at me.

'No, you're not coming,' he said quickly. 'I told you, you need to rest. This won't take long and I'm not going to make you climb the tower with a broken rib.'

'You made me climb right after I got shot,' I pointed out. I meant it as a joke but he didn't seem to get it as he frowned at me.

'That was different,' he said flatly, offering no further explanation. 'I have to go but just . . . stay here.'

He watched me with slightly narrowed eyes and I could tell he was thinking of how I'd betrayed his trust. He was hesitant to leave me completely alone even after all we'd just gone through. I resisted the urge to roll my eyes as I propped myself up on my elbow.

'I'm not leaving, Hayden.'

He continued to watch me and frowned slightly, drawing his lower lip between his teeth before he released it and nodded resolutely. 'All right.'

He turned from me and started to walk away before he seemed to change his mind. He spun around to face me and paused, opening his mouth to speak before clamping it shut once more. An amused grin pulled at my lips as I watched his internal battle, finding his rare awkwardness endearing. He sighed heavily and shook his head before taking purposeful steps towards me. I barely managed a breath before I felt his hands on either side of my face gently. He pressed his lips

23

into mine, letting them linger there for a few seconds and sending my pulse pounding. My eyes drifted closed for the few moments as he kissed me gently before he pulled back, keeping his hands on my cheeks.

'I'll be right back, Bear,' he said quietly. His thumbs ran across my cheeks once before he released me, cutting off my chance to reply before I could even catch my breath. He turned and moved quickly out of the hut, leaving me alone in his bed.

HAYDEN

An adrenaline rush I hadn't been expecting pumped my blood through my veins, the last-second decision to kiss Grace goodbye causing my pulse to skyrocket. I felt like an absolute idiot for being so indecisive about it at first, but couldn't say I regretted the final decision. Every time her lips touched mine, it was like someone set off a round of fireworks in my heart.

The last thing I wanted to do right now was check on the tower, but I couldn't ignore my duties just because Grace was hurt. All I wanted to do was comfort her and hold her in my bed, but I couldn't. At least not yet.

I shook my head vigorously as I began the ascent of the tower, my pace quick in my haste to get it over with. I needed to stop with these pathetic thoughts. It was one thing to finally admit I had feelings for her, but quite another to want to drop everything just so I could be around her. This was exactly what I'd been afraid of back when the stirrings of emotion had started, but I was determined not to neglect my duties. I'd given up trying to resist my feelings for her, but that didn't mean I had to completely lose focus.

It was completely dark now as I climbed, and the only light that could be seen was the light from the moon and the few scattered lanterns that flickered throughout Blackwing. A gentle breeze seemed to pick up the higher I climbed, and it ruffled my hair around my face. Finally, I reached the top to see Dax manning the post, his back to me as he surveyed the area.

'Hey,' I said. He jumped and jerked around to face me, clutching his chest dramatically as he stared at me with wide eyes.

'You scared the hell out of me,' he said, blowing out a huff of breath. I chuckled for what felt like the first time in years.

'Sorry.'

'Hmm, no you're not,' he grumbled playfully. 'What if I'd jumped so badly that I fell off the tower and died? You'd be real sorry then.'

'I think you're being a bit dramatic,' I told him, shaking my head and grinning all the same.

'We'll see how dramatic it is when I'm dead.'

'Okay, princess. You all good up here?' I asked, raising an eyebrow at him. I was eager to get back to Grace but I didn't want to appear so.

'Yeah, no action tonight. How's Grace doing? Broken ribs are no fun,' he said, watching carefully for my reaction.

'She's all right. Pretty banged up but Docc said it's just one most likely so I guess that's good.'

He nodded thoughtfully, glancing out into the distance for a few seconds before he returned his gaze to me. 'So . . . are you going to stop lying to me and tell me what's up with you two or not?'

He pinched his lips together and raised his eyebrows sceptically as if daring me to deny it. I sighed and pinched my fingers over my brow before shoving my hand through my hair.

'I don't even know,' I said honestly. I knew felt far more for her than I had anyone else, and I knew I liked being around her, but that was about it. We seemed to have fallen into some unspoken, pseudo-relationship that I had no idea how to handle.

'But you're *something*! Ha! I knew it,' he said, clearly satisfied with himself. I glared at him.

'Shut up, Dax.'

'I'm just saying, mate. You two are pretty obvious about it,' he said, shrugging.

'No we're not,' I argued flatly.

'You kissed her right in front of me,' he pointed out. He sounded extremely smug and it exasperated me.

'Well, then you should know something's going on, you idiot.'

He just shrugged again and grinned at me. 'I like it. I think she's good for you. Maybe you'll stop taking everything so seriously for once.'

'It doesn't change anything,' I rebuffed. 'I still have to do what I was doing before.'

'I know, I know. All I'm saying is I'm happy for you, all right? You deserve to be happy at least some of the time even if you insist on being miserable.'

I shook my head and let out another chuckle, pleased Dax approved even if he'd already made it clear he would.

'Just . . . don't tell anyone, all right? I'm not sure how people would take the whole thing since she's technically still a prisoner.'

He nodded easily. 'Yeah, sure thing.'

'Thanks.'

I was about to say my goodbye when a flicker of light

caught my attention. It had flared up for only a second before someone smothered the light quickly, but it was enough for me to catch. My face fell as I squinted into the night, something Dax noticed immediately.

'What is it?' he asked, turning around to glare in the same direction.

'There was a light over there,' I said, pointing towards where I'd seen it, which was not very far away at all. My heart dropped as I realised what direction it was in: the same direction as Greystone.

Dax picked up the rifle that was leaning against the railing and looked through the scope. He searched around in the darkness for a few seconds before he spoke.

'I can't see anything, it's too dark. Are you sure you saw something?'

'I'm sure,' I said, my voice low and serious.

I'd seen something, all right, and if the direction they were coming from told me anything, it was what was maybe most important. It appeared that soon, we'd have some unwelcome visitors from Grace's home – Greystone.

Chapter Three – Bedlam
HAYDEN

Wind rushed past my ears, blowing the dark strands of my hair into my vision as I squinted into the darkness. I was certain I'd seen a light; it hadn't been very far away, which meant that whoever it belonged to was far too close for comfort. My heart pounded as I considered the possibility of another Greystone raid, the thought of Grace alone, injured, and in an easily escapable position only adding to my distress. I only hoped my suspicions were wrong.

'Dax, we have to get down there,' I said quickly as I continued to survey the area. It was too dark to see anything, and I felt my anxiety creeping up at the uncertainty. 'We're useless up here in the dark.'

'Yeah, here, take a gun,' he said quickly, as he passed me a handgun and an extra magazine full of bullets. I stuffed them into my pocket and prepared the weapon before taking off at a sprint down the stairs. Dax followed close behind, and I could hear him speaking into the radio that usually remained at the top of the tower.

'Raiders coming in, everyone get into a building and secure your doors. Lights out, and be quiet. Again, raiders coming in,' he said clearly, stating the usual protocol for when we had enough of a warning to issue it. Usually it didn't come to this – we either took care of raiders before they got close enough, or we had no warning at all and had no time to prepare.

Radios were distributed throughout the camp, one in every communal building and every third hut. Those with the radios in their huts were responsible for telling those without. They were used only for emergencies, as the batteries drained quickly and were very difficult to come by. I prayed the one situated in my own hut was on, and that Grace would hear the warning and hide without figuring out exactly who was most likely leading the raid – someone from her home.

The countless stairs never seemed to end as we practically flew down them. I skipped two at a time in my haste to reach the bottom before the raiders reached the camp. Their stealth concerned me, as if they were being extremely cautious about being caught. I had no clue how many there were or what they were coming for, but a nagging thought in the back of my mind refused to subside as I tried to focus on simply protecting Blackwing.

They're coming for Grace.

No matter what I did, my mind refused to think of anything else. My thoughts flashed to the night I'd thought I'd seen something in the trees just beyond my hut only to discover the area deserted upon closer inspection. Had I missed something? Had someone actually seen that she was here?

It wasn't impossible, in fact, it was almost likely, and the thought haunted me as we finally reached the bottom of the tower. Every fear I'd had about Grace's presence putting so many lives in danger was potentially playing out right now, and I was in the worst position: torn between protecting my camp, and selfishly hiding Grace.

Dax's muttered words into the radio ripped me from my thoughts as we sprinted across the clearing surrounding the tower. My legs stretched and revelled in the ache that seemed to ease out of my muscles, and breath moved evenly in and out of my lungs as I ran. My back collided with the side of a building a second before Dax joined me.

'Hayden and I are by the tower. Get some people to run patrols,' he said, his voice a hushed whisper as he held the radio to his lips. He then held it to his ear, listening closely to the reply that I couldn't make out thanks to how far he had the volume turned down.

'Tell them to stay hidden. It'll be easier to get rid of them if we're stealthy rather than an all-out gun fight,' I whispered. Dax nodded and relayed my message. I assumed he was talking to Kit now, or potentially Barrow. Either way, I knew those that defended Blackwing would be prepared in a matter of minutes, a fact that gave me great pride to call myself their leader.

I felt a rush of pride for the people I protected. Not a single person could be seen on the pathways between the buildings, and the camp was plunged into near complete darkness thanks to everyone extinguishing the lights before we'd even reached the bottom of the tower. They'd reacted immediately, taking the necessary precautions and trusting those who were sworn to keep them safe.

'It's going to be hard to find them,' Dax muttered to me, keeping his voice low and his gun drawn as he, too, searched the area for movement.

'I know,' I replied grudgingly. It was nearly pitch black, something that would hinder both sides but them more than us; I knew every single inch of this camp, as did Dax, but they didn't. Not knowing where exactly they'd come in, how many there were, or what they wanted put us at a bit of a disadvantage, but I was confident we'd be able to defend our camp.

30

My eyes jumped to where I saw a flash of movement. It was a mere shadow shifting in the darkness, and I lost it as quickly as it had arrived, but I had seen it. Between two huts about one hundred feet away, something had moved.

'There,' I breathed, nodding in the direction I'd seen movement. 'Someone's over there.'

We remained hidden by the shadows cast over us as we observed, but no further movement could be detected.

'Let's circle around. You go left and I'll go right,' I instructed, holding the gun in front of my face to double check that it was loaded and ready.

'All right,' Dax whispered. I could barely make out the focused nod he gave me before melting back into the shadows to peel off from me. Careful to stick to the shadows myself, I kept my eyes locked on where I suspected movement while I crept ever closer.

My back pressed into the walls of whatever building I skirted behind, pausing long enough to glance around for any more movement before darting to the next landmark. I was nearly where I'd seen movement, but nothing had emerged from between the huts. Dax was nowhere in sight, but I knew he would be somewhere similar on the other side.

My ears pricked as I listened closely, but heard nothing besides the soft rustling of the trees from the wind. Slowly, cautiously, I stepped away from the final hut, gun raised and aimed into the dark gap.

A flash of movement caught my attention immediately, and my finger tightened on the trigger. On the other side of the gap, where I'd seen the movement, stood Dax, with his gun trained on me just as I had mine on him. I lowered my gun immediately and let out an exasperated huff.

'Son of a bitch,' I muttered, frustrated that after all that, there was nobody there. The second flash of movement I'd seen had only been my best friend.

'Jesus,' he breathed, his eyes wide as if his life had just flashed before his eyes. He physically sagged as he exhaled. 'Thanks for not shooting me.'

'Same to you,' I muttered distractedly. I moved to the edge of the gap and peered out into the path to search for more movement. 'All right, let's split up again and head towards the main buildings.'

'What do you think they want?'

'I don't know,' I muttered. I had the odd sensation that I was lying, even though technically, I had no confirmation as to why they were here. 'You take the left again and stay hidden. Use the signal if you need help.'

He nodded instantly. 'You got it, sir.'

I barely caught the sarcastic grin he shot me before darting away into the darkness. He knew how much I hated to be called sir. I shook my head, blown away that he could still joke around in the middle of being raided.

After glancing around one last time, I bolted from my hiding place toward the centre of camp. Every instinct I had was begging me to go to my hut, to check on Grace, but I ignored it. I had to put my people first.

My muscles were starting to really warm up as I reached the main buildings, and when I threw myself behind a large barrel that served as a rubbish skip, I felt pure exhilaration. I saw two shadowy figures dart across the path. It was difficult to tell if they were friend or foe, so I didn't fire.

I hunched low to keep myself hidden as I crept forward, following the path they'd taken. They didn't appear to notice as I followed, keeping about thirty feet behind them as I surveyed their shadows moving through the gaps in the buildings. They didn't enter any of them and seemed unsure where they were going, which told me they were most likely from Greystone. It surprised me that they appeared to have no gear with them besides the weapons they clutched in their hands.

I focused on keeping my breathing low and even as I followed, and I was surprised yet again as they ignored basically every storage building we had, passing up opportunities left and right to raid us for supplies. This could only mean one thing, and it made my blood run cold. My thoughts seemed to be confirmed as I observed them from my perch behind a stack of crates near the storage building.

I watched in horror as they pressed their faces into the windows to look inside. Never before had I seen raiders search through huts – they were usually more concerned with getting supplies and getting out.

Not these raiders. They were searching for one thing, and it had been the first thing I'd feared: Grace.

My stomach flipped over as I looked down the row of huts; the two were only five away from my own, where I prayed Grace had hidden herself. A brief feeling of relief washed through me as I saw that no light came from the window, but the hut was considerably larger than those around it, which would make it stand out. I had to get to it before these two, and they couldn't see me.

The two men moved away from the first hut and towards the second. I kept my gun trained on them but hesitated to fire. I didn't want to shoot and make my location known, especially if it would only draw more unwanted attention to my hut. My best bet would be to get there first, hide her, and defend her if necessary, especially since they didn't make any attempt to enter the other huts. At least whoever was hiding inside remained safe.

I needed some type of distraction. I frowned as I looked

around me in the dark, silently celebrating when my eyes landed on a rock in the dirt next to one of the crates I was hiding behind. My fist closed around it as I picked it up. I glanced at the raiders one last time to make sure they wouldn't see me as I rose to my feet.

Their backs were turned to me as I threw it as hard as I could in the opposite direction, pleased when I heard it clang loudly against some source of metal. I dropped back down to kneel behind the crates. I saw their heads whip around towards the sound. One of them nudged the other and pointed, to which he nodded before they set off the way I'd thrown the rock.

Pleased at my success, I waited just long enough until they disappeared between two buildings before I bolted from my hiding place. Dirt flew up from beneath my feet as I sprinted towards my hut, my legs carrying me silently through the dark. I knew it would only take them a few minutes to discover there was no one there and return to their search, and I didn't want to waste any time.

In a few short seconds, I'd reached my hut and landed silently outside the door. After one quick glance around, I opened the door and slipped inside, closing it quickly behind me. My back pressed into the wood and I immediately felt something sharp dig into the skin of my neck. It was too dark to see, but there was no mistaking the cold edge of a blade forced against my throat.

My adrenaline, which was already pumping ridiculously fast, seemed to skyrocket as I took in the situation. How the hell had someone got inside? Where was Grace?

'Hayden?'

I recognised the voice instantly and sagged against the door as a breath of relief washed through me.

'Grace,' I whispered, taking a deep breath as she dropped

the knife from my throat. I squinted into the dark but was unable to see her.

'Sorry, I thought you were a raider,' she hissed quietly. I didn't miss the strained tone to her voice and I remembered she must still be in considerable pain after getting herself out of bed.

'You were going to kill whoever came through that door?' I asked, momentarily forgetting our current situation and finding myself both in awe and impressed by her tenacity.

'Yes,' she said simply. I could practically see her shrugging even though it was pitch black. A thump from outside jerked me back to reality, ripping me from my consideration. It sounded like it was at the hut next to mine, which would be Dax's, and also meant the raiders had returned from their distraction.

'Shit, come on,' I said, reaching forward to where her voice had sounded. She hissed sharply as I accidentally nudged her ribs before finding her arm and gripping it firmly. 'Sorry.'

'It's okay,' she replied. She didn't resist as I tugged her through the darkness, thankful for my years of living in this very hut and my ability to navigate through it. There really was nowhere to hide as it was all one room, but my feet carried me automatically to the bathroom. At least that way, I could hide her in there and fight off the raiders if necessary.

I had just managed to rip the door open and shove our bodies through the frame when I heard mumbled voices from outside my front door. A quiet click sounded as I closed the door, my ears tuned for the tiniest of sounds. My hand remained on Grace's arm as I steered her into the corner, pressing her against the wall as I positioned myself between her and the door.

'No matter what happens, you stay in here, okay?' I

whispered, my voice so quiet it was almost inaudible.

'But Hayden—'

'No. You stay put, Grace.'

She was cut off from responding, at the sound of my front door opening. I squeezed my hand lightly and let my thumb trace over her skin before releasing her arm and turning around. My gun was aimed at the door, prepared to shoot if someone came through. The stakes were higher than ever.

The heavy footfalls of raiders' boots landed on my wood floors. They moved around inside my hut, every now and then rustling or banging something as they searched. I cringed as something crashed to the floor right outside the door, and I knew it was only a matter of time before they tried the door itself.

'You sure you saw her?' a voice said, the tone low and even despite the tense situation.

'I'm positive. She was here,' the other grumbled, clearly frustrated.

It was impossible to miss the gasp that Grace tried to stifle behind me, and I felt my heart plummet. She realised what I had already figured out – they were looking for her. It was also confirmed now that someone had been lurking just behind the tree line, but had somehow managed to escape before I came looking.

'But you don't remember which hut?' the first voice asked. It sounded as if he were trying to maintain his patience.

'It was one of these on this side, that's all I know. We don't even know if that's where she's being kept,' the second said defensively. I heard a soft rustling from behind me as Grace took a step forward before stopping herself. Her hand landed softly on my back before curling into a fist, and I could feel her forehead press into my shoulder blade. I

36

could practically hear the inner battle she was waging, and I couldn't blame her.

Mere feet away were two people from her home camp, searching for her, while I forced her to hide in a bathroom. She had to be feeling torn in two completely opposite directions, and I suddenly found myself terrified she would choose to make her presence known and leave me.

'I just find it hard to believe she's been here this whole time. The Grace I know would have escaped by now,' the first voice said sceptically. The mention of her name sent a dagger of fear through my heart. Grace's breath warmed the fabric of my shirt that covered my back, and I felt her press harder against me as if holding herself back.

'I'm telling you, it was her. And she was with their leader.'

Their footsteps had stopped moving, as if they had taken a moment to pause their searching to discuss. My eyes had adjusted to the darkness now, and a tiny sliver of light leaked through the roof to provide just enough illumination to make out whatever was within a few feet of me.

Grace's fist thumped lightly into my back in frustration before I felt it slide down slowly and fall to her side. My heart pounded once, anxious as to what her silent actions meant. Bravely, I turned slowly on the spot, lowering my gun to my side. She leaned back as I moved, and her face quickly came into my line of vision. Her brows were knit tightly together and her jaw was clenched firmly, her gaze blazing into mine even through the near complete darkness. My eyes flitted quickly back and forth between hers, desperately trying to read her thoughts as the conversation carried on just outside the door.

'His name is Hayden. How do you know it was him?' the first voice, the calmer of the two, asked. A brief flash of disappointment flooded through me that they now apparently knew what I looked like; in this world, it wasn't a bad thing to be anonymous.

'I just know,' the second voice growled. 'I can't believe Grace was stupid enough to get herself caught.'

'Maybe she wouldn't have got caught if you hadn't left her behind.'

My head jerked to the side as I absorbed the words. They sounded distinctly familiar to something I'd said to her, and I knew she heard it, too. There was no surprise in her face, however, as she had surely recognised the voice a long time ago.

These weren't just any raiders from Greystone. One of them, the angrier one, was none other than her brother, Jonah.

I caught the flicker of the silent battle going on in her head as she saw me make the connection. She was so close to me – only a few inches away – but I suddenly felt like she was about to slip through my fingers. I could see the way her chest heaved slightly as her breathing increased, the stress of the situation clearly getting to her. I could see the tension on her face and the way she both tried to hold my gaze and drop it all at once.

'Yeah, I got it,' snapped Jonah. It was very clear from the tone of the conversation that he'd heard this more than once. 'Believe it or not, I want her back, too, you know.'

The first voice muttered something I couldn't hear, but I saw the weight of the words reflect on Grace's face. Her eyes pinched shut and her nostrils flared as she drew a deep breath, as if trying to calm down. I couldn't imagine how she felt at that moment; to be so close, *so close*, to a member of your family but unable to reach them must have been the most painful thing imaginable. For a second, I considered what I'd do if I were in her situation.

I had no family left, but if I had, there was nothing that could stop me from getting to them. The fact that she still stood here, internally debating on what to do, seemed to speak volumes. I felt a surge of guilt as I realised that the only reason she'd have to stay where she was would be because of me. Surely if she revealed herself, they'd find me as well, and there was no telling what would happen then.

She really did care about me, and it was currently breaking her in half.

Despite knowing how torn she was, I wanted her to stay, and I wanted it desperately.

She held my gaze throughout this thought process, and I knew she could make out enough of my face to see my reactions. She still appeared torn, her body leaning forward slightly as if tempted to run past me while her fists remained clenched by her sides in an attempt to keep her there. There was no way I could stop myself from shaking my head slowly, silently pleading with her to stay.

She drew a silent breath, and I caught the way her jaw quivered and she tried to rein in her emotions. It was impossible to tell which choice she was leaning towards, but I prayed she'd choose to stay. Slowly, I raised my free hand and placed it on her cheek, the tips of my fingers brushing lightly over her skin before sliding back into her hair. She sagged under my touch, as if it had melted part of her resolve, and her eyes drifted closed momentarily.

'I just want my little girl back.'

She squeezed her eyes even more tightly as the words took effect. Just as with the first voice, she had identified it long ago, and it explained why she was having such a hard time. The pieces fell into place; I realised just who was standing only feet away from us: Celt, Grace's father, and the leader of Greystone.

Any hope I had plummeted to the pit of my chest. I could maybe compete with her arsehole of a brother, but her father, who she'd only spoken highly of and obviously missed desperately? I didn't stand a chance. My only question now was why she'd waited so long.

Green irises, nearly gone now from her widened pupils, were revealed to me as she opened her eyes again. Her lips parted silently and closed once again as if stopping herself from speaking, all the while her eyes remained focused intently on my own. My hand lingered on her cheek, my final silent plea for her to stay. The tension between us seemed to electrify the air, and I felt as though we were stuck in a kind of vacuum that sucked out all meaning of time. My breath stalled in my lungs, and I found myself more anxious than I had been in a very long time.

She was still my prisoner, but there was no denying she'd grown to be something much more important to me. I'd never felt the things I felt for her before, and I'd never wanted so badly to keep somebody safe. It felt wrong, frankly, to consider her a prisoner, and I couldn't find it in my heart to force her to stay if she truly wanted to leave. She was too much to me now to do that to her, and despite feeling weak, I knew if she chose to go, I would let her, even if it broke me to do it.

'I know,' Jonah said quietly. He sounded slightly less angry now than before, as if Celt's sincere statement had sunk in. 'Let's move on. We'll find her.'

'Good idea,' Celt said calmly.

The front door opened, and I heard them move through it. This was it – the moment Grace decided if she'd stay with me or reveal herself to the only living members of her family left.

My hand on her cheek seemed frozen in place, and

my thumb had stopped the careful tracing of her skin as I waited for her to decide. I held my breath in my chest, and I felt the depth of her gaze down to my toes. She had a pained expression on her face, brows pulled low over her beautifully green eyes. Emotions were rolling off the both of us, colliding and mixing in the air between us.

Even though we were silent, so many thoughts and unspoken words were flowing between us, the silent conversation riveting, captivating and heart breaking all at once. I knew what I wanted to say, what I wanted to beg of her, but I couldn't do it. She had to decide on her own, leaving my fragile heart on stand by, ready to shatter at the word.

Stay. Please, Grace, stay.

Chapter Four – Pronouncement
GRACE

The overwhelming silence between Hayden and I seemed to stretch on for an eternity. I could feel the weight of the silent conversation we were having as it filled the space around us and settled on my skin. This moment, right here, would determine my future. He'd made no moves to restrain me or stop me other than the silent plea communicated by his eyes. I could feel the tension radiating off him, see the desperation he tried to hide in his gaze, and practically hear his heart hammering as he awaited my action.

Or maybe that was my heart.

I heard the heavy footsteps of my father and brother growing distant, each step carrying them closer to the door and away from me. I hadn't been expecting to hear voices I'd recognised, let alone the only remaining members of my family.

Upon hearing Dax's warning over the radio I hadn't known existed until that moment, my first instinct hadn't been to hide, but to find Hayden. It had surprised me greatly when I found myself jumping out of bed, causing my ribs to ache with pain, and look for a weapon rather than hiding immediately. After extensive searching, I'd found Hayden's knife in the pocket of his jeans on the floor, and had been just about to run outside to find him when I'd heard a loud clang. The shadow I'd seen streaking through the darkness approached the hut I was in, though it was unidentifiable. It wasn't until he'd burst through the door and I had my knife at his throat that I realised it was only Hayden.

Now, looking into his eyes through the darkness, I felt like I was being torn in two directions at once. Half of me longed to push past him and follow my family, while the other half wanted to stay rooted on the spot with Hayden. It didn't seem fair that I had to make such a difficult decision, nor did it seem right that I was so torn.

Surely the decision was easy: family should win out over someone who used to be an enemy. But the pounding of my heart and the heavy thudding of my pulse in my ears seemed to indicate otherwise. His hand remained on my cheek, the warmth of it seeping into my skin as I listened to the front door of the hut swing open.

'Grace,' he whispered so quietly I almost couldn't hear. His voice was dripping with emotion and positively loaded down with pleas that somehow managed to squeeze into a simple word: my name.

All I could do was feel – feel the weight of the decision, feel the pounding of my heart, feel the warmth of his vicinity. All I could comprehend was the way he made me feel – alive, happy, respected.

Loved.

I heard the door slam shut, the sound of it jolting me from the trance I'd fallen under. My body seemed to decide before my mind did as I reached up to hold either side of his jaw and pull him down to me. His lips landed on mine, instantly sending my heart into a wild flutter. Hayden's arm wound around my waist while the other remained on my face, pulling me tightly against him as he kissed me. It was like every emotion we'd felt in those silent moments was poured into the kiss.

I could practically feel the relief flowing through him as he held his lips to mine, neither of us moving as if too over-come to fully react. My eyes squeezed tightly shut. He was everywhere – lips on mine, hand on my cheek, arm around my back, chest pressed to mine. He filled the air around me, smothering any thoughts I had of leaving no matter how ir-rationally I was thinking. It didn't matter that my father and brother were only yards away, getting nearer and nearer by the second; in that moment, all I cared about was Hayden.

Hayden made no effort to deepen the kiss as he held me to him, and my arms moved against my will to wrap around his neck. A bolt of pain shot through my ribs but I ignored it, the sensation dimmed in comparison to the fireworks going off in every cell of my body. It was irrational, spontaneous, and utterly compulsive, but at that moment, I couldn't find a single ounce of regret within me. Without a word, Hayden knew I'd chosen him.

Finally Hayden pulled back and sucked in a deep lung-ful of air. I felt like my entire body was shaking under the weight of what I'd just decided, but there was no denying the thrill that rushed through me every time Hayden kissed me. Every touch made me crave another, my desperation for it growing more and more insatiable by the day. Even light touches like his palm to my cheek seemed to set me on fire, and I knew that wasn't a normal thing.

How could I leave when I felt such things with Hayden?

His forehead dropped to mine and his eyes blazed into my own, the current of electricity between us almost over-whelming as I struggled to draw an even breath. It was a strange moment, hidden away in the darkness of his bath-room while Blackwing was being raided by my family, but in that moment it was as if the entire world dropped away, leaving us alone with our wildly beating hearts.

The deafening bang of a gun going off, however, was enough to rip us from our serenity as the sound echoed through the camp. Hayden jerked upward, his peacefully relieved expression falling from his face to be replaced once again by the intensely focused one I'd seen so many times.

'Shit,' he breathed, as if just appreciating what was going on. I couldn't subdue the panic that flared through me as I realised the likelihood that someone I knew had just fallen. My eyes flicked towards the door as my body lurched forward, ripping myself from Hayden's grasp as my instincts to run towards the action kicked in.

'No,' Hayden said, gripping my wrist lightly between his fingers.

'I have to see who that was,' I said. The warm feelings from moments ago disappeared completely as fear and confusion started to set in. What if that was my father? Brother? What about Dax? Kit? There were far too many people here that I cared about, no matter what camp they were from, and I didn't want any of them to get hurt.

'I'll go,' he said quickly. He tugged on my arm and pulled me back from the door once more, turning me to face him. 'You're still hurt and it's dangerous out there right now.'

'I'm not trying to leave but I need to know what's happening,' I pleaded. I had no intention of leaving him now that I'd given in to just how much I wanted to be there with him, but I had to see it for myself.

'You're not going to leave?' he asked, his voice cautiously hopeful despite the situation.

'No, I'm not,' I reassured him. My voice, which had been strongly urgent before, now held a softness as I realised just how relieved he was that I had chosen to stay. My heart

45

flipped over, as his lips pulled gently to one side in a soft smile.

'Good,' he said simply, his grip on my wrist still lingering in the dark.

Another bang jolted us once again back into the harsh reality of the moment. I heard a loud shout that was indecipherable echo through the camp, and adrenaline flooded through my veins.

'Please stay put, Grace,' he begged. I noticed the change in his demeanour as he, too, processed the sounds. His muscles tensed and his actions seemed more rushed, as if he wanted desperately to sprint outside but wanted to make sure I didn't follow.

'No,' I said defiantly, frowning at him. He pressed his lips tightly together and blew out an exasperated huff.

'Please?' he said through gritted teeth. He was clearly running out of patience, and I could feel his mounting frustration.

'No, Hayden, I'm going out there and you can either tie me down to try and stop me or come with me.'

He looked almost pissed off now as he glared down at me, his brows pulled low and jaw set sharply. His free hand shoved through his hair once before he nodded shortly.

'Fine, but you're staying right behind me.'

'Fine,' I muttered grudgingly. His hand slid up my wrist to clasp my own, tangling his fingers between mine as he turned on the spot and opened the door. I watched him reach behind his back to pull free the gun he'd stowed in his waistband, which reminded me to take the knife I'd dropped on the ground after nearly cutting Hayden. I stooped quickly on the way and retrieved it, arming myself as we moved out of the front door of his hut.

A quick glance around told us no one remained around here, and the loud bangs echoing from across the camp seemed to indicate where the majority of the action was. Hayden's hand remained locked with mine as he tugged me out across the path and through the gaps between buildings. The gun he held was raised and continuously sweeping, though it was becoming more and more obvious that no one was around here.

'You okay?' he asked, throwing a glance over his shoulder as we moved quickly towards the source of the struggle. The pain in my ribs hurt, but it seemed that adrenaline and the aftershocks of the way Hayden made me feel had numbed it slightly. That, in combination with the meds Docc had given me, made everything bearable.

'I'm fine,' I said honestly. He nodded curtly and continued to pull me along after him as yet another bang echoed out, followed quickly by muffled shouting. We had nearly reached the other side of camp now.

'They're getting away!' someone shouted, their voice understandable now as we drew nearer.

My heart leaped, but I wasn't sure if it was with relief that they'd got away and left Blackwing or disappointment that it appeared my family, if they had even survived, was now gone. A final bang rang out, the source of it clear now as Dax came into view holding a gun, just as Hayden and I came to a stop next to him. Kit and Barrow stood with Dax, all holding weapons as well.

'They're gone,' Barrow said, wiping sweat from his forehead. Grey hairs stuck out in all directions, as if he'd jumped up from his sleep to defend the camp. For a man in his mid-fifties, he was in excellent shape. I hadn't seen him for a while, but there was something daunting about him that was impossible to forget.

47

'What happened? Anyone hurt?' Hayden asked immediately.

Dax suddenly cleared his throat, drawing Hayden's attention and mine. His eyes widened and darted down to our hands, which remained linked. Instantly, Hayden and I dropped our hands and shifted away from each other, but it was obvious what had been happening before. Everyone seemed to be staring at us, though no one spoke. Hayden stared firmly back at everyone before he repeated himself.

'Well? What happened?'

'Greystone raiders,' Barrow muttered, choosing not to comment on what he'd just seen. He glared at me as if I had invited them over, knowing I was from Greystone. 'No one is hurt, but we didn't get any of them, either. They're sneaky bastards, the lot of them.'

I was torn between insult and pride as Hayden let out a silent sigh of relief, pleased that no one had been killed as he nodded. 'Did they take anything?'

'No. Curious, isn't it? That Greystone would raid but not take anything,' he said before pointedly glaring at me once more. I narrowed my eyes at him, not liking what he was insinuating. He clearly blamed me for the raid, and he was at least partially right. They had been here to search for me, but I had done nothing to encourage this.

'Well, it's a good thing no one's hurt and nothing's gone, then,' Hayden said sharply, jerking Barrow's attention back to him. I couldn't help but notice he stood a bit taller, his pride making him defensive even though I could tell he was trying to stop it.

'Yeah or maybe they just couldn't find what they were looking for,' Barrow said. 'Or rather . . . who they were looking for.'

'What are you saying? Out with it then, don't beat around the bush,' Hayden demanded, taking a defiant step towards Barrow. Kit and Dax remained silent as they watched the quickly intensifying exchange.

'I think they were here for her,' he grumbled, throwing his head in my direction while continuing to glare at Hayden. 'And I think she had something to do with it.'

I couldn't stop the derisive scoff that forced itself from my lips. It seemed painfully obvious that I'd done no such thing, but after all, I was still just a prisoner from the enemy camp, no matter what I'd done. Barrow glared at me once more before Hayden stepped into his line of vision. Though Barrow was more muscular, Hayden was taller, and his height proved to be quite intimidating as he towered over him.

'She had nothing to do with this,' Hayden said through gritted teeth. I watched in a slight stupor as the muscles in his back flexed tightly beneath his T-shirt.

'No? She's from *Greystone*, Hayden. The enemy. Or have you forgotten that since you've been living with her? She looks pretty now but I bet she's just waiting for the chance to slit your throat and run home to spill all our secrets.'

I couldn't help but think how badly he'd react if he knew just who my family was. If he was this upset at me for simply being from Greystone, something he'd known all along, I didn't want to see what he'd do if he ever found out who I really was.

Hayden took yet another step forward, his entire body tense as he tried to restrain his obvious anger. I wanted so badly to rush forward and place my hand on his back to calm him down, but I couldn't with so many pairs of eyes present. They'd seen us holding hands, but that could be written off as Hayden forcing me to stay near him. Actually, that still might have been what he was doing even with the hidden meaning behind it.

'Do you even know what she's done, Barrow? How many lives she's saved or how much she's helped us here? No one forced her to do any of it, but she did it. You don't know what the hell you're talking about, so I suggest you shut your mouth before I make you,' Hayden hissed. He seemed personally offended by Barrow's verbal attack on me, and even I had to admit how powerful and intimidating he looked and sounded at that moment. Barrow's glare faltered for a second and he took a step backward out from under Hayden's shadow, widening the distance that had somehow shrunk to only a few inches.

'All right, all right,' Barrow said, backing down. Hayden's hands remained clenched into fists by his side as he continued to glare at him. 'All I'm saying is . . . don't forget who she is, Hayden.'

'Got it, thanks,' Hayden snapped sarcastically. 'Why don't you go home, now, Barrow.'

His words were more of a command than a suggestion, and it seemed insane to defy him. There were times when I forgot that Hayden was the leader of Blackwing, and was so for a reason, but now it seemed impossible that I'd ever forgot. His tone held obvious authority and his body language clearly revealed just how in control he actually was. Barrow's small attempt at defiance had been smothered almost immediately despite being more than twice Hayden's age.

Hayden continued to glare at him as he backed away into the dark. Barrow slung his gun over his shoulder and gave a minute shake of his head that was not missed by anyone. He clearly didn't believe Hayden but wasn't brave enough to defy him. Hayden remained where he stood, practically seething on the spot, as he glared after him.

'Jesus,' Kit muttered, speaking for the first time. I found it difficult to tear my gaze from Hayden's obviously tense shoulders but finally managed to look at Kit and see his eyes widened in surprise.

'What?' Hayden snapped, jerking his head towards Kit accusingly.

'Nothing, chill, mate,' Kit said, raising his hands by his side. His gun was still clenched in his right hand, useless now that the raiders had got away. 'Barrow was out of line.'

It surprised me to hear Kit agree with Hayden. He hadn't been my biggest fan at first, but I liked to think he was coming around to me. He must have started to trust me more than I realised for him to not immediately agree with Barrow.

'No shit,' Hayden muttered grimly. He pushed his hand roughly through his hair, something I'd quickly come to know meant he was stressed. Again, my urge to rush forward and comfort him flared up, but I subdued it.

'What do you think they wanted?' Dax asked, joining the conversation. He had dirt smeared across his cheek and a dark purple bruise forming along his jaw, hinting at a fight of some sort.

'I don't know,' Hayden said, his voice still tense. He turned and cast a short glance at me before averting his eyes back to Kit.

That was a lie, though. Hayden knew exactly why they'd come, but he couldn't tell them why without revealing the fact that they knew I was here. It occurred to me that he would probably have to tell them at some point, but I knew he wanted it to be on his own terms that he could control. 'But at least everyone's okay, right?'

'Um, no, I got hit in the face,' Dax said, pointing at his jaw and raising his eyebrows. I couldn't stop the snort of laughter that burst through my lips. All three of them turned to

51

look at me, and a grin pulled at Dax's lips, pleased he'd succeeded in lightening the mood.

'Sorry,' I murmured quietly, waving my hand casually at him.

'Think it's funny?' he joked, pretending to glare at me.

'No, don't you see my own face? Nothing funny about it,' I said lightly, pointing at the bruises that surely covered my skin. It was odd that the damage to my face didn't seem to hurt, but I suspected my body was too focused on the pain in my ribs to really notice much else.

'You did get worked over,' Kit said as if noticing for the first time. 'Badass.'

He sounded highly impressed, which made me grin. I prided myself on my ability to fight and defend myself, never having liked the idea of being considered weak just because I was a girl. I could deliver a hit and take one just as easily as a guy could.

'Thanks,' I said happily. It was then that I noticed Hayden glaring at Kit, as if he disapproved of the new friendly tone he used when speaking to me. Only moments ago, he'd been pleased Kit had sided with him, yet now he appeared annoyed again. His eyes flicked to me, catching me watching him, and he blinked once before wiping the glare from his face. I tried not to smirk as I detected his jealousy.

It was completely misguided and not at all founded in reality, but I couldn't help but feel a flutter of satisfaction at the thought of Hayden being jealous. It wasn't the first time I'd seen flashes of it, but it was more and more gratifying each time. It seemed like something so trivial and normal in comparison to our world, which made it all the more fulfilling.

Poor Hayden had been through quite the emotional rollercoaster this evening, and I was almost completely to blame. I felt guilty for being happy about it, but I couldn't deny that I liked knowing I had such an effect on him, because it was exactly how he made me feel.

'All right, well, since everyone's okay, we're going back,' Hayden grumbled, speaking for me as well as himself. He stepped towards me and gripped me by my arm, steering me away from the circle. My shoulder jerked automatically, ripping my arm from his grip even though he hadn't hurt me in any way. I didn't like being led around like a child, and he needed to realise that. He blinked in surprise as he glanced down at me before letting out a sigh of resignation.

'See you, guys,' I said, waving over my shoulder at Kit and Dax. They both watched our silent exchange with slightly stunned looks. It occurred to me how strange it must seem – Hayden giving in to me so easily after backing Barrow down intimidatingly in a matter of seconds – but no one said anything.

'Bye,' Kit said, recovering from his slight shock.

'Bye, kids,' Dax said lightly, a knowing smirk on his face. I frowned at him as I remembered his question earlier.

You two . . . you're like . . . together, aren't you?

Dax seemed to have a pretty good idea of what was going on – a better idea than I did, in fact – but he didn't say anything else as Hayden and I disappeared into the darkness without a word. He marched stonily next to me, and made no attempt to touch me again after I'd broken his grip on my arm. I tried not to giggle at his bad mood, knowing I was partially to blame. Actually, mostly from me, but his anger at Barrow had darkened his mood considerably.

We made it all the way back to his hut before he said anything, even then it wasn't until he'd opened the door and followed me through that he spoke. I sat on the edge of the bed, relieved to finally be off my feet. The door shut a bit harder than was necessary, and it was obvious he was still in a bad mood. I frowned as he stalked over to the table to light a candle. I was pleased he was so affected by me but slightly put off that he was so crabby after I'd just chosen to stay for him.

'Hayden—'

'Do you like Kit?' he asked sharply, cutting me off and surprising me with his question. I blinked.

'What?' I asked blankly.

'Do you like Kit?' he repeated, his tone more tense this time. I frowned, surprised he even had to ask such a ridiculous question. At first it had been flattering to see him jealous, but now I just felt guilty that such a thought had even crossed his mind.

'Of course not,' I said slowly, hoping to stop this train of thought before it took off.

'Are you sure?' he demanded, glaring at me from across the room. I remained seated on his bed as I rolled my eyes.

'Yeah, Hayden, I decided to stay at Blackwing even though my father and brother were here so I could get to know Kit.'

He didn't say anything as he watched me. He leaned against the door now and crossed his arms over his chest before he blew out a deep sigh as if just realising how ridiculous he sounded.

'Well . . . I had to ask.'

'No, you didn't,' I said flatly. I still found it shocking he'd even thought that could be possible. It was one thing to get a little jealous over something, but another thing entirely to think I actually liked Kit. He didn't say anything but I could feel his gaze on me as he studied me silently. 'You're being paranoid.'

'Well, I've been through a lot of shit tonight, okay?' he

said exasperatedly. His frown softened a bit and his head tilted back to lean against the door, causing his skin to tighten over his sharp jaw. I had to shake my head once to tear my gaze away from it to refocus on his face.

'Oh, *you've* been through a lot of shit tonight?' I asked incredulously. I wasn't mad, but I had the odd sense that I was dealing with a stubborn child. His eyes, which had drifted closed momentarily, shot open as he snapped his head forward to look at me once more.

'No, shit, I'm sorry,' he said quickly. He pushed himself off the wall and took a step towards me before he stopped himself. 'You've had a more difficult night than I have.'

It was my turn to remain silent as I simply raised my eyebrows once at him and pinched my lips together. My gaze dropped to the floor, where I focused on a knot in the wood.

'It's just . . . I don't know. I've never felt jealous of someone before,' he admitted, sounding vulnerable. My eyes rose to meet his once more and I saw the obvious change in his expression. It was pained and confused all at once.

'I'm here for *you*, you know,' I told him firmly. My tone sounded almost spiteful, but only because I was frustrated with him for not seeing that. 'You. Nobody else, just you.'

I suddenly realised what I'd just admitted without really meaning to. I couldn't take it back even if I wanted to, though, as the words drifted through the air between us.

'You're really staying?' he asked quietly, as if afraid to. I sighed and rose from my perch on his bed to move towards him. He met me in the middle after seeing what I was doing, stopping only a few inches away from me.

'Yes, Hayden. I want to be here . . . with you.'

My stomach flipped over, and all the annoyance or frustration I felt seemed to melt away as he stepped even closer. He seemed to invade my senses as I felt his chest press to mine and his hand land on the side of my jaw gently. My gaze was locked on his as he gazed down at me, and I felt the connection that always seemed to be buzzing through me intensify. His words were just a quiet whisper as he said them, but they managed to set my heart aflutter.

'I'm glad you stayed, Bear.'

He sealed his words with a kiss as he ducked down and connected his lips to mine, erasing any doubts that may have started to creep up. Being there with Hayden was the happiest I'd felt in a long time, and I wasn't about to lose that feeling, no matter what it cost me.

Chapter Five – Intimate
GRACE

The world seemed to move in slow motion around me in a surreal blur, each second that ticked by seeming longer than the last as time stretched on infinitely. I couldn't quite wrap my head around how I'd wound up in this position, willingly choosing to stay in a camp with a boy rather than going back to my home with my family. The rational side of me was positively screaming at me for being so illogical, while the side I'd only recently discovered revelled in the inner warmth provided by my decision.

It had been made with my heart rather than my head, and I was still trying to figure out exactly how I felt about staying. I was still torn and very much terrified that my decision would come back to haunt me, but at the moment there was nothing but happiness as I felt the warmth of Hayden's chest pressed lightly to my back, something that was still so new and surreal yet wonderfully familiar all at the same time.

My body rested between his legs as he leaned back against the wall on his bed, and his arms were curled lightly around my waist where he was careful to avoid my broken rib. We hadn't said much after he'd kissed me, and I could tell that he, too, was having trouble sorting out what exactly tonight meant. Instead of tormenting myself further by overanalysing the situation, I decided to focus on how he felt, holding me, comforting me.

Hayden's hands were folded together over my stomach as he hugged me from behind, and I could feel every breath he drew as his chest expanded against my back. My head rested back on his shoulder while my hands traced absent-mindedly up and down the backs of his forearms. His legs stretched out on either side of my hips, and my knees bent to keep me propped up against him. My stomach flipped when I felt his lips press lightly at the base of my neck, such a gentle gesture from someone who was usually so resilient.

My eyes drifted closed as I enjoyed the sensation and re-laxed into him even more. It was almost like our bodies were cut to fit together, each curve and groove seemed to suit the other's. I loved to feel his heat through the light clothing I wore. His shirt had been discarded, leaving him in just a pair of shorts, as he so often was, and I'd found it difficult to tear my gaze from his lean, toned torso before he'd pulled me onto his bed and into this position.

Hayden's lips pressed to my shoulder once, the tank top I was wearing exposing a considerable amount of skin to his warm mouth. He let them linger against my skin, resting his lips there while he inhaled slowly. I felt his lips open as he drew a breath, as if he were about to speak, before he de-cided against it and closed them again where they remained pressed lightly to my shoulder. A soft laugh floated from my throat at his reluctance to speak.

'What, Hayden?' I prodded gently, making it clear I knew he was having some type of internal debate.

'Do you want to see something?' he asked quietly. His fingers unfolded from themselves and stretched upward to intertwine with mine, the palms of my hands resting on the backs of his.

'Does it require getting on a motorcycle?' I joked lightly. Curiosity flared inside me as I remembered the last time he'd shown me something. He chuckled softly and I felt the warmth of his soft exhale drift over my skin.

'No, it does not.'

'Good, I don't know if I could handle that,' I said. 'Yes, I want to see.'

'Okay,' he replied gently.

His lips pressed lightly against my neck one last time, hinting at the vulnerability he'd felt earlier before he shifted himself out from behind me. His long frame unfolded from the bed as he stood, his shoulders shifting and muscles flexing smoothly as he straightened up. He truly was the most graceful kind of powerful. He moved effortlessly to his desk that sat along the wall, and pulled open the bottom drawer. My heart leaped when he pulled out the photo album I'd retrieved for him and leaped again when he pulled out something else from beneath it.

The excitement I'd felt at seeing the photo album washed away briefly when he put it back in the drawer and closed it, leaving him with the other item he'd retrieved: his journal. The excitement and curiosity peaked again, though I tried not to look too eager as he crossed slowly back to me. He sat down on the edge of the bed and faced me, causing it to sag under his weight.

He held it gingerly between his hands, his eyes focused on the worn cover as if it might burst into flames. I didn't speak for fear of him changing his mind. I desperately wanted to know what kinds of things he wrote in there, as the last time I'd asked he'd been extremely vague and changed the subject almost immediately, even though it had been the night he'd revealed to me that he'd lost his parents.

'You can't read it,' he started out suddenly. I watched him carefully as his gaze flicked up to mine once before lowering back to the journal. 'Well, not all of it.'

'Okay,' I said calmly. I was more than willing to accept whatever he wanted to show me. He nodded once and blew out a deep breath. Green eyes focused intently on the book as he opened it. The worn cover opened to reveal the first page, which was filled with messy, scrawled handwriting that I couldn't read.

'I've had this forever,' he explained. 'Docc brought it back from a raid for me when I was about seven. The first twenty or so pages are just what Kit, Dax and I did that day because I was still practising my writing.'

I felt a soft smile pull at my lips as I listened. It was almost scary how easily I could picture a young Hayden bent over the book, concentrating on writing each letter correctly to record his day. I hoped it was filled with happy memories like going to the pond, among other things that normal kids should get to do. He held it closer to show me the scratchy handwriting.

'Then I got a bit older and I realised I had a sort of responsibility to keep track of things because no one else seemed to . . .' he trailed off as he flipped a few pages. The handwriting seemed to progress before my eyes, getting neater and more uniform the further into the book he got. 'So I wrote the memories I had of my parents.'

My heart clenched in my chest and I drew an involuntary breath as I realised the stories this journal must hold: things he could remember from before, what they looked like, how they died . . . It made me feel horribly sad for him to have to record such a thing at such a young age simply because he didn't want to forget.

My gaze flicked up from the pages to find him watching

me closely, a soft, sad smile tugging at his lips. I couldn't find words that would do justice to how tragic this actually was, but I did allow my hand to drift across the space between us to land lightly on his knee. My thumb brushed over his skin, which was warm to the touch, and again I felt a light spark shoot up my arm at the contact. His lips pressed together once before he continued again.

'When I started going on raids, I started to see people die first hand . . . so I wrote that down, too,' he said, flipping through a few more pages. He'd dropped my gaze once again, so I studied the obvious pain in his features that he was trying to hide, before letting my eyes land on the pages.

'Oh, Hayden . . .' I said quietly. 'It's everyone you've lost, right?'

He didn't look at me as he nodded at the list. There were two columns on the page: the first showed a name, and the second had a short description. I felt myself pale as I read a few of them, my heart clenching each time for the people I would never know.

John Garrity – raid into the city
Maria Fedderson – raided by Greystone
Bernard Olsen – raided by Whetland
Violetta Arendt – raid into the city
Sergio Koffman – raid to Greystone

On and on the list went, seemingly endlessly. He'd flipped more pages before he finally reached the end, and I realised with a jolt that the last name on the list was one I'd witnessed myself.

Helena Trodder – raided by Greystone

Maybe it was because I was sensitive to the name, but it seemed to me that Greystone had been on the list far more than any other, including the city. Irrational guilt flooded through me as I realised just how many lives had been lost because of my home. I shuddered at the thought that I could have potentially contributed. It wasn't unlikely that at least one of the names on that list was there because of me.

I suddenly felt sick as images of bodies stacked up around Greystone bombarded me, the countless faces unfamiliar yet no less impactful. So many people had died, and for what? Simply trying to survive and provide for those they loved? The carnage seemed so unnecessary, so wasteful, and I suddenly found it impossible to understand how our world had got so out of hand that it had come to this.

There was a reason Greystone and Blackwing were bitter enemies, and the proof was right there in front of me. Far too many humans had been slaughtered by each side to be forgiven. Hayden was the first person I'd ever come across who'd felt it necessary to actually make a record of some kind. The haunting truth reverberated through my skull, and I found it impossible to ignore as the grim reality I'd always known really set in for the first time: we were losing our humanity.

'Hey,' Hayden said gently, drawing my attention from the depths of my dark thoughts. I blinked once and refocused. 'I didn't mean to upset you.'

A jolt of heat shot up my arm as his hand landed on mine, covering it lightly with his while his thumb traced the back of my own.

'It's just . . . it's sick, isn't it? What a shambles of a life we have now?'

I didn't know where this was coming from; I was usually on the other end of the spectrum, insisting there were things to be happy about and to embrace in life, but seeing the physical evidence of just how many people had been senselessly killed, from a single camp, no less, seemed to make that type of thinking seem laughably naïve.

Hayden frowned at me and set the journal down in his lap before leaning a little closer to me, his hand still covering mine. 'No, Grace, you said it yourself. We still have so much to live for even if things are . . . harsh.'

'Harsh,' I repeated slowly, testing the word. It fit our world but didn't seem to do just how barbaric it had become any justice.

'Look, it's not all bad, see?' he said, squeezing my hand before releasing it to pick up the journal once more. He flipped to about the middle and scanned the page before turning it to me to read. His finger tapped to indicate I start reading.

Took Jett on his first shooting lesson today. Went dreadfully. Not a single ounce of natural talent, though he was happy and enthusiastic the entire time. He'll be ten next week and Maisie's managed to get ingredients for a cake. Found a toy helicopter on a raid yesterday for a gift. Hope he likes it.

I couldn't help but smile as I read the small excerpt. Immediately, the memory of seeing the exact toy helicopter Hayden had written about surfaced as I remembered the night Hayden had carried him home after falling asleep. To this day, he adored that toy and kept it where he could see it. I could easily picture how excited Jett must have been both about the cake and Hayden's gift, and it helped erase some of the crushing weight that had started to settle over me.

'Did he like his helicopter?' I asked, smiling softly at Hayden. He let out a low chuckle and shook his head.

'Loved it. The kid carried that thing around for over a year before one of the blades finally fell off. Dax fixed it up for him and he's still got it by his bed, last I checked.'

'I thought so,' I laughed. Hayden flipped a few more pages, scanning the words as he did so. He snorted a laugh suddenly before flipping it around to show me what it was.

Caught Kit and Malin sleeping together today in the back of the storage unit. Never want to see that again.

I burst out laughing as I finished reading, somewhat shocked that Kit, who was usually so serious, had been daring enough to have sex in one of the communal buildings. 'You caught them?!' His eyes crinkled slightly in the corner as he laughed at the memory and nodded.

'Yeah, would have been impossible not to. They were being so loud people thought there was an animal trapped in there so I had to go and investigate. I would have preferred to see an animal,' he said, shaking his head and chuckling once more.

I grinned, thrilled to hear that despite what it looked like, things weren't always so serious around here. There were indeed good memories scattered in with the bad, and the basic nature of humans had persisted even though our world had changed.

'It was scarring,' Hayden added lightly before flipping through the pages once more. My heart leaped as I caught my own name scrawled among the words as we reached the most recent pages. He didn't pause long enough for me to see what it said, but twice more I was certain I saw my name written down. When he reached the last page, he tilted it towards himself so I couldn't see at all.

'This is . . . amazing, Hayden,' I said with quiet sincerity. The air between us seemed to thicken, and it was as if, once again, the entire world had fallen away.

'Yeah?'

I nodded earnestly and let my thumb drag across his knee once more. 'Yeah. The fact that you've taken the time to record so much . . . the good and the bad . . . it's just amazing. People need to know.'

'That's why I do it — so people don't forget what happened . . . who we were.'

'It's admirable, Hayden.'

He paused for a few seconds as he returned his gaze to the page, resuming the internal debate he'd held earlier. He pulled in a deep breath before his gaze flicked up to meet mine, where I studied him closely. Then he turned the book slowly towards me. I saw a single word, which caused me to suck in a gasp of air when I recognised it.

Bear.

My heart thudded erratically as my eyes locked on his. It was such a simple gesture, just a single word, but the fact that I'd been included in the journal, more than once it would seem, made me realise just how real my feelings for him had become. More so, it seemed they were returned.

The space between us, which had shrunk to no more than a few inches, disappeared as I leaned forward to press my lips against his. The vulnerability necessary for him to show me the single word on the last page spoke volumes, and I couldn't ignore the palpable tension lingering in the air around us.

He responded immediately, setting the journal on the bed beside us as he leaned into the kiss. Warm hands clasped either side of my face, and his lips moulded perfectly against my own. There was a certain sensuality to the kiss that hadn't been present earlier, and I felt each cell in my body waking up as his lips parted mine gently to deepen it. It wasn't rushed, but there was an undercurrent of urgency there that spread from my lips throughout my entire body.

Both of my palms landed on his knees now, pressing flat to his skin as the fabric of his shorts rode up on his thighs. He leaned forward again, erasing even more space between us as he kissed me. The gentle swipe of his tongue pushed into my mouth, and the strangely intoxicating haze started to roll into my mind as my body took over.

Light pressure was applied to me as Hayden shifted his weight forward to lay me down. My back landed gently on the mattress as Hayden's body followed, hovering over me and holding himself up so he wouldn't put any weight on me. Even now, in the heat of the moment, he was aware of my injury and constantly cautious.

A soft gasp left my lips as Hayden's hips landed between my thighs, the pressure sending a spark through my body. His hands clasped either side of my head while mine reached up to rope around his neck and haul him down to me. Our kiss reconnected, and Hayden's tongue pushed lightly against mine as my hands tangled into his hair. It seemed like I couldn't get him close enough, because my fingers clutched the strands of his hair and my head rose from the mattress to kiss him fervently.

The only weight he rested on me was between my legs, even though I craved the pressure, the heat, though I knew I couldn't. The pain in my ribs was almost completely masked now by the endorphins that flooded through me, but I knew if he were to actually let his weight rest on me, it would be unbearable.

My heart was racing faster than normal as Hayden tugged lightly on my lower lip, before releasing it. In a split second, our eyes connected, and I caught the hint of lust that flashed through his gaze before he dropped his lips to my neck. Hot kisses were pressed to my skin, and my head instantly rolled to the side to allow him more access. My eyelids fluttered closed as I felt his lips part over my skin to allow his tongue to dart out and wet the surface before he slid down a few inches and repeated his actions.

A trail of wet kisses was made down my neck, covering every bit of skin before he reached my collarbone, where he nipped lightly and ran his tongue over the area to soothe the light sting. I completely lost my ability to think as I let my body take over. Soft strands of hair slipped through my fingers as my hands roamed down his neck, across his shoulders, and down his back at their own will.

Each kiss he pressed into my skin dipped a little lower and effectively chipped away at any ability I had to maintain control. I felt the shift in the mattress as Hayden slid his body downward, holding himself on one elbow now as his other hand snaked beneath the hem of my shirt. A soft gasp left my lips as I felt him push it upward, revealing my stomach to him inch by inch.

Just as he had before, he studied the dark bruise along my ribs as he hovered over me, his face level with my stomach now while I floated between watching him and darkness as my eyes closed against their will.

I managed to force myself to look down now, where I could see Hayden's lips pressing into my stomach, my skin revealed all the way up to the bottom of my bra where he'd pushed up my shirt. Dark hair sprawled across his forehead as he shifted downward. Again and again, his mouth connected with my skin to take away some of the ache lingering beneath, his weight shifting down my body each time his lips dropped lower on my stomach until he reached my hipbone where it met the waistband of my shorts.

Slowly, torturously, he pushed his hands up my thighs from where he rested between my legs until his fingers dug beneath the band. He paused, waiting for me to stop him. My lip bit into my mouth and I tried to force myself to breathe normally as I gave the tiniest of nods, giving him silent permission to continue. His lips tugged up mischievously at the side and I felt his gaze positively burn through me before he dropped his lips once more to my skin, probably searing a hole straight down to the bone.

Hayden tugged slowly on my shorts and underwear, pulling them down inch by inch tantalisingly slowly as he revealed myself to him. Kisses followed the band, his lips pressing into the skin as each new part was bared. He leaned backward as the layers passed my thighs so he could tug them off completely. My heart was beating so loudly that I could barely hear the sound of the fabric falling to the floor.

He held me firmly as he turned his head to my inner thigh, where his lips dragged slowly upward towards where I wanted him desperately. His thumbs rolled tiny circles over my hips as his tongue darted out to wet my skin; every second that ticked by seemed torturous as I silently begged to feel the heat of his mouth on me.

He was close, *so close*, to where I needed him, and I felt his lips pucker one last time at the place where my hip met my pelvis as I sucked in a deep breath to try and prepare. I could feel the hot warmth of his breath wash over me when he paused, flicking his burning green eyes up to meet mine.

'You need to be quiet, Grace,' he murmured, the tone of his voice sending a bolt of fire through my entire body. It was absolutely dripping with lust, and the quiet desperation was enough to make me lose control before he even touched me.

'Okay,' I breathed, unable to speak any louder than a

whisper because of the way he'd already stolen my breath. His eyebrow cocked upward in recognition, and that was all the warning I got before he dragged the flat of his tongue up my centre.

My head fell backward onto the mattress almost immediately as I felt his tongue flatten out against me again. My breathing, which had already been irregular, seemed to grow even shallower as he pressed his tongue to my clit, simply putting pressure on the bundle of nerves. Each tiny movement of his tongue sent a wave of pleasure through me; it was like every little flick of his tongue was working to unravel me, something he was accomplishing quickly.

My hands, which had been abandoned by my side after he'd slid out of my reach, clutched desperately at the blanket covering the bed while I tried to keep my hips from moving beyond my control. Hayden's tongue swirled around my clit again, the smooth circles building up the pressure that had started to grow in the pit of my stomach. His palms flattened out over my hips, putting enough pressure to hold me down while his tongue flicked relentlessly.

A strangled moan left my throat as his lips formed around the nub and sucked lightly, nearly sending me over the edge in a split second. I could feel my chest rising and falling quickly, and I could hear the moans I tried to suppress breaking through, but there was nothing I could do about it.

'Quiet, Grace,' Hayden murmured against me, the deep rumble of his voice sending shiver-inducing vibrations through my core.

'Shit, okay,' I panted, trying to collect myself.

I squeezed my eyes tightly shut and tried to keep quiet as he dragged his tongue up the length of my centre once more, his pace more eager and desperate than before. He alternated between using the flat of his tongue and the point of it to circle over my clit. His hands pushed down firmer on my hips as they struggled under his hold.

My hands started to shake slightly by my sides, their grip on the blankets not enough to subdue the buzz. I gave up trying to get a grip of myself and surrendered, tangling my hands desperately into Hayden's hair as he moved between my thighs – there was too much heat, too much pressure, too many deliciously agonising movements of his tongue for me to resist.

His grip on my hips was the firmest it had been yet as they attempted to rise off the mattress only to be shoved back down. The loudest moan yet burst from my lips as I tried and failed to stifle it when Hayden's tongue ran up my centre one last time before his lips closed around my clit and let his tongue flick over it to send me tumbling over the edge.

My hands shook in his hair and my vision blurred slightly as I felt the orgasm rocket through my body, taking over every single cell and nerve until I was completely enveloped in idyllic indulgence. Pants and gasps were all I managed as I struggled to breathe through it.

Finally, I started to come down and felt Hayden circle my now very sensitive nerves one last time with his tongue before he pressed a light kiss into my hipbone. I was positively gasping for air as he shifted himself up my body, pressing random kisses into my skin until he drew even with me. His face was flushed and his eyes looked wildly alive as he looked down at me, beyond thrilled to see me in such a euphoric state.

He dropped his lips to the hollow below my ear, kissing the skin once before I felt his mouth hovering at the edge of it.

'You weren't very quiet, Bear.'

I let out a wispy gasp of a laugh, still too overcome with what he'd just done to me to be embarrassed. It seemed like every cell in my body was singing with joy, rejoicing in the afterglow of my high. I felt light as a cloud, and all I wanted to do was revel in that moment with Hayden forever.

Chapter Six – Tantalise

HAYDEN

My chest pressed into her back, and I could feel every inch of where her body was in contact with my own, as if an electrical current was running between us. The skin was soft on her neck where my face had buried itself, and her hand remained tangled with mine even in the depths of her sleep.

Grace slept soundly, her body worn out after what I'd done to her, and I couldn't help but bask in the satisfaction that I was responsible for how quickly she'd fallen asleep. Just the thought of the way she'd reacted to my mouth was enough to drive me wild. Without really meaning to, I felt my lips pucker against the soft skin covering her neck, letting them linger there for a few seconds before dragging them upward.

A quiet hum sounded from her throat and she shifted ever so slightly, tugging my hand to cradle closer to her chest. I couldn't stop myself from dragging my lips further up her neck. A gentle shift in her breathing alerted me to her waking, and I took the opportunity to nip lightly at her throat, earning another quiet hum of satisfaction.

'Graaace,' I breathed into her ear quietly before tugging on it lightly with my teeth.

'Hmm,' she hummed softly. I smiled as her eyes squeezed tightly shut, as if fighting off my lips subconsciously. Her voice was scratchy and weak. 'What are you doing?'

'Nothing,' I said innocently. I managed to slip my hand out of her grip to trail my fingers lightly over her side, skimming over her skin enough to raise goosebumps on the parts of her that were exposed. Her tank top had ridden up to her ribs, revealing the dark splotches of bruises.

'Bullshit,' she murmured. My hand touched her hip and squeezed gently before she managed to catch it with her own, gripping it tightly as if to stop me. I grinned into the kiss I placed on her throat again, very much enjoying knowing that she was, once again, reacting to me.

'Good morning to you, too,' I said. I couldn't remember ever feeling so contented after waking up. She surprised me by twisting in my grip, landing on her back. My lips pulled from her skin and my arm remained draped over her, resting on her stomach now as she settled into the mattress. She narrowed her eyes at me suspiciously as she studied my face.

'What's wrong with you?' she asked accusingly, noting the grin on my face.

'Nothing,' I said honestly. She frowned at me playfully.

'You sure?'

'Yeah, why?' A light chuckle slipped past my lips as I gazed down at her.

Her green eyes seemed to sparkle a bit in the soft light that broke into the hut, and her cheeks still held a hint of a glow from the night before. *God, she was fucking beautiful.*

'You're being so . . .' she paused, searching for the right word as she studied my face. 'Happy.'

'Am I not allowed to be happy?' I asked, my grin widening on my face. It amused me that she found it so suspicious for me to be happy. She shook her head.

'Of course you are, it's just different. It's nice,' she concluded, finally breaking into a smile. My hand rose to toy with the hem of her tank top. My knuckles grazed lightly over her stomach as I did so and I saw her suck in the tiniest of breaths at the contact.

'Mmhmm, it is,' I agreed. I couldn't seem to rein in the light feeling flooding through me as I ducked my head down to press my lips into hers. She returned my gentle kiss for a few seconds before I pulled away.

'Now get up. I'm starving and I haven't eaten since last night,' I said, biting my lip to halt the grin trying to break through. A blush crept up her cheeks, freezing her in place in my bed as she understood.

'Hayden! Oh my god, who are you?' she asked, letting out a disbelieving gasp of a laugh. Her cheeks were bright red as I let out a burst of laughter, highly amused at myself and finding her embarrassment beyond endearing. She tucked her hair behind her ear in a flustered manner before sitting up gingerly and shoving the blankets off her, wincing briefly at the pain in her ribs. She shot me another grin, stilling my worry before it fully set in. It felt so good to laugh, even if it was over something so stupid.

'I had to,' I said, letting out one more solid laugh before turning toward the bathroom. Grace cut me off, however, as she scooted forward and reached the door first.

'Nope, I get to go first since you said that,' she said, a wry grin on her face. She slipped behind the door and was about to close it before she paused, leaving a crack open wide enough to show her face. 'Pervert.'

With that, she slammed the door shut and set me into another round of booming laughter. I loved that she didn't take me seriously and that she was able to laugh with me, even if she'd been slightly embarrassed by it. I felt light as a feather, lighter than I had in ages, as I crossed to my dresser to get dressed for the day.

Twenty or so minutes later, we were heading towards the mess hall for breakfast. There seemed to be an awful lot more activity than usual, and I had the distinct feeling I was forgetting something rather important. Groups of three or four people rushed by, chatting excitedly and carrying odd items to unknown locations. Some of them said hello to me while others seemed too preoccupied to even notice me.

'Does everyone seem . . . excited today, or is it just me?' Grace asked, frowning in confusion as three girls a few years younger than us rushed by practically squealing with delight.

'I noticed that, too,' I muttered. My eyes landed on two older men carrying a large barrel toward the centre of camp.

'Is something going on?' she asked, glancing at the same men I was watching.

'I don't know,' I admitted. She surprised me by snorting a laugh. My eyes widened as I looked down at her next to me.

'Aren't you supposed to be in charge? Know what's going on?' she said, letting out a very uncharacteristic giggle as she nudged me lightly in the ribs. I couldn't help but grin down at her.

'Watch it, Greystone,' I said, nudging her back while being careful to avoid her injured rib. I'd had to practically force her to take her pain meds earlier as she claimed she didn't really need them. It was only after she had been unable to put her shirt on by herself that she'd finally caved in and swallowed them.

'Really? Still?' she asked. It was difficult to tell if she was offended or not, but a hint of a smile remained on her face so I chose to drop it and made a mental note not to say that again. She hadn't really been offended, but she hadn't liked it either. *Shit*.

We were silent the rest of the way to the mess hall, which

was strangely empty thanks to all the people milling around outside. Only about ten people remained in the building eating, one of whom was Maisie standing behind the serving counter.

'Grace, Hayden,' she said brightly, nodding at us. 'Are you two getting excited for tonight?'

I finally realised what was going on. Maisie had asked nearly two weeks ago about this, but I had been distracted and agreed without really listening. A certain prisoner had been occupying more than her fair share of my mind, making it difficult to focus on other matters.

'Yeah, definitely. How's everything coming along?' I asked, pretending like I'd never forgotten. Grace stood silently next to me, clearly oblivious to what was going on.

'Well! I've been working on the food for days and Perdita has finished up her barrels of hooch for everyone. We're just working on setting up and it should be all finished!' Maisie was practically glowing with excitement as she spoke, and I was surprised when I felt a flash of legitimate enthusiasm.

'Sounds great. If you need anything, let me know,' I said, nodding as I accepted the plate she held out to me. Grace smiled at her as she took her own.

'Thanks. Just make sure you're in the centre of camp this evening for the fun!' Maisie said brightly before waving a small goodbye as Grace and I nodded in agreement and turned to go sit down.

'So,' Grace said, as she sat down across from me on the rickety wooden table. 'What's going on?'

'I totally forgot about it until now but Maisie is throwing a party, I guess you'd call it. She asked me weeks ago but I didn't even remember until right now.'

'A party?' she repeated. She sounded very perplexed by the idea. 'What for?'

'I don't know, really. She just thought things had been pretty . . . serious lately and wanted everyone to have a good time. She used to do them about once a month but we haven't been able to for a while now because we haven't had the supplies,' I explained. It had been at one of these 'parties' about a year ago when I'd discovered Kit and Malin in the storage unit.

'That actually sounds fun,' Grace mused, grinning at me before she took a bite of her food.

'Yeah, I guess,' I said, shrugging. I had never really got too into them before because I'd always been too preoccupied keeping an eye out for everyone. With most of the camp out at night and drinking the homemade hooch, it was more important than ever for me to keep everybody safe. 'Perdita makes this hooch that's pretty disgusting but gets people drunk, so it's always interesting by the end of the night. It's kind of like wine and whiskey mixed together.'

'Who's Perdita?' Grace asked, as if trying to remember if she knew her or not.

'You haven't met her,' I said, shaking my head as I took a bite quickly. I swallowed before continuing. 'She's about eighty-five and she's kind of insane, but she's really good at making explosives, which comes in handy. And . . .'

Grace's gaze jerked from where it had been focused on her food to meet mine as she caught me trailing off. 'And?'

'She did all my tattoos,' I said, watching her closely. Her eyes widened slightly as they darted to the ink staining my skin, which was most heavily focused on my left arm. I knew she had to be wondering how I'd got them, but she'd never asked.

'You let a slightly insane, eighty-five year old woman who makes explosives and hooch tattoo you?' she asked, a grin pulling at her lips.

I shrugged. 'That makes it sound bad, but yeah. Basically.'

'How does she do it?' Grace asked, curiosity clear in her features.

'Nails and animal blood, mostly.'

Her eyes widened and her jaw fell open. '*What*? Really?'

'No,' I said, laughing. 'She has a tattoo gun. Took the damn thing with her when everything fell apart and has kept it working since.'

'You idiot,' she said, grinning at me while she shook her head.

I felt a wave of happiness wash through me as she sat across from me, smiling and laughing lightheartedly. I almost didn't feel like myself as I indulged for a moment and took in the way her cheeks held a bit of a glow and the way her eyes lit up when she looked at me. It was such a surreal thing to feel so happy simply because of another person, in such a casual moment, and I never wanted it to go away.

She seemed to catch the wistful thoughts running through my head, because the light grin on her lips faded and her eyes grew more serious. I wondered desperately what was going through her head, the pace of her breathing hastening a little, indicating she had deep thoughts of her own. It was like we were sitting in a bubble that could burst any moment.

Our moment was interrupted by a sudden appearance to my left.

'Hayden!'

Grace jumped slightly and blinked, as if realising she'd been pulled under some sort of trance just as I had. I tried to ignore the slight disappointment I felt as the tension fizzle away. Turning to look at who had broken our moment, I quickly saw that it was a very excited looking Jett. I resisted the urge to sigh as I leaned back, unaware I'd been leaning so far forward. Across the table, Grace mirrored me, as if she, too, had been leaning inward.

'Hey, Jett,' I said casually.

'Are you excited for tonight? Maisie said I can stay out until it gets dark!' he said enthusiastically. At previous parties, Maisie had forced him to retire to their hut as the sun went down, claiming it was too dangerous for him to be out too late.

'Did she?' I asked, surprised. He nodded excitedly, practically bouncing up and down.

'Yeah! Grace, are you excited?' he asked. He still looked slightly afraid as his eyes widened, but he watched her determinedly. I suspected he'd got less wary of her ever since she saved him from the intruder from Whetland. I noticed he didn't wear a bandage around his neck anymore, showing only a faint line as evidence of that very incident.

'I don't really know what happens but sure, I'm excited,' she said, grinning at him.

'You'll see! It's so much fun!'

Her eyes were light and filled with admiration for Jett as she watched him speak. Her cheeks were pulled wide as she smiled back at him, unable to resist his enthusiasm as it infected her as well.

'Well, I can't wait then,' she answered happily.

'I've got to go. I'm in charge of setting up the chairs,' he said proudly, beaming at Grace before turning his attention to me. I quickly averted my eyes from Grace's face to meet his and nod reassuringly at him.

'Sounds good, little man.'

'Hayden,' he whined, unhappy with the nickname. I chuckled.

'All right, sorry. Sounds good, Jett. Run along, now.'

'See you later!' Jett said, grinning widely at us before practically sprinting out of the mess hall.

'That kid, I swear . . .' I muttered, trailing off. I scooped the last bit of food into my mouth as Grace let out a light laugh, her plate cleared as well. 'You finished?'

She nodded, gathering her plate and utensils as I copied her to dump them in the dishes bin. Together, we made our way outside where the hubbub continued. Excitement was palpable as people continued to set up, the centre of the camp being transformed before our very eyes.

'Should we help?' Grace asked.

'Yeah, I guess so,' I said shrugging.

Our afternoon passed quickly as we hauled seemingly endless equipment into the centre of the camp. Chairs, logs, and basically anything that could be used for seating, as well as several tables from the mess hall to hold the endless food Maisie had slaved away to prepare. The first barrel of hooch we'd seen earlier seemed to multiply as three more appeared, the last one carried by an obviously excited Kit and Dax. Massive logs were piled into the middle that would become a large bonfire later, and lanterns were scattered around to provide light once darkness fell. Much to Grace's exasperation, I made sure she did nothing that could potentially cause her any pain from her broken rib.

Evening was fast approaching when Maisie recruited Jett, Kit and Dax to help carry out the food while Grace and I were put in charge of setting it up. People had started to arrive, and before long, nearly all of Blackwing, except those on duty, had gathered in the centre. The mood, which was already light, seemed to lighten even more when music started playing. Several people had arrived with instruments and had set up to play them, entertaining everyone present and giving a relaxing vibe to the atmosphere.

It wasn't long before the party really began. People started to help themselves to food and drink, milling around excitedly while Kit lit up the massive bonfire to cast everyone in a warm glow in the diminishing light. Grace suddenly appeared beside me as I stood watching over the party, returning from her last trip to the kitchen.

'Wow,' she said simply, looking around in surprise. 'You weren't kidding when you said it's a party.'

I chuckled lightly and took in the scene, noticing that people of all ages had come out to enjoy the festivities. 'Yeah. It's a good thing, what Maisie does. It's so . . . normal. It's good for people to have something normal to look forward to.'

'I agree. We never did anything like this in Greystone,' she said softly. I glanced down at her to see her face illuminated by the firelight. A small, close grin remained on her lips, and I had to resist the urge to let my hand snake around her shoulders.

Too many people, Hayden.

'Well, you're here now,' I said gently, unable to tear my gaze from her face. As if she could feel me watching her, she turned slowly to look at me. A bolt of electricity seemed to jolt through me as her gaze landed on mine, and again I found myself physically holding back from getting closer to her.

'Hayden!'

Dammit.

I tried not to feel the irritation that flashed through me as our moment was yet again interrupted. I didn't even have to look to know who it was.

'Yes, Jett, how can I help you?' I said, a bit sharper than I intended to. Grace shot me a disapproving look. Jett seemed to shrink slightly under my gaze as I turned to look at him.

'I, um, I wanted you to come and dance with me,' he muttered, his excitement slightly diminished now as he pointed vaguely over his shoulder. I glanced up to see people of all ages dancing playfully to the music that reverberated through the camp. I was about to answer, an unintentional scowl on my face, when I was cut off by Grace.

'I'll dance with you, Jett,' she said warmly, smiling softly at him. He lit up immediately and a blush crept up his cheeks.

'You will?' he asked. His voice was slightly higher now as if he were nervous.

'Yeah, come on,' she said brightly. She tugged him away and cast the shortest of glances over her shoulder at me, so short it was difficult to read though I did manage to catch the smile on her face. I sighed, disappointed that she was once again being taken from me. My eyes scanned the crowd before they landed on Kit and Dax, who were sitting at the edge of the crowd with glasses of hooch in their hands. I moved to join them and sat down on the free chair to Dax's left.

'Hey,' he said, belching after. I cast a sceptical glance at him that he returned with a very wide grin.

'Hey, drunkard,' I said, clearly noting his current state. 'Not wasting any time, huh?'

'Where's the fun in that?' he said with a sly grin. His eyes dropped to my empty hands, noticing my lack of drink. 'Where's yours?'

'Here,' Kit said, jumping in and handing me a cup filled to the brim with a dark, brownish red liquid. My nose wrinkled as the putrid scent hit my nostrils.

'Thanks,' I muttered, taking a reluctant sip. The liquid burned on the way down, nowhere near the quality of the stuff Dax had found on our raid into the city, but for being homemade it wasn't that terrible. Dax seemed to be enjoying his enough, anyway.

'Anyway, as I was saying. You don't know how hard it is to run with your pants around your ankles . . .' Dax said, returning his attention to Kit as he carried on with a story I had missed the beginning of. Despite the promising start, I couldn't find it in myself to focus as my eyes landed on Grace.

Her hands were clasped around Jett's as she waved their arms in the air. A grin so wide stretched across her face I thought it must hurt her cheeks, but there was no denying how incredibly beautiful she looked in the soft lighting. Her blonde hair had fallen out of its ponytail a while ago and drifted over her shoulders as she swayed to the music, keeping both her and Jett in time with the rhythm. It was impossible to ignore the fluid way her body moved even though she was only dancing playfully. I found myself transfixed by the way her head was thrown back in laughter when Jett pulled some silly dance move out of nowhere.

As she raised her arm on her good side over her head to spin Jett in a circle, the hem of her shirt rode up over her stomach to reveal a thin strip of skin. The bruise from her rib had barely made an appearance before her shirt lowered again.

The world seemed to disappear around me. Every move she made reminded me of the way she'd writhed beneath my mouth last night. Every laugh and smile that crossed her face reminded me of the way her lips had parted and she'd gasped for air as she unravelled beneath my tongue. I had no control over the dirty thoughts flooding through my mind as I watched her in front of me.

She was so incredibly beautiful yet so devastatingly sexy

all at the same time, a potent combination guaranteed to ruin me completely.

Before I knew what I was doing, I dropped my drink unceremoniously to the ground and launched out of my seat. Her eyes never left mine as she tried to carry on dancing with Jett, but I could tell she was distracted.

The people I passed blurred as I moved. My heart pounded heavily as I finally reached her, coming to stop behind her. She remained facing Jett, her body tense as she froze and held her breath while my chest pressed into her back. Jett took no notice of my sudden arrival as he continued to dance, equally oblivious to his hands being dropped by Grace's as she stiffened when my hand landed on her hip. He danced away, distracted by a new partner who appeared.

'Come with me,' I whispered into her ear. My lips brushed against the shell of it and I felt a shudder run down her spine. Her heart, I noticed, was also pounding faster than it should have been as her back pressed to my chest.

'Okay,' she breathed.

She barely managed to suck in a breath before my hand slid around her back and down her arm to grab her hand, linking it with mine and tugging her silently through the crowd. No one seemed to take notice of us; everyone was too distracted by their drinks and their dancing to bother. My eyes were locked forward on the trees that bordered the camp just beyond the ring of the buildings in the centre, too impatient to make the walk all the way back home.

Neither of us spoke as we moved quickly through the now darkened area, the light of the bonfire not reaching here as we moved further and further away from the crowd. Finally, mercifully, we reached the tree line, and I pulled her with me into the dark shadow to hide us from view.

'Hayden, wha—'

Her words were cut off, however, as I spun around sharply and slammed my lips down onto hers, her face cradled desperately in my hands. She responded immediately as sparks exploded inside me, setting off a chain reaction and waking my entire body with one kiss. Her arms locked around my neck as she hauled me closer to her, and I couldn't help but push her backward until her back collided with the thick trunk of the tree we were behind that cut us off from the view of the party.

It was what I'd been desperate to do all day, driven nearly to the point of insanity before I finally caved and let myself do it. The stolen moment in the darkness was enough to breathe life into me again as I kissed her hungrily, my body unwilling and unable to stop craving hers. We'd opened a dangerous door last night, and somehow I knew that it was only the beginning of a desperate need I would constantly feel the need to satisfy.

Chapter Seven – Insatiable
GRACE

Hayden kissed me hungrily, deepening the kiss almost instantly as he let his tongue drag across mine. My body pressed into his desperately, using the tree as leverage to shift my hips against his. My hands tangled in his hair and tugged lightly, which only served to encourage him further. I felt my heart hammer erratically as he let his hands leave my face to rake down my sides, careful even now in his heated state to avoid my ribs.

Rough bark from the tree scratched into my skin as Hayden pressed me into the trunk, a sharp contrast to the heated warmth of his body pressing into my front. His lips moulded against mine desperately, and the wet heat of his tongue met my own. There was an urgency to the kiss that I had been craving without even knowing.

Breathy gasps ripped from my throat as Hayden tore his lips from my own to trail them greedily down my neck, devouring as much of my skin as he could with his painfully beautiful mouth. His hands landed on my hips, clutching them through the fabric of my shorts as he pushed against me to grind me further into the tree. The sensitive skin on my neck stung as he sucked harshly, earning a moan I tried and failed to stifle before releasing it into the warm night air.

'D-don't,' I managed to pant. The last thing we needed was a spot on my neck as evidence. 'They'll see.'

Hayden's warm breath washed over my neck as he exhaled sharply, frustration catching him as he detached his lips from my skin.

'I don't care,' he muttered, nipping at my neck just below my ear before tugging the lobe between his teeth. His mind was clouded by the obvious lust he felt at the moment, but his unadulterated words sent a bolt of electricity straight down to my toes.

It hadn't been my intention to put him in this current state, but I couldn't help but be grateful. It was unexpected, desperate, and undeniably, hot.

I managed to suck in a short breath before his lips landed on mine once more. His tongue delved into my mouth immediately, as his hand left my hip to trail over the front of my thigh. Without hesitation, I felt his palm slide between our bodies to slip between my legs, putting pressure on my centre and causing a surge of heat to run through me.

As much as I enjoyed Hayden's urgent touch, I couldn't ignore the obvious bulge between us as Hayden kissed me. With every ounce of self-control I could muster, I ripped my hand from around Hayden's neck to grasp his wrist. My efforts to tug it away from between my legs were met with resistance.

'Grace—'

I cut off his protest with my lips, kissing him impatiently as I finally managed to rip his hand away from me.

Before I could have any second thoughts, I reached between us to run my hand over his front where the obvious bulge protruded against my palm. His grip on my hip tightened as he tried to pull me against him, craving more contact as my hand slid away momentarily to trace the waistband of his jeans. I worked quickly to undo the button and zip of his jeans, Hayden's ragged breath washing down over me as he watched me intently.

I leaned forward to reconnect our lips as my hand traced over the band of his boxer briefs. My back pressed even harder into the tree as he pushed me against it. I slipped my hand beneath the fabric and wrapped my fingers around his length, the skin smooth beneath my palm. Hayden's chest rose and fell dramatically, and his deep moan was muffled as he kissed me harder.

I felt strangely powerful as he pressed his body against mine, hardly leaving enough room for me to stroke my hand over him. He was practically panting as I pulled my hand from him to push his shirt upward, ducking my head down to press my lips into his firm, flat stomach. Finally, I dropped to my knees in front of him, resting between him and the tree.

'You don't have to,' he whispered, his voice laden with lust and hope I wouldn't decline despite his words. I leaned forward and pressed my lips into his hipbone, letting them linger there for a few seconds as I tugged down enough on his layers to free him from their tight confines.

'I want to,' I answered honestly.

My eyes connected with his one last time as I sucked in a deep breath before shifting forward to run my tongue up the entirety of his length. As soon as my lips closed around the tip, he blew out an intense exhale above me.

'Jesus, Grace,' he muttered, his voice deep and gravelly as his body shifted against his will. I could sense the tension pent up in him as I pushed forward, taking more of him past my lips. My hands pushed up his thighs as I bobbed forward, sliding him in and out of my mouth in a fluid motion.

Each time I lowered my lips around him, he seemed to grow more and more restless above me.

I wanted to make him feel like he'd made me feel, but there was a selfish motivation to my actions, my desire to see him come undone because of me so overwhelming that I became consumed with the idea.

He struggled to stifle low groans, which only encouraged me further as I drew as much of him into my mouth as I could. Each time I pulled back, my cheeks hollowed out as I sucked, causing Hayden to draw his lower lip harshly between his teeth and his eyes to close before he forced them back open to watch.

'Oh, shiiit,' he groaned. Each word he uttered sent a bolt of excitement through me, pushing me even further. My grip on his thigh remained firm with my left hand as my right wrapped around his shaft, gripping him firmly as I tended to what my mouth couldn't fit. I could feel his body jerk uncontrollably now as he tried to resist his end, causing me to increase my pace as I let my tongue circle around his tip, delving around the curves and ridges to his length.

He was close, I could tell easily by the way he struggled to draw a full breath and the difficulty he was having controlling his hips. He slammed his fist into the trunk of the tree in an attempt to control his body, but it didn't work. I could feel his muscles straining beneath my palm as my other continuously rolled down his shaft in rhythm with my mouth.

'Grace, I'm—'

His warning was cut off, however, by a sharp hiss as he inhaled suddenly, his body tensing. I continued my actions until he was done. With one final swipe of my tongue along his length, I pulled back. I had just enough time to tug his layers back up to cover his now sensitive area before I was ripped upward, Hayden's hands gripping me easily to pull me up and push me back against the tree.

Immediately, Hayden's lips slammed into my own as he kissed me roughly, not caring about where my mouth had been only seconds before. His body pinned mine to the trunk of the tree, pressing into every single inch of me but somehow managing to avoid causing me pain. When he pulled back, his face was practically glowing as a beautiful flush crept up. I couldn't help but smirk slightly, beyond pleased with myself for putting him in this electrifyingly beautiful state. He hovered inches away as he tried to catch his breath.

'You're going to kill me,' he breathed. His head gave the tiniest of disbelieving shakes as my lips split into a satisfied grin.

'Not purposely,' I said as a half laugh, half exhale blew past my lips. The corner of his lips quirked up before his teeth raked over his lower lip. He blew out a final soft exhale of incredulity before he closed the distance between us one last time, his hand landing on my cheek to pull me into him.

My eyes had just drifted closed to enjoy the gentle kiss when he pulled away, hovering an inch away from my lips.

'We have to get back,' he said reluctantly. The disappointment was clear in his voice, but I understood why. We'd been gone far too long, and to remain shrouded by darkness any longer would become too obvious.

'Yeah, okay,' I agreed, nodding slowly. His eyes held my gaze for a few seconds longer, darting back and forth between my own in the close proximity before his hand dropped from my face. His touch slid down my arm and I felt a happy warmth travel through me as his hand claimed mine. Hayden tugged on it lightly as he turned reluctantly away from me and started heading back towards camp.

A soft glow emitted from the enormous bonfire at the centre of camp, making it easily located among the huts and buildings we wove through. Hayden held my hand as we walked, and I could feel the quick pulse that lingered in his veins in his thumb as it rolled smoothly over my own. I sneaked a glance up at him, unwilling to miss the lasting beauty his release had given him.

'What?' he asked suddenly. He didn't even have to look at me to know I was staring. His eyes flitted down to catch me, their green irises seemingly illuminated in the dim light. A ghost of a smirk settled on his face as he busted me studying him.

'Are you aware of how ridiculously attractive you are?' I said, throwing caution to the winds as I spoke without a filter. I was too exhilarated from what had just happened to hold back.

Hayden snorted a laugh and looked at me sceptically. His eyebrow kinked up as he looked down at me while we walked. 'Right. I don't think so.'

My jaw actually dropped at his denial. There was no way he didn't know. The way he moved sometimes seemed directly intended to make me sweat.

'I'm serious. You're just so . . .' I paused, searching for the right word. 'Beautiful.'

Hayden let out a low chuckle and squeezed my hand. 'No, Grace. That's you.'

All I managed to do was gasp quietly and shake my head in disbelief at his modesty as we approached the edge of the party. His compliment sent a wave of butterflies through me, and I could feel the warmth from it radiating through my heart. It seemed impossible that he didn't see what I saw, but it didn't surprise me in the slightest that he felt that way.

We had reached the outskirts of the party now, and I felt my hand swing free as Hayden smoothly released it. I instantly yearned for the connection again even though I understood why I couldn't have it.

We passed through little gatherings of people, each happier than the last as they relaxed and enjoyed the proceedings. Laughter, children's squeals of delight, acoustic music, and even some singing rang out into the darkness of the air, casting a festive atmosphere over the glowing camp. All of this only added to my elation as we made our way through the throngs of people.

'Hayden! Grace! Where did you guys go?!'

I turned to see Jett jogging excitedly towards us, coming to a halt a few feet away. He was slightly sweaty and had dirt smudged under his eye, but he looked thrilled to still be allowed outside. I felt a blush start to creep up my cheeks at the horror of Jett knowing exactly what we'd been doing.

'Don't you worry, little man. Looks like you've been busy enough without us,' Hayden said smoothly, noting his current state. 'What have you been doing?'

'Dax started a game but then he got too drunk to play so I had to take over,' he said proudly, grinning widely as he puffed out his chest. I bit back the laugh that tried to burst forth; I could only imagine the state of Dax right now.

'Of course he did,' Hayden chuckled. 'Well get back to it – can't let everyone down, now, can you?'

'No sir!' Jett said excitedly. I couldn't help but smile when for once, Hayden didn't correct him for calling him 'sir'. With that, Jett turned and ran back towards the small crowd of younger kids playing some game I couldn't follow.

'Please let us go and find drunk Dax,' I begged, grinning widely at Hayden. He drew a deep breath before blowing it out and widening his eyes at me, brows raised.

'You asked for it, keep that in mind,' he joked. His head ticked to the right and he started to move in that direction. I fell into step with him, but our journey was cut short as a loud burst of laughter reached our ears. I wasn't surprised when a laughing Dax came into view, a drink in his hand as he chatted animatedly with Kit, Malin, Docc and an elderly woman I did not recognise.

'—and then I swore to myself I would never try to wear a shirt as pants again,' Dax concluded dramatically as we approached. He raised his drink to his lips and took a long sip before his eyes landed on Hayden and me as we joined the circle, which was bursting with laughter at whatever Dax had said. A knowing glint sparked in his eye as he observed us.

'Well, well, how lovely of you two to join us,' he said smugly. Panic flared inside me as I remembered how much Dax actually knew, and I was suddenly terrified he would spill a secret that wasn't his to reveal. Hayden stiffened momentarily beside me before he recovered, his reaction nearly invisible to the rest of the crowd.

'I heard it was Dax's Story Hour so I just had to come over,' Hayden said coolly.

'I'm afraid you've missed the riveting tale, son,' Docc said, his deep voice calm even now as he let out a quiet chuckle.

I could feel someone watching me, and I quickly discovered who as I scanned the circle. A pair of deep brown eyes was focused on me, framed by wrinkly skin and wispy white hair that fell around her wizened face. As my gaze met hers, she smiled a nearly toothless grin at me.

'Nights are full of whispers, aren't they?' she said suddenly, as if she hadn't been listening to the conversation in the slightest. I blinked, both surprised and confused.

'Uhh . . .' I had no idea how to respond to such a statement as she continued to stare at me.

'Grace, this is Perdita. Perdita, this is Grace,' Hayden introduced, saving me from responding.

'Nice to meet you,' I said politely, grinning tentatively at her.

'The whispers of the night speak the truth, my dear,' she responded, nodding wisely at me as she closed her eyes. I felt my brows furrow as my jaw fell open before I quickly clamped it shut again.

'Sure do,' I agreed, even though I had no clue what she meant. Hayden ducked next to my ear to murmur to me.

'Ignore that — she says things like that a lot and no one has any clue what she means.'

'Ah,' was all I said, nodding. I recalled that Hayden had said she was slightly crazy, so I accepted that I would probably be very confused by a lot of what she said.

'But she's a badass, aren't you, Perdita?' Dax said, grinning widely at her. She didn't speak but nodded solemnly, closing her eyes as she did so. When she opened them, her gaze landed on Hayden.

'Hayden, you're looking refreshed on this whispery night.'

Again, a blush crept up my cheeks. This was the first thing she'd said that made some sense, and I prayed the others didn't catch on.

'I think I need a drink,' Hayden said, changing the subject quickly. Almost immediately, Kit handed him one, leaning forward from the chair he was sitting in. Malin stood behind him, her hands massaging lightly over his shoulders as she observed everyone in quiet happiness.

'It won't help with this crowd, trust me,' Kit joked, a wry grin on his face. 'Want one, Grace?'

'Sure,' I said, accepting the mug he handed me after grabbing it off the table the crowd was gathered around. I sniffed the murky liquid and immediately wished I hadn't as the scent stung my nostrils, but I braced myself anyway and took a drink. The hooch was bitter and harsh with a slight fruity undertone, unlike anything I'd ever drunk before, but there was no denying that it was potent. I sniffled once after I swallowed, attempting to keep my face blank under the careful scrutiny of the entire group.

'It's good,' I lied, causing the entire group to burst out laughing, including Hayden.

'No, it's not but it does the trick,' Dax said happily before taking another swig. I grinned and managed to take another sip, the second no easier than the first.

The mood shifted slightly when the music picked up from across the area as the group of people with instruments started up a lively song. The instruments consisted of a few acoustic guitars and a violin, and their sound reverberated easily through the camp. Dax made several people jump as he sprang to his feet suddenly, spilling half his glass.

'Let's go. Everyone. We're dancing,' he demanded. His hands landed on the people nearest to him, who happened to be Perdita and Hayden, as he tried to tug them with him. Perdita followed happily, raising a finger in the air to point in time with the music, but Hayden resisted immediately.

'No thanks,' he said, shaking his head. I was surprised when Kit allowed Malin to pull him from his seat, an appeasing smile pulling at his lips. Even Docc, who I had expected to remain where he was, humoured Dax and moved toward the quickly growing crowd of people dancing.

'Come on! Everyone's coming, you have to,' Dax said, throwing his hands dramatically in the air. The rest of the group had melted into the dancing crowd now, leaving just Hayden, Dax and me.

'I don't have to do anything, I'm in charge,' Hayden said with a slightly smug look. Dax scoffed loudly and waved off Hayden's excuse.

'Your girl wants to dance, don't you, Grace?' Dax said casually, causing both panic and elation to flare up inside me all at once. I resisted the urge to shush him.

'Dax—' Hayden started as his eyes darted around quickly to assess that no one was within earshot.

'Don't even deny it,' Dax said, cutting him off. Hayden huffed a sigh but didn't protest. Dax grinned smugly at him. 'Now, as I said, your girl wants to dance.'

My heart leaped at the simple fact that Hayden no longer denied Dax's statement. In a flash of bravery, I spoke.

'Come dance with me, Hayden.'

Hayden's gaze, which had been switching between Dax and the people around us, flashed to me suddenly. He frowned, his arms crossed over his chest as he observed me.

'I don't dance,' he said simply.

'Hup, you've had your chance, mate. She's mine now!' Dax exclaimed, linking his arm with mine and jerking me away from Hayden unceremoniously. I barely managed to cast a deliriously amused glance over my shoulder before

I allowed Dax to pull me towards the group of dancing people. I couldn't contain my laughter when Dax spun in a quick circle, jerking me along with him in an attempt to twirl me.

My body was thrown away from his, and the only thing keeping me from landing in the dirt was his hand clinging to mine. His free hand waved around in dramatic fashion, and he maintained an overly serious face as if giving the performance of a lifetime. I thought for sure he was going to spill his entire drink on me as he suddenly threw his other arm behind my back and tipped me down, so low that I felt my hair graze the dirt. I was suddenly extremely grateful for the pain medication I'd taken earlier.

I was laughing hysterically now as Dax tried and failed to dance with me, finally giving up on his pretend seriousness to burst into a wide grin. Much of his drink had splashed onto me, and I felt myself getting dizzy, but I couldn't find it in me to care as I laughed along with him. Finally, the upbeat song ended and I had an excuse to pull myself from the mess that was Dax's dancing.

'I knew that would work,' he said, his voice filled with satisfaction. I tilted my head to the side in confusion, unsure what he was referring to just as I felt a pair of hands land lightly on my waist. Dax shot me a final grin before speaking again. 'Have fun, kids.' With that he moved away.

My body turned suddenly, from Dax to Hayden, as a mellow song started around us. Large, gentle hands reached out to draw my wrists around his shoulders before he dropped his hands to my waist and pulled me softly against him. He was close, but not so close as to arouse suspicion. I hardly noticed, but people were pairing up all around us to dance to the slower song that allowed us to melt into the crowd unnoticed.

'Thought you didn't dance?' I asked softly, smiling up at Hayden as my heart beat heavily.

'I don't. Only for you, Bear.'

Chapter Eight – Nostalgia
GRACE

The heat of Hayden's hands on my waist seared through my clothes as we moved slowly to the music. I resisted the urge to pull him closer as my arms remained looped loosely around his neck. It felt almost silly that so many butterflies had erupted in my stomach at his sudden appearance, but I couldn't deny that it made me practically glow with joy.

I don't. Only for you, Bear.

Every single time he used his nickname for me I felt a flash of warmth flood through me, something that only grew stronger with every repetition. It was difficult to rein in the smile on my face as I looked up at Hayden, beyond surprised and thrilled that he'd broken his 'I don't dance' rule just for me.

'I thought you'd be worse at this,' I admitted quietly. A soft smile pulled at the corner of his lips and his eyes were practically glowing as he watched me.

'There's not much to it, is there?' His voice was low and deep, meant only for me to hear amongst the crowd that carried on blissfully unaware around us. His hands slid further down my waist before coming to rest on my hips, and I didn't miss the slight pressure he put there to tug me a little closer to him.

'I guess not,' I admitted, dropping my voice softer to match his. We were only separated by about six inches now, and the people around me began to fade away, the music meshed together into an indistinguishable blur, and every other detail that wasn't Hayden seemed to drop away as I felt myself slip into the bubble that often surrounded us.

'Did you have fun tonight?' he asked. A ghost of a smile lingered on his face as he watched me closely.

'I'm still having fun,' I told him, grinning even wider. I could practically see all the thoughts racing through his head, though each and every one was a mystery to me. My heart pounded a little harder as he pulled me even tighter against him, pressing my front into his as he ducked his head next to my ear. I sucked in a breath involuntarily as I felt his jaw press lightly into my temple.

'I really want to kiss you.'

My heart thumped heavily into my ribs as he lingered a moment longer at my ear. Every cell in my body was screaming to hug him tighter, press a kiss into his neck, pull back and kiss his lips, *something*, but I knew I couldn't. Despite being completely enveloped in all things Hayden, I knew in the back of my mind that we remained in the middle of a camp full of people who knew nothing about us.

'Kiss me later,' I whispered, my mouth hidden by his shoulder.

He let out a deep sigh before finally retreating to a less suspicious-looking distance. His gaze found mine. The way he was looking at me sent chills down my spine, like every thought and feeling he was having were channelled into one look. I felt sure he wanted to say something but was struggling with himself to hold it in.

A flash of movement to my left broke the spell I'd fallen under as Dax swooped by. Perdita's hands were clasped in his as they danced by far too quickly for the pace of the song, and a ridiculously wide grin was plastered across his face. He manoeuvred them closer to us and dipped her backward so quickly I feared he'd injure her frail body. His head ducked towards us, pausing with Perdita in mid-dip.

'Hands,' he said, shooting a wink at us before his eyes darted to where Hayden held me. With that, he scooted away, whipping Perdita back upward and whisking her back into the thick of the dancing.

Both Hayden and I let our eyes dart to my waist, where I noticed Hayden's hands had fallen dangerously low and were holding me far too close. Immediately, Hayden shifted back up to a respectable height and moved even further away from me. I let out a quiet chuckle, grateful for Dax's small intervention and resenting it all at the same time.

'Of all people to know . . .' Hayden muttered, shaking his head gently as his gaze fixed itself on Dax. I couldn't help but smile softly at Hayden's obvious disappointment at being interrupted.

'How does he know?' Dax seemed to have picked up on the subtle moments between Hayden and I a long time ago, but I wasn't sure how he'd reached such certainty about whatever exactly it was going on. Dax seemed better informed about it than I did, quite honestly.

'He's an idiot but he's a smart idiot,' Hayden said. 'He figured it out a long time ago and . . .'

'And?'

'And only recently got it confirmed,' Hayden said mysteriously.

'Got it confirmed?'

'Yes.'

'By you,' I guessed, unable to suppress the grin pulling at my lips. Hayden let out a sharp exhale before reconnecting his gaze with mine.

'Yes.'

The song we'd been dancing to ended as a faster one picked up. I was disappointed when Hayden's hands dropped from my waist. I pulled my arms from around his neck and frowned gently at him. I hardly had time to process any of our conversation before Hayden flicked his head to the side and started moving through the crowd, indicating I follow.

Hayden's shoulder shifted easily beneath his shirt as he moved deftly through the crowd. My mind was preoccupied as I tried to think clearly. Hayden's statement just now told me that he'd admitted to Dax that we were . . . whatever . . . which made me incredibly happy and very confused all at once. It seemed like such a normal issue to have – how to define the terms of a relationship – and I found myself wondering if these were a girl's biggest problems before the world fell apart.

Hayden's sharp jaw came into view as he glanced back over his shoulder, making sure I was following, as we reached the edge of the crowd. Docc had returned from dancing and was joined by several people I recognised but didn't know. He nodded calmly at Hayden and I before returning his attention to the group while we sat down on a log a few yards away from the small group.

We'd hardly been seated for when Jett appeared for what felt like the hundredth time that night, a piece of flat wood in his hands. He looked at us excitedly, still very dirty but slightly less sweaty than the last time I'd seen him.

'Hi, Jett,' I greeted with a small smile. His gaze connected with mine before blushing furiously and averting his attention to Hayden.

'Hi,' he said quietly. He hugged the piece of wood in his hands to his chest.

'What have you been up to?' Hayden asked. I caught the hint of amusement in his tone and felt his gaze flit to me briefly before refocusing on Jett.

'Maisie set up a craft station,' Jett said, still avoiding looking at me. 'I made you something.'

'What did you make?' Hayden asked patiently. It was the gentlest I'd seen him with Jett, something I hoped stemmed from his overall good mood.

Without a word, Jett slowly flipped the board to reveal the other side. He watched us both carefully, judging our reactions as we took in what he'd created. My lips parted involuntarily as my eyes took in what appeared to be a painting made with mud.

Jett's painting consisted of three people. The first stood tall, with wild waves of hair atop his head, and what I assumed to be a gun in his hand. The second figure was much shorter with equally wild hair. The third figure took my breath away. It was clearly a female as the triangle dress indicated, with long hair and a large, unmistakable 'G' painted on the front of her dress.

'It's not very good,' Jett started when neither of us spoke. 'We only had mud but I—'

'Is that us, Jett?' I asked, cutting off his disclaimer before he could go any further. He blushed once again and managed to look at me. 'You, me, and Hayden?'

'Yes,' he finally answered, a small, sheepish grin pulling at his lips. I felt a smile break out on my face as I studied the painting more closely. I noticed now that all three of the figures were holding hands, their little stick arms joined between the depictions.

'I love it,' I answered honestly, awe stealing some of the volume from my voice. Not only had he included me with him and Hayden, but he'd made our figures hold hands. A feeling of acceptance and happiness rushed through me as I realised how significant that really was.

Jett appeared stunned as I reached forward suddenly, pulling him into a hug. He barely managed to get his artwork out from between us before his small chest pressed into mine. His body remained frozen for a few seconds, surprised and unsure of what to do before I felt a tiny arm snake tentatively around my waist to return the hug. I was feeling overwhelmed with emotion when he roped his other small arm around me to hug me even tighter.

After a few seconds, I pulled back, holding him at arm's length. 'Thank you.'

'F-for what?' he stammered, his eyes wide and face flushed. I shook my head slowly.

'Just . . . thank you.'

I couldn't put into words how much his small gesture meant. Not only did it mean he liked me, but it meant he thought of me as a part of the family he'd formed here. It was something I'd been missing and craving ever since I'd left home – the feeling of inclusion, acceptance. The feeling of family.

It wasn't until I released Jett fully that I became aware of Hayden watching me closely. His gaze was trained tightly on me, brows pulled low and lips set. He looked thoughtful for a few seconds before blinking once and looking to Jett.

'This is for us, right?' he asked, reaching his hand out for the board. Jett placed it in his hand and took a small step back, his fists closing behind his back as he smiled at Hayden.

'Yes! For both of you,' he announced proudly.

'Thank you. We'll hang it up in my hut, all right?'

'Really?!' he asked excitedly, as if having his artwork hung up on the wall was some huge honour.

'Really,' Hayden agreed, smiling widely at him. 'Now you'd better go and find Maisie. The party's winding down.'

Jett nodded vigorously. 'Okay. See you tomorrow, guys!'

'Bye, Jett,' I managed to say before he bolted away, his feet carrying him faster than necessary in his excitement.

'What was that?' Hayden questioned. I could feel his gaze on me once again and a gentle smile played on his lips. A hint of embarrassment crept up as I thought of my overly emotional reaction.

'It's just . . . nice to be included,' I said calmly, glancing at Hayden once with a soft smile before returning my gaze to the party. Hayden was right, I saw, as I noticed people calling it a night. Small groups of people were saying goodbye to others, some groups carried items back to their rightful places, while still others stumbled home drunkenly, the effects of the hooch obvious in their staggered steps.

My attention was suddenly commanded by a middle-aged man moving through the crowd. In his arms was a small child of about five or six with light blonde hair flowing down her back. Her head was resting on his shoulder, and his hands held her securely as he moved. His hand moved easily down the back of her head soothingly, her position making it obvious she'd fallen asleep. The light kiss he pressed to the top of her head forced a wave of nostalgia through me as a memory surfaced.

'Dad, I'm not tired,' I argued sleepily, the yawn that followed my statement effectively negating it.

'Shh, Gracie. It's time for bed.'

'But Jonah's still outside,' I mumbled. My head felt far too heavy for my body as I let it rest against my father's shoulder as he carried me inside. At eight years old, I thought myself far too old to be carried by my father but couldn't find it in me to force him to put me down. I really was very tired.

'Jonah is a bit older than you, sweetheart,' he cajoled gently. His hand ran lightly down the back of my hair as he manoeuvred us inside our home, backing easily through the doorway. 'Hush now, your mother is sleeping.'

I remained quiet as I fought to keep my eyes open, the gentle thumping of my father's heart lulling me easily into submission. The familiar setting of my home flashed through the small gap my almost-closed eyes allowed, and I saw the dark mass that was my mother as she slept in my parents' bed. She seemed to be sleeping a lot more lately, and was always too tired to play with me.

'Daddy I'm not tired,' I argued weakly. We'd reached the small room that I shared with Jonah now, and I felt my body being lowered gently into bed. Covers were pulled over me and I snuggled into them despite my statements to the contrary. 'I was about to beat Jonah.'

'Shh, I know, Gracie.'

We'd been in the middle of a heated game that involved 'swords' that were really sticks, and I'd been on the verge of finally defeating my big brother when my father had intervened and stopped him from hitting me in the leg with his stick. I hadn't been scared, and was more than determined to beat Jonah.

'I was!' I replied indignantly.

'Yes, Grace. You'll always be my brave little girl, won't you?'

I sighed and pressed my face into the pillow. It really was very comfortable, and as much as I didn't want to admit, I really was tired.

'Yes, Dad. I'll always be brave.'

'Grace?'

I sucked in a gasp of air as I was ripped from my memory, by the real-life echo of my name. I blinked furiously before looking around to see the caller sitting next to me. Hayden.

'Sorry, what did you say?' I asked, trying my best to sound casual. My heart seemed to throb in my chest at the memory, and the sight that had triggered it was no longer around. That father had successfully taken his daughter to safety, just as mine had years ago.

Hayden was watching me closely again, and I couldn't miss the soft frown that had settled over his features. He was observant, far too observant, and I feared he had seen just how much the sight of the father and his daughter had affected me.

A few more seconds passed where I tried to appear casual but Hayden didn't seem to buy it. Finally he repeated himself. 'I asked if you were ready to go.'

'Yeah!' I said, a little too enthusiastically. 'Yeah, let's go.'

His eyes narrowed slightly before nodding once. He rose smoothly from the log and I copied him, smiling softly as I saw he had the board Jett had painted in his hands. Silence enveloped us as we moved from the crowd. A few wordless greetings were exchanged as Hayden nodded casually at passersby, but he didn't speak as we walked through the camp towards his hut.

The shift in the atmosphere was palpable now, and I couldn't ignore the lingering hint of sadness that had fallen over us. Despite my best efforts, I couldn't shake the memory that had surfaced so suddenly. Ever since my decision to stay with Hayden had been made, I hadn't found myself doubting or regretting it, even for a moment. Now, however, I couldn't help feel the flicker of apprehension as we strolled silently through the dark.

Had I made the right decision in staying here? Every moment I spent with Hayden, I felt myself falling deeper and deeper into whatever it was I felt for him, but that bliss made it easy to ignore the glaringly obvious: staying here with him meant I would never see my family again. I'd known what the decision meant all along, but I hadn't truly felt it until now. Memories like the one I'd just experienced would remain just that: memories.

No new memories would be made, no new moments to re-member fondly would arise, and there would be no looking back on them with family. A dull ache settled into my heart, and a sadness I couldn't ignore seeped through me. This new life I'd chosen here had seemed so right at the time, and for the most part still did, but it was slightly tainted by the bitter knowledge that I was leaving behind my former life completely.

I swallowed the lump that had formed in my throat as we reached Hayden's hut. His saddened gaze fell on me as he opened the door and pushed through, as if he could sense the inner heartbreak I was struggling to mask. I felt a flash of guilt run through me as I realised what he must be feeling and I resolved to stop letting these thoughts con-sume me. The last thing I wanted was for Hayden to feel guilty for influencing my decision, even though the truth was obvious: if it weren't for Hayden, I never would have stayed.

I had made my choice, and I was here for good.

Hayden didn't speak as he moved through his hut, lighting a few candles to cast a warm glow over us. There was a visible slump to his shoulders, and I was struck by how much my sudden mood change seemed to have affected him. He couldn't have known what I'd been thinking, but somehow he'd picked up on it enough to know I'd been saddened by it. I felt yet another flash of guilt for potentially ruining his good mood.

Hayden stood at his desk, lighting a candle there with his back to me. Silently, my feet carried me across the space until I paused right behind him. My hands pushed up his back once before trailing down to wind loosely around his torso. Leaning forward, I pressed my lips lightly into his shoulder blade, where I could feel the heat radiating off him even through his shirt. He put the match down on the desk, before clasping my hands, much tighter than necessary, as if he were desperately trying to stop me from slipping away.

'Hayden,' I whispered quietly, my lips mumbling against his back. He turned slowly in my grasp, keeping my arms looped around him as his broke free. I felt the familiar spark shoot through me as his hands slid to either side of my face. Despite my best efforts, I couldn't bring myself to wipe the lingering traces of sadness from my features. The memory stood too starkly in my brain to be ignored.

It was like a weight had fallen onto both our shoulders, when all we wanted to do was rise up and be free. Every moment of happiness we shared seemed to be negated by something that demanded attention as payment for daring to feel happy. A bitter resentment at the world settled into my stomach. Why couldn't we just be happy for the sake of being happy? Why must every good feeling be smothered by something darker, something heavier, fighting for attention when all we wanted to feel was the light?

'I don't know what happened, Grace,' Hayden finally said. His words were pained and heavy, as if it hurt to admit he'd noticed the obvious shift in my mood. I just wanted to feel happy without feeling like I was doing something wrong.

I hesitated to respond to his statement, certain any mention of missing my father would be like a dagger of guilt straight through his heart. I didn't want to miss my family, my home, or the future I might have had there, but I couldn't ignore it as I looked up at Hayden.

His jaw was clenched tightly and his brows were pulled low as he watched me, obvious concern and sadness written across his features. I let out a deep sigh, determined to shake any doubts from his mind. I wanted to be there with him and I was happy there with him. It wasn't fair of me to choose him then make him doubt himself.

'Do you still want to kiss me?' I asked quietly, my voice no louder than a mere whisper thanks to the emotions loading it down. Hayden's lip tugged lightly between his teeth before he released it while studying me.

'I always want to kiss you, Grace.'

My heart, which had been torn in several directions tonight, seemed to glow at his admittance. His words were so bold, yet they carried a ring of truth that couldn't be ignored. The gentle strokes of his thumbs over my cheeks warmed me to the bone, and I felt each and every gentle action he gave as it reverberated through my body.

'Then kiss me.'

I needed to feel the reassuring way his lips fit with mine, feel the heat that would surely spread though my body at the contact. I needed to feel the emotion behind the kiss that would reaffirm my decision and erase the doubts. What I needed, desperately needed, was to lose myself in Hayden and remind myself that there was a reason I'd chosen to stay here, with him.

The doubt I'd fought off lingered in his gaze, and the sadness I didn't want to feel was reflected in his features, as if everything I was feeling, he was feeling, too. Slowly, cautiously, he lowered his lips to mine, pressing them gently against my own so they fit perfectly how they always did.

Sure enough, the moment he made contact, heat seared through my veins. Every pessimistic thought and doubt that had crept into my brain was fought off by the light that took over, brightening every cell in my body where before there had only been dark, stormy clouds. The kiss was simple and gentle, but I felt it down to my toes as he held me close. It was like everything I'd just been worrying about disappeared, confirming that I'd been right all along to stay.

The things he made me feel weren't normal, of that I was certain. Never before had a person taken such hold of me, and never before had I been so terrified and exhilarated all at once by how I felt. This thing between us had taken over my life, and although I couldn't imagine how we'd got to this point, there was no denying it now. We'd skipped right over any normal semblance of a friendship, bypassing normal milestones that may have existed in a previous life, but that didn't make it any less real.

In that moment, I could feel it – the desperate longing to be near him, the reliance I'd formed without even realising, the haunting ache that settled in my heart when I thought of being away from him. It was something I'd felt for a very long time and had refused to acknowledge, but now seemed pointless to ignore. The fact was simple, and it was staring me right in the face as I kissed Hayden back.

I loved him.

Chapter Nine – Promise

HAYDEN

There was an undeniable pull drawing me deeper into the kiss as I held Grace's face between my hands. She leaned gently into me, her torso pressed to mine as she gripped my hips lightly.

Something had happened tonight, and it made me apprehensive. There had been a subtle shift in her mood, so small it was almost undetectable, but it was impossible to ignore. From the moment I'd seen it, it only became more obvious. Each passing second seemed to pile a weight onto my shoulders, crushing downward. *Something* had changed.

She'd been practically glowing all night, and her mood had been infectious as we'd danced together. Despite my best efforts, I hadn't been able to resist going to her. Seeing her with Dax, no matter how friendly and unromantic, had caused a surge of jealousy to sear through me. She'd looked so beautiful as I danced with her that it had been almost impossible not to kiss her; only the lingering sliver of sense in my brain had held me back.

Her blissful mood had changed, however, when we were sitting together. I wasn't sure what triggered it or what it was she was thinking of, but something had brought her down, bringing me down with her. Whatever she'd thought of had saddened her greatly, and no amount of effort on her part to hide it could stop me from seeing that.

She'd become lost to me for a few moments, stuck in her own head with whatever was going on inside. The light that blazed inside her had dimmed, and when she finally came back to me, she wasn't the same. Our walk back had been silent, and the quiet between us had seemed to swell to breaking point until I couldn't take it any longer. It felt like she was slipping through my fingers, and I was unable to stop it. It was impossible not to feel the weight of whatever had happened in her mind.

The quiet vulnerability when she'd asked me to kiss affected me now as I did, her lips pressed in a soft desperation to my own. It was as if a great importance weighed on the kiss, like whatever she'd thought of had made this one so much more essential than all the others we'd shared.

When she pulled back, I found myself breathing more heavily than I should have been. Heavy thuds beat against my ribs as my heart pounded erratically, and I felt a strange hint of nerves tightening in my stomach. My eyes opened slowly to see hers doing the same, gradually revealing the green irises that I found so beautiful.

Relief flooded through me as I saw that the sadness from before had been eradicated in her eyes, leaving them free to glow happily at me as they had been doing all night. A soft smile pulled at her lips, and I felt her hands slide around my waist to bring herself into me. She didn't speak as she hugged me tightly. It took me a moment to respond, surprised by the hug but no less thrilled to embrace her as I wound my arms around her shoulders.

She still didn't say anything, but I felt her sigh contentedly as she nuzzled her face lightly into my chest. My lips automatically pressed into the top of her head, a gentle action that should have felt so foreign to me but only felt right. Even without words, it was clear that there were so many emotions flooding through us both at that moment.

I held her like that for a long time. Neither of us spoke, and we let our bodies communicate silently as we stood locked in our embrace. I found my hand trailing lightly down her back before returning to her shoulder to start the descent all over again. With every passing moment her grip on me tightened a little bit more. I desperately wanted to know what it was that had caused this rollercoaster of emotions tonight, but didn't want to force her to talk about it if she didn't want to.

Finally, she pulled back from me, her eyes meeting mine once again.

'Bed?' she asked simply, smiling softly up at me. My arms remained looped around her shoulders and her hands reached up to trail lightly down them.

'Yeah.' My voice sounded deeper than usual, thanks to the emotional strain I'd just endured. She nodded once with a small smile before ducking out of my grasp and heading to the bathroom.

I was still confused about why her mood had shifted at all. I tried to let it go as I peeled off my shirt and jeans, kicking them to a pile on the floor, before pulling on a pair of shorts, leaving my torso bare. Grace emerged from the bathroom, and cast me a small smile before heading to bed.

'I'll be right there,' I told her before heading to the bathroom.

'Okay,' she said.

A few moments later, I returned to see her snuggled under the covers, lying on her good side as she faced the middle of the bed. I moved around the hut to blow out the candles, plunging us into darkness, before I made my way into the bed. I felt her gaze on me as I slid between the covers across from her.

'Are you okay, Grace?' I asked softly, going against my better judgement not to pry.

'Yeah, why wouldn't I be?' she responded quietly. Even though it was dark, I could see the faint outline of her features thanks to the light of the lanterns outside.

'I don't know . . . it just seemed like tonight was going so well but then you got really . . .' I paused, searching for the right word. 'Sad.'

She was quiet for a long time as she thought about my statement. The silence stretched on for so long I began to wonder if she had fallen asleep before she spoke.

'You noticed,' she stated. It sounded like she was confirming a suspicion she had.

'Of course I did,' I said, almost offended she'd thought I wouldn't. I noticed everything about her. She didn't answer me again, so I reached slowly across the space to let my hand cover hers that lay between us. My thumb ran a light trail down the backs of her knuckles before I squeezed gently.

'Why were you sad, Bear?' I asked carefully. It hurt me to know she was sad when all I wanted was for her to be happy. This realisation sunk in as I waited for her response: all I wanted was for her to be happy. It seemed insane to think that after how she'd come to be here, but it was the truth. The absolute truth.

She drew in a deep breath and blew it out slowly before speaking. 'It's nothing, Hayden.'

She was lying, I could tell. Whatever it was that had caused her sudden change in mood had definitely not been 'nothing', no matter how contented she seemed now.

'Grace . . .' I trailed off. My tone clearly indicated I didn't believe her.

'Hayden . . .' she said, mimicking my tone before letting out a soft, uncharacteristic giggle. 'Honestly. It's nothing. I'm fine now.'

'Yeah, *now*,' I mumbled, discontented she wouldn't talk to me. 'I wish you'd tell me.'

She let out a heavy sigh and I was surprised when she picked up my hand to press a kiss into my knuckles. 'I just . . . I saw something that reminded me of my dad but seriously, it's all right.'

It was like a dagger of guilt speared through my chest as she finally admitted what it was that had changed her mood. Of course she'd become sad after seeing something that reminded her of her dad. I didn't know much about their relationship, but from what I could tell, she loved him a lot. His words when he'd been searching for her confirmed that he, too, loved her equally. Again, my decision to keep her here and my hopes that she would stay sent a flare of guilt through me.

'Hayden, don't do that,' she said seriously. 'Don't guilt trip yourself.'

'I'm not,' I lied. She rolled her eyes at me, unconvinced.

'You are, I can tell. I don't know how many times I have to say it but I'm happy here with you, Herc.'

My heart thumped once in my chest; it was like she could read my very thoughts.

'You're happy?' I prayed what she was saying was true, because I didn't know if I could handle the guilt of making her unhappy.

'I'm happy. I love my father and I will miss him, and I love my brother too but . . .' Her words trailed off and she paused, her gaze holding mine tightly through the dark. My stomach flipped over in my abdomen as if she were about to say something important.

'But . . .?'

'But I have you.'

For some reason, my heart plummeted in my chest. That wasn't what I thought she would say, and I shouldn't have been disappointed, but I was. I'd thought she was going to say something I'd never heard from anyone but my parents, but I was wrong.

'You do have me,' I agreed quietly. She had no idea just how much she had me.

'Then I'm happy.'

I could see the truth of it behind her eyes, and I took in the soft smile she gave me. I shook off my disappointment, telling myself I was being irrational. Of course she wouldn't say that. I hadn't earned that from her.

She wouldn't say she loved me.

'I've been thinking about something,' I told her, changing the subject away from the dangerous topic I'd been thinking of.

'What's that?'

'When your mum died . . . did you get to say goodbye to her?'

My words were cautious and light in tone. It was probably a horrible time to bring it up seeing as she'd just been upset about her father not even an hour ago, but it was something that had been weighing on me for a while now.

'Yes,' she answered. 'The day she died, my dad, Jonah, and I were all there. I don't know how but she just knew it was her last day. We all got to say goodbye.'

'You're lucky,' I told her even though I knew she already knew. She was too smart not to realise how fortunate she was that she got to say goodbye.

'I know,' she responded softly. 'You didn't get to, did you? Say goodbye to your parents.'

My heart clenched as the flashes of images that always seemed to haunt me returned. Fire, bombs, blood, bodies falling, falling, falling all around me. Faces I didn't know, faces I did, faces of those I loved. To say the words out loud made it feel like I was reliving the experience all over again, and the images never seemed any less torturous as they flashed before my eyes. The chaos swirled around my head like an unrelenting tornado, wiping all my thoughts blank before Grace's hand touched my cheek lightly, bringing me back to her.

'No, I didn't.'

She was quiet as she waited patiently, seeing if I wanted to continue. I drew a sharp breath and tried to subdue the dull ache that rose whenever I spoke of my parents. It made me feel weak, so incredibly weak, but I couldn't help it.

'They were both there one second, running with me to take me somewhere safe, and the next thing I knew my dad was dead. Just like that . . . in a split second, he was gone. We didn't make it much further before my mum was dead too. What kills me is that it could have been me so easily. A bullet two feet to the left or right and maybe they'd still be here instead of me.'

Grace had shifted closer to me as I spoke, and her attention was focused entirely on me. It was something I'd only discussed a few times before in my entire life, but I trusted Grace. Fully, completely, I trusted her.

Her hand pushed my hair lightly back from my forehead in a soothing gesture, and she snaked her body so it was pressing comfortingly against mine.

'No, Hayden, don't think like that,' she said quietly. 'They wouldn't want that. You're here for a reason and you've done something incredible with your life, okay?

They would be proud of you, Hayden. *So* proud.' Then she added, quietly, 'I'm sorry you didn't get to say goodbye.'

I nodded silently before draping my arm over her lightly, hauling her even further into my chest.

'That's my point with this,' I started. 'I didn't get to and I don't ever want that to happen again. This world we live in . . . it's so unstable and you never know what's going to happen so I want you to promise me something, okay?'

'Anything, Hayden.' She spoke without hesitation and it made my heart pound even harder.

'Promise me you'll always say goodbye like it's the last time because it really could be. You promise me that and I'll promise you the same.'

I was surprised when I felt her shift forward and press her lips suddenly to mine. Her hand remained on her face as she drew me closer and held the kiss for a few moments. When she pulled back, my lips remained parted as my breath blew out in shallow pants.

'You can't think like that, Hayden. Yes, this world is dangerous and yeah, there's a high chance of something bad happening but . . . you have to see the good. You can't focus on the bad or it'll drown you.'

'I'm not, I'm being realistic,' I said, frowning when she wouldn't consent to my request. The idea of losing her sent a bolt of pain through my body so sharp it caused me to physically recoil. 'Please promise me. I don't want to lose you without saying goodbye.'

Grace looked saddened by my insistence, and I could tell that her usually optimistic outlook was being damped by this, but it was important to me. If something were to happen to her and I never got the chance to say goodbye like I hadn't countless other times, I'd never get over it.

'You're not going to lose me.'

Her words did little to comfort me though they did send sparks jumping through my veins.

'Promise me,' I requested softly. My brows were pulled low as I watched her carefully, and I could see that she knew just how serious I was. She sighed softly and pushed her hand back through my hair once more.

'I promise.'

A wave of relief washed over me at her words and I immediately rushed forward to kiss her again, sealing her promise with a kiss. Her lower lip was folded perfectly between my own, and my hands flattened out on her back to pull her against me. I did nothing to deepen the kiss, satisfied by the simplicity of it and the meaning it held.

'Thank you,' I whispered as soon as our lips parted. It didn't completely shake the weird feeling of unfinished thoughts I'd been having, but it helped. I'd lost too many people without getting the chance to say goodbye, and I refused to let that happen with Grace. She was too important to me, something that seemed to surprise me and comfort me all at once.

'Get some sleep, Herc,' she said gently, a soft smile playing on her lips. Her eyes lingered on mine for a moment before she snuggled further into me, draping her arm loosely over my torso.

'You too, Bear.'

A few days had passed with no further mention of that night's revelations. The opportunity to uphold the promise we had made to each other had yet to arise. The camp was relatively quiet, something that both relaxed and stressed me out at once. Things were never quiet for long, and I knew it was only a matter of time before we'd have to go on our next raid. Supplies had to be running low, especially after the success of Maisie's party.

Rain drizzled down from the sky, flattening my hair to the back of my neck as Grace and I moved through the camp. I tried to keep my eyes from drifting to where her shirt stuck plastered against her stomach, but it was impossible to resist the beaming smiles she kept offering in my direction.

'I like the rain,' she said happily. 'It makes everything look clean.'

'Hmm,' I agreed, ripping my eyes away from her chest where the wetness made her skin glisten. She was only wearing a thin tank top and shorts. I pushed my hair out of my face and continued walking. We were on our way to see Docc so he could look at Grace's ribs and cut.

'Hmm,' she repeated, laughing as if mocking my lack of words. She shot me an amused look, and I couldn't help but grin back at her. She'd been in an incredibly good mood ever since our late-night conversation, and more than once I'd caught her smiling happily to herself. She gave no explanation, however, and I didn't want to press her and risk spoiling things. After all, all I wanted was for her to be happy.

As we walked, we passed several people, most of them making no impact. An upcoming pair, however, caught my attention. A middle-aged man was leading a blonde haired little girl along, both of them laughing as they skipped to avoid puddles from the rain. Immediately, my eyes darted to Grace where I saw, sure enough, that the smile had slipped from her face.

Her eyes were trained on them, watching their happy interaction closely as they neared us. I desperately wanted to distract her from whatever memory she was surely reliving, but I couldn't. Her walking slowed and her actions became stiffer as the pair got closer, her eyes never leaving them.

'. . . and when we get home, we'll get you some warm clothes, how's that sound?' the man said, as he passed. The little girl's response was inaudible as they moved by, but the delight was clear in the tone that reached both of our ears.

It took everything in me not to turn around and swear at them for reminding Grace, once again, of what she'd left behind. Guilt had been eating away at me for a few days now no matter how much I tried to ignore it. Grace insisted that she was happy and she certainly looked it, but it was hard to believe when her mood had once again plummeted into the mud along with the rain that pelted down on us.

'Grace,' I said gently, watching her closely. She blinked once as if she'd forgotten I was there and forced a smile.

'Yeah?'

I frowned, wishing more than ever that her smile was real and reached her eyes, but it didn't.

'Um, we're here,' I said lamely. I opened the door and allowed her to move through first, returning the small smile she shot me as she did so. We were greeted almost immediately by Docc.

'Grace, Hayden, hello,' he said casually, nodding at us both. 'Aren't we looking like a couple of drowned rats today.'

'Funny,' I said flatly, my mood somewhat sombre again. Grace shot me a silent scolding look for being rude.

'How are you, Docc?' she asked politely.

'Fine, fine. How's that rib of yours?'

'That's why we're here,' she explained. 'It feels a lot better and I'm out of pain meds but I don't think I really need anymore. Could you look at it?'

'Certainly,' Docc said, waving his hand at the bench

nearest him. Grace followed his instructions and lay back, peeling her wet shirt off her stomach to fold it up around her chest so Docc could examine her injury. I moved to stand by her side but didn't say anything as Docc leaned closer.

Grace stared up at the ceiling as Docc's fingers gently poked and prodded her rib, and her face stayed carefully set in determination. The bruises had faded slightly over her side, but a faint purple remained beneath her skin. Whenever I asked, she claimed it didn't hurt anymore, but I knew it was a lie. Every once in a while I caught her wincing if she moved too quickly or twisted a certain way. Getting her to take her pain meds had been like making her drink acid, but eventually she gave up fighting me and took them. She'd taken the last one this morning.

'Well, it's still broken,' Docc said, straightening up after finishing his assessment. 'But I'd say it's healing nicely. Are you still having as much pain?'

'No—'

'Yes,' I interrupted, frowning at her. She glared at me, upset I'd interfered. 'She still has pain.'

'It's not as bad as it was, really,' she insisted. I knew she didn't like being injured but that didn't take away from the fact that she was.

'But it still hurts you—'

'Okay, you two, that's enough,' Docc said, interrupting our bickering. 'Grace, take it easy for another few days and then you can start running wild again like before. I'll give you a few more pills.'

'I don't need anymore,' she said, sitting up and pulling her shirt back down over her stomach. She winced slightly as she did so, negating her statement.

'Hayden will make sure you take them, won't you, son?' Docc said, glancing at me quickly.

124

'Yes, I will.'

She shot me another glare as if she didn't like that Docc and I were ganging up on her. I shrugged, and a loud huff emerged from her lips before she nodded.

'Fine.'

'Excellent. Now that that's taken care of . . . Hayden, I'm afraid we need some things again. Maisie, Barrow and I are all running low.'

My heart sank as Docc announced the inevitable raid I knew was coming sooner or later. 'You have a list?'

'Here,' he said, nodding as he reached in his pocket and pulled out a slip of paper to hand to me. 'Can you go tonight?'

I unfolded the paper and glanced over it, taking in the necessary items. I nodded. 'Yeah, should be fine.'

'Thank you. I'll go inform Dax and Kit, then?'

'Sounds good. Tell them to be ready in a half hour.'

With that, Grace thanked Docc for the pills he handed her and we made our way out the door back into the rain. We moved quickly down the path back towards my hut.

'So where are we going for this one?' she asked, raising her voice to be heard over the rain that only seemed to grow heavier.

' "We're" not going anywhere,' I said firmly.

'What?' she asked incredulously.

'You're not going.'

'What? Hayden, I'm coming with you,' she argued. I could feel her staring at me but I marched on, focusing on my hut that had just come into view.

'No. You're still hurt and I'm not risking it getting worse.'

'Hayden—'

'No! You're not coming, Grace. That's final.'

We reached my hut now and I threw open the door, but Grace refused to move as she planted herself outside the door. Rain pelted down on her and she was practically seething as she glared at me with her arms crossed tightly over her chest.

'Come inside, Grace.'

'No.'

I exhaled sharply in exasperation and pushed my hand through my hair. '*Please* come inside?'

'Hayden, I want to go with you,' she said firmly. I could tell how much she meant what she said.

'And I want you to stay here. You're hurt, Docc *just* said so.'

She stared at me for a long time, her jaw set and eyes blazing, as she held her ground. I sighed as I took a step out of the doorway and moved back into the rain where I stood right in front of her. Her head tilted back as she looked up at me, soaking wet hair plastered around to frame her face.

'Please stay here,' I requested, softening my voice. My eyes pleaded with her silently, and finally I saw her harsh exterior start to crack. Her arms unfolded from her chest and her shoulders sagged slightly as she finally gave in.

'Fine,' she said in defeat. I let out a sigh of relief and nodded before taking her hand lightly and pulling her inside.

Once inside, she surprised me by immediately pulling off her soaking wet shirt and flinging it to the ground a little harder than necessary, as if frustrated by my instruction. She moved to the dresser and pulled out a fresh, dry shirt that she pulled on and cut off my view of her exposed skin. She shot me a challenging look as she then moved to pull off her shorts, which were also sopping wet, and she held my gaze as she slid them down her legs.

I shook my head and let out a huff of frustration before turning away from her, denying myself the show she was purposely putting on to torture me. Payback for making her stay, I supposed.

'That's not nice,' I told her gruffly. She shrugged as she buttoned the shorts she'd slid on.

'Sorry,' she said. She did not sound the least bit convincing.

'I just don't want you to get hurt again, okay? It's not because I don't think you can handle it or anything. It's just to keep you safe,' I explained.

She let out a heavy sigh before crossing the space between us to come and stand in front of me. 'I know, Hayden.'

My hands rose to cup her face gently, drawing her into me. 'Remember our promise?'

'Hayden—'

'You promised,' I reminded her sharply.

'Goodbye, Hayden. Please be careful,' she said, finally letting go of her resentment to loop her arms around my waist. 'I'll see you when you get back.'

My heart pounded a bit harder as I ducked down slowly to press my lips into hers, my hands light on her cheeks. I held our kiss for a few seconds before I pulled back.

'Wait for me and I'll come back to you, Bear. I promise.'

Chapter Ten – Anxiety
GRACE

'Wait for me and I'll come back to you, Bear. I promise.'

I was fairly certain I had never heard more beautiful words in my life, particularly aimed at me. I could feel the weight of the promise, the determination in his voice to keep his vow, but it didn't stop the trepidation creeping up inside me. I did not like this idea in the slightest.

'You'd better,' I whispered. I let myself feel the vulnerability in the words. His hands were warm on my cheeks as he held them there, his face lingering inches from my own.

'I will. Just stay here, okay? Don't go wandering around by yourself.'

'No way, I'll go crazy,' I said, shaking my head. His brows, which were already pulled down, lowered even more as he frowned at me.

'It's not safe for you to be alone out there.'

I rolled my eyes and shot him a faint smile. 'I may have a broken rib but I can still protect myself.'

'I don't doubt that but you're still hurt. Will you at least *try* to stay here?' he asked, clearly frustrated by my lack of cooperation. His muscles flexed as he blew out an exasperated sigh and I could feel them contract beneath my palms that lay over his hips.

'How long will you be gone?' His answer would greatly influence my own.

'We should be back tonight. Just a few hours.'

'And where are you going?' I pressed, nerves making my stomach twinge.

He was quiet for a long time, as if debating whether to tell me at all. I had just opened my mouth to demand he explain when he responded.

'The city.'

My stomach clenched as he finally answered. The city. Great. Just about every single trip we'd made to the city had either had some type of complication or ended horrifically. This conversation was doing little to calm the quiet storm brewing in my mind, and I could feel more and more storm clouds rolling in.

The roar of the truck's engine outside jerked us out of the spell that always seemed to enrapture us both. Hayden's thumbs trailed lightly over my cheeks and my grip tightened on his waist, pulling him even closer against me.

'I have to go,' he whispered. He was only an inch or two away from me, and his reluctance was clearly written all over his face. Even though he didn't want to, he would go, because it was his duty. I took a deep breath and pushed myself up to my toes to press my lips lightly into his. He ducked down to meet me, and his shoulders hunched forward as he did so.

'Come back to me,' I whispered. The world was dark thanks to my eyes drifting shut and my lips fumbling against his, but I could feel every single syllable we exchanged. There were too many emotions rushing through me to process; anxiety, fear, resistance, determination, love all mixed together to form a swirling mass of feeling that seemed to fight the very air in my lungs.

'I will, Grace,' he promised.

My eyes finally flitted open to find him running his thumbs across my cheeks once more before he ripped himself away. He cast me one final look over his shoulder before moving out the door. I heard the sound of the engine continue to roar, accompanied by obnoxious honking from the impatient driver.

Hayden's shirt whispered across his back, the light fabric masking the defined muscles and jagged scars beneath. I watched as his hair curled up at the back of his neck, noticing the way it pulled away from his scalp when he ran his hand through it once. He reached forward to open the door to leave the hut. To leave me.

The door shut behind him, officially separating us and twisting a knot in my stomach almost immediately. He was still there, just feet away, but as soon as it shut I felt like he was gone, and there was nothing I could do to protect him. I didn't like being separated from him at all, much less separated while he went on a dangerous raid and I sat hiding in his hut. My newly discovered emotions seemed to rush back in full force, and I fought the urge to chase him down.

'I love you,' I whispered quietly. Too quietly, for he was no longer there, and the hushed, terrifying words were too weak to break through the physical barrier between us and the emotional one around my heart.

It felt strange to say it out loud. I could count the number of people I'd said it to on one hand, all of whom were family. My mother, my father, and once or twice, my brother, were the only ones who'd ever heard such a thing from me, though even then it was a rare occurrence. That love was different to what I felt for Hayden. Familial love was something that bound children to parents, siblings to siblings, and it was strong, so strong, but it was undeniably different to what I was feeling now.

This love for Hayden was much more emotional than anything I'd ever felt. It was draining, really, to care so much for another person, especially when it had been so easy to only think of myself before. To feel this way made me want so many things: to keep him safe, to lighten the endless burdens placed on his shoulders, to make him happy – and they were things I never dreamed I would nor wanted to feel until I felt them.

But still I couldn't tell him. The rumbling of the truck had disappeared now as it carried him away, leaving my whispered words lingering in the air, unheard by the only one they were meant for.

Hayden's words echoed relentlessly in my head, feeding the anxiety that had begun gnawing at my stomach the moment he walked out the door. He was adamant that I stay put, locked away in his hut like a scared little girl. I knew that wasn't what he thought – never for a second had he made me think he believed I was weak – but it was impossible to stop the thoughts from returning. I hated being left behind because of an injury, unable to help or protect the people I'd come to care for so dearly. If there was any consolation to be had, it was that Hayden cared enough about me to not risk my safety.

Rain pelted down on the roof of Hayden's hut, each and every ping of the raindrops only adding to my stress. With Hayden's last kiss still sizzling on my lips, I forced myself to move back to the bed. My movements felt stiff and unnatural as I unlocked my legs from where I'd stood in the same place since Hayden left. It was with a heavy sigh that I threw myself onto the bed, wincing involuntarily when I collided with the mattress and sent a sharp bolt of pain up my side.

I wasn't exactly sure how he knew, but Hayden was very aware of the fact that I was still experiencing pain despite my best efforts to play it cool with Docc. True, the pain had lessened and it was more than bearable now, but it was still there. The combination of rest and the pills Docc had given me had done wonders, and I expected a few more days would make things even better. Hayden was, I hated to admit, right. I needed to sit the raid out.

I tried to distract myself by staring at the ceiling, examining the strange patchwork that created the roof, but it didn't work. All I could focus on was what Hayden and the others were doing. How long had it been since they'd left? Five minutes? Ten? It felt like it had already been hours, though I knew that wasn't true. They probably weren't even out of the trees yet.

This was going to be a long day.

I rolled to my side and huffed in frustration as time refused to pass. All I had to do was make it until night-time and he would return to me. It struck me as odd that my natural thought was that he'd return to me, not just return in general. Odd, but right. Those had been his words, after all.

Wait for me and I'll come back to you, Bear.

He would come back. The raid would go just fine and he would come back.

I blew out a heavy sigh and tried to force myself to believe it. Images of the past raids I'd gone on with him and things I'd seen from raids before my life here began flashed in front of my eyes, mixing together to form a horrific waking nightmare that predominantly featured Hayden. I saw him getting shot, stabbed, clubbed, beaten brutally by fists. No matter how tightly I squeezed my eyes shut, the images refused to subside.

Without deciding, I shot up in bed. There was no way

I could obey Hayden's wishes and remain alone in the hut with only my thoughts to distract me or I'd surely drive myself insane. The knot in my stomach already sat like a rock, and I knew the feeling would only get worse as time wore on.

Before I was really aware, I was marching back out into the torrential downpour, wetting the dry clothes I had just put on. My hair was instantly plastered to my head as I hurried down the path, not exactly sure where I was heading but not caring as long as it got me moving. I desperately wanted to go for a run to clear my head, but I knew my ribs wouldn't tolerate it. I longed for the day I could start training again, because I was certain I'd lost a bit of my edge.

I wasn't paying much attention to where I was going, my legs carrying me aimlessly through the camp, when I heard a muffled voice calling out through the rain.

'Where do you think you're going?'

I turned toward the sound to see Barrow standing between two huts. Rain pelted down on him and seemed to deepen the scowl on his face as he glared at me.

'To see Docc,' I lied easily. I kept walking, attempting to brush him off, but he followed and fell into stride with me.

'Aren't you supposed to be a prisoner? Where's Hayden?'

'On a raid,' I answered flatly, ignoring his first question.

'So he just lets you walk around on your own?' he pressed, glaring at me from beside me. I kept my gaze trained forward.

'Not usually,' I said. I could see his train of thought and the last thing I wanted was Barrow thinking Hayden was an unfit leader because of me. I hissed involuntarily when he jerked me suddenly so I was facing him, his grip on my arm far tighter than necessary as his fingers dug into my skin. I glared angrily up at him and tried to pull my arm away.

'There's something off about you. I don't trust you for a

second,' he accused bitterly. I jerked my arm again but still he didn't let go.

'I haven't done anything but help since the day I got here,' I shot back, anger creeping up inside me. I couldn't blame him for not trusting me; I was from the enemy camp, after all, and if I were in his shoes I'd probably think the same, but it frustrated me that what I'd achieved seemed completely lost on him. It might not make me his best friend, but it at least shouldn't make me his enemy.

'I think you're hiding something from us, and I think it's going to get a lot of us killed,' he said, his voice deadly calm and quiet. I held my ground and resisted the urge to throw my knee into his groin, uncertain of my ability to fight him off when I wasn't at a hundred per cent. He glared at me, his grip tightening on my arm. Picking a fight with Barrow while my one true ally was gone was not smart.

'Barrow!'

The sudden announcement of his own name stilled his action, as his gaze ripped away from me to squint through the rain. My eyes followed to land on Docc emerging before us.

'Let the girl go, Barrow,' he said calmly. His voice was deep and mellow as ever, and it held a certain authority that seemed impossible to ignore. Aside from Hayden, I'd never seen anyone who was obeyed so quickly as Docc. Barrow released my arm and he took a step back. I shot him a glare as I folded my arms over my chest.

'There's something she's not telling us, I know it,' Barrow muttered bitterly. Docc watched him coolly.

'I'm sure there's a lot she's not telling us, but that doesn't make her a danger to us.'

Appreciation for Docc rushed through me as he came to my defence. Barrow muttered something I couldn't hear over the rain before scowling at me one last time and walking back in the direction we'd just come. I turned to Docc and squinted up at him through the rain.

'Thanks.'

As much as I didn't like getting help, it was lucky for me that he'd come along.

'You shouldn't be out here,' Docc said, ignoring my thanks. 'Let's get you inside, yes?'

I nodded and tried not to feel like I was being scolded as I followed him back to the infirmary. I began to wonder if he ever left the place, because he always seemed to be there. Neither of us spoke as we moved through the paths, which had quickly turned to sticky muck thanks to the unrelenting rain. It wasn't until we were inside and he'd handed me a towel to dry off with that Docc spoke.

'You should be in Hayden's hut,' he told me. I was immediately reminded of Hayden's words before he left, renewing the anxiety I'd momentarily been distracted from.

'I couldn't stay in there,' I said honestly. I sat down on a stool across a small workbench as he mirrored me on the other side. He studied me closely as I tried to look casual by running the towel roughly over my hair. It did little good as I was soaked once again, so I gave up and set it on the table.

'You're worried about Hayden,' he said slowly. I blinked and felt my breath hitch in my throat.

'Erm, no . . . All of them,' I answered. It was true, but it was also a massive lie. While of course I wanted them all to return safely, I couldn't deny that this had been nearly my first thought of anyone besides Hayden. Docc's gaze stayed trained on my face as he observed me further.

'Hmm.'

I blinked, unsure of how to respond. I could feel the

135

seconds ticking by, as if each one that passed only made it more and more obvious how I felt. I could feel the tension gnawing at my stomach, and the knots there seemed tighter than ever.

'They'll be back tonight, right?' I couldn't resist asking, needing to hear the confirmation one more time. Docc nodded slowly.

'If all goes well, yes, they should return in just a few hours.'

I let out a deep sigh and nodded, dropping my gaze to focus on the table between us. Just a few hours. That was all the time I had to kill before he'd be back.

I could feel Docc's gaze on me still and knew he was surely seeing the anxiety written on my face. Docc was a very smart man and surely not fooled by my lies, but I couldn't bring myself to admit my feelings for Hayden aloud.

'It's not my place, but I'd like to say something if you don't mind,' Docc said slowly, snapping my attention back up to him.

'By all means,' I said, waving my hand casually in the air before pressing my fingers into my temple. A dull headache had started to creep up, the stress of waiting making its physical presence known.

'Hayden deserves someone like you to care about him. The boy has had a rough deal and I think you're just what he needs.'

I could feel my lips part as I blew out a shaky exhale, Docc's words stunning me into silence – his gaze calm and peaceful while mine surely was intense and shocked.

'You don't have to explain anything to me, and frankly I don't want to know, but it's clear that he cares for you far more than you realise.'

'I don't . . . I'm not . . .' I stuttered, unsure of how to

respond to his bold statement. His lips pulled into a soft smile as he shook his head slowly.

'You don't need to say anything. I just wanted you to hear that. Now, how about you help me with some organising?'

I blinked, surprised by his abrupt subject change but I managed to nod. It was a lot to process. I already knew Hayden cared for me quite a lot, but it made it seem so much more real when Docc said it himself. My mind flashed back to when Hayden had carried me into this very room and been more supportive than I could have asked for without a second thought for Docc's presence. It made a bit more sense when I thought of how that must have looked from Docc's point of view.

The thought of Hayden caring for me so gently made me ache for his presence, and again I felt the anxiety heighten in my stomach. It was impossible to ignore as I pulled myself from my seat to follow Docc to a cabinet where he showed me to organise the vials by medication class. He didn't speak of Hayden again and neither did I, but it was constantly on my mind. Nearly an hour of silent sorting and labelling had passed before I broke the silence, in an attempt to clear the image of Hayden dying a particularly bloody imagined death that was haunting me.

'Is Docc your real name?' It was something I'd wondered for a while but never really had the opportunity to ask.

'No. My name is Doccrie,' he said casually as he picked a handful of vials out of a basket he'd brought over. He squinted at the label before placing it on the shelf.

'Doccrie?' I repeated, frowning. It seemed odd to call him anything but Docc. 'You were a doctor named Doccrie?'

'Trust me, the irony was lost on my colleagues,' he said, letting out a light chuckle. 'It got shortened to Docc while I was in medical school and I've been Docc ever since.'

I let out the first laugh in what felt like years. I was surprised it managed to work through the nerves; it felt slightly unnatural, but it did make me feel a little bit better. Unfortunately, Docc and I had finished our task. Without a distraction, my every thought returned to what Hayden was doing and if he was okay.

My hands twitched by my side as I tried to keep myself calm and rational, but it was difficult. No matter what I did, I couldn't stop seeing Hayden getting killed, injured, captured, something. Every bad thing that could possibly happen flashed through my mind, and I had myself all but convinced he was already dead when Docc interrupted.

'Let's get some food,' he said, studying me closely. I nodded and followed him as he started to move towards the door.

Dinner was a bleak affair, with few words and far too much tension and anxiety. Despite his best efforts, Docc was unsuccessful at diverting me. They'd been gone over three hours now and it was dark by the time Docc and I left the mess hall. The food had tasted like sand, and I hadn't managed to get more than a few bites down before giving up and letting my stomach twist itself into knots.

'Hasn't it been long enough? Shouldn't they be back?' I asked, unable to resist. Docc was accompanying me back to Hayden's hut, where he insisted on depositing me for my night vigil. I shoved my hand hurriedly through my hair as we walked and I was immediately reminded of Hayden doing the same thing when he was stressed.

'Soon, yes. Though sometimes it takes longer than expected, as you know.' How he always managed to be so calm was beyond me, because I felt like a nervous wreck. All I managed to do was huff out a deep breath as we finally arrived at Hayden's hut.

'You go in and get some rest, now. Don't worry yourself sick like you're doing right now,' Docc said kindly, casting a sympathetic smile at me. 'They're tough boys. They'll be all right.'

I nodded and closed my eyes for a few seconds as I tried to believe him. He was right: they'd been on an infinite number of raids and always come back. This time would be no different.

'Thanks, Docc. For everything.'

'Any time, child. Any time.'

With that, he nodded once and turned to head back into the night. The pounding rain had been reduced to a light mist that cast an eerie glow around the camp as it reflected the light of the lanterns. I closed the door behind him, locked it, and started towards Hayden's bed before I remembered Barrow. Without hesitation, I retrieved the knife I'd stashed in my dresser drawer and slipped it under my pillow.

My clothes were still uncomfortably damp from earlier, so I draped them over the back of the chair at Hayden's desk. As I went about my night-time routine, every second seemed to drag by. All I wanted was for Hayden to return and hug me close. I wanted to hear about the raid and something sarcastic Dax probably said. I wanted to hear how Kit remained reasonable and efficient as he always did. I wanted to tell Hayden just how much I felt for him.

That was what was haunting me the most as I crawled into bed – the fact that he might not come back and I had been too scared to tell him. It was almost as if the promise we'd made had been exactly for this situation, but I hadn't upheld it. If he didn't come back and I never told him just how I felt . . .

I shuddered in bed, horrified at the thought. He *would* come back. In an hour or two, he would be here, and things would go back to normal. Or rather, as normal as they possibly could be in this situation. Then, this horrible, gut-wrenching ache would dissipate and I would be free to feel happy with him once more.

But an hour or two passed and there was no whisper of a return. It took everything in me to stay rooted in bed, and more than once I had to physically stop myself from running up to the tower to watch for them. I had been lucky earlier with Docc's intervention, and though I was confident in my abilities, I knew it wasn't smart to go messing around outside. Alone. At night.

Three hours had passed since I lay in bed. A weird kink had settled into my neck from the rigid way I was lying, and my head was positively pounding thanks to the throbbing headache that had developed.

At five hours since I lay down, about eight or nine since their departure, I couldn't lie there any longer. I rose from the bed and immediately began pacing. My feet carried me in a tight line, back and forth, back and forth, until I was certain I'd worn a path in the floor. My hands twisted anxiously in front of me and I found myself silently cursing Hayden for making me stay behind.

If he ever came back, he was going to get a piece of my mind for putting me through this.

When the sun started to creep up in the sky, I'd lost track of how many hours it had been. Far too many, in my opinion. My legs ached from my pacing and my head felt like it was about to fall off my shoulders, but there was nothing I could do. Never in my entire life had I felt so nervous, and it was a feeling I prayed I would never have to feel again. Never again would I stay behind on a raid, because this emotional turmoil was ten times more taxing than any physical pain could ever be.

'*We should be back tonight,*' I muttered bitterly. This was what it had come to: talking to myself.

The sun was fully up in the sky now and it streamed through the windows as if mocking me for my decidedly un-sunny mood. Mixed with the anxiety and nervousness now was anger. Anger at myself for listening to Hayden, anger at Hayden for taking longer than he'd said, and anger at the world.

'What is taking so long?' I demanded to no one in particular. My foot caught on the ground and I stumbled before righting myself. I threw a harsh glare at the ground and resisted the urge to actually growl in frustration.

To say I hated this was a massive understatement. I hated feeling utterly helpless as I waited for him to return. I hated the corrosive anxiety eating away at my stomach. I hated how I was physically unable to sit still without feeling completely insane. I hated everything.

Lunchtime came and went, yet still I paced the hut. I gave up seeking any sort of distraction, the masochist in me choosing to voluntarily wallow in my stress. The more anxiety that built up, the more determined I became to never let this happen again. Black seemed to cloud my vision, now and then, as my thoughts grew impossibly dark. I refused to consider the possibility that Hayden wasn't coming back, because even the very thought of something happening to him made me feel light-headed and impossibly weak.

It had been nearly twenty-four hours since he'd left. An entire day had nearly passed when he was supposed to be gone for only a few hours. There was no way I could deny that something had gone wrong. *Something* had happened, and I felt physically ill at the thought. My stomach churned and I felt like I was going to expel what little food I'd managed to eat over the past day.

Wait for me and I'll come back to you, Bear. I promise.

'You promised,' I muttered as I paced. 'Come on, Hayden. Keep your promise.'

The physical manifestations were even worse than before. My heartbeat was too fast while my lungs felt too slow, as if I was constantly struggling to draw a full breath of air. Knots had appeared in my muscles, and my legs felt shaky from the constant pacing for hours on end. I was certain my insides had dissolved, thanks to the stress eating away at me. I'd never felt anxiety like this before.

A sudden low rumble halted my pacing, jerking me to a stop as I tilted my head toward the sound. Had I just imagined that in desperation, or was that really the rumbling of the truck I heard approaching? My ears pricked as I remained perfectly still, and sure enough, the deep roar of the engine could be heard from far away.

Without a moment's hesitation, I bolted from the hut, flinging the door open as I sprinted outside. My muscles screamed in protest but I pushed forward as I ran towards the sound. If I hadn't been in such a hurry, I'd have noticed that it was now evening, meaning they'd been gone more than a day. The rumbling of the truck grew even louder, but I was yet to see it as I flew between the huts.

My lungs burned and my legs felt like they were going to give out as I pushed on, and the sigh of relief I let out when I saw the truck's glowing headlights nearly knocked me to the ground. Finally, the vehicle came into view in a beam of headlights. My heart pounded heavily, still not quite believing they were back. I needed to see him before I could take a full breath.

All the tension and anxiety seemed to accumulate in that moment and pile on my shoulders as the truck finally pulled to a stop about twenty feet away from me. My feet jerked forward, carrying me on. The headlights blinded me on the approach and it wasn't until I finally drew even with the truck that I could see anything when I gazed up through the windows.

Kit sat in the passenger's seat with a large amount of blood streaked and dried across his cheeks, but alive and well. The bandage on his neck had fallen off to reveal a jagged scar that would probably be there for the rest of his life. In the driver's seat sat Dax, who looked relatively unscathed.

But Dax wasn't supposed to be in the driver's seat. Every raid we'd been on, someone else had driven. Someone whose absence was obvious as I glanced at the back of the truck. My heart shattered to dust before falling through my abdomen, the fine shards shredding every organ on the way down, ripping me apart.

Hayden was gone.

Chapter Eleven – Emotion
GRACE

The images in front of me swooped together and blurred into a dizzying chaos as I stood beside the truck, too shocked to move from where my feet had become rooted to the ground. There was no Hayden driving the truck as he should have been, no Hayden in the backseat, no Hayden anywhere to be found. My body seemed to be revolting against what my eyes were seeing as my heart attempted to break out of my chest, and my stomach twisted violently in my abdomen.

This was not happening.

This couldn't be real.

Hayden was not missing.

But it was happening, it was real, and he was missing.

I finally managed to tear my eyes away from the empty backseat and looked to Dax, who was climbing out of the truck. His face looked serious, which only caused the panic that was rising in my body to intensify.

'Where's Hayden?' I managed to choke out, my words thin and strangled as if my throat was fighting to keep them in. Dax took a cautious step toward me before pausing.

'Grace . . .'

Darkness started to creep into my vision as I stared at him, certain I looked absolutely insane but unable to find it in me to care. I could feel my hands starting to shake by my sides, matching my jerky breathing.

'Where is he, Dax?'

'Grace, just listen—'

'No! Tell me where he is!' I shouted, hysteria edging into my voice. Dax watched me closely, an unreadable expression on his face as he took another step closer.

'Hey, let's just calm down for a sec—'

He was cut off, however, when I threw my hands against his chest to shove him as hard as I could. He stumbled backwards and collided with the side of the truck, causing a loud metallic crunch to echo out over the rumbling of the engine which was still running. I didn't care that I looked crazy, or that this behaviour would raise a lot of questions with Kit, who was surely watching this whole thing. All I cared about was getting answers and finding Hayden.

'Don't do that. Don't you dare tell me to calm down,' I seethed. All my fear, panic, fury, rage, terror and anxiety surged into a physical force as I shoved my hands into Dax's chest again.

'Where is he?' I demanded as I glared up at him. My entire body shook as my hands fell from his chest.

'Grace . . . he didn't make it.'

No.

My feet stumbled backward, away from Dax as his words crashed violently around my skull.

No, no, no, no . . .

I could feel my chest caving in with every gasp of air I took, each one less successful than the last as I tried and failed to breathe. My heart surely would have been beating a thousand miles per hour if it weren't for the fact that it had absolutely disintegrated in my chest, leaving only a gaping black hole where it should have been.

He didn't make it.

It was as if my senses had disappeared, too; everything in front of me muddled together into an indistinguishable blur; the sounds I heard transformed into petrifying screams, each shrill and gut-wrenching sound driving a spear into where my heart should have been. The air around me, which had been warm only moments before, now felt freezing cold, as if trying to suffocate the life out of me.

He didn't make it.

A muffled sound I couldn't make out confirmed that Dax was calling my name, but I was too shocked to reply. I struggled to keep down the bile that rose in the back of my throat, though my still hands clutched my stomach and lips. I felt dizzy, and the black creeping in told me I was on the verge of passing out.

A loud rumble, different to the one emitted by the truck, managed to infiltrate the suffocating haze that had settled over me. I blinked, my jaw quivering as I tried to draw a full breath. After a few attempts, I managed to clear away the fog that had settled over my vision as the rumbling grew even louder. I managed to turn my head towards the source, the muscles in my neck screaming in protest, before they settled on what was causing the new noise.

It was hard to make out as my vision was still rebelling against me and blurring every few seconds, but what I saw nearly made me fall into the dirt. There was one beam coming from the headlight of this other vehicle, so bright it nearly blinded me from seeing who was in control of the noisy four-wheeler.

Surely I was seeing things.

Surely this wasn't what I thought.

Surely this was my vision playing tricks on me.

But the vehicle came closer and closer, there was no denying who it was.

Hayden.

My eyes narrowed in confusion, not daring to believe what I was seeing.

Hayden?

I turned back to Dax, still pressed against the truck and now sporting a ridiculously wide, self-satisfied grin. His arms were crossed over his chest and he looked incredibly pleased with himself. Without deciding, my feet started carrying me briskly towards him.

'Got you,' he said smugly.

My body had felt only rage as my fist rose, drawing back before swinging forward to forcefully connect with his jaw. His head whipped to the side as my punch landed with a dull thud, and I was vengefully pleased to see the smirk had been wiped clear off his face.

'What the hell is wrong with you?!' I shouted, shaking with fury now that I started to put the pieces together. Kit, who I hadn't seen but knew must be close by, cursed loudly in surprise.

'Jesus, chill, Grace, he's fine!' Dax said, throwing his hand in Hayden's direction. The rumbling of the four-wheeler was especially loud now, telling me he was almost upon us, but I couldn't rip my furious glare from Dax.

'That's not fucking funny, Dax!'

Livid was not even close to describe what I was feeling.

'All right, all right, it was a bad joke,' he said, raising one hand in surrender while the other lightly massaged his jaw. He didn't seem upset that I'd punched him, only surprised. 'You didn't have to punch me, damn.'

'You're lucky that's all I did, you little—'

'Hey, what's going on?'

Hayden's voice cut me off, jerking my head towards the source of the sound. It was only then that I noticed the rumbling had disappeared as the engine stopped and the driver started to climb off the seat. My relief that he was alive and relatively unharmed was short-lived, however.

Again, I found myself storming towards someone, only this time it was Hayden. A grin pulled at his lips, clearly oblivious to what I'd just gone through, and he opened his arms as if to receive a hug. The closer I got, the more I felt the furious shake returning to my limbs. At the last second, Hayden's grin faltered as he seemed to notice I was not rushing forward to embrace him.

'Grace, what—'

'You—'

Shove.

'Stupid—'

Push.

'*Arsehole!*' I finished with another solid shove, my hands colliding heavily with his firm chest. Much to my frustration, he hardly moved despite my best efforts.

'What the hell!' he said, throwing a bewildered look in Dax's direction, which only served to piss me off more. I was feeling more than irrational and ridiculously emotional, but it was justified. My rage was directed at every single person in my vicinity, whether they deserved it or not.

They all deserved it.

They were all dickheads.

I let out a furious yell as I shoved my hands at Hayden's chest once again. This time he seemed to pull himself out of his shock to catch my wrists and stop them from hitting him again. I struggled against his grip and tried to free myself.

'Let me *go*!'

'No, Grace,' Hayden said, his voice strained as he tried to subdue my tantrum.

'Stop,' I demanded, twisting this way and that, in an attempt to throw his hands off my wrists, but still he held on. I could feel the hysteria I'd given into changing now to something else, something deeper.

'No,' Hayden rebutted, fighting me all while being careful not to hurt me. I could feel my throat tightening, burning as I tried to free my hands. I needed to shove him, push him, hit him. I needed him to feel an ounce of the pain I'd just gone through when I'd thought for a few devastating moments he was dead.

But my actions had slowed, my attempts to attack less vigilant as I gave a half-hearted shove.

'Stop,' I repeated. My voice was losing its angry conviction as I struggled to hold down the sob I felt fighting to break through. Hayden's gaze held mine, still slightly confused but blazing. It was like he could feel me breaking down and was waiting for the moment I started to fall to pieces completely before he rushed in to catch me.

'Grace, stop,' he said gently. My last effort to shove him off me was the weakest yet, and all it took was a soft pull of his hands on my wrists to send me crashing into his chest. The moment I gave in, I did something that I hadn't done once since arriving in Blackwing: I cried.

His arms wrapped around me immediately, enveloping me in his warmth as I clung to him. Once I let the tears start, they seemed to take over my entire body as sobs ripped from my lungs and shuddered through me. Tears wet Hayden's neck as I buried my face there, but he gave no notice as he held me tightly to him.

'It's okay, Bear,' he whispered so no one other than me would hear.

The use of his endearing nickname for me only set me off again as I tried and failed to draw an even breath. It was the weakest I'd felt in a long time; the broken rib had felt like a mere annoyance when compared to the pain of momentarily losing him. After all I'd gone through here, after all the decisions I'd made, this was what had broken me down and made me cry.

I didn't care that we were standing right in front of Kit and Dax. I didn't care that I looked absolutely crazy. I didn't care that I was crying like some pathetic little girl. All I cared about at that moment was that Hayden was back, and he was alive. Hayden didn't seem to mind our stunned audience either, because he continued to hold me as tightly as I held him, while he murmured quiet words into my ear.

'It's all right, Grace, I'm fine,' he whispered, once again quiet enough for only me to hear. My face stayed hidden in his neck and my grip on him never loosened as I cried, the shaking in my body making my muscles ache even more than they did from the stress. One of Hayden's arms unwound from my waist to rake his hand lightly down the back of my hair soothingly, his actions repeated over and over as he tried to calm me down.

It could have been minutes or hours, I had no way of knowing just how long I stood like that. Clinging to Hayden, his arms locked around me, was the most emotional I could remember feeling in a very, very long time. Finally, I managed to draw a full, shaky breath that seemed to stretch my lungs and sniffed once before I loosened my arms just enough to pull back.

Hayden looked down at me with a gentle, slightly confused expression. His arms looped lightly around my waist, and mine fell from around his shoulders to land weakly on his chest.

'I thought you were dead,' I muttered, shaking my head slightly as if still not fully believing he was there.

'Why would you think that, Grace?' Hayden frowned.

'Dax said you didn't make it.' Anger was returning now as it struck me just how awful that had been. I didn't see how anyone would find it amusing even in the slightest.

'What?' Hayden's lips parted in surprise and he shot a confused look at Dax.

'Hey, I thought it would be funny,' Dax defended. He sounded like he very much regretted it now after seeing how I'd reacted.

'It wasn't funny,' I spat, throwing a glare in his direction. I was vaguely aware of Hayden's arms falling from around me and I took a small step away from him now that Kit and Dax seemed to be back in the picture.

'That was a dick move, mate,' Kit said. He'd climbed from the passenger seat in the truck to stand with us all. He shook his head slowly as if disappointed. It occurred to me that Kit seemed to know more than he let on, making me think he was much more observant than I'd previously realised. He didn't seem shocked by much of this, something I didn't really know how to react to.

'All right, I get it! I didn't think she'd freak out like that,' Dax said. His eyes were wide as if still surprised. 'I'm sorry, Grace, but you did get a good punch in so that should help.'

'You deserve another one,' I told him.

'I'm sure I'll get one sooner or later so justice will be served, don't you worry,' he said, shrugging. An angry red blotch had formed over his jaw, though I felt no guilt for it. He deserved it, and even he couldn't deny it.

'Good,' I muttered.

'You can put away all the stuff then, Dax. Serves you right,' Hayden said, flicking his head toward their truck and the four-wheeler they must have acquired on the raid. I resisted the urge to walk over and kick it, irrationally blaming the inanimate object for Hayden's late arrival and my subsequent panic attack.

'Fair enough,' he mumbled. It was clear he felt bad after seeing what his 'joke' had done to me.

Kit jumped behind the wheel of the truck while Dax took over driving the four-wheeler. They both called out goodbyes to me as they passed, Dax's sheepish and guilty, before they disappeared down the path to leave Hayden and I alone.

'Come on, Grace,' Hayden said gently, placing a hand on my lower back to steer me back down the path. It was as if he could tell how fragile I still was, which I had begun to feel embarrassed by. I had completely lost my cool, making me look far weaker than I ever wanted to be seen. But Hayden was back and that was all that mattered.

The return to his hut was silent as I tried to gather my thoughts. I vowed silently never to be left behind again. Back at Hayden's home we moved through the door without a word. Immediately, I crossed the room and sat on the edge of his bed, too exhausted to stand any longer. I watched, feeling slightly numb, as Hayden kicked off his boots that were caked with mud. Finally, Hayden moved to stand in front of me, gazing down at me gently while I looked up at him.

'I can't do that again, Hayden,' I told him truthfully. A shaky breath blew past my lips as I felt his hand cradle my jaw lightly. I could see he knew how much it must have scared me as he peered down at me.

'I couldn't let you go, Grace,' he explained gently. His thumb dragged over my lower lip once before he crouched down in front of me. His touch left my face and he let his hands hook lightly around my knees while he watched me closely.

'I won't do it again, I mean it. I can't . . . It was way too hard. You can't leave me behind again,' I said, feeling the tears starting to creep up once more as I tried to force them down. I refused to make a habit of this crying thing. 'Every second you were gone, all I thought about was how you were going to get killed. It was *hell*, Hayden.'

'Hey,' he said gently, moving closer and reaching up to push my hair lightly out of my face. 'I promised I'd come back to you, didn't I?'

My eyes squeezed shut momentarily and I blew a light breath from between my lips to try and calm my heart, which had started to race once more. I nodded slowly and let my hand fall to cover his that was resting on my knee. 'You did.'

'Yes, I did. And I came back to you,' he said softly.

I swallowed harshly, his gaze melting me from the inside out as he watched for my reaction. The emotions had rushed back in full force, though I was fairly sure they had never really left. Silently, I reached forward and looped my arms around his neck to hug him to me once more. He obliged, scooting me closer to the edge of the bed so he rested between my thighs while he hugged me.

Without really deciding, I shifted backward, pulling him with me so he hovered over me as my back struck the mattress. I never loosened my hug, nor did he, as we held each other close. His body came to rest between my thighs, and much of his weight settled onto me comfortably. Almost no pain came from my ribs despite this, a sure sign of healing and probably, distraction.

'Don't ever leave me again, Hayden,' I whispered, my words muffled by my lips at his neck.

'Grace . . .' he trailed off, reluctant to promise me such a thing.

'Please, Hayden,' I begged quietly, pulling my face from his neck to look up at him as he hovered over me. 'Please.'

He frowned down at me, his hair falling down over his forehead like a halo. His eyes searched mine deeply, and it was obvious he saw just how serious I was. 'I won't leave you.'

A rush of relief flooded through me, and my arms pulled on his neck to bring his lips to mine. It was the first kiss we'd shared since he'd come back, and I could feel all the emotions I'd experienced pouring into it. There was a quiet desperation, a subtle hint of the promise he'd just made beneath the motions as he kissed me slowly.

His actions were gentle and smooth, as if savouring every whisper of our lips against each other's. My eyes squeezed shut and my hands tangled lightly in his hair, holding him to me as his lips captured mine gently. It still seemed like such a miracle that he was back, and I relished the chance to hold him and kiss him once more, determined to never let go of him.

A quiet groan rumbled from his throat as he pressed his hips lightly into my own, increasing the pressure between us and instantly building the heat that had been simmering beneath the surface. I craved more contact, needed more pressure between us. I needed the confirmation that he really was breathing, warm, alive. I needed to feel it.

My lip was tugged between Hayden's teeth as he pulled it back, nipping lightly before releasing it to trail his lips across my cheek. I could feel the warmth of his breath at my ear as he let his lips close around the lobe lightly, and a wet heat when he continued his path on my neck. My head rolled to the side as my eyes drifted shut, in pleasure.

Without really deciding to, my hands slid down his back to grip the hem of his shirt. I started to tug it upward, revealing his marred back inch by inch, until I had it up to his shoulders. He finally seemed to realise what I was doing, because he pulled his lips reluctantly from my neck to pull it off, casting it to the floor and revealing his toned torso to me.

He paused for a moment, before his hand snaked under my shirt. His fingers grazed my stomach and my ribs lightly before he gripped the fabric and pushed it up my abdomen. His lips found mine again as he kissed me gently, all the while pushing my shirt higher and higher. When I felt it reach my bra line, I pulled my hands from where they'd landed on his neck to take over. Sitting up just enough to pull it over my head, I managed to free myself of the shirt before Hayden's bare chest pressed back against mine.

Raised scars and jagged edges passed beneath my palms as I slid them slowly down his back. I sucked in a breath when his hips rolled into mine, more purposeful this time than the first. All the emotion and stress I'd experienced over the past day and half seemed to leach out of my system as I began to lose myself in Hayden, every action on his part chipping away at the anxiety.

I could feel the heat building between us and the desperate need that was growing as he kissed me fervently, dipping his tongue into my mouth in time with his hips grinding against my own. A very prominent bulge had appeared between us, sending a wave of anticipation through me. My hands moved over the warm skin to land on his waistband, fingers digging beneath the fabric before sliding around between us.

I tried not to remember the first time I'd attempted this, a time that felt like years ago now when he'd stopped me.

So much had changed since then and so many more feelings had developed that I was even more terrified of the same rejection. Much to my horror, Hayden's lips paused against mine, a sure sign of hesitation, when my fingers began to undo the button of his jeans. My heart sank as he stopped kissing me.

'Grace, we can't,' he murmured, his voice loaded with disappointment. I felt an embarrassed blush creeping into my cheeks.

'Why not?' I asked. My voice sounded small.

'We don't have . . . anything,' he said vaguely. Again, I felt a rush of heat to my cheeks.

'Um . . .' I trailed off, unsure of how to tell him. 'Don't be mad but . . .'

He paused and gazed down at me, his eyes slightly wild thanks to his heated state. 'What?'

'I kind of . . . got a birth control shot from Docc,' I said, barely able to hold his gaze as I spoke. He blinked once as a flicker of confusion crossed his face.

'You did?'

'Please don't be mad,' I said, wincing slightly. He studied me for a few long seconds, sending my heart into yet another fit of nervous pounding. I was suddenly very afraid he'd be angry at me for doing something so bold, for not telling him, for potentially letting someone else know about our . . . relationship.

'I'm not mad,' he said finally, his voice soft. My eyes examined his, searching for signs of deception. I found none.

'You're not?'

'No, I'm not,' he said, cutting off my response by kissing me once again. His lips melded with mine and his hips pushed against me once once, earning a soft moan from me.

Relief so strong flooded through me that it made it difficult to draw a breath as I returned his kiss and let my hands splay out across his lower back once more.

I felt the heat of his hand as it trailed down my side before coming to rest over my hip. My skin felt like it was on fire when he dug his fingers beneath the waistband and tugged it down, taking my underwear with it. My hips lifted off the mattress to ease the process, and soon he had them cleared from my legs, leaving me in just my bra. Feeling braver now that he'd reacted well to my revelation, I resumed my work of unfastening his jeans.

His lips pulled from mine as I undid the zip and slipped my hands beneath the band to push them down his hips along with his boxers, shifting his weight slightly until he helped me remove them completely. I could feel the warmth of his breath over my skin, his uneven panting as he rested his weight on top of me. His hand snaked behind my back to undo my bra, releasing the clasp and pulling it from between us to leave us both completely naked.

One final kiss was pressed into my throat as he raised his head in front of me, gazing down at me intently.

'Are you sure you're okay with this?' he asked softly, so softly. I could feel every inch of his body that was pressed into mine, and I could feel just how ready he was if I were to give him permission. I had never been more okay with anything in my life.

'Yes. I want this so badly, Hayden,' I answered honestly. My voice was no more than a mere whisper. He paused, making sure I really meant it.

'Please, I just want to feel you,' I begged. I was so desperate to share this with him that it made me feel like I was going to burst into flames if I didn't. 'Don't you want this?'

'You have no idea how much I want this, Grace,' he answered honestly.

His gaze was practically burning a hole through me, and I could feel him pressing lightly at my entrance. My hips shifted, sending a flicker of pleasure flitting across his face as he blew out a sharp breath. I pulled down on his neck once more, bringing his lips to mine. I pressed a feathery-light kiss, holding it for a few seconds before I pulled back just enough to mumble against his lips.

'Then show me.'

He gave the smallest of nods before reconnecting our lips once more, kissing me deeply and smoothly as his tongue slid slowly across my own. My entire body was buzzing with anticipation and I felt like I was actually going slightly mad, but the moment his hips shifted forward to slowly push into me, everything felt right. I gasped, our kiss broken. We were both breathing shakily, our lips parted and pressed together but not moving as he moved slowly, so carefully and slowly, until he had filled me completely.

'Hayden . . .' I breathed, overcome by the beautiful way he stretched my body. His hips pulled back slowly, his body rolling easily before pushing back into me again. We resumed the kiss that had been interrupted moments before. He supported himself on his elbows, one either side of my head, as he rolled smoothly over me, driving himself in and out of me slowly, his chest pressed to mine.

'Oh my god, Grace,' he groaned. I was unable to respond as his body moved over mine, each and every roll of his hips sending a wave of heat through me. My hands roamed down his back to feel the muscles that allowed him to move so fluidly. Again and again, his hips surged forward.

It seemed like such a long time coming, even overdue, yet exactly right at the same time. To give in to this earlier would have cheapened it, diminished it. Waiting until now made it feel so utterly perfect and beautiful that I wouldn't have changed a thing. Now, when the feelings between us were so strong, it felt like it was exactly what we were supposed to do.

The pace was slow, lingering, burning, and more emotional than anything I'd ever felt. His lips moved against mine in steady rhythm with his hips, creating a beautiful fluidity of movement. It was like every move he made was intended to show just how much he cared about me. Every time he pushed into me felt even better than the last, quickly adding to the pressure building in the pit of my stomach as well as the warmth radiating from my heart.

Hayden's hand lifted from the mattress to cup my face gently as his hips shifted forward slowly, dragging out each and every thrust to unwind me completely. He kissed me deeply, held me gently, rocked into me slowly. My breathing was shallow and weak as I tried to hang on.

My legs wrapped around his waist, bringing our bodies even closer together. His hand left my face to find my fingers. His fingers tangled with my hand, pressing the back of it into the mattress above my head as his body rolled smoothly once again.

'Hayden, god,' I panted. My lips pulled from his as my back arched, tilting my head back even farther. He took the opportunity to trail his lips down my neck, allowing his tongue to dart out here and there to wet my skin as he continued to roll his hips forward. I knew I wouldn't last much longer with this devastatingly deep and slow pace.

'Hang on, Grace,' he whispered, his voice strained as a low groan escaped his lips. My eyes squeezed tightly shut as I struggled to resist, and my legs tightened even more. My breathing was positively ragged now and the pressure in my stomach was begging to be released. My hips jerked involuntarily and my limbs started to shake.

'I can't—' I was cut off, however, by a moan that ripped from my throat as Hayden pushed deep into me, sending me over the edge and releasing the pressure that had been building up. Relief coursed through me, making my muscles practically vibrate and my limbs shake even more. Heat seared through my veins, and I couldn't stop the strangled gasps and moans that tumbled from my lips.

The sounds were briefly stifled by Hayden's lips pressing to mine, kissing me desperately as he rocked forward into me one last time. His muscles tensed before he let out a gasp and hit his high, stilling inside me as he let go. My legs, like jelly now as they shook around his waist, struggled as I tugged him tightly against me, while my body started to come down.

Finally, after a few moments of unadulterated bliss, he let himself collapse against me, resting his weight once again on his elbows before pressing his lips to mine heavily. He held himself there for a few seconds, revelling in the effects of his high while I tried to stop my body from shaking. He pulled from me and pressed one last kiss to my lips before finally opening his eyes to meet my gaze.

His eyes were blazing and a glow had settled over his skin, illuminated by a thin sheen of sweat. We were both panting through parted lips as we recovered. A look of bliss, slight surprise, and captivation settled on his face; he looked absolutely amazing. I struggled to take a breath as I felt his hand gently push my hair off my face, my heart beating a thousand miles an hour.

'You are so beautiful, Grace.'

A grin pulled at my lips as I let out a blissful gasp of a laugh, still unable to respond other than to pull his lips down to mine once more in a delicate kiss. No one had ever made me feel like this before, and there was no doubt in my mind that I was absolutely in love with him.

Chapter Twelve – Irreversible
HAYDEN

Surely this was a dream.

Surely this girl I was seeing now wasn't real.

Surely the heat I felt coursing through my body was a simple trick of the mind and not the result of her skin pressing into every inch of my own. It didn't seem possible that this had happened; it wasn't planned, wasn't anticipated, wasn't even really conceivable, but it had been, without a doubt, absolutely perfect.

I could feel the thin coat of sweat over my skin, feel the strands of hair sticking to the back of my neck, and feel the way my heart hammered violently. I could feel the sizzling warmth that burned through my veins and consumed me in flames, tearing through my limbs and igniting my heart. My body was still coming down from its high and my mind whirred in a thousand directions all at once while surrounding one single topic: Grace.

Every cell in my brain was certain that she was the most beautiful I'd ever seen her as she gazed up at me now, a light flush creeping up in her cheeks that seemed almost dim in comparison to the blissful glow that emitted from her eyes. I felt too mesmerised by her to even move.

'You are so beautiful, Grace,' I told her, awe stealing the volume from my voice. How could I not be in awe? Never once, in my entire life, had I felt anything close to what it had just felt like to be with her. Previous encounters had been coldly detached, a weak excuse at best for what it should have felt like. There had been the sense of going through the motions, but the deep, burning, emotional connection I'd been unknowingly craving had been missing.

Until now.

Until Grace.

A soft gasp of a laugh blew past her lips, the sound almost angelic as it floated through the air. She smiled gently at me before tightening her arms and drawing me back down to her. My lips pressed to hers gently and yet another spark erupted at the contact, shooting through my body that still rested on top of hers. It was like she had some strong gravitational pull that drew me in more and more – the closer I got, the more impossible it became to pull myself away.

I could still feel the way we'd fitted together, the way our bodies had moved; the inevitability of it felt too strong to resist, though the build-up had been the most exquisitely beautiful part. It was as if waiting had made the moment all the more perfect, and all I wanted to do was sink into that space for the rest of my life. I wanted to let it weigh me down and to revel in the comforting pressure of it. I wanted to block out the world and linger with no one but Grace, the pressures and responsibilities of my everyday life forgotten for those short moments in time because I was with her.

When my lips finally separated from hers, it felt far too soon. I wasn't ready to let go. Reluctantly, I ducked my head forward to press one last lingering kiss at the hinge of her jaw before I shifted sideways, landing on my side to climb out of bed. I moved to the drawer and pulled on a pair of boxer briefs before tugging out one of my shirts and a pair of shorts as well.

I turned to see Grace sitting up slightly in the bed, the blanket held loosely over her chest as she watched me. With a soft grin, I tossed her my clothes. My grin widened even more as I watched her pull the shirt over her head, something about seeing her in my clothing making me very happy. She wiggled under the blanket as she pulled on the shorts before she settled back into the mattress. Without a word, I returned to the bed and climbed back in next to her. She rolled over, mirroring me so she, too, was lying on her side as she pressed into me with my arm draped over her hip.

My eyes found hers, the stunning green of them bright despite the dim lighting of the hut. I suddenly found myself at a loss for what to say as I studied her features closely, memorising every detail in the perfectly serene moment.

'What?' she asked with a soft laugh as she noticed me studying her. I shook my head in slight disbelief.

'I just . . . I've never felt something like that before,' I admitted, the residual high from what we'd just done together making me vulnerable. I didn't even have time to feel nervous at having said that before she responded.

'Neither have I,' she whispered softly.

I felt her fingertips run along a jagged scar covering my skin. Her statement was basically confirmation of what I already strongly suspected but hadn't asked: I wasn't her first. I didn't know how to feel about this revelation, so I just chose to ignore it. She wasn't my first, after all, yet she was the only person I'd come across yet in this world to make me feel anything. That was all that mattered.

'Hayden . . .' she started before drawing a deep breath. Her gaze dropped momentarily as she seemed to collect her thoughts before flitting back up to mine. 'You have no idea how scared I was when I thought you weren't coming back.'

I could feel the intensity of our words as they sizzled between us.

'You don't know what it was like sitting here all day waiting for you to come back and then when Dax said you didn't make it, I just . . . I broke, Hayden.'

Her words were laced with a dangerous emotion, and I could sense that she was close to letting herself slip into the fear I'd seen written across her features when I pulled up earlier.

'Hey, shhh,' I whispered, drawing her closer so her chest pressed into mine. My hand smoothed gently down the back of her head and I felt a small spark as her lips pressed shakily into the base of my throat. Earlier tonight was by far the most vulnerable I'd ever seen her and it was tearing my heart in two. She finally drew one full, shuddering breath and pulled back far enough to look me in the eyes once more.

'I've never seen you cry before tonight,' I told her quietly. There weren't enough words to describe the pain I'd felt when I saw her breaking in front of me. It had been so clear that she wasn't okay, despite her determination to remain so strong. It wasn't until the last second that she'd given in and shattered, but luckily I'd been waiting at her feet to pick her up again. Or at least, to try.

'That's because of you, Hayden,' she answered seriously. 'What I felt when I thought you were dead . . . it was enough to rip me in half.'

It was one thing to see how distraught she'd been and feel the physical shake of her body when she broke down, but another thing entirely for her to admit it. She was always so brave, but this was a different kind of brave we both struggled with: bravery to admit our feelings. The strength it took for her to admit such a thing was astronomical, and I felt even more in awe of her than I already was.

'I never want to see you cry again,' I said honestly. It was an unusual brand of pain to feel something on someone else's behalf – a deep, guttural pain that seemed even worse than the kind derived from one's self.

'Just . . . never leave me behind again, okay? If I'm with you, I'm happy.'

Again, my heart thumped so hard it felt like it was trying to jump in my throat. I wished I had the words to explain how happy she made me – happier than I ever remembered feeling.

'I promise. I'm so sorry, Grace,' I murmured, unsure of what else to say to take back the horrible things she'd gone through earlier. 'I'm seriously going to kick the shit out of Dax for this . . .'

'Let me do it and it'll help,' she said, letting out a wispy laugh. I chuckled quietly as my lips pulled up to one side, and my hand rose gently to brush her hair back behind her ear. She was so strong, so resilient, so ferocious.

She was my Bear.

'Deal,' I obliged easily. She shot me a small, satisfied smile that warmed me from the inside out before speaking again.

'But I'm mad at you, too,' she said, frowning suddenly in an overly serious fashion as if scolding me.

'Me? Why?' I asked, my tone light.

'You said you'd be back in a few hours. That was so much more than a few hours,' she accused fairly.

'I know,' I admitted. 'I'm sorry.'

She sighed heavily and continued to tickle her fingers absent-mindedly across my chest. 'You're back now, that's all that matters. What took you so long, anyway?'

I'd been hoping she wouldn't ask; I'd wanted to forget the things I'd seen and leave them behind forever, sparing the details from Grace, but I knew that wasn't right. I didn't want to tell her how many we'd been forced to kill, how many pointless lives had been lost simply because we were all in the wrong place at the wrong time, and I certainly didn't want to tell her that those killed were from her home.

'Hayden?' Grace prodded gently. Her face was pulled in a light frown, and her brows were knit together over those captivating eyes.

I hesitated as the events of the raid flashed through my head. Everything had started off so well and we'd collected half of our supplies with no interruptions — until *they*'d come from an alley, surprising them and us alike. There had been so many of them, so many to fight and so many to fall, so many faces to be forever ingrained in my mind as the dead stared blankly up at the sky.

'Hayden,' she repeated, a bit more forcefully this time. 'What happened?'

'Grace . . .' I sighed, unable to stop myself from using the tone I knew she hated. The tone that promised bad news. Her face tightened as she recognised it, bracing herself.

'What? What happened, Hayden?' she pressed, her body physically tensing against my own. Guilt flickered inside me because I knew I was about to bring down her blissfully light mood.

'Things were going fine until we went to the third pharmacy . . . We ran into some people and everyone just started shooting. They kept falling and falling, at least ten of them . . .'

I trailed off, squeezing my eyes shut against the image of a boy too young to be on a raid, a thin trickle of blood leaking from his chest as he fell to the ground. He was too young, too inexperienced, too slow, and now he was dead. He'd been killed by someone, though it hadn't been us. Not only had we run into a pack of Greystone, but we'd become

167

caught in a crossfire with a small group of Brutes.

'Then when they were gone, the Brutes came and we got stuck in this building. We had to wait until morning to leave and then we still had half of the stuff to get. We found the four-wheeler so I offered to drive it back but I didn't even think how it would look if our truck pulled up without me. I was just so distracted by everything to think straight . . .'

I paused again, frowning as I remembered the gruesome events of the raid. It seemed so long ago that I was in the ruins of the city fighting so many when now I felt so content to hold Grace against me. Her gentle touch on the side of my face brought me back, eradicating the visions as I refocused on her glowing face.

'Who is "them", Hayden?' she asked quietly.

I didn't answer but frowned gently at her.

'*Who?*'

I remained silent, my face pained. My silence was confirmation of what I knew she suspected.

'Greystone,' she stated slowly. Her eyes flitted quickly back and forth between my own. 'My father—'

'He wasn't there,' I reassured her quickly, catching her train of thought and cutting her off. I shook my head and cupped my hand around her face, running my thumb over her cheek to calm her. 'Neither was your brother, don't worry.'

She blew out a gentle sigh of relief and sagged forward slightly. I hated reminding her of what she'd lost and given up, but at least she knew they were alive.

'How many?' she asked, her voice slightly subdued. Her eyes closed as she waited for me to answer, already cringing slightly as if she knew it wouldn't be good.

'At least ten,' I answered honestly. 'Maybe more.'

'*Ten?*' she repeated tightly.

I pursed my lips together and let them drop onto her forehead, letting them linger there in my unwillingness to answer. I simply shook my head, something I knew she'd feel even though her eyes were closed. She surprised me by pulling back and reconnecting our gaze. Her hand once again reached up to run her fingers lightly along my jaw.

'Are you okay?'

I blinked in surprise. I just told her I'd helped kill ten people from her home and she wanted to know how I was?

'I'm fine,' I answered automatically. She studied me closely, her gaze burning intensely into mine. After a few seconds, she shook her head minutely.

'No, you're not,' she assessed. I tried to keep my face blank as she continued to scrutinize me, but it was useless. The guilt I felt was eating me up as it always did; there were some things I could never get used to, and killing was one of them.

'You hate it, I know you do,' she said quietly. 'The violence and the killing . . . You hate it.'

Again I didn't say anything. I couldn't deny her statement, so why bother speaking at all? Every life that was lost seemed utterly pointless to me; what made one person's will to survive more deserving of life than another's? What was the determining factor? Stepping left instead of right and into the line of fire? There was no justice left, only the unwritten laws of the sadistically cruel realm we'd fallen into.

'You deserve so much better than this world, Hayden.'

My eyes, which had drifted to focus on the space between us, snapped back to hers. 'Don't say that. I'm no more deserving than anyone else, all right?'

She shook her head gently. 'I just wish you could see how incredible you are. You have absolutely no idea.'

She was wrong, though. If I was half the man she thought

I was, I would have been able to tell her the one detail I'd left out. It was the one phrase I'd heard that could have given warning to their arrival if only it hadn't taken me by surprise. It was what seemed to taunt me now, mocking me for being too afraid to tell her because I knew what it would do to her, what it would make her want to do.

Celt's sickness is getting worse. We need the medicine before he's too far gone.

If what I heard before the chaos was true, her father was very sick, and I couldn't bring myself to tell her. I was weak, selfish, greedy, and the farthest thing from what she thought of me.

'I wish I could be the man you think I am, Grace,' I said quietly. 'I wish I could be that for you.'

'You already are. Always so stubborn . . .' she murmured, shaking her head gently. The tiniest hint of a smile pulled at her lips as she let her hand snake back into my hair, raking her fingers soothingly through the strands.

Neither of us said anything for a few moments, caught in a stalemate while we both firmly believed ourselves to be correct. I knew, deep down, she was wrong. If I had any strength, I'd have let her go a long time ago, but I hadn't. I'd clung to my desperate desires and selfish urges, keeping her here against her will, and begging her to stay when she finally was presented with the choice to go. My rejoicing in her decision was evidence of my flawed character, as I was only selfishly happy she'd given up so much to stay with me. Me, who didn't deserve someone like her for even a second of time.

I wasn't exactly sure when it had happened, but she'd done something to me, changed me and melted the cold layer of ice around my heart, and there was no going back. The more I'd resisted, the harder I'd fallen until I lay crumbled in a heap on the floor, shattered into a thousand pieces until she made me feel whole and then fragment all over again. I was broken, beautifully broken, yet so completely whole all at once.

Despite all my lies and attempts to convince her otherwise, she'd seen through my façade easily. All my bullshit about not caring for anyone was dismissed almost instantly as she challenged the beliefs I'd grown up with. It was something I'd firmly believed until she'd come along only to be completely shattered now that I felt this way about her.

Just as I knew I would do anything for those in my camp – Jett, Dax, Kit, Docc, Maisie, any of them – I knew I would for Grace, too. If I was being totally honest with myself, I knew I would do more. I would sacrifice anything for her, pay any price to keep her safe, and I had been right about one thing: caring makes you weak. I was weaker now than I had ever been as I found myself putting her life before mine, yet at the same time, I had never been stronger.

There was a certain strength to be drawn from our feelings, and it was something I'd never dreamed of. She lightened me, challenged me, and taught me so much more than I probably even realised at that moment. There was something undeniable between us, and it was so strong that no amount of resistance on my part could have stopped it. As much as I had fought it, resisted it, and tried to ignore it, there was no denying it.

Grace had captured my heart, and I was indisputably, irreversibly in love with her.

Chapter Thirteen – Resolute
GRACE

I huffed in frustration as I sat perched against the back of the mess hall, the shade from the roof keeping me cool. Despite my efforts to help, I'd been banished to the sidelines to watch while the three boys built a small fence for Maisie to house the chickens. Their old pen had finally broken and they'd almost escaped before a valiant rescue by Jett and several other younger members of Blackwing.

The moment I'd lifted a large fence post and carried it over to them, Hayden had practically scolded me and told me I wasn't allowed to help because of my rib. The last few days, I'd hardly felt a thing, which made me feel relieved because I could finally get back to training again. As much as I appreciated Hayden's concern, it was a bit much and made me feel relatively useless.

For now, I watched Hayden work. He'd long ago shed his shirt, leaving him in just a pair of black athletic shorts and tennis shoes, and a thin layer of sweat had formed over his skin. The dark smattering of tattoos seemed even sharper, but his scars weren't visible as his muscles flexed along his arms and chest when he hammered a pole into the ground. I was slightly transfixed by the way he moved, and it was nearly impossible to stop myself from gaping at him.

'Grace,' he called suddenly, without looking at me as he frowned at the fence he was constructing.

'Yeah?'

'Would you bring me those nails?'

'Sure,' I said, rising from my position to gather the box at my feet before carrying them over to Hayden. He raised his hand to wipe it across his brow, then flashed me a grin as he accepted the nails I handed him.

'Thanks.'

'Mmhmm. You know I really could be helping with this and we'd all be done that much sooner,' I offered hopefully.

'Yeah, we'd all be done much sooner,' a voice chimed in from a few yards away.

Dax had dared to speak to me. His careful grin turned to a grimace as he caught my harsh look, and he returned to his work. He was yet to offer me a sincere apology; the half-hearted one he'd said jokingly when Hayden and I arrived this morning had fallen very short.

'Watch it, mate,' Hayden warned.

His voice seemed playful, but there was an edge to it that made it clear he hadn't forgiven him either. I heard Kit mumble something to Dax, followed by a heavy sigh as Dax pushed himself off the ground where he'd been kneeling. He approached us slowly, as if we were a pair of cobras about to strike him down.

'Look, guys, I really am sorry,' he said sincerely. His gaze flitted back and forth between Hayden and me, a united front against him. I felt Hayden's shoulder nudge mine slightly as he moved a bit closer to me.

'Don't apologise to me – apologise to her,' Hayden said sharply.

Dax sighed again and shifted his gaze to me. My arms

crossed automatically over my chest and I cocked an eyebrow at him expectantly.

'Grace, I'm sorry. I know it wasn't funny and I shouldn't have made a joke like that. I honestly don't know what I was thinking. But I never would have guessed you'd react like that. I'm so sorry.'

'I just don't see why you'd do that, Dax. You know . . .' I trailed off, frustrated by this entire situation. Now that the agonizing pain had gone away, all I felt was bitterness towards him after what he'd put me through even though it had ended well. I took a deep breath and shook my head to refocus. 'You knew that would hurt me.'

'I know,' he agreed solemnly. He looked like a kicked puppy and I felt a bit of sympathy for him, though it was still outweighed by resentment. 'I really am sorry.'

I could feel Hayden watching me closely as I considered Dax's apology. I really did like him and didn't want to be angry with him, but it had really been a dick move to make me think Hayden was actually dead.

'You want to punch him again? Because I'd be fine with that,' Hayden added, a tiny hint of amusement creeping into his voice.

'Please, no, my face is my money-maker and you've already got a good one in,' Dax said lightly. He clasped his hands in front of him as if begging for his life. Despite my reluctance, I let out a quiet chuckle.

'It's all right, Dax. Just don't pull something like that again or I will beat the hell out of you.'

'Never again will I make the mistake of messing with you two,' he said, raising his hands by his side in surrender. His eyes widened as he glanced back and forth between us, playfully taking a step backward. Hayden let out a low chuckle as he shook his head.

'You're an idiot.'

I couldn't help but agree. Dax was an idiot, but he kept the mood light and it was nearly impossible not to like him. He shot us one final smile before retreating to rejoin Kit and finish their work on the fence. Hayden hammered a few final nails into his side. When he straightened up, he shot me a tight smile. I returned it but couldn't help think that his felt a bit forced.

'Shall we head back? Kit and Dax can finish up.'

'Yeah, sounds good,' I agreed. We called our goodbyes to Kit and Dax before heading back towards Hayden's hut. Evening was quickly approaching, and the sun was already starting to dip lower in the sky.

Today with Dax was the most animated Hayden had been for a while, but now it appeared he'd retreated back into his shell. Ever since he'd returned from the raid and we'd finally slept together a few days ago, something in him had changed. It was difficult to pick it out, and sometimes he hid it almost completely, but he was different. He'd been quiet, even quieter than usual, and I often found him either staring at me or off into the distance as if lost in his own head.

Did he regret our time together? Were his thoughts clouded with remorse and a desire to take it all back? These thoughts unsettled me, and were impossible to shake, especially at times like this when he was so inexplicably quiet. A nervous twinge ticked at my stomach as we finally entered his hut.

'I'm going to take a shower,' he said evenly. He shot me the smallest of smiles before disappearing behind the door, leaving me once again with my thoughts.

'Okay,' I said. It felt so strange to have been so intimate with him only days ago and now struggle to simply communicate. It was like he was locked in his own head, barricaded against me.

I could hear the water from the shower through the door as I flopped backward onto Hayden's bed with a soft sigh. I felt very conflicted; I wanted to flat out ask Hayden what was wrong and stop tiptoeing around everything like a scared little girl, but I was also afraid of what he'd say.

Seeing as I had relatively no experience with things like this, I had no idea what to do. My feelings for him hadn't changed, and I was still just as certain that what I felt for him was love, but his behaviour lately had scared any thought of saying it out loud from my mind.

I jumped when the bathroom door opened, revealing a slightly damp Hayden with just a towel around his waist. Water droplets glittered across his chest, and his hair hung down in wet strands around his face as he moved towards the dresser. Again, he flashed me a tight grin before letting his gaze flick away, halting my chance to return it. I averted my eyes as I saw his towel drop out of the corner of my eye. It felt wrong to watch him get dressed when he'd been so distant lately.

Lying on my back, I focused on the ceiling and tried to talk myself into believing everything was fine. The nagging feeling in my stomach refused to subside, however, and my efforts made no improvement on my thoughts. I was surprised, therefore, when I felt the bed sag slightly as Hayden climbed onto it next to me. He landed on his side, facing me as he let out a deep sigh.

I felt his arm snake around my waist, tugging me into his chest and shifting me so I faced him. Suddenly my face was only inches from his and his eyes were locked on mine, the closest he'd been in days. I couldn't help but let out a shocked breath.

'Hiii,' he said softly. I felt a flash of confusion but was more than willing to accept this change in mood if he was going to actually talk to me again.

'Hi back,' I replied. His hand was warm as it moved slowly up and down my back.

'I, um, I know I've been kind of weird lately,' he said, surprising me yet again.

'Yeah, I noticed,' I agreed gently. My hand landed lightly on his ribcage as I let my thumb run slowly across his skin, occasionally finding a bump or ridge of a scar. 'Why is that?'

He paused, frowning softly at me and holding my gaze. 'I don't know. I just have a lot on my mind, I guess.'

'I wish you'd tell me, Hayden. Maybe I can help?'

Again he was quiet for a few moments as he considered my words. 'It's just something I need to decide on my own.'

His words confused me, their cryptic meaning lost on me. All I wanted was to go back a few days and get that feeling again – the absolute certainty that I was supposed to be right there with him and the unparalleled happiness I'd felt – but it was so hard when he was so obviously burdened.

'I want to take you somewhere,' he said suddenly, watching me closely. 'Will you come with me?'

'Yes,' I answered immediately. Maybe this would be a step in the right direction. A small smile pulled at the corner of his lips as he nodded slowly.

'Now?' he asked.

'Yeah, if you want to.'

He didn't speak but nodded once more before pulling his arms from around me. I felt a wave of disappointment that it was over so soon, but I told myself that whatever we were doing would hopefully provide some relief of the tenseness that had settled over Hayden.

He moved back to the drawer to pull a black T-shirt over his head before stuffing his feet back into his tennis shoes. His gun was pulled from where he stored it and tucked beneath the waistband at the back of his shorts. I lifted myself off the bed and started to follow him as he moved toward the door. His hand landed on the handle before he retracted it and turned slowly to kiss me.

There was a certain desperation to the kiss, yet he made no effort to intensify it. When he finally pulled back, I felt myself fall forward into his chest as if too dependent of the pressure of his lips on mine to remain balanced. I sucked in a breath at the loss of his kiss and opened my eyes to see him hovering just a few inches away, his hands still on my face. My mind felt hazy as I held his gaze.

'Ready?' he asked, his voice deeper than usual, thanks to the melancholy of our kiss. I nodded slowly.

'Yes.'

His thumb ran over my cheek once and he aimed a soft smile at me before dropping his touch and turning away again to head out the door. Once outside, I drew even with him as he led us down a path that led out of camp. Again, he was quiet. It was like the silence was pressing in on me, threatening to suffocate me after so much struggling against it.

We moved through the woods now, leaving Blackwing behind. Every silent step we took chipped away at my self-control, but I clung to the feeling of Hayden's arms around me as they had just been. I wanted to help ease whatever was on his mind so he could be happy again.

'Where are we going?' I asked cautiously.

'You'll see.' His words were short, offering no further explanation as we continued to move through the woods.

We walked for another thirty minutes with no further communication, and the knot in my stomach had grown even larger with anxiety. I was so distracted by my thoughts, I had absolutely no clues as to what direction we were moving in.

Hayden's steps slowed before he stopped walking altogether in a relatively unremarkable looking section of the woods. Confusion washed over me as I looked around; I could see nothing of importance, and my lack of knowledge of our location didn't help.

'Where are we?' I asked. He stood a few feet away and he was watching me closely with a tight look on his face. A dark shadow was cast down his neck thanks to the tightness with which he held his jaw, and his shoulders were visibly tense.

'We're at the edge of the woods outside of Greystone,' he said slowly. 'You're going home, Grace.'

It was like I was hit with a semi from two different directions at once. My lungs were forcibly emptied as I blew out a harsh huff of air, and I felt a wave of dizziness sweep through my brain. I suddenly felt like I was going to throw up.

'What?'

'You're going to go home.'

His words were cold, detached, unfeeling, just like his gaze. His figure swam before my eyes. I shook my head vigorously, my body rejecting the idea before my mind could catch up.

'No,' I said in disbelief. He continued to watch me with the hard expression on his face. I didn't like that look – it was like the first few days I spent in Blackwing when I was nothing more than a prisoner to him, a debt to repay before he lost the chance.

'Yes, you are,' he said firmly. 'You're going to walk out of these woods and run home. You'll tell them we kept you blindfolded and that you saw nothing, and you'll go *home*.'

'No, Hayden, I don't want to—'

'Too bad,' he cut me off sharply. He looked, if possible, even colder now as he stared at me. His gaze was so different, so incredibly different, than it had been only a few days ago. What had once been so tender and affectionate was now hardened, cold, and unwelcoming.

It was clear now what had changed: he didn't want me there with him anymore. I couldn't stop myself from taking a tiny step forward, my heart plummeting to the ground as I saw him retreat as I approached.

'Hayden, if this is about what happened . . . I'm sor—'

'I think you should just go, Grace,' he said, cutting me off yet again.

'Why? Why now?' I asked, confusion flooding through me along with pain and the humiliating sting of rejection.

He didn't respond and every second that stretched on with no answer felt like it added a thousand pounds to my shoulders, physically dragging me down into the dirt.

'If this is some kind of retribution for feeling guilty for keeping me here . . . then don't do it. I chose to stay here. I chose to stay with you,' I said quietly. My voice sounded weak and thin as I spoke despite my best efforts to remain strong. His jaw ticked slightly as it clenched, and his eyes stayed firmly locked on my own.

'You chose wrong,' he said flatly. His hollow tone reverberated down to my bones, chilling every cell along the way.

'No I didn't,' I said desperately, my voice no more than a mere whisper as I shook my head.

I took another step forward and was minutely relieved

when he didn't step back. My heart thrashed against my ribcage even more, and I was physically unable to tear my gaze from his. His arms were crossed tightly over his chest, closing him off from me as his cold glare met my vulnerable one.

'I want to be here with you. I don't want to go back,' I said honestly. The emotions I was struggling to subdue had tightened my throat now, straining my voice and stealing the volume.

We were a complete contrast: Hayden stone cold, shattering my heart with every hard word he spoke and me, dangerously weak and on the verge of complete collapse as I tried to cling to my strength.

'You're going back,' he said harshly. 'You don't have a say in the matter.'

I shook my head fervently. 'I can't go back, Hayden, I'm in lo—'

'Don't,' he said sharply, cutting me off yet again. For the first time, a flicker of emotion flashed across his face before he masked it behind his harsh exterior. His words were deadly quiet and thick with tension as he spoke again. 'Don't you say that to me.'

'I'm not leaving you. I don't know what this is or why you're doing it but I know you don't mean it . . . You can't mean it,' I said desperately, praying that my words were true. His expression remained as cold as ever as he stared down at me, the hint of emotion I'd thought I'd saw long gone now.

'I'm telling you one last time, *go*.'

I felt a shiver run through my body, shattering my bones and organs alike as it travelled up my spine. My heart already seemed too damaged to respond as it thumped pitifully, like every word he'd said had been a dagger straight through it until it was nothing more than a mangled heap of flesh and blood incapable of sustaining anything at all.

I was physically unable to move as my chest caved in over and over in an attempt to draw a full breath. I stared up at him in shock, disbelief, and utter heartbreak, yet he showed no empathy or emotion. A flash of movement interrupted my vision as his hand flew behind his back quickly; I was only about two feet away from him when I found myself with the barrel of his gun pointed straight at my heart.

Disbelief, shock, and anger surged through me as I took a tiny step backwards.

'I'm not joking, Grace. Go. Now.'

He was almost unrecognisable now as he glared at me. Never before had I seen this side to him; he was cold, cruel, and devastatingly dangerous to me in just about every single way. The Hayden I knew and loved would never pull a gun on me, yet here he was, aiming the deadly weapon straight at me.

'You're not going to shoot me,' I said, not as confident as I would have liked. I swallowed harshly when I heard the soft metallic click of the gun as he loaded the bullets into the chamber with a small tick of his thumb.

This wasn't my Hayden.

'Try me.'

A hot, wet streak ran down my cheek as a tear I hadn't been aware of fell. This was it. He really, truly did not want me with him any longer, and he was willing to shoot me over it. His gaze didn't waver from mine as I shook my head slowly, too shocked to register any more emotion. I took a step backward, my throat tight and heart absolutely shattered.

'Tell Herc I said goodbye, will you?'

The tiniest flash of emotion appeared on his features, but his cold gaze quickly covered it once more as I turned my back on him. My steps were jerky and unnatural as I walked back towards Greystone, leaving my bloody pulp of a heart in the dirt at his feet where it belonged.

Chapter Fourteen – Agony
HAYDEN

Agony.

Excruciating agony.

No other words could possibly do justice to what I felt, their empty meanings utterly pointless and wasted now that I'd done what needed to be done. It was with one final shocked, heartbroken look that she turned from me and muttered the words that drove a white-hot spear straight through my heart.

Tell Herc I said goodbye, will you?

She threw our promise to always say goodbye to each other in my face. She meant it to hurt me, to dig at any shred of humanity I might have had left despite my attempts to hide it behind my cold exterior, and she had succeeded. It was like she was saying she didn't even know me, like the person she'd come to care about so much had abandoned my physical form. I was a stranger to her, my harsh words and blatantly cold actions doing exactly what I intended – to drive her away from me.

She'd been gone for nearly an hour now. But I still lingered, planted to the ground. I was unable to move, unable to think, unable to breathe. The only thing I could do was feel. Feel the agonising pulverisation of my heart, feel the rotting ache in my stomach, feel the chilling cold that had settled into my bones the moment I started speaking to her.

She was the only girl I'd ever loved, and she was gone.

Of everything I'd done in my life, that was without a doubt the hardest. All the fighting, stealing, and killing seemed like child's play when compared to how hard it had been to let Grace go. Even thinking her name now mangled the hopelessly abused flesh of my heart even more. She could never understand it at the time, but everything I'd done had been for her. Everything was completely for her benefit, paid for by my loss.

Ever since the moment I realised I was in love with her, I knew I had to do it. It had taken me far too long to gather up the courage, my selfish weakness stopping me from doing what I knew was right. I wanted it too much, wanted her too much, and I almost didn't do it, but after days of agonising internal debate, I had finally decided: I would do what was right for her and let her go. It was for her own good, even if she couldn't see that yet.

Every second I spent with her after we'd come together as one had been so stunningly exquisite and horrifically terrorising all at once – a living, breathing paradox that demanded to be pulled apart at some point. It was like I could feel the clock ticking, every second that dragged by berating me more and more for being greedy and weak, for keeping her to myself when I knew what she was losing even if she wasn't aware of it herself.

Every moment she spent with me was one less she'd get with her father before the inevitable happened and she truly lost him forever; it was my own selfishly desperate need to be with her that kept her from him.

She had clearly picked up on my anxiety, and I hated myself for making her think she'd done something wrong. But how was I supposed to act when I knew I had to let the person I was so ridiculously in love with go? How was I supposed to pretend that I didn't feel the excruciating throbbing in my heart every single time I looked at her, touched her, kissed her, because I knew my opportunities were running out?

Once again, my weakness had won out and I acted against my will, kissing her one last time before I broke both of our hearts irreparably. Every bit of love I had for her had leaked into it, the emotion nearly overwhelming the both of us without my intention. I had to do it; I had to kiss her goodbye. I knew it wasn't fair to her – to pour such emotion into a kiss and then force her to leave.

The walk to this place, where I now stood frozen, had been the toughest test yet. Every step we took was like we were shrinking the distance between us and the edge of a cliff, the inevitability of having to jump off getting closer and closer. It had been so hard not to hold her hand, not to turn around and run in the other direction, not to tell her how much I loved her and how much it hurt me to do this. I wanted nothing more than to hide away with her forever, shielding us from the horrors and heartbreak of the world, but I couldn't do it.

She deserved to see her father before he died, and this was the only way I could guarantee that she did. I couldn't tell her he was sick; I couldn't put that weight on her and make her choose, once again, between her father and me. She'd already had to choose once and it had nearly broken her in half. I wouldn't do that to her again, refused to do that to her again.

Everything about this situation rode on my ability to convince her I didn't care, didn't want her, didn't love her. She had to believe that or she would never go. By pretending I didn't love her, the choice was made for her. She would feel no indecision or trepidation about leaving, and feel no guilt for choosing her father over me. I loved her too much to make her choose, and I loved her too much to make her feel any sort of remorse or guilt for a decision she should never have to make.

It was the biggest lie I'd ever told and it had absolutely destroyed me to do it, but she'd believed me. How had she believed me when it felt so glaringly obvious how in love with her I was? How could she doubt for a second that my entire world hadn't started to revolve around her? How could she not see that every single breath I had was dedicated to keeping her safe, keeping her alive, keeping her loved?

But it had worked, and it had worked too well. She had fallen for my lies, hook, line, and sinker, and I had absolutely destroyed her the way I'd intended. If she knew just how much I loved her and how much I needed her, she never would have left. Every word I spoke was a dagger to not only my heart, but hers as well. Every plea she gave in response tore me to shreds, and it had nearly been enough to make me cave in on my resolve.

The hardest test of them all had been when she'd started to say the phrase I'd been craving to hear. I'd ached for it for so long only to have to cut her off before she finally said it. I couldn't hear her say it, couldn't watch her as her world shattered around her. To hear those words leave her lips would have broken me in half. I couldn't hear her say she loved me without going back on my every word and destroying what I was trying to do for her.

Grace was lucky to still have her father and brother, and I wouldn't rob her of that. Family was a rare thing, these days, and I'd taken that from her by begging her to stay.

She'd made it so much harder on both of us by refusing

to leave, but that was what I loved so much about her. She was strong, resilient, defiant. She was tougher than anyone I'd ever met, and I was constantly in awe of her tenacity and fortitude. She deserved so much that I couldn't give her, but there was one thing I could: I could give her back her family.

To pull a gun on her had destroyed me. Never in my life would I have been able to actually shoot her, I'd rather put the gun to myself than her. It had been the last straw, the final warning before she dropped the line that had shattered me to bits and left. At least she had not really believed I would kill her.

I'd finally won, but it didn't feel like winning; it felt like annihilating, soul-crushing torture, as if my entire body had been dipped in flames and left to char until I was an unrecognisable, blackened pile of flesh and blood and bones.

I'd lost track now of how long it had been since she'd left, yet my feet still remained firmly planted to the ground. If I moved just ten feet forward, I would see her home. I would see the place she'd returned to only after I'd forced her, and it would crush me all over again. To know she was right there, just out of arm's reach, yet still able to do nothing about it was a sick test I knew I would fail if I moved forward. With every bit of self-control I had, I finally managed to jerk my foot upward and turn around, my unnatural step leading me away from the only girl I loved.

She's home where she belongs. She's going to see her father before it's too late. You can give her that, Hayden.

These were the thoughts I forced myself to think as I walked jerkily back towards Blackwing. The trees around me seemed to swoop in and out and I was pretty sure I stumbled far more often than I should have, but I couldn't help it. It was like my body had been taken over by some foreign presence, working the controls but without any expertise or skill to make movement fluid and natural. I was a walking shell, hollowed out and emptied, able to feel only the crushing pain of what I didn't think I was strong enough to do.

She'll get time with her father. She didn't have to choose. She'll feel no guilt for leaving you because she thinks you don't love her.

Over and over, I reiterated my train of thought. I had to keep myself convinced I'd done the right thing or I would run straight back for her.

You had to do it. There was no other way. This is what's best for Grace.

A rock in the dirt caught on my toe and I stumbled forward, catching myself blindly against a tree stump at the last second before righting myself and carrying on. The sharp edge of the bark bit into my palm but I felt nothing despite the droplets of blood that leaked out. My pain was mental, far too advanced to be interrupted by a measly cut on my palm.

You love her. You love her more than you even know. You had to let her go. For her.

It was like the world had been drained of colour as I moved through the woods. The greens seemed duller, the browns dirtier, the blue of the sky grey and bleak. What usually sounded so light and relaxing now sounded completely flat, as if I'd been sucked into a giant vacuum that drained all the beauty from the world. How fitting as I'd lost the beauty from my own life.

Never in my life had I felt more emotionally drained as when I finally reached Blackwing again. I took absolutely no notice of the faces that passed by, too consumed by my own heartbreak to care about anything else. My legs carried me methodically back to my hut, which would surely be

189

haunted with her image, her smell, the residual sound of her laugh. She would positively surround me the moment I entered, but the masochistic side of me craved it; at least I'd have her in some way.

I was nearly home and fully prepared to isolate myself with my sorrows for the rest of the day when a stooped figure appeared in front of me, cutting off my path. Wispy white hair framed her wrinkled face as she gazed up at me, her expression placid.

'It hurts when our light is smothered, doesn't it?' Perdita said wistfully. I blinked in surprise. I was used to her non-sensical statements, but this one felt too close to home, like she was seeing right through me, feeling what *I* was feeling. My light, my Grace, had indeed been smothered, leaving me dark, empty, desolate.

I didn't respond to Perdita, nowhere near strong enough to have a conversation right now, especially if she was rambling with uncanny accuracy. I tried to dodge past her, but she stepped in front of me once more.

'Oh yes, it hurts to be smothered.'

'Yeah . . .' I muttered, holding her calm gaze for a fraction of a second before stepping around her once more. I couldn't take any more from her.

I closed the remaining steps between my hut and myself before throwing my shoulder into the door harsher than was probably necessary. The door swung open only to be slammed quickly shut again, blocking out the light that insisted on streaming in. I wanted darkness, total darkness, but it wasn't dark enough to match how dark I felt inside.

I moved to the edge of my bed to sit down and was immediately greeted by the memory of her lying there mere hours ago, watching me carefully before I joined her and pulled her close. What I would give now for one last chance to hold her, one last chance to feel her heartbeat and the heat that radiated off her body. What I wouldn't give for the chance to tell her I loved her.

A deep sigh pushed past my lips as I leaned forward to rest my head in my palms. My elbows dug into my knees as I hunched over and tried to block out the memories, but they never relented. Such a strange journey had now come full circle, and I was right back where I started. I was still the leader of Blackwing, Grace was home, and things around camp remained exactly the same, but I was completely different — so completely different.

Grace had changed me. She made me feel things I'd never felt before even though they were so natural and human: happiness, joy, reliance, trust, love. So many things that I'd been missing without even knowing had been found in her, yet I was back to where I started: alone, cold, empty.

She'd let me feel like a human being, embracing my weaknesses and showing me that what I thought of as weak was really only human. She let me lean on her, opened me up, and challenged me. Out of all the things I needed desperately in this world, she was every single one combined into one stunningly beautiful person.

My throat felt dry and tight, as if it might crack at any second. I could feel myself crumbling yet I gave no effort to stop it. I would take this pain, this wretched, obliterating pain, if it meant Grace could be with her family. I would suffer this hurt for her and only her, certain she deserved what I had nearly killed myself to give her.

A sudden knock at my door jerked me from my inner turmoil, though I made no move to answer it. Ignoring it completely, I dug my palms even further into my eye sockets. Little white lights burst into the darkness of my closed eyes at the pressure, but it did nothing to block out the second round of knocking that sounded at my door.

'Go away.'

My voice sounded tight and gravelly, as if I hadn't spoken for years.

'Hayden, open up.'

Dax.

'Go away, Dax,' I repeated, more forcefully this time. Putting on a front for Dax was the absolute last thing I felt like doing, much less explaining why Grace had suddenly disappeared. The thought of how my camp would respond to this news hadn't even crossed my mind until right now, but I couldn't find it in me to care. I almost relished the idea of someone challenging me so I could take out some of this pain on them.

'I just have to ask a quick question then I'll go!' he called, clearly oblivious to what was happening on the other side of the door. I'd told no one about my plan, so he was completely clueless.

'No, Dax—'

The door opened, despite my protests. Anger surged through me that he disobeyed, though it was quickly stifled by the crushing weight of sadness. I remained still, head resting in the palms of my hands, hunched over on the side of my bed.

'Hey, what's up?' Dax said brightly, clearly not processing anything yet.

'I thought I said go away.' My words were slightly muffled and bitterly dark.

'I just wanted to ask – wait,' he said, pausing. 'Where's Grace?'

My chest physically caved in at the sound of her name, and I was pretty sure I was actually bleeding from the gaping hole where my heart had been. Slowly, I forced myself to sit up, letting my hands drag down my face before falling to my lap. Dax stood just inside my doorway, the door closed once more to shut out most of the light.

'Home.'

Dax blinked in surprise before a deep frown settled over his face, brows pulling low in confusion.

'What do you mean, "home"?'

'I mean she's home, Dax. She's gone,' I snapped, my patience incredibly thin.

'She's gone?' he repeated. He looked completely stunned.

'Yes, Dax, she's fucking gone, all right?'

Every time I said it made it feel more and more real, digging deeper and deeper into my pain.

'But . . . what . . . how?' he stammered, dumbfounded.

'I let her go.'

'And . . . she was okay with that?' he asked slowly. He took a few steps forward before sinking down onto the bed a few feet away from me. I could feel his eyes on me as I stared blankly forward.

'No. I had to pull a gun on her.'

I still can't believe you did that to her, arsehole.

I shook my head, chasing away the thoughts. I had to do it or she never would have believed me and gone.

'*Why* though? Why let her go now? And why the gun?' Dax asked. I could feel him gaping at me but still I ignored it. I couldn't tell him the entire truth without revealing who her father was, but he didn't need to know his name.

'Her father is dying,' I said simply. Dax would understand the weight of this and the importance it held with me. I had seen my parents die, but Dax didn't remember his at all. 'I couldn't make her choose between us. No matter what she chose, she'd feel guilty for picking one over the other. I couldn't do that to her.'

'Oh,' he said solemnly. He was quiet for a few long moments as he let that sink in. 'You gave up your happiness so she could see her father?'

I sighed and dropped my forehead to my hands once more. I didn't need to reply. My silence was my confirmation. Any flicker of happiness had been extinguished the moment I made her leave.

'Jesus . . .' Dax muttered. 'You selfless bastard. I don't know how you do it.'

'It hurts so fucking bad, Dax.'

My chest seemed to contract as I spoke the vulnerable words and my breath was cut short as I tried and failed to breathe normally. Again he didn't respond as he mulled the situation over. My heart beat feebly, the damage inflicted upon it far too great to allow it to function properly.

'You're in love with her, aren't you?' Dax said quietly, more of a statement than a question. 'Like, really, truly in love with her.'

I drew a shuddering, shaky breath between my lips as I nodded, my head moving in my hands as I continued to attempt to block out the world. The darkness of my vision still seemed lighter than how I felt inside. Oh yes, I was really, truly in love with her.

'Wow,' Dax said softly. I imagined him shaking his head in disbelief, unable to see him thanks to my position. 'Just . . . wow. I'm so sorry, mate.'

'Yeah,' I muttered flatly. I squeezed my eyes shut even tighter against my palms but it did nothing.

'If anyone around here deserves to be happy, it's you. I'm just so . . . I don't know. I wish it didn't have to be this way for you, mate, I really do.'

'Thanks.' My tone was, if possible, even flatter than before. I was talked out, exhausted, drained. Utterly and completely drained.

Dax's hand clapped once on my shoulder, the touch making me jump slightly as I pulled my face from my hands.

'Sorry,' he murmured. 'If you need anything . . . let me know, yeah? Don't suffer through this alone like you always do.'

'Okay,' I said, knowing it was a lie. I wouldn't seek out him or anyone else. I would endure this pain alone in solitude. The agony would eat me alive, but I would endure it.

He nodded once and pressed his lips together in a sad expression before blowing out a deep breath. He cast one last saddened look at me before moving to the door, murmuring a soft 'bye' before slipping out and closing it behind him.

Despite it being the most painful thing I'd ever done, I didn't regret it for a second. Grace was home, where she belonged, and she deserved to see her father before he died. It was the absolute best I could do for her even though it was tearing me apart to do it.

This was what my life would be like from now on. There would be no happiness, no warmth, no playfulness. There would be no one to lighten me, no one to teach me to see the beauty in the world. Most devastatingly, there would be no love, because there would be no Grace.

No love. No Grace. No Bear.

Chapter Fifteen – Numb
GRACE

My mind had yet to process what had just happened as I walked stiffly back toward Greystone. There were no words to do justice to what I was feeling, of that I was certain. Hayden's strange mood over the last few days had finally been explained as he absolutely destroyed me bit by bit. He'd made it perfectly clear in his words and actions that he no longer wanted me with him at all, much less loved me the way I'd fooled myself into thinking he maybe would.

He'd said nothing about loving me, nor had I told him how I felt, but some small fragment of me believed maybe he would say it someday. Some tiny, hopeful part had thought maybe he would say the words I so desperately wanted to hear, but I could not have been more wrong.

Hayden didn't love me the way I loved him. He didn't love me at all.

I should have felt something – pain, hurt, embarrassment, *something*, but I felt nothing. I was numb. Hollow. I was an empty shell stumbling back towards the place I'd grown up in, not giving a second thought to what I'd say when I showed up with no explanation at all. There was no way my mind could process any more information after what I'd just gone through. I knew the pain would come, but it lingered behind, waiting and swelling until the right moment to demolish me completely.

It should have occurred to me to be careful, to make my presence known somehow so I wouldn't be shot, but the blank void of my mind made rational thought impossible. I was nearing the edge of the camp now, the rounded buildings easily defined. Each step I took away from Hayden only added to the odd, emotionless weight that had settled over me.

The whizzing of a bullet a few inches to the left of my head jerked me out of my stupor, sending my body crashing to the ground on instinct. I landed in the dirt with a huff that sent a dulled wave of pain up my side before my head jerked upward to see which moron had shot at me. I couldn't make out whom it was, but a shadowy figure stood between two shacks, clearly aiming a gun at me.

'Don't shoot me, you idiot!' I shouted, feeling angry, of all things. The shadow faltered and lowered their gun momentarily before raising it once more.

'Who are you?' the voice called back uncertainly.

'Grace,' I spat.

'Grace who?'

'Grace Cook.'

The person gave no response but I could hear the muffled sound of footsteps as they rushed toward me. I pushed myself out of the dirt and straightened up, the flash of anger subsiding as quickly as it had come. Once again, all I felt was numb.

I stared blankly as the person approached, quickly identifying them as one of Celt's trusted confidants. He was Harvey, and he was about sixty years old with extremely grey, unkempt hair.

197

'Grace, oh my god, I thought you were dead,' he said, a sense of awe in his voice as he stared at me.

'I'm not,' I said flatly. Funny, because I felt absolutely dead inside.

'Where have you been?' Harvey pressed, staring at me incredulously. He looked like he was seeing a ghost.

'I have to go and see my father,' I said, ignoring his question and continuing on with my jerky, unnatural movement as I brushed past his shoulder.

'Wait, Grace . . .' His voice trailed off as I moved farther away. I felt like an absolutely horrible person for feeling no relief, no happiness at being home again and desperately hoped seeing my father would snap me out of this feeling. Seeing my family was the only positive to come out of being completely shattered by Hayden.

I moved through the camp, which now felt so strange and unfamiliar with its cold, unwelcoming buildings and its linear set-up. The stark landscape and buildings matched how empty I felt inside. Everything felt off, unnatural, wrong.

I probably should have come up with some sort of story or explanation, but all I could do was feel the blank expanse overtake my body and the crushing numbness infiltrate my brain. I supposed that was about right – wasn't I supposed to have been a prisoner for months? Wouldn't a prisoner be broken in absolutely every sense of the word? I fitted the part perfectly.

I hadn't made it very far when my name was called out, a mixture of shock and relief leaking into the tone.

'Grace?'

I turned slowly toward the sound, unable to move any faster thanks to my hollow shell of a body. Jonah.

He gave me no chance to respond before I was wrapped

tightly in his strong arms; his hug was too tight, too rough, as if he didn't know the proper way to hug a person. It felt cold even though it was probably the most affectionate he'd ever been towards me. I couldn't find it in me to reciprocate, and my arms lay limply by my sides as he held me tightly.

'You're alive,' he murmured in relief. 'I knew you were alive!'

I remained silent as I let him hug me. I gazed blankly over his shoulder, flat and void of any emotion as I waited for the hug to end. I desperately wanted to feel something — some flash of happiness or relief — but I still felt nothing even though it was my own brother.

'You're alive,' he repeated yet again, his voice a mere whisper now.

I don't feel alive.

Jonah pulled me back at arm's length, his hands on my shoulders as he studied me. I took in the green of his eyes, the usual stubble along his jaw, and the light brown hair atop his head. How long had it been since I'd seen him up close? Three months? It felt like a few days and a lifetime all at once. My entire world felt flipped upside down.

'I missed you so much,' he said sincerely. It was probably the nicest thing he'd ever said to me, the shock of my arrival making him honest.

'I missed you, too,' I managed to say. My voice sounded tight and rough as if I hadn't spoken in days. He continued to stare at me in shock and awe, his hands planted firmly on my shoulders. I felt a tiny, almost unidentifiable flicker of happiness in the pit of my stomach for a moment before it was quickly smothered by the cold, numb grip of suffocation.

'We have to get you to Celt,' he said as if suddenly realising what had actually happened.

It struck me as odd now that both Jonah and I, more often than not, referred to our father as 'Celt' rather than 'Dad'. Surely most children wouldn't call their fathers by their first name, but it had always seemed normal growing up. It was yet another reminder of our cold, detached way of life here. But after spending so much time with Hayden and seeing what family really meant it him, it felt wrong to call him by his first name.

I nodded slowly, unable to speak again as he released me completely and steered me in the direction I'd already been going. Despite being away for months, I could think of literally nothing to say. It was like the life had been sucked out of me, shattered and drained from my body faster than I ever thought possible.

'I can't believe you're here,' Jonah murmured. I wasn't sure if he was talking to me or just thinking out loud so I ignored him; I wouldn't have been able to form a response anyway.

I hated myself for feeling this way – resenting where I was because I wanted to be somewhere else. What an awful person I must be to still want to run back to Hayden after what he'd just done. What an awful person I must be to feel no joy at seeing my own brother again. Maybe I did deserve this desolation.

I was hit with an odd sense of déjà vu as we arrived at Celt's office. Flashes of the first night I'd seen Hayden in my own camp came flooding back: catching him after hearing a loud clatter in the building, discovering he wasn't alone, letting him go. Jonah calling me out for letting him go and being weak. Telling Celt. I remembered the anger I felt at the implication that I wasn't as strong as everyone else and the determination, if given the chance, to reverse what I'd done and redeem myself.

The thought alone seemed laughable now. There was absolutely no way I could have known I would fall so deeply in love with the man I nearly killed that very night, only to be irreparably shattered by him now. Of course I would never have been able to kill him, however. Even though I was broken now, every moment that had led up to it had been completely worth it in every way fathomable.

A sharp knock on the door jerked me from the thoughts that were starting to roll in relentlessly, and I blinked to try and focus.

'Come in,' he called softly from inside. Jonah cast me a look that almost counted as a smile before he pushed the door open, leading the way and blocking me from sight with his muscular frame.

'Celt,' he said quietly. I could just see around Jonah; his head was lowered as he studied what looked like a map, and his fingertips pressed into his temple as if he had a headache.

'Just a moment,' he responded, not looking up as I closed the door softly behind me. Still, I remained quiet. Quiet, and tragically numb.

He studied his map for what seemed to drag on for an eternity before letting out a deep sigh and running his palms over his face, closing his eyes as he did so. His hands dropped to the desk and his eyes remained closed for a few moments longer as if storing away his thoughts for later. When he finally opened them they landed on Jonah briefly before flitting immediately back to land on me.

'Grace,' he whispered, a stunned expression falling over his face as he gaped at me. For the first time since arriving back, I felt a heavy thud of my heart – proof that I was still alive. He seemed frozen in his seat as he stared at me for a few seconds before something jerked him out of it.

'Grace,' he repeated before bolting from his seat to move hurriedly around his desk. 'My little girl.'

With that, he closed the distance between us and wound his arms around me, tugging me into him. That touch, that one embrace, was all it took for the wall holding back my emotions to crumble into dust. They hit me like a wave, physically knocking me over and sending a choking sob through my throat. The only thing that kept me from crumpling to the floor was my father's hug. Supported by his embrace, I finally managed to react and threw my arms around his torso.

'Dad,' I choked, my words stifled by his shoulder as I let the gut-wrenching sobs loose. I felt dizzy, like the entire world was spinning around me and attempting to drag me with it only for me to fall to pieces and crumble to the floor. Wet, hot tears soaked my cheeks and it felt like a hole had ripped open in my chest as my heart felt the full force of what it had been numb to for so long.

'It's okay, Gracie, you're safe now,' he whispered kindly.

He held me tightly against him and let me sob into his chest, misinterpreting my tears. In all honesty, I didn't know what I was feeling. The devastating pain of losing Hayden had finally hit, as I knew it would, but there were other emotions as well. There was relief, a flicker of happiness, and the tiniest, thinnest sliver of love at being reunited with my father and brother.

I sniffled once, attempting to get myself together long enough to take a full breath. My throat burned with the effort and I was certain my eyes were bloodshot and puffy, but it couldn't have mattered any less. This was only a taste of the anguish I would feel later, of that I was certain.

Celt finally released me and pulled back enough to look down at me with a soft, shocked smile. His hands ran soothingly over my shoulders the way he used to do when I was younger and upset about Jonah or some other issue. 'You're back where you belong, Grace.'

It didn't feel like where I belonged. Even now, I felt the undeniable pull to return to Blackwing. So much had happened there and I'd changed so much that it felt like that was where I was supposed to be. In Blackwing, with Hayden.

But that wasn't a possibility now. Things had come full circle and I was back at Greystone, yet everything, absolutely everything, was completely different.

'Here, sit down. You must have been through so much,' he said kindly, ushering me into a seat across from his. Jonah, who had remained silent during our entire exchange, sat next to me in another chair while my father returned to his. He peered at me gently across the desk before sliding his own mug towards me.

'Here, have some tea. I just made it but it'll help you more than me,' he murmured. My eyes landed on the mug and I was instantly reminded of the night Hayden had made hot cocoa for Jett and me. It was such a simple memory – experiencing something new for the first time – but it stood out as one of the happiest moments I'd had in Blackwing because it felt so normal.

'No thanks,' I replied softly. I felt too weak to even manage to lift the mug.

I could feel both of their eyes on me and could tell they were both greatly restraining themselves from asking me a thousand questions at once. I sat blankly, unable to block out the overwhelming emotion now that I'd let it in. Jonah cracked first as he spoke after a few moments of silence.

'You were at Blackwing, weren't you?'

My heart thumped weakly at the sound of the place, and a dull ache spread through my abdomen. If hearing

'Blackwing' was enough to do that to me, I didn't want to know what would happen once the reality of what Hayden had said to me set in. Minutes seemed to pass before I managed to weakly nod my head, confirming his statement.

Even now, after everything I'd been through, I resolved to reveal no information about Blackwing. I didn't care what they asked or what they thought, I would not tell them anything and put anyone I cared about in danger. Hayden may not love me or care for me, but that didn't mean I wanted him hurt. Him, or any of the other countless people I'd come to care for. Dax, Kit, Docc, Maisie, Jett . . .

Jett.

Oh god.

Jett surely would not understand, because I myself did not. The image of the painting he'd made for Hayden and I flitted through my mind, each of our stick figures holding hands as if in some type of family. He would be crushed by this, and it broke what remained of my heart all over again.

'Grace?'

'What?' I replied, not having heard the question. I blinked once and tried to refocus on my father's face, hoping some of the minuscule good feeling I'd felt would come back to help drive out this pain.

'What happened?' my father asked kindly. I took a deep breath that burned my lungs as they expanded. What happened? What hadn't happened was a better question.

'I . . .' I paused, trying to recall how this journey had even started. I had to be careful, very careful about what I said to save Blackwing from any retribution.

Celt's green eyes, so similar to my own, were locked on mine as I pondered what to say. It wasn't until that moment that I realised something looked different about him. I studied him carefully, taking in the differences between how I remembered him to look and the man sitting in front of me now. I'd been gone for a while, but not long enough for such a drastic change to occur.

'Are you okay?' I asked, ignoring his previous question as I frowned at him. Jonah shifted beside me and Dad blinked before smoothing out his facial expression once again.

'I'm just fine. Now why don't you tell us what happened?' he said calmly. I got the distinct impression he was not being truthful, and the evidence was right in front of my face. He was thinner, much thinner than he had been. His previously firm muscles had atrophied and his face had narrowed out, leaving him looking gaunt and slightly sunken.

'But—'

'All in good time, love. Tell us what you've been through.' His words were placid and he encouraged me to continue with a silent nod. I would tell my version of the story only so he would admit what was wrong.

'I was shot in the city on that raid with Jonah,' I started. I was unable to stop myself from casting a sideways glance at him. He did not react at the reminder of him leaving me.

'Go on,' Celt urged kindly.

'And H – they found me,' I explained. I almost said Hayden's name before I managed to correct myself. 'They took me back to their camp and kept me prisoner.'

There. Long story short. Almost no details, yet still technically the truth.

'But you were shot,' Jonah pointed out. 'Wouldn't you have bled out?'

'Someone stitched me up,' I admitted reluctantly.

'Where did they keep you? Did you see anything? Did you see how things work? How did you escape?' Jonah pressed, leaning in eagerly as he impatiently waited for my response.

Escape. Ha.

'Jonah,' Celt scolded. 'She's been gone months. Don't pressure her. She'll tell us everything in her own time.'

No, I won't.

'Fine, where did they keep you?' he said through gritted teeth, obviously frustrated that I was being so unforthcoming.

'I don't know,' I said stubbornly. 'I never saw anything.'

'You were there for over three months and you never saw anything?' Jonah pressed sceptically, eyeing me warily.

'No.'

My voice was flat, and I forced myself to ignore the pain radiating through my body. Every word I spoke was breaking me more and more, and I could already feel another collapse threatening to occur.

'But . . . I saw you with him!' Jonah burst, frustration taking over. 'You were with their leader and you were just walking around. Not tied up, no blindfold, just walking around. You must have seen something.'

I tried not to react to this statement. I had to lie. 'The only place we ever went was to the mess hall to eat. I didn't see anything.'

'But surely you heard something—'

'That's enough,' Celt said firmly, cutting him off. Jonah's gaze, which had been locked intently on mine, jerked to our father's. He leaned back, and blew out a frustrated sigh.

'It's just she's been in our enemy's camp for three months. We'd be stupid not to try and get as much information as possible,' Jonah said. 'Think how much we could use that!'

'She's been through a lot. There's no need to pressure her tonight when she's probably exhausted.'

They were talking about me as if I wasn't there and I

was reminded of when Hayden had done that with various members of Blackwing in the first week or so. Yet another stinging ache rocketed through my body at the thought.

'She could at least tell us what their leader is like,' Jonah huffed. I couldn't stop myself from physically wincing at his words. Luckily they were too busy staring at each other to notice.

'Not tonight,' Celt stated. 'Grace, let's get you home. You need to rest.'

'Wait, what about you?' I asked, eyeing him nervously. Concern forced my brows to pull low over my eyes as I studied his sunken face across the desk. He sighed heavily and sent me a soft smile.

'Don't you worry about me just yet. We'll get you to bed and then we'll talk tomorrow, yeah?'

Something was off, and it was very obvious things were not fine, but I couldn't find the strength in me to argue. The pain I'd been trying to fight off twisted at my stomach and tore at my heart, begging to be acknowledged and really, truly felt. I would go to bed, but rest would be the very last thing I'd do. The knowledge that I was about to go through absolute hell wasn't what scared me – what scared me was that I almost welcomed it.

I nodded weakly, agreeing with almost no objection to my father's suggestion.

'That's my girl,' he said softly as he pushed himself up from his chair. I followed silently as they led me back outside. It wasn't really that late but the sun was just starting to lower in the sky as evening approached. I was exhausted. Physically, mentally, and emotionally exhausted.

The few people we passed were probably shocked to see me, but I took absolutely no notice of anyone as I moved methodically after my family. What should have been a happy reunion was tainted. It was selfish of me to feel this way, but I couldn't shake it.

We approached the home we all technically shared but rarely inhabited at the same time. Celt spent most of his nights in his office, working and planning with other leaders in Greystone. Jonah spent most of his nights roaming the camp on duty. It seemed that we were as separate as can be.

My father led me down the short hallway to my room – the same room I'd had since I was a little girl when I shared it with Jonah. It was my own now, as Jonah had moved into a different area of the small shack, yet it didn't feel like mine anymore. What had once felt so familiar and welcoming felt foreign and mysterious, like a girl I'd never met lived there and I was intruding on her personal space.

Jonah had paused at the doorway and was watching me closely while my father appeared behind me and put a gentle hand on my shoulder, spinning me round to him. He shot me another small smile before dropping his touch. People in Greystone didn't touch unless in exceptional circumstances, such as returning from the enemy camp after months and months. Celt seemed to be the only one who'd ever shown even the slightest bit of affection.

'Get a good night's sleep. We'll talk tomorrow,' he said warmly. I nodded once in response.

'I'm glad you're home, Gracie,' he said sincerely. He was still obviously slightly shocked I'd arrived, but there was no denying the obvious relief and delight in his features as he gazed at me.

'Me too, Dad,' I managed to reply with a forced, weak smile. I wasn't sure if it was a lie or not. He gave me one last endearing look before joining Jonah at the door, who called out a soft 'goodnight' before they both disappeared and closed the door behind them. I hoped after adjusting a bit I would feel happy to be home.

Home.

What a weird word. What a weird, perverse, inconceivably twisted word. How was it decided where one's home truly was? What were the requirements that made a place the one you were meant to be? How was I ever supposed to know for certain where my home was?

These thoughts knocked me backward, my legs stumbling blindly until they collided with the side of my bed and I collapsed onto it. Without warning, the choking sobs I'd experienced earlier returned tenfold. Strangled cries ripped through my throat as I let the tears fall unrestrained. Annihilating pain like I'd never felt before seared through my every cell, shredding them to bits only to dig deeper and deeper into my being until it had burned a hole straight through me.

I knew the answer to my questions. Home was where you felt accepted. It was where you knew what you were supposed to do and who you were supposed to be with without a shadow of a doubt. Home was where you were the best you could be and managed to make others better with you; you could grow, learn, laugh, play. Home was where you were safe, happy, and alive. Home was where you were loved.

Hayden was my home. Being with Hayden was the only time in my life when I felt like the best version of myself. I had been free to be myself completely, with no pressures of those around me, and I'd been free to live the way I thought life should be lived. Being with Hayden made me happier than I'd ever felt in my entire existence, there was no denying that. I'd grown more as a person than I ever could have imagined.

The love I felt for Hayden remained, lingering and burning in my veins as if to mock me for what I'd lost. Agonising jolts cleaved through my heart, ripping it to shreds only to start the process all over again and mangle me even further. It was brutal, everything that had happened, but what caused me the most agony was glaringly obvious: Hayden didn't love me back.

Home was supposed to be a place where you felt like the happiest and most complete version of yourself. My issue wasn't that I didn't know where my home was; my issue was that I did, and that I had lost it indefinitely.

Chapter Sixteen – Insidious

GRACE

Ten days.

I'd been back in Greystone for ten days, yet it felt like an absolute eternity. Time seemed to drag on slower than I ever thought possible as I experienced confusing waves of blank numbness and crushing agony over and over again. The few moments I managed to feel happy again were the moments I spent with my father, though they were few and far between.

He appeared busier than I ever remembered, locking himself away in his office with a few trusted colleagues and Jonah for hours on end only to emerge at night and go straight to bed. Dark circles lingered under his eyes at all times and he seemed to grow thinner and thinner by the day, like he was wasting away in front of me. It was impossible to ignore the nagging suspicion something was wrong with him, but he still refused to acknowledge me when I asked.

'*Later, Gracie,*' he'd say, brushing me off with a gentle touch of his hand to my shoulder. His blatant avoidance of the subject did little to settle my growing anxiety.

Jonah, I could tell, was making an effort to be nice to me, but it was clear it didn't come naturally to him. His words were overly formal and smiles were forced, but at least he was trying. We'd always had a tense relationship, fuelled by competition and a never-ending rivalry to be the best. His obvious belief that being a girl made me weaker than him was something that constantly grated on me, now more than ever.

No matter what I did or how I tried to distract myself, I couldn't force my mind off Hayden. I couldn't stop wondering what he was doing, if he was safe, how things were going. I felt weak for wanting it after what he'd done, but I wanted to be there for him and help him with the burdens he constantly faced. All I could think about was how he was back to handling it all alone, because I knew he would never let anyone in to help. A dull thud pounded against my ribs at the thought and the ever-present ache in my chest seemed to swell a bit more as I thought of him.

'Grace?'

I blinked, refocusing quickly on the face in front of me. Light blue eyes framed by long, beautifully wavy brown hair stared back at me. My only friend, Leutie, sat across from me as I picked at the measly helping of food I was trying to choke down.

'Sorry, what did you say?' I attempted to sound normal and withheld the heavy sigh fighting to break forth.

'I asked if you were done,' she said sweetly.

Leutie was about as opposite from me as anyone could possibly be. Sweet, gentle, earnest, and undeniably beautiful, she held so many qualities I lacked. Or at least, had lacked until a certain someone had brought out things I didn't realise I'd had. Before I'd known Hayden, the idea of me being caring or gentle seemed almost ridiculous, but he brought it out in me. He made me feel beautiful when I'd never considered myself anything close. That was gone now, however, as I felt myself retreating back into my cold shell as before.

'Yeah,' I answered, hurriedly tucking my hair behind my ear before standing up to return my plate. I felt bad for wasting food but I hadn't had an appetite since I'd returned.

We left the building we ate in and strolled quietly through camp. Yet again, Jonah and Celt were locked away in the office. It felt odd, as though they were spending more time in there than usual, but then I remembered I'd been gone over three months; I'd forgotten how Greystone worked.

'So,' Leutie said lightly. 'How are you feeling today?'

'Fine,' I answered automatically.

She'd been trying for a few days now to open me up and I knew it was solely out of concern for me, but I couldn't bring myself to tell her anything. I didn't know with absolute certainty that she wouldn't betray me, so I wouldn't tell her anything.

We settled under the shade of one of the few trees that managed to grow in our camp, sitting amongst the cool grass.

'You're not fine, Grace,' she argued gently. She knew me well enough to see that even if I hadn't intended for her to. My performance wasn't very convincing. She was right: I wasn't fine.

'I just don't want to talk about it, okay?' I said, slightly more aggressively than I planned. She shied away somewhat as if I'd snapped at her and swallowed harshly.

'You don't have to but . . . can you just tell me what happened? They didn't . . . torture you or anything, did they?'

I resisted the urge to snort derisively in her face. I'd been tortured, all right, just not until I returned to Greystone with an absolutely shredded heart.

'No, Leutie,' I told her slowly.

Her eyes widened with relief. Yet another aspect we differed in so much was our experience with the brutality of our world; I'd been on more raids and killed more people than I could count while she'd never even left camp. She was, for lack of a better word, weak, but she was also so positive about everything that it was impossible not to let it influence you. She was the reason I could still see some of the good in the world, some of which I'd tried so desperately to get Hayden to see.

Hayden.

Ugh.

Stop thinking of him, Grace.

'Did they hurt you?' she pressed gently. I could feel her watching me closely despite looking elsewhere. I stalled, picking at the blades of grass next to my leg.

'No,' I answered quietly.

'What's it like there? Is it like here?' she asked, curiosity getting the better of her.

'I said I don't want to talk about it, okay? Let it be,' I snapped before letting out a heavy, frustrated sigh. I'd managed to avoid Jonah's questions for the last few days and didn't want to have to deal with Leutie starting in on me as well.

'Okay, okay, sorry,' she said sincerely. 'It's just . . . you're the only person to ever come back from a hostage thing like that, you know?'

Hostage. The word sounded odd as I repeated it in my head, the usage striking me as incorrect. I'd been a prisoner, yes, but not a hostage. Not once had they even considered using me in any way against Greystone. At least, Hayden hadn't. His intention from day one had been to repay me for sparing his life.

'I know,' I said, not bothering to correct her. The less I revealed, the better.

'It's a good thing you came back when you did, honestly. What with Celt being sick and all,' she said casually, leaning back against the trunk of the tree. For the first time, my gaze snapped to her intently.

'What?'

Her eyes connected with mine suddenly before widening in realisation. 'What?'

'What do you mean, "what"? Celt is sick?' I demanded, sitting up straight. I'd known he didn't look right so this shouldn't have come as a surprise, but to hear the words confirmed out loud was terrifying.

'Oh my god, Grace, I'm so sorry, I thought you knew,' she rambled on quickly, placing a hand in what was supposed to be a comforting gesture on my knee.

'No, he never told me,' I snapped. My words were rushed as I heaved myself to my feet quickly. I was already hurrying away from her as I called over my shoulder to her, 'I have to go.'

'Wait, Grace—' she called after me, her voice disappearing as I burst into a run. I had to hear it from him.

Shacks and people alike flashed by as I sprinted through the camp, my muscles stretching and lungs burning thanks to a lack of use lately. If Leutie had tried to follow me, she was far behind now; she'd never been able to keep up with me. Fear was creeping up higher and higher as I finally arrived at Celt's office, and my breath ripped from my lungs far harsher than it should have. I didn't even bother knocking before throwing myself at the door to burst inside.

It was much darker inside and it took a moment for my eyes to adjust before I saw Celt, Jonah and several other men huddled around the desk studying countless maps and other papers. Every single one of them jerked to face me as I slammed the door shut behind me.

'Grace, what—'

'Are you sick?' I demanded, cutting my father off as he tried to speak.

'Grace—'

'Are you?!' I practically shouted. My chest heaved as I stared at him, brows pulled low on my face and hands clenched by my sides.

'Would you gentlemen give us a moment?' Celt said, ignoring my question. I drew a shaky breath and tried to remain calm as everyone filed neatly past me, including Jonah. The fact that no one put up any sort of fight scared me greatly. Jonah's green eyes locked on mine in a momentary expression of dejection before he disappeared out the door, closing it behind him. This was not good.

We were left alone and the silence seemed to swell around us as I waited for him to speak. Even now, it was obvious he was ill. He was pale, dangerously pale, which made the dark circles under his eyes seem more defined than ever. His cheekbones were sharper than they should have been thanks to the sudden weight loss, and his eyes were rimmed with red where they should have been white.

'Grace, maybe you should sit down,' he offered kindly.

'No, Dad, just tell me,' I begged, my voice thin and weak as I waited for him to confirm what I already knew. 'Don't avoid it anymore, please.'

He stared at me for a long time, an unhappy expression falling over his face as he studied me.

'Yes, Grace. I'm sick.'

His verbal confirmation caused my chest to cave in,

lungfuls bursting out. He couldn't be sick – he was our unyielding leader, our unflinching commander. He was my indestructible father.

'What's wrong?' I managed to ask, forcing myself to hold back the tears I could feel rising once more. I felt like I'd cried more in the last week than I had in my entire life.

'We think it's endocarditis,' he said slowly. I felt the blood drain from my face as I realised what that meant: he had an infection in the inner lining of his heart, something that was nearly always fatal in our world.

'But don't we have antibiotics? Can't that help—'

'No, sweetie,' he said calmly, shaking his head slowly. 'I'm afraid it's too late for that. I know you can understand it. You're a smart girl.'

'But – no, you – you can't just give up, Dad,' I begged. Tears finally spilled over my cheeks. My voice was desperate and watery as I spoke.

'I'm not giving up. I'm just accepting what's going to happen,' he said as he stepped closer to me and placed his hands gently on my shoulders.

'No, there has to be something we can do—'

'There's nothing, Grace. You know that. Times are different now, and I've accepted it.'

My eyes squeezed shut as my face contorted with tears. As much as I wanted to argue and fight, I knew he was right. There was no denying he was wasting away in front of me. The telltale signs were impossible to ignore: weight loss, paleness, the swelling in his arms and legs that always indicated heart failure, all of it. There was more proof than I needed to confirm what he said but I couldn't accept it. He couldn't die – he was Celt, my valiant, resilient father – it wasn't possible such a man could die.

But he would. He and I both knew it.

Sooner rather than later, he would die.

A shuddering gasp of a sob ripped through me before I launched myself into his arms. He collected me and hugged me tightly, though it was impossible not to notice it wasn't nearly as tightly as it should have been. He was weak, so very weak, and it was obvious in everything that he did as I sobbed into his shoulder.

I'd just got him back and now I was going to lose him again.

What perfect timing, indeed.

'You can't die, Dad,' I pleaded weakly, my words muffled by his shoulder. Tears poured from my eyes as I hugged him close. 'I just got back, you can't die.'

'Shh, Grace,' he murmured. He didn't even bother to denying my statement.

'You can't . . .'

'Hush, it's okay,' he said calmly. His voice was strained, as if he, too, were fighting off tears. 'You got back just in time. A few more days and I never would have got to say goodbye.'

Just in time.

A flicker of confusion sparked in my brain as I hugged him and let more tears fall.

Just in time.

What were the odds that Hayden would decide to send me home days before my father's impending death?

No, Grace. You're dreaming.

There was absolutely no way Hayden could have known about this. My arrival back at Greystone was purely coincidence, of that I was certain. How could he have known such a thing?

He couldn't, you idiot. He just didn't want you there anymore.

I waved the irrational thoughts from my mind as I hugged

my father more tightly, the protruding bones even easier to feel as I held his weak, thin frame. Choking sobs continued to rack through my body, the pain and terror I was feeling blinding me from any further thoughts. The opportunities I had to hold my father in such a way were quickly running out, as I suspected in just a few short days he would be gone.

That was it. A few more days. Just a few more days until my father, the one person who'd managed to make me happy since my return, would be dead. Just a few more days before I truly lost everything.

HAYDEN

A scowl remained plastered on my face as I stalked through the camp. To say I'd been in a bad mood ever since forcing Grace to go home was the understatement of the century. Everyone was more than aware of it now as I moved through the camp, and people went out of their way to avoid the raging storm that was myself as I approached.

I'd hardly spoken to anyone since my time with Dax. My conversation with him had been the only time I'd shown any emotion at all, and I'd now closed myself off completely. I was left as a shattered shell of a man with absolutely no patience for anything. Rage seemed to be the only emotion I was capable of conveying, my heartbreak manifesting itself unfairly into insidious wrath.

I was on my way to do my usual rounds when someone dared to approach me. The small body appeared by my side and I felt the apprehensive glance he cast up at me even though I stared blankly ahead.

Go away, kid. Save yourself from me.

'Hayden,' Jett squeaked nervously. He was practically running as he tried to keep up with my brisk steps.

'What?' I snapped. I couldn't help it. I snapped at everyone these days.

'I was wondering . . .' he trailed off, testing my non-existent patience. 'Where's Grace?'

The sound of her name sent a thousand daggers into my body, piercing every possible inch of me and ripping me apart. I forced myself to remain blank.

'Gone.'

'But . . . why? Didn't she like it here?' he asked quietly, obvious sadness leaking into his voice. The tiny pang of guilt I felt was quickly wiped away by the residual hurt I felt inside. I could easily see his train of thought: Grace didn't like it here, meaning she didn't like him, and wanted to leave. I couldn't bring myself to correct him.

'I sent her home,' I said shortly.

'Why?'

His questions were grating on me and I had to grit my teeth to stop from shouting at him. 'Because.'

'But . . . I thought you liked her? And she liked us? I thought we were like a fami—'

'A what? A family?' I snapped, unable to control myself. 'You're fucking kidding yourself, all right? We're not a family and we never were. Now get lost.'

A tiny squeak from beside me finally managed to draw my burning gaze, and a flash of guilt erupted in my stomach as I saw Jett's face twist in sadness. Tears leaked from his eyes and he swallowed harshly as he started to shrink away from me.

'I'm sorry,' he choked out, his voice strained with tears before he turned sharply and ran away back in the opposite direction.

I let out a heavy sigh and hated myself even more for hurting him, but he had to know. He was too soft, too weak, and he needed to realise things didn't always turn out to be all rainbows and sunshine. The world was a shitty place, with shitty people and shitty things in it. People don't always get what they want and the sooner he learned that, the better.

My scowl deepened as I arrived at the main part of the camp. I was surprised and annoyed to see that there were far more people than usual gathered around. The last thing I wanted was be bothered with a crowd. I had all but decided to turn around to avoid them all when someone called my name.

'Hayden!'

I gritted my teeth, setting my jaw and flaring my nostrils as I huffed out a deep breath and tried to stay calm. It seemed impossible to keep my emotions in check these days. My feet carried me to the middle of the crowd to where whoever had called my name stood. I quickly identified Barrow in the middle, watching me approach with narrowed eyes.

'What?' I said, my voice darkly deep and flat. Morbid.

'Care to explain?' he demanded, his voice harsh and accusing as he glared at me. I noticed those gathered around had hushed dramatically as they listened to our exchange. A feeling of unease joined the constant agony that lurked in my stomach.

'Explain what?' I snapped.

'I think you know,' he accused sharply. I felt countless pairs of eyes watching me but I maintained my unflinching glare at Barrow. I knew what he meant. It was fairly obvious he was talking about Grace's absence, something I'd been able to avoid until now, but I wasn't about to volunteer information.

221

'If you have something to say, spit it out,' I dared. I almost relished the thought of a confrontation to use up some of this unrelenting anger.

'Well, I can't help but notice you're significantly lacking a prisoner and I know I'm not the only one,' he said darkly, glancing around dramatically as if looking for something he knew wasn't there: Grace.

'How clever of you,' I shot back, anger creeping up in my system. 'Any other astute observations you'd care to share?'

'I'm just wondering what you've done with her, seeing as she's the enemy.'

'I don't think I have to explain myself to you or anyone, Barrow. Need I remind you who the leader of this place is?' My attempts to sound cool and collected were negated by my fists balling tightly by my sides and the unmistakable hint of a threat to my voice.

'What kind of leader are you if we can't trust you? What are you hiding from us, huh? Where did your pretty little prisoner go?' he pressed. I couldn't help but notice more than a few people nodding in the crowd, siding with him as they decided that they, too, wanted some sort of explanation. It struck me as odd that all my allies – Dax, Kit, Docc, anyone who could have backed me up – seemed to be missing.

'You've got some nerve,' I growled. I was positively livid now. How dare he challenge me in front of so many people?

'I'm not the one keeping secrets from his camp,' he accused, narrowing his eyes even further at me.

'I'm not,' I spat, even though it was a lie. 'She's gone, that's it. There's nothing to discuss.'

'So you're not denying you let the enemy go after *months* here? After getting so much essential, potentially devastating information about us, you just let her go?'

A shocked gasp seemed to spread through the crowd as people realised just what Barrow was saying. What they didn't know, however, was that Grace would never betray any of us. I had no doubt in my mind that we were as safe as ever, but these people didn't know that. They trusted me to keep them safe, but in their eyes, I'd just thrown them all into the lion's den.

I stalked forward suddenly, stopping inches away from Barrow's face as my gaze seared into his own. 'You don't know what you're talking about, *Barrow*, so I suggest you shut your mouth. We're in no more danger than we were a week ago, and you're starting shit that doesn't need to be started. Don't make life harder on yourself by being a complete idiot.'

He returned a derisive sneer as an almost inaudible scathing chuckle floated through his lips. 'You're just a boy.'

'And you're a coward, challenging me in front of people who have no idea what's going on,' I spat, my head ticking upward as a disbelieving gasp of a cold laugh forced itself through my lips.

'Whose fault is that? Shouldn't they know what their leader's been up to?'

A low rumble of assent drifted through the crowd as people seemed to agree with Barrow. Fury rolled through me, momentarily blinding me as black started to creep in around my vision.

'They should know I'm keeping them safe. That's all that matters,' I said firmly.

'Why let her go then, huh? Sick of screwing her?'

My mind had barely absorbed the words before my body reacted. Without my control, my fist flew forward in the air before connecting with a sickening thud against his jaw, sending him flying in the opposite direction before he crumpled to the floor. The sting in my knuckles was completely lost on me as rage seared through me, leaving me positively seething on the spot. Breath ripped from my lungs and I was seeing odd flashes of light as I forced myself to turn around and stalk away from Barrow, who was heaped on the ground.

Surprised gasps and murmured whispers were hushed suddenly as a derisive laugh rumbled over them, silencing the crowd immediately. I didn't look back as I walked away, certain I'd be unable to restrain myself from hitting him again if I did.

'Oh, Hayden,' he called, his voice light and mocking even though he was still in the dirt.

With an impossibly heavy sigh, I forced my eyes closed to gather myself before stopping and spinning on the spot to face him. I saw a thick trail of blood leaking from his mouth and an angry red blotch over his jaw. He held himself up as he sat in the dirt and stared at me with dark amusement written across his features.

'Aren't you going to tell them the best part?' he asked, the devious enjoyment he was having leaking into his tone. I stood frozen in place, heart thumping wildly and lungs practically ripping to shreds.

'I learned something interesting the other day on a raid . . .' Barrow started, watching me closely for my reaction. I seethed, too angry to move or speak.

'Not only did our Hayden here let our enemy go with more information that she could ever dream of . . . but turns out she's someone quite important.'

No.

'Precious Grace has quite the family over there . . .' he continued. His audience was silent, absolutely riveted as he spoke.

Shut up.

'You see, she's their leader's daughter, and Hayden just gave him the key to all of Blackwing.'

Chapter Seventeen – Pivotal
GRACE

Every aspect of my world felt like it was caving in around me as I felt the cold, clammy hand of my father squeezed too tightly in my own. In the two days since he'd told me he was sick, he'd deteriorated so rapidly that I felt like I was counting the seconds until he was gone forever. He was a mere shadow of the man I remembered as I watched him now, too afraid to take my eyes off him in fear he'd pass without me noticing.

Never in my life had I felt so helpless than the last two days. There was absolutely nothing that could be done, something I'd finally come to accept just as he had. There were no medicines that could bring him back from the brink of death, no surgeries that could even be dreamed of attempting under such circumstances. Any attempts to do so would have killed him within minutes. There was nothing to do but wait – sit and wait in devastating agony and grief for the moment he finally succumbed to his illness and truly left me with nothing.

How could I go on without my father? He was my one ray of sunshine, my one sliver of happiness after what I'd gone through. Our time was short-lived and rushed, however, thanks to the crippling illness squeezing the life out of him. I'd come back just in time to lose him.

I sat by his bedside now, as I had been for the last twenty-four hours when he became too weak to walk any longer. His hand was held in mine too tightly, but I couldn't help it; my grasp was a desperate attempt to stop him from slipping away, but physical strength did nothing to hold off the inevitable end that we both knew was coming.

He was awake now, the discomfort of his illness making sleep impossible, though his eyes were closed as he drew shallow breath after shallow breath. A thin sheen of sweat covered his pale, sunken face, and his chest moved quickly up and down as he breathed far too quickly. I wavered between covering him in as many blankets as we could find and peeling them off his sweat-soaked body, unsure of what made him the most comfortable. No matter what I said or did, he insisted he was fine.

Jonah lingered out in the main room, unable to watch as our father slipped further and further away. He'd already said his goodbyes. I, on the other hand, couldn't look away. In some way, I was grateful to Hayden for this. His decision, whatever his motivation behind it, had allowed me to at least see my father before he died. What a lucky coincidence that he chosen to force me to leave right before this happened. I still believed it to be a coincidence, refusing to even entertain the alternative. It would break me even further.

'Grace,' he whispered, his voice thin and wheezy as he spoke.

'Yes?'

'I'm so happy you're back.'

'Me too, Dad,' I agreed softly, already fighting to hold back the burning creeping up in my throat. I'd been on the edge of tears all day and knew I wouldn't be able to hold them off long. His eyes flitted open with much effort as they locked on mine.

'I just want you to know how proud I am of you, Gracie,' he said in a hushed voice.

'Dad, don't, it's okay,' I said quietly, shaking my head as I drew a shaky breath. I didn't know if I could handle this – saying goodbye.

'No, I need to say this,' he said weakly. His eyes should have shown determination but there was no strength behind them; he was too weak to even muster that. 'I'm so proud of you. You're so strong. *So* strong. You're too young to have gone through what you've gone through and I'm sorry for putting you in that position. You're too young to have such burdens on you.'

He drew a gasping breath, as if speaking had winded him greatly. Tears welled in my eyes, blurring his pale face in front of me as I fought to hold them down.

'You didn't put me into anything,' I told him as my heart clenched in my chest. I sniffed once before continuing. 'I wanted it, you know that. I wanted to be included and to fight. You didn't put anything on me, Dad, I promise. You let me be who I wanted to be.'

He needed to know that. He needed to know he hadn't ruined my life by letting me do the things I'd done growing up. He needed to know he'd made me stronger, tougher, better. I was thankful for all he'd let me do because it made me who I was. The last thing I wanted was to be weak, and he'd let me be anything but.

'Always so strong,' he whispered weakly. His eyes were pained as he studied me, and his breath seemed shallower than ever. 'So beautiful and brave and strong.'

'I'm strong because of you,' I told him. My voice broke on the last word as tears started to fall and my throat tightened uncontrollably.

'Promise me you'll stay that way. Things are about to get

very difficult and I need you to promise you'll stay who you are,' he said, his voice even weaker though his eyes burned into mine. His words had pauses between every second or third, as if speaking was causing him to use vast amounts of effort.

'What do you mean?' I choked out, my words strangled by my ever-tightening throat.

'Just . . . promise me you'll stay strong.'

His insistence was stronger than ever, though his words were even weaker. I didn't want to waste time arguing or pressing him.

'I promise, Dad.'

'That's my girl,' he said, finally relaxing back once again as his eyes drifted closed. 'My little girl. So happy I got to see you one last time.'

'Dad . . .' I whispered before another gasp ripped through my throat. It was like I could see the light draining from him as his skin grew, if possible, even paler. 'Dad, please, I love you . . .'

'I love you too, Gracie.'

His voice was so soft now it was nearly inaudible. What little colour remained in his face began to disappear, and his grip on my hand slackened immensely.

'I'll always be with you,' he murmured softly, opening his eyes just enough to connect with my teary ones. I nodded and drew a shaky, uneven breath.

'I know, Dad,' I choked. My jaw quivered as I cried silently, the only sounds escaping me were my shuddering, gasping breaths as the tears continued to fall.

'I love you,' I gasped, blinking away the tears that were blurring my vision. They fell silently down my cheeks and splashed onto our linked hands. He began to drift away. I knew it was happening; I'd seen it far too many times.

'I love you so much, Dad.'

I couldn't stop saying it. I hadn't said it enough in my life and he needed to hear it now.

'I love you,' he returned weakly, holding my gaze for a few seconds before closing his eyes once more. 'My beautiful daughter . . . I love you.'

My heart panged painfully as a soft wisp of an exhale blew past his lips as his chest sank down. I watched through blurred eyes as it didn't rise again, allowing no more oxygen to flow into his lungs. The colour was gone from his face now as a stark grey replaced it, and he was completely still, as his hand relaxed its grasp of my own. The tiny flicker of light that had managed to cling to life inside him was extinguished, leaving him cold and empty.

He was gone.

My eyes squeezed shut tightly, blocking out the image as my head fell forward to land on his chest. Tears poured out of my eyes as I cried. These tears were different from the choking, body-racking sobs I'd experienced a few days ago; these were tears of grief, of acceptance, and they ripped through me silently as my jaw shook silently.

That was it. No more dad. No more Hayden. No more anything.

My father's hand grew colder and colder in my own and his chest continued to stay still and lifeless as I cried countless tears. The achingly cold numbness I'd felt days ago seemed to be battling for attention once more as it started to creep in, but the pain managed to hang on as my insides shredded themselves to bits.

This wasn't something I'd ever thought about before. Who really plans to lose a parent so young? How does one prepare for that? Even after going through this once before with my mother, I was no better prepared the second time around. To think of the finality of it all was starting to make me sick to my stomach. He was dead, and there was no coming back.

I didn't know how long I sat there, sobbing seemingly endless silent tears and trying to make sense of it all, but eventually Jonah came in to discover what had happened. He took a deep breath and placed a somewhat awkward hand on my back as he approached, causing me to weakly lift my head from where it had fallen.

'Grace, come on,' he said gently. It was the softest I'd ever heard his voice.

'No,' I said pitifully, sniffing harshly and wiping my hand quickly across my cheek.

'I know it's hard but . . . we have to let him go.'

'He can't be dead,' I murmured flatly, shaking my head in disbelief. Despite my better judgement, my eyes drifted up his body to land on his face. My stomach flipped over violently as I took in the grey pallor, the obvious lifeless-ness, and the way his jaw hung open slightly as it had when he'd taken his last breath. I felt like I was going to throw up.

'He is,' Jonah said quietly. He ran his hand across my shoulders once before stepping between the edge of the bed and where I sat. His hands landed lightly on mine that still held my father's as he gently removed my grip.

'Dad's dead, Jonah,' I said, my voice completely hollow and flat. It didn't feel real.

'I know,' he said solemnly. 'Please . . . let me do this. I need to do this.'

I didn't know exactly what he meant but I assumed it was something to do with moving his body. I'd got to share the last moments of his life with him so I could give Jonah that. I nodded slowly, leaning back in my chair for the first time in what felt like days. My back ached and my body felt stiff as I tried to look at anything other than my father's body. The image was burning itself into my brain, never to be forgotten.

At some point the tears seemed to have dried up, leaving my cheeks feeling tight and salty. Jonah inhaled a deep breath as he took in the heart-breaking image of our once strong father lying completely broken. Stiffly, I managed to rise from my seat. A deep breath pulled into my lungs as I leaned forward, forcing myself not to cry again as I did so.

'I love you, Dad,' I whispered so quietly it was almost inaudible. My body felt like it was shaking as I ducked to press a light kiss onto his forehead; his skin was cold against my lips. My eyes squeezed shut to fight off the tears once more as I straightened up and turned away, unable to look at the image before me. I sniffed and wiped my hand under my nose as I nodded to Jonah and forced myself to leave the room.

It took every ounce of strength I had to not look back, determined to leave in peace. As heartbroken as I was, there was a small silver lining; I'd got to say goodbye, something I would be eternally grateful for. I'd told my father how much I loved him and how much he meant to me before he'd died and that was all that mattered.

A shaky breath pulled through my lips as I walked through the camp. I was too distracted to focus but had to move so I wouldn't be crushed by the impossibly heavy sadness weighing down on me. My throat felt like it had been shredded to bits and my heart felt non-existent, but no more tears fell. The all too familiar numbness deluged me.

I didn't even realise where I was going until I arrived,

the door I now stood in front of confusing me slightly. How many times had I barged in here without announcing my presence? How many times had I seen him hunched over his desk, poring over papers, maps, and whatever else he was always studying? It seemed like far too many to count.

Without deciding to, I leaned my shoulder into the door, pushing my way inside. It looked as it always did: dim, slightly cluttered, and very worn in. My father's office. Or rather now, just an office with no owner to occupy it. I moved slowly to step deeper inside, taking in the small details that seemed so normal before: a mug half filled with tea, a small collection of pens scattered around the desktop, countless stacks of papers detailing who knew what.

Most poignantly, however, was the single photo that stood in a silver frame on the corner of his desk, as it had for as long as I could remember. My legs carried me to his desk where I sank down numbly into the chair. There was just enough light filtering through the windows to make out the four smiling faces in the photograph.

It was the only photo I'd seen of us, and as far as I knew it was the only time the four of us had been completely happy together. My mother and father both had wide grins plastered across their faces, my father's arm slung lovingly over my mother's shoulder as she held me in her arms. I was maybe two years old, only recognisable by the wisps of bright blonde hair adorning my head. Jonah stood in front of my father, holding one of his hands in both of his smaller ones. He was maybe six or seven, and was missing several teeth in his gap-filled smile.

Half of the people in that photo were dead.

I reached a shaking hand forward to pick it up when I

accidentally knocked over a stack of papers, sending them tumbling across the desk in a haphazard manner.

'Shit,' I muttered, upset with myself for disturbing things the way my father had left them. I hastily tried to reorganise them, my shaking hands flying out uncoordinatedly while I felt the return of the stupid tears welling up again.

Well done, Grace. Mess up the one thing you have left of him.

I silently berated myself as I tried to organise the papers, fighting off tears again as my emotions started to get the better of me. I had just about stacked them back into place when my eye caught the much larger paper unfolded beneath the sprawling pile. I froze, staring intently at the tiny area of the paper I could see.

Not a paper.

A map.

With shaky hands, I started to clear away the piles and piles of papers that covered the map I now discovered took up most of the desk. I began to realise exactly what it was, and my actions became quicker and sloppier. Finally, I'd cleared nearly the entire surface, so it was revealed in its entirety.

There, unfolded on the desk with countless scribbles and symbols, was a very detailed map of Blackwing.

Fear started to creep up in my body as I took in more and more details. Arrows were drawn coming in from all sides, cohering together at certain points around the border. Areas of the camp were highlighted and labelled in bold. I saw captions like 'ammo' and 'food supply' before I saw one that made my blood run cold: 'Leader.'

The more I pored over it, the more I realised what it was. The lines and arrows connecting to certain words made it clear that this wasn't just a distribution map; this was something much, much worse. This was a battle plan.

A loud bang of the door being forced open made me jump, and my eyes jerked up to see the source of it. Jonah stepped slowly through the doorway, his eyes taking in the scene before him as he realised what I'd just discovered. It explained so much — why Celt had been so busy lately, why he'd kept himself locked up in here until the very last possible moment, why he'd chosen a select few to divulge information to.

They were planning to go to war, and he was setting up his successors to carry it out after he was gone.

'What is this?' I demanded, my voice tight and low as I stared at Jonah. Jonah, who had been included in nearly all the meetings.

'What are you doing in here?' he shot back, ignoring my question. He clearly hadn't been expecting to find me here and was still struggling to make sense of things.

'What is this, Jonah?'

He sighed heavily and ran the palm of his hand down his face. 'It's what it looks like.'

'I want you to tell me,' I hissed. Fear was taking over now as I thought about what this would mean: an attack on Blackwing didn't just mean an attack on those who fought, it meant an attack on everyone. Men, women, children, young, old, it didn't matter. If Greystone launched a war against them without warning, they would all suffer.

They would all die.

'We're running out of everything, Grace. We're coming home empty from raids more and more often . . . We all knew the city would run out eventually, right? Well . . . it's happening.'

'So you're just going to start a war with Blackwing?!' I all but shouted, my voice rising in volume against my will. Jonah blinked once.

'Why do you care?' He sounded genuinely confused.

'Because . . . you can't just do that! Don't you know what that means? You start a war with them . . . they'll all die. Those who don't right away will die when you take everything they need to live. They're *people*, Jonah,' I said hurriedly. How could he not see that? How could he not see how wrong it was?

Steal a little on a raid, sure. Take a few things here or there, fine. But start an all out war to clean out a camp?

It was inhuman.

'We're people, too, Grace,' he reminded me, his face darkening slightly as he took in what I said. 'You'd rather our people die than theirs?'

'I don't want anyone to die,' I said firmly. My jaw tightened and I could feel my nostrils flaring as I blew out uneven breaths.

'Well, someone has to because there's not enough to go around. It's us or them, Grace,' he said flatly, as if explaining to a five year old.

Logically, I knew he was right. We all knew it would come to this eventually; the city would run out of things to raid and soon we'd have to figure out other ways to survive. The time had finally come.

'No, you can't do this,' I said, shaking my head again. 'You can't kill them. They're good people.'

'They held you captive, Grace!' he roared, apparently fed up with me arguing.

'And I'm still alive, if you haven't noticed! They did nothing to harm me and actually kept me alive after *you* left me!' I yelled, unable to hold back any longer.

He stared at me incredulously as if he couldn't believe what I was saying. His jaw hung open slightly as he scoffed at me.

'Something happened with their leader, didn't it? I saw you with him and you didn't look the least bit like a captive,' he accused, narrowing his eyes.

'He's a good person,' I said sharply, ignoring his assumption.

'He's a *killer*, Grace. Just like you. Just like me. He's no better than anyone else,' he spat.

'You're wrong.' My voice was a mere whisper, tight with tension as I shook my head in denial. 'He's not like either of us. He's not a killer like us.'

'You're in denial! He's hurt people, yes?' he hissed.

'Yes,' I spit reluctantly.

'And he's killed people, yeah?'

'Yes, but—'

'But nothing, Grace. That's it. Your precious whatever the hell he was is no better than we are. Why does he deserve to live more than we do?'

'He doesn't deserve to die. None of them do.'

My entire body was shaking now, a combination of fear, rage, and devastating loss doing more than enough to destroy any control I might have had. We glared at each other, at a standstill with our arguments while the tension in the room whirled around us like a monsoon.

'It doesn't matter. This was my idea. It's happening and there's nothing you can do to stop it. I'm in charge now, whether you like it or not,' Jonah said through gritted teeth. The veins in his neck and forehead bulged beneath his skin, and his muscles in his arms were firm as he clenched his fists by his sides. He, too, seemed absolutely livid.

'Is this what Dad wanted?' I demanded. I needed to know if he'd been supportive of this barbaric scheme.

'Dad's dead,' Jonah replied, avoiding answering my

question but confirming it all the same. My father had not wanted this.

'What happened, you and everyone else tried to plan this while he tried to stop it?' I accused sharply.

As the words spilled out, I knew they were true. Jonah didn't reply and simply stared at me, confirming my guess. I shook my head slowly, unable to believe someone so brutal and violent had come from my own flesh and blood. I finally dropped his gaze as my head tilted forward. A light scoff blew past my lips as I shook my head.

'Dad would be disappointed, Jonah.'

He didn't respond as I shot him one last derisive look and shifted to move past him. I couldn't be in the same room as him anymore, not now that I knew what he was planning to do. Silence so loud echoed around us that it was almost deafening as I opened the door and slipped through it. I expected him to say something, anything really, to defend himself, but he said nothing. He felt no need to defend what he clearly thought was right.

The sky had started to darken outside now as evening fell. Thick clouds were rolling in, blocking out the bright blue of the sky to more appropriately match how I was feeling inside. A faint hint of thunder in the distance could be heard, rumbling menacingly as I stalked purposefully through camp.

That was it. I couldn't stand by any longer while these people, who now felt like strangers, plotted something so disgustingly inhuman that it made my stomach tie into knots. I couldn't let so many innocent people be slaughtered with absolutely no warning. I couldn't be completely and utterly helpless when there was something I could do.

Wind whipped past my head as I picked up my pace. My feet moved faster and faster, carrying me from a brisk walk to a jog before finally breaking into a sprint. I pushed harder and harder, determined to get away from there.

Away from Greystone.

Back to Blackwing.

Chapter Eighteen – Dire
GRACE

My lungs were starting to burn with the effort of running as I propelled myself towards Blackwing. It had been a long time since my body had had to work so hard thanks to my injury, and as difficult as it was, I had to admit it felt good to use my muscles again. I moved as quickly as I could through the thick brush along the wooded floor, and the browns and greens of the trees blurred as they flew past my line of vision. These woods that had started to feel so much like home now felt like barriers as I darted in and out of them, pushing ever closer to my target.

I didn't have time to think whether I'd made the right decision or consider going back; it was what needed to be done. No matter what the reasoning behind it, I just couldn't stand by while my brother planned the slaughter of another camp. Yes, there were only enough dwindling supplies left to sustain one camp, but that didn't mean that everyone had to die in order to earn it. It was wrong and it was only further evidence of what I'd started to see about our world: the fast deterioration of whatever humanity remained.

The trees started to look more and more familiar as they flew by, and the distance I'd covered started to show in my muscles. I felt my adrenaline spike in my veins. My heart pounded harder, sweat pricked at my forehead, and my breathing ripped roughly from my lungs as I pushed forward. I began seeing flickers of lights leaking through the trees.

Almost there.

I threw caution completely to the winds as I burst from the tree line into the camp. There was no one around, but I was still on the outer edges. I rushed forward, sprinting past huts as I flew down the dirt path. It was evening now, the light was slipping low in the sky, which meant Hayden would probably be somewhere in the middle of the camp. I headed in that direction.

A few people here and there appeared as I pushed on, doing startled double takes as they saw me sprint by. I took no notice of them, too determined to get to Hayden and warn him of what was coming. The path I was on turned sharply left, carrying me closer to the centre of the camp. As soon as I rounded the corner, my field of vision opened up to reveal the hub of the community about a hundred yards away.

My feet snagged suddenly in the dirt as my eyes landed on him. Hayden stood in the middle of a group of people. His back was to me and even from this distance, it was easy to see his tension. With his shoulders hunched forward and the haphazard way he dragged his hand through his hair, it was clear to me whatever he was doing was causing him great stress.

I assessed all this as I ran. He was fifty yards away now but still he hadn't seen me. No one in the group did either, all of them too focused on whatever he was doing in the middle. My lungs were burning now with the effort of running and my muscles felt like they might give out, but I was nearly there.

Twenty-five yards away.

Twenty.

Fifteen.

I had just opened my mouth to call out to Hayden and get his attention when a large hand clamped over it from behind, yanking me forcefully backwards. My body was dragged out of the line of trajectory, and the side of the building I was hastily jerked behind cut off my line of vision, blocking out Hayden from my sight.

Limbs fought automatically against whoever was restraining me – kicking, pulling, scratching, punching – but it was no use; I was too worn out from running to use my full strength, and whoever had hold of me was much stronger than I was. I huffed desperately, my nostrils flaring thanks to the way my mouth was covered. A rough, stubbly chin grazed my temple as my captor lowered their face next to mine.

'Just where do you think you're going?'

My blood ran cold in my veins as I recognised the voice instantly. How could I forget the first time he'd asked me nearly the exact same question? There was no mistaking the seedy voice, the strength required to restrain me, and the prickly stubble currently scratching into my skin.

I'd just encountered probably my worst enemy in all of Blackwing when I'd been mere yards from Hayden: Barrow.

HAYDEN

My jaw clenched harshly as I tried to force down my frustration. Darkness clouded my vision as I closed my eyes and blew out a sharp exhale in an attempt to calm myself down. There were too many people, too many voices, too many demands for information I could not and would not give. They were all around me, fighting for my attention and calling out my name as they tried to get me to respond.

'How could you do this to us, Hayden?'

'Are we in danger?'

'She's the enemy, Hayden!'

'If we die, it's on you.'

'Why, Hayden?'

These questions and more were hurled at me repeatedly, bombarding me from every direction as I tried and failed to block them out. In the hour since Barrow had made his declaration, I'd been attempting to calm everyone down and reassure them, but it seemed to be completely pointless. No one would listen, and the panic Barrow had wanted to instil had forcefully taken hold of all those present.

His motivations were pretty clear to me; he didn't think I was suited to be the leader anymore and wanted it for himself. The truth was, I'd never asked for it. I'd been thrown into this situation too young, too inexperienced, too weak. Eighteen is not old enough for someone to become a leader, but in the three years that had passed since then I'd learned more than enough to keep people safe.

Besides, it didn't matter if I asked for it or not: I was their leader now, and I would be their leader until I died. That responsibility was mine and I wasn't about to brush it off because of a few obstacles and a broken heart.

Someone reached out and placed a hand on my arm, forcing me to look at them. It was like all the sound of their desperate cries rushed back in at once, hitting me full force as I blinked and tried to refocus myself. The person who had touched my arm came into focus as I took in the dark brown eyes framed by lighter brown skin. Docc.

'Hayden,' he said calmly. 'They'll listen to you if you explain. Not everything, just enough to settle them. They trust you.'

His words were so mellow and the total opposite of the rest of the crowd that they brought me instant comfort. To hear the heavy accusations being flung in my direction had only dug the pit of despair and hurt more deeply around me.

'Everyone shut up!' I roared suddenly, unable to take the deafening noise any longer. An awed hush fell over the crowd as they all, miraculously, stopped their chattering. Every single pair of eyes was focused on me as they waited for me to speak.

'I know you're all confused and pissed off and scared, but I promise you're safe. Yes, I let Grace go, and yes, she's someone of importance, but it doesn't matter. If any of you here talked to her, you know what I'm about to say is true: she's no danger to us. She's done so much for everyone here, saved so many of our lives when she didn't have to, and she won't betray us. She's gone back, but she won't do anything to endanger anyone. Trust me.'

No one responded to my speech at first, although a few seemed placated by my words as they seemed to remember seeing Grace around or hearing stories of what she'd done. Others, however, remained sceptical as they frowned at me.

'Look, you know all I want is to keep everyone safe. Do you trust me to do that?' I demanded, glancing around the circle that had formed. I was relieved to see most people now nodding or at least softening their stubborn looks. Few remained of those who doubted my qualifications. I was just about to speak to continue my argument when the sound of my name cut me off.

'Hayden!'

The breathless voice sounded far away. Immediately I saw people parting as they let a slightly sweaty, very winded Dax through the crowd.

'Hayden, you have to come quick,' he said urgently,

wiping sweat from his brow as he stared at me intently.

'I'm in the middle of somethi—'

'No, really, come with me, *now*,' Dax said directly, his voice tightening with tension as his eyes widened. He nodded quickly as if urging me on.

'Dax—'

'Hayden!' he shouted suddenly, cutting off my protests. 'It's Grace.'

I halted at the sound of her name, and it felt like someone had dumped a bucket of ice-cold water over me. Immediately, without hesitation, my body jerked towards Dax. A look of relief washed over his face as I finally listened to him. He turned quickly, darting back the way he had come, as people started to question me again, though the murmur of their voices was completely lost on me as I hurried off after Dax.

Once free of the crowd, our pace increased to a quick run as I drew even with him.

'What do you mean?' I demanded, following him as he moved through the huts.

'It's Grace,' he repeated sharply, accelerating even more.

'Yeah but *what*?' My frustration intensified as he stalled. My heart seemed to pound harder than it had in years at the thought of something bad happening to her. Dax and I sprinted forward, I didn't really care where we were going.

'Barrow has her.'

My body seemed to paralyse as his words thundered over me.

Oh no.

Oh no, no, no, no, no.

Barrow, who had just declared he knew exactly who she was and what that could potentially mean, had the girl I loved more than I ever thought possible.

I couldn't even find words to respond as I pushed my body even harder, running faster and faster as Dax navigated the course. My hands started to shake as my arms pumped by my sides and crippling anger and fear flooded through me. If he hurt a single hair on her head, I would fucking kill him.

Vague shouts could be heard as we ran on, though the words were difficult to make out. It was a male voice, clearly laced with anger. I heard a second, slightly deeper voice, growing louder and louder as we approached. Again, the words were muffled, as though they were inside.

'You can't do this!' the first voice shouted, finally distinguishable as Kit's as we neared the source they were coming from: Barrow's hut.

'I'll do what I like, *boy*,' the second voice, Barrow, yelled back. He'd just finished speaking when I reached the front door. Without a moment's hesitation, my shoulder slammed into it to throw it open. A loud bang sounded as it bounced off the inner wall, silencing the yelling inside.

'You,' I spat harshly, unable to control myself.

Fury nearly blinded me as I scanned inside quickly, my eyes landing on Barrow first. He whipped around, blocking whatever was behind him from view while Kit stood next to him, glaring at him and clearly about to punch him. Before I could even think of anything to say, my feet carried me forward in blind rage. My fist cocked back and swung forward, connecting with Barrow's jaw for the second time today as he stumbled backward into a table.

I was about to unleash an unrelenting storm of punches on him when a quiet whimper drifted to my ears, drawing my attention to what I should have seen in the first place. My head jerked in the direction of the sound before my eyes landed on her.

Blood turned to ice in my veins as I saw her, and a new kind of fear ripped through my entire body. She sat on a chair, both her hands tied behind her back by thick rope, similar to the one that bound each of her legs to a post in the chair. A thick trail of blood poured down the left side of her face, and she appeared slightly dazed.

'Hayden,' she breathed as her eyes fluttered weakly for a moment before her head lolled forward for a moment. She recovered and righted herself, but it was very obvious that she wasn't fine at all.

'Grace,' I gasped in shock. I managed to recover finally as I lurched forward, immediately taking her face between my hands as I crouched down in front of her. Her eyes fluttered once again before she managed to focus on me. Her pupils seemed to contract and dilate repeatedly as I studied her intently.

'Grace, are you okay?' I asked firmly, desperate for her to be okay. She had to be okay.

'Hayden,' she repeated. An unmistakable flicker of pain crossed her eyes as she held my gaze, ignoring my question completely. I forced a sharp exhale from my lips as I tried to remain calm. 'I have to tell you . . .'

She trailed off weakly, however, as her eyes drifted shut once again.

'Shit, okay, Grace, hang on,' I said urgently, releasing her face from my hands as I moved behind her to start untying the knots there.

'Kit, Dax,' I said distractedly. 'Take Barrow to the top of the tower and tie him up. I don't want him talking to anyone, understand?'

'Yeah, of course,' Dax said quickly, moving to grab one of Barrow's arms while Kit took the other. He'd been slightly dazed by my strike but was starting to come around again.

'Sure you don't want us to just push him off?' Kit offered seriously. I contemplated taking him up on his offer before I shook my head.

'No, just tie him up then tell Docc to go to my hut,' I answered sharply as my fingers tugged on the knots. I groaned in frustration as my shaking hands struggled to undo them.

'You fool. You total, complete fool,' Barrow hissed, finding strength to speak again. I ignored him, too distracted with untying Grace to bother with him.

'Shut up, dickhead,' Kit muttered as he and Dax dragged him from the hut. I could hear them bickering spitefully as they moved outside before the door shut and cut them off.

Another tiny whimper creaked from Grace's throat as I finally succeeded in undoing the ties around her wrists, freeing her arms. She managed to pull them back around in front of her, massaging her wrists weakly as she struggled to stay conscious. I shifted so I was in front of her again and began working on the ties on her right leg.

'What are you doing here, Grace?' I muttered, more musing aloud than asking her. She was clearly not completely alert thanks to whatever Barrow had done to her, so I wasn't surprised when all she did was groan quietly in response. My fingers worked furiously, successfully undoing the second tie much faster than the first. I moved to the final tie and started to work.

'Stay with me, Grace, I'm almost done,' I murmured, glancing up at her to see her barely clinging to consciousness. If the blood streaming from her temple was any indication, she'd taken at least one heavy blow to the head.

I was going to burn Barrow alive for this.

A heavy sigh of relief pushed past my lips as I finally undid the final tie, even though my hands still shook with anger, shock, and fear. I couldn't even absorb the fact that she was right in front of me let alone process any of the countless emotions I was feeling; all that mattered was keeping her safe.

I stood up immediately and slid my arms around her shoulders and beneath her knees to scoop her up, standing to lift her from the chair. Her head rolled to land on my shoulder and she let out another quiet groan as she winced slightly. As soon as I had her settled in my arms, I started manoeuvring us out the door, and towards my hut.

'Grace,' I said gently, trying to subdue the panic I was feeling that she seemed to slip further and further away. She didn't respond though her eyes were fluttering, telling me she was still conscious.

'Grace!' I repeated a little more firmly as her eyes squeezed tightly shut, as if struggling internally, still not responding.

'Bear,' I tried. My voice hushed automatically as my endearment for her hit me like a ton of bricks. A flash of green appeared as her eyes opened, finally responding to my calls. My shoulders sagged momentarily with relief as she looked at me with some actual conviction for the first time.

'Herc,' she whispered weakly. It was like she'd never left as my feelings for her surged forward in full force, even stronger now than they'd been when she left.

'You're all right, Grace,' I told her, refusing to believe anything to the contrary. To think about the potential outcome would absolutely paralyze me with fear, something I couldn't have as I carried her warm body back to my hut.

'Hayden, I have to tell you—'

'Shh, just wait, all right? It can wait until you're okay,' I said, cutting her off. Whatever she had to say couldn't possibly be as important as making sure she was safe. 'Just rest, we're almost there.'

And we were. My hut finally came into view as I rounded

the final corner. Hasty, rushed steps brought us on to the door. A candle I'd forgotten to blow out earlier cast a soft glow around the small space as I carried her to the bed and laid her down gently. A sudden, deep rumble from the sky sounded ominously as the incoming storm approached.

She was silent as I settled her onto her back, resting her head on a pillow. I sat down, and leaned over her, one arm reaching across her weakened body, our faces level. Her eyes managed to find mine in the dim lighting. I knew I shouldn't, but I couldn't stop my free hand from rising to brush her blood-streaked hair off her face.

Neither of us spoke as I repeated my silent actions over and over. Not once did my eyes leave hers. It was like the air had thickened around us to encase us in that bubble I had begun to miss, as if no time had passed at all and none of the heartbreaking agony had ripped us apart.

Our moment was broken, however, by my door whipping open suddenly. My gaze jerked from hers, ready to attack whoever intruded before I saw it was just Docc, carrying a small bag with him. Ignoring me, he rushed forward. He shoved me unceremoniously aside, forcing me to sit up, as he inched forward to inspect the damage.

'What happened?' he inquired without looking at me. He immediately started digging in his bag, pulling out gauze pads, antiseptic and bandages.

'Barrow,' I hissed angrily. 'He had her tied up and I think he hit her on the head.'

Grace fidgeted at the sound of my voice though I couldn't see her face now as Docc leaned over her.

'You're a tough girl, aren't you?' Docc murmured. He inspected her temple and I found myself almost painfully anxious. Automatically, my hand that had been moving along her face reached to clasp her fingers between my own. I squeezed once, holding my breath silently until she returned the light pressure and sent a wave of warmth through my body. It felt like it had been decades since I'd been able to do something so simple with her.

Docc worked quickly and silently, assessing her pupils and breathing for signs of internal trauma before he moved to clean the cut. She was nearly completely unconscious now and pretty much unaware of what he was doing.

'It doesn't need stitches,' he said as he wiped away the remaining blood. He spread some of the antiseptic on the cut before placing a bandage over it. 'And I don't think she has a concussion. Just a good knock on the head, which is pretty disorienting.'

A sigh of relief so huge forced from my body that I sagged forward low enough to bring Grace's hand to my lips. I pressed a lingering kiss to her knuckles as I let my eyes close for a moment, beyond grateful she would be okay. With a deep breath, I sat up and glanced at Docc.

'Thank you.'

'You're welcome. Let her sleep a bit. I know you'll take care of her,' he said calmly, nodding at me once before he finished gathering his supplies. With that, he straightened up and moved toward the front of my hut.

'And Hayden,' he said, pausing as he reached for the door.

'Yeah?'

'Don't let her go again. You're better off together.'

My jaw fell open at his words, unsure of what I'd been expecting though it definitely hadn't been that. He didn't wait for me to recover from my shock and respond, however, before he slipped out the door and into the oncoming storm, leaving us alone once more.

Once again, Grace's eyes were closed and her lips parted slightly as soft, even breaths blew from her lungs. It appeared

251

as if she'd finally given up holding on to consciousness.

It was then that it really started to sink in. Grace was right in front of me, albeit unconscious, in my bed rather than at home with her father like she should have been. A sharp pang struck me at the thought that maybe he wasn't around anymore – but I desperately hoped that wasn't the case for Grace's sake.

Docc had cleaned the blood away, so my eyes roamed across her features as I tried to sort out my thoughts. I had so many questions to ask her but at that moment, all I could focus on was how incredible it was to see her after convincing myself I'd never see her again. She was there, *right there,* and she was alive.

I resumed my position from before Docc's arrival, leaning over to study her as one hand lifted again to trail lightly over her features. Her jaw, cheeks, brows, nose and finally her lips passed under my fingertips, just as I'd memorised them so long ago. It was as if no time had passed at all since she'd left as every thought, feeling, and emotion rushed back to fill my shriveled, broken heart.

It was with a deep, heavy sigh that I managed to finally pull my hand away from her face. I allowed myself to duck down and press one feather-light kiss on her forehead that she would not feel as she slept, before forcing myself to stand from the bed.

I still didn't know why she was here. Her sudden reappearance didn't change anything if her family was still alive. Once again, I feared making her choose between her family and me.

My feet carried me back and forth in a short line around my bed as I paced, desperate for her to wake up and explain, while also hoping she'd stay asleep for hours to delay her inevitable departure once again.

She'd tell me what she had to tell me and leave, I was certain. I had to start to prepare myself to lose her all over again.

Much to my surprise, however, she stirred after only a few minutes. A low groan rattled from her throat as she shifted in the bed. I rushed forward again, sitting on the end of the bed this time rather than right next to her. Might as well start the separation now.

A soft frown crossed her face as she took in how far away from her I was sitting. She managed to prop herself up slightly once she seemed to have got over the initial disorientation of her injury. In fact, she looked more focused and determined than ever.

'How do you feel?' I asked slowly, my voice low and soft as I studied her closely.

'A little woozy but fine,' she said, her gaze intent on my own. 'Listen, I know you don't want me here and I'll leave but I just need to tell you something—'

'Jesus, Grace, this wasn't supposed to happen.'

'What do you mean?' she asked, confusion flitting across her face.

'You, you're . . . you're not supposed to be here,' I said slowly, dropping her gaze for a moment in distraction before I refocused on her.

'I get it, okay? I said I'd leave, I just have to tell you—'

'What are you doing here?' I asked, unable to stop myself from interrupting her. I could feel my emotions starting to get the better of me and I feared that I wouldn't be able to let her go a second time without actually caving in and dying. 'This isn't . . . you're supposed to be home with your family. I wasn't supposed to see you again.'

My breathing felt like it was too fast now and my hands started to feel clammy as I slammed them onto my thighs in frustration. She watched me closely and I could tell she wanted to interrupt me so I continued before she could.

'You weren't supposed to come back. You weren't supposed to get hurt. You were supposed to stay safe, Grace. None of this was supposed to happen,' I rambled on. I could feel myself getting carried away but I couldn't seem to stop it. Having her right there in front of me yet still so untouchable was going to drive me mad.

My breathing grew even more irregular when she surprised me by sitting up and scooting closer to me, moving so she sat right in front of me now. Gingerly, she reached forward and took my clammy hand in hers.

'Hayden, I need you to listen to me,' she said firmly, peering intently into my eyes. 'Things don't happen how they're supposed to, okay? I'll go after this.'

'God, Grace, I don't want you to go.'

It was the last thing I should have admitted when I was trying so hard to do what was best for her but it was impossible to stop. Her breath hitched in her throat as she absorbed the words, her gaze locked firmly on mine.

'You don't?' she whispered, her voice loaded with emotion. She was too close now, and her vicinity was clouding my thoughts. My throat felt tight as I shook my head. I couldn't keep up this façade any more. I found it impossible to think that she still had believed my lies. She still thought I didn't want her there with me.

'No, I don't,' I admitted. 'You're right, things don't go how they're supposed to.'

'Yeah . . .' she said softly, waiting for me to continue. I pulled my hand from hers and reached up automatically to cradle one side of her face. I let my thumb drag along her lower lip. She returned my look, utterly captivated by my every move just as I was with her.

254

'You were never supposed to be here. You were never supposed to see the things you did, never supposed to become a part of the camp . . . You were never supposed to come back . . . and . . . I was never supposed to fall in love with you.'

There it was, out in the open. I'd pulled the pin on the grenade and launched it recklessly into the air, throwing all caution to the winds as I finally, finally, told her exactly how I felt. She sucked in a quick gasp and her eyes widened in surprise all while my ribs practically vibrated with how hard my heart was beating.

'You're in love with me?' she finally asked, her voice so quiet I could hardly hear.

'I'm so in love with you it hurts, Bear.'

It felt so good to say it, finally say it, that I had to physically restrain myself from leaning forward to kiss her right that second.

'Hayden, I'm in love with you, too.'

My heart leaped into my throat and I seemed to lose the ability to breathe as her words nearly knocked me over.

'You are?' I asked, too shocked to believe her. Her eyes were narrowed intensely as her gaze burned into mine while she nodded.

'Completely.'

That confirmation was all it took to send shockwaves burning through my body. I leaned forward, erasing the space between us. My other hand rose to cradle the other side of her face. I leaned forward, pausing just a fraction of an inch away from her lips as if to make sure this was actually real.

She was there, warm, alive and safe, and she was in love with me.

This was real.

I pressed my lips to hers. The moment we made contact, fire erupted in my veins and the entire world fell away, leaving me alone with Grace and the way she made me feel. Every cell in my body seemed to be celebrating as I kissed her, rejoicing in the reunion I never thought would happen. In that moment, she was all that mattered, and for the first time in what felt like years, I felt whole again.

Chapter Nineteen – Impending
GRACE

Hayden's lips were warm against my own as he kissed me, the feeling enveloping me from the inside out as he poured every emotion into his actions. I could feel the relief, the stunned disbelief, and most importantly, the love all at that moment as he held my face between his hands. A dull haze started to creep over my brain, threatening to pull me completely into his spell. Only a soft nagging in the back of my mind stopped it, reminding me that as exquisite as this reunion was, there was a bigger purpose to my return.

With every bit of will power I had, I managed to pull back just enough to release my lips from his and whisper softly, 'Hayden.'

'Hmm?' he hummed softly, leaning forward again to try and reconnect our lips. My hands drifted lightly to his chest and put soft pressure there. The touch seemed to surprise him, and his eyes finally flitted open. 'What is it?'

His thumbs ran across my cheeks gently as he studied me, concern etching into his features as he took in my expression.

'I need to tell you why I came back,' I said firmly, forcing myself to stay focused.

'It's not just because you love me?' he said with a hint of a smile. My heart fluttered at his words.

'Of course I do. But . . . that's not why I came back.'

'Then what is it?' he asked. A strange hint of fear crossed his features and I wondered what he was thinking of. His hands finally dropped from my face to squeeze my thigh gently.

'Something bad is going to happen . . . My brother, Jonah . . . he's planning to attack Blackwing.' My body tensed as I said the words. I watched him closely for his reaction, nervous for how he'd take it. The ache of losing my father surged forward as I thought of how he hadn't wanted this, but I forced it down. I couldn't deal with thinking of my father now or I'd completely break down; this had to be taken care of, first.

'Like a raid?' Hayden asked, a frown creasing his face.

'No, Hayden. Not like a raid. Like a . . .' I paused, searching for the right word. 'Like a war.'

Hayden's frown deepened as his brows pulled low over his blazing green eyes. His voice was a carefully controlled calm. 'Why?'

'Because they're running out of everything and it's harder and harder to find stuff in the city. He wants to take everything from Blackwing and leave everyone else to die,' I explained. Hayden was quiet for a few moments while he absorbed what I was saying.

'Let them try,' he finally said. 'People have been attacking us for years and we're still standing.'

A flash of panic rose inside me. He didn't seem to understand how serious this was.

'No, Hayden, you don't get it. They have plans drawn up – like actual battle plans with front lines and stuff. This isn't just a raid – they want to wipe us out.'

'Us?' Hayden repeated, blinking once and studying me closely. I couldn't help blow out a frustrated sigh and roll my eyes.

'Not the right time, Hayden. But yes, us. You, me, every-one out there – they'll kill them all to get what they need. Do you understand? It's not a game,' I said urgently, my tone now clearly laced with frustration.

'Okay, okay,' he soothed, squeezing my thigh reassur-ingly. 'I know it's serious, all right?'

He dropped my gaze and frowned as he chewed his lower lip. I prayed the weight of the situation was finally starting to hit him.

'How do you know all this?' he finally asked, snapping his gaze back up to mine.

'I saw the maps. Then when Jonah caught me, he con-firmed everything. I don't know when but I know where.'

'Show me,' he commanded sharply.

I was pleased he finally seemed to see how serious it was. My legs unfolded from the bed as I stood, the room swim-ming through my vision as my head panged sharply. Barrow had hit me over the head hard enough to raise a small lump and knock me out, but it wasn't the worst injury I'd ever sustained. I suspected it would feel better tomorrow.

Hayden followed me to his desk before pulling out a scrap of paper and a pen, handing them to me so I could show him what I'd seen. My hand scrawled feverishly across the page as I recreated the map that was, thankfully, now burned into my brain. I sketched out Blackwing quickly before adding the arrows and lines meant to represent scores of Greystone members attacking. Just as I remembered, lines converged from all sides to overcome Blackwing. A shudder ran through me as I finished the last arrow and straightened up for Hayden to see.

'Shit,' Hayden breathed. His eyes were focused intently on the paper as he took in the numerous advances and real-ised this attack would be far worse than any faced before.

'How many people live in Greystone?'

'At least six hundred,' I answered. 'If not more.'

'*Shit*,' he swore again, pushing his hand roughly through his hair. 'That's more than we have.'

I was quiet as he continued to study the map I'd drawn. The visible tension that had started to ease from his body had returned in full force, and it was clear he was very stressed by this new development. My hand reached up automatically to run down his back, feeling the tight muscles there as I tried to soothe him.

'Who will they bring? Just raiders, adults, what?'

'Everyone,' I said slowly. If there was one thing I knew, it was that my brother wouldn't care who he put in danger. He would bring every single person able to wield a weapon, be they eight years old or eighty.

'*Everyone?*' he repeated incredulously. It must seem crazy to him, because I knew he would never expose people to such grave danger. Yet more evidence that he was better than the rest of us. I nodded solemnly as he glanced quickly in my direction.

'Okay,' he nodded, as if talking to himself. 'You're sure about this? It's going to happen?'

'*Yes*, Hayden,' I said urgently. 'I wouldn't have come back if I wasn't sure.'

A flicker of hurt flashed across his face at my confession, but it was true.

'You sent me away,' I reminded him softly, my own pain still very fresh in my mind. Despite hearing Hayden tell me he was in love with me, I knew it would take some time to get over what he did.

'I know,' he said quietly. Now sadness flitted across his features. 'We'll talk about that later, okay? Right now . . . we need to start planning for this.'

260

I nodded in agreement. Now was not the time to discuss our heartbreak. He surprised me by ducking forward suddenly, kissing me firmly as his hand landed on the side of my neck.

'You just saved us all, Grace.'

I drew a shaky breath, the weight of the words really starting to sink in. He didn't wait for my response, however, before he reached down to grab my hand. With his free hand he stuffed the piece of paper I'd drawn on into his pocket, then tugged me briskly up and out of the hut.

Almost immediately, we encountered several people milling around outside. Most were visibly confused or upset about whatever had happened before I'd arrived. More than a few suspicious looks were cast in my direction, and I couldn't help but notice a lot of the questioning looks were aimed at our linked hands.

'Hayden—' I started as he pulled me along, attempting to tug my hand free, only for his grip to tighten. He didn't seem to care that people could see, something that made me both elated and terrified all at once.

'Everyone, come to the middle of the camp,' Hayden called sharply, addressing those that had appeared around us. 'I have something important to say.'

His voice held such command and authority that people immediately started following us, alerting those who hadn't heard. I was surprised when Kit appeared suddenly, falling into step besides Hayden.

'What's going on?' he asked quickly.

'I'll tell you in a minute. I need you and Dax to get everyone who's not on patrol in the middle of the camp, all right?'

'Okay,' Kit said, nodding sharply before veering off the path to alert more people.

My stomach twisted into knots as more and more people

threw unhappy looks in our direction. I couldn't shake the feeling that it was something deeper than simply seeing Hayden and I together. Barrow seemed to know exactly who I was when he'd attacked me, but did everyone else . . .?

I finally pulled my hand from Hayden's, unable to take the surly looks any longer. Hayden seemed surprised but so much confusion remained between us that it was almost overwhelming. What had changed while I was gone? Why did Hayden force me to leave in the first place if he loved me? Did he even love me then or did he only realise it after I was gone? I needed to know, but now wasn't the time to ask.

'They know,' Hayden murmured quietly. We were nearly to the centre of the camp now, and a large crowd had quickly gathered in anticipation of Hayden's announcement.

'What?'

'They know who you are,' Hayden explained further. 'Barrow found out somehow and told everyone.'

I was prevented from responding, however, as we reached the largest group I had seen since the bonfire ages ago. Familiar, friendly faces were few and far between as most of the crowd was restless with tension. I spotted Docc, Maisie, Kit, Dax and several others I knew by sight but not by name. Most of the faces were unfamiliar or ones I'd only seen once or twice before.

Hayden moved to climb on top of a large crate propped against one of the buildings and offered a hand to pull me up after him. All I could think of as I settled slightly behind him was how that these people, every single one of them, knew my secret. Would they treat me differently now? The answer was fairly clear in the mistrustful glances being aimed at me now.

'All right,' Hayden called out sharply, quieting the soft

rumble rolling through the crowd. I swallowed nervously as I awaited his announcement. His shoulders were tense and I had to subdue the urge to reach out and touch him.

'As you can see, Grace is back,' he started. He waited a few moments before the quiet mutterings calmed down again. 'Now I know you've all recently become aware of who her father is—'

Was.

'But as far as anyone should be concerned, that doesn't change anything. She has never been a danger to us and she never will be, something more than one of you can attest to from the fact that she saved your lives.'

My eyes automatically found Kit, where I was pleased to see him nod in agreement. Several others glanced in his direction as well to see his reaction, the evidence made clear by the thick scar running along his neck.

'If any of you still have trouble trusting her, you can answer to me. If anyone, and I mean *anyone*, threatens her or tries to harm her in any way, they can join Barrow at the top of the tower. Is that clear?'

Hayden's voice was strong with conviction and authority, and I found it difficult to repress my sudden flare of desire for him. There was something so sexy about the way he was in control and knew it, even though I knew this wasn't the time for such thoughts. I blew out a sharp exhale and shook my head once to clear my mind.

Later, Grace. Focus.

A quiet murmur of assent came from the crowd, though it was clear from the few unhappy faces that not everyone agreed so readily to Hayden's terms.

'Now that that's settled, I have something important to tell you all and I need you all to stay calm.'

My heart picked up speed a bit as I waited anxiously for

263

him to tell them. Unease was palpable in the air as people shifted nervously. If they'd reacted in such a way to simply discovering who I was, how would they take the news of Greystone's impending attack?

'I don't know when, but we're going to be heavily attacked.'

Hayden might as well have dropped a bomb on everyone for how quickly the uproar started. Confused, scared words were shouted out from every direction as people demanded more information. Flashes of sentences fought for attention as I tried not to make eye contact with any one person.

'How do you know?'

'This is her fault!'

'Can we trust her?'

'Who's attacking us?'

'Why?'

I bit my lip into my mouth to stop from shouting at everyone to shut up and calm down. It irritated me that they didn't even let him finish before exploding into questions.

'Hey!' Hayden shouted suddenly, quieting the crowd once more. 'Look, I know you're all scared, but what I said earlier still stands. I've kept you all safe this long and I'm not going to stop now, all right?'

A few mumbles and groans sounded but most people waited with bated breath for him to continue.

'Grace came back to warn us. If that isn't further proof that we can trust her, I don't know what is. Greystone will attack with the intention to wipe us out, but thanks to Grace, we'll be ready. We'll fight, and we will win.'

Chills rose on my arms as I listened to him speak, his forceful words playing on my emotions. Not only did I know he meant it, but I believed him. If there was anyone in this world I trusted to keep everyone else safe, it was Hayden.

'I want double the patrols around the clock. I want you all to be extra alert at all times. If you see anything even slightly suspicious, tell me or any of the raiders immediately. Don't hesitate. We'll start training anyone who wants it, and we'll keep kids and people who can't protect themselves with someone else at all times. Just use common sense, and be cautious, everyone understand?'

Everyone nodded, and their panic that had risen quickly seemed to be dying down because they trusted Hayden and what he was saying. A sense of relief swept through me as they seemed to believe in him once again.

'Things are going to get tough, there's no doubt about that, but if we stick together, we'll make it. We always make it.'

It amazed me that he could continue to be so strong and in control after enduring so much. There was no doubt in my mind that he was the most incredible man I'd ever met.

'All right, good. If you have questions, you know who to ask. Everyone just stay smart and stay strong.'

With that, he nodded once and turned to face me, stepping a bit closer than was probably necessary. His back was turned to the crowd, blocking me out from most of their view. His voice dropped low as he spoke, intended for only me to hear.

'Was that all right?' he asked nervously, showing insecurity for the first time since arriving here.

'You were perfect,' I told him honestly. My hand rose to twist the hem of his shirt lightly around my finger once before releasing it. 'You're so good at this, Hayden.'

'At what?' he asked, his brows pulling downward.

'Leading them. They trust you even now, it's obvious.'

'I hope so,' he murmured quietly, glancing sideways tensely.

I wanted to grab his face and gently turn him back towards me, but I resisted.

'They do,' I said simply. He blew out a heavy sigh as he shoved his hand through his hair yet again. A small, unconvincing smile pulled at his lips before he jumped down off the crate, offering me a hand again as he helped me follow him down.

Almost immediately, we were joined by Kit, Dax and Docc, all of whom looked very concerned.

'What's going on, mate?' Dax asked quickly.

'Not here,' Hayden murmured. 'Let's go to the ammo building.'

Everyone nodded and moved together as a group, away from the crowd. We hadn't made ten feet when a small body collided heavily with me out of nowhere. It wasn't until I felt a thin pair of arms wind around my waist that I realised who it was.

'Grace,' he choked, his words muffled as he hugged me tighter. A dull ache remained in my rib, but it had pretty much healed completely now and was easy to ignore. The wave of emotion that rolled through me appeared so quickly that I had no time to think as my arms encircled the thin, frail shoulders.

'Jett.'

'You're back,' he sniffed, squeezing me one last time before releasing me enough to peer up at me with watery eyes. He was too fragile for his age, sheltered by Hayden and the others from the horrors of our world. He hadn't seen what we'd seen, hadn't trained as we had, hadn't grown up too quickly like the rest of us. He was still pure and child-like as children his age would have been in a normal world.

'I'm back,' I agreed, smiling. I could feel everyone's eyes on us and was surprised no one hurried us along.

'Are you back for good? Hayden said . . .' he trailed off, cringing at whatever memory struck him. What had Hayden said?

'Yes, I'm back for good,' I answered. I'd left once and had no intention to ever again.

'I missed you so much.'

His brown eyes were wide with truth as he finally released me completely and took a shaky step backward. He was an undying source of light in the darkness of our world, something I hadn't fully appreciated until I realised I wouldn't get to see him again.

'I missed you too, Jett.'

He beamed up at me, wiping a tear away hastily as he did so. I returned it as I looked down at him.

'I have to go now, Jett, but I'll find you later, okay? We'll catch up,' I promised.

'Okay!' he said excitedly, his old enthusiasm coming back in full force.

'Good. Now stay with Maisie,' I instructed, pointing to where she stood a few yards away. Jett nodded and bounced on his feet once before bolting away, joining Maisie quickly. When I looked back, I was surprised to find them all studying me closely.

'Sorry,' I murmured. 'Let's go.'

We resumed our path toward the ammo building, arriving quickly. Everyone hurtled inside and gathered around the single table there, illuminated by a candle that Docc lit.

'Okay, so,' Hayden started. He pulled out the now crumpled paper from his pocket and smoothed it out on the table. Everyone leaned in closely to study it.

I listened as Hayden repeated what I'd told him, filling them in with more details than he'd given to the general public. They were all quiet until he'd finished speaking, taking in the information tensely.

'You're certain, Grace?' Docc asked slowly, his voice deep and, amazingly, calm.

'Yes, I'm positive.'

'I think we all knew it was only a matter of time before it came to this,' he said matter-of-factly. 'Thanks to you, we stand a chance now.'

A blush crept up on my cheeks. It felt so strange to hear praise when it felt like something any normal person would do. I jumped slightly when I felt Hayden's hand land on my lower back offering silent reassurance. It was unusual for him to do such a thing in front of so many people, but I realised that everyone present was very much aware of whatever was going on between us.

'I think we have a little time to get ready,' I said. 'They hadn't really started training or anything but it won't take long.'

'That's good news,' Kit muttered. A deep frown was pressed into his lips as he studied the map I'd drawn. 'We need as much time as we can get.'

'Agreed,' Dax muttered. His eyes were wide as he ran his palm down his face. 'We'd better start now. I'll join the patrols tonight and set up a new schedule.'

'Good idea,' Hayden said, nodding at him. Dax pushed away from the table and started toward the door before pausing and turning to me.

'Good to have you back, Grace. Hayden can be happy again.'

My lips parted in surprise at his bold statement, but he slipped quickly out the door before I managed to reply. Docc let out a low chuckle and shook his head in amusement before also making to leave. Hayden's hand pressed firmer against my back.

'I'll round up what I can to have it ready,' he said gently. 'Just in case.'

'And I'll go do an inventory. We might have to go on a run before this gets too serious,' Kit said. Hayden agreed with them both before they headed out, leaving Hayden and I alone once more.

Tension was practically radiating off him as he let out a heavy sigh next to me. Without hesitation, I moved closer and wrapped my arms round his neck, hugging him tightly. I felt the warmth of his arms as they wound around my waist and pulled me to him.

His skin was soft as I buried my face in his neck, unable to resist pressing one small kiss to his throat before letting out a deep sigh.

'It'll be all right, Hayden,' I whispered softly. My lips fumbled over his skin. His grip on me tightened, drawing me even tighter against him.

'How do you know?' he asked quietly. For the first time, he sounded afraid.

'I don't,' I admitted. 'But we have you. There's no one I'd trust more to keep us safe than you.'

Hayden pulled back just enough to study me closely. 'You know I'll protect you, right? I'll never let anyone hurt you, Grace.'

'I know,' I whispered. There wasn't a single doubt in my mind that he meant every word he said. 'And I'll protect you.'

Concern flashed across his features and I could practically hear his thoughts before he even protested. He would think that by protecting him, I'd be in danger.

'Don't even say it,' I said. 'This goes both ways, yeah? We protect each other.'

He let out a heavy, frustrated sigh in acceptance of my statement.

'I love you, Grace.'

My pulse quickened as my heart fluttered erratically. There was absolutely no way I'd ever get used to him saying that; I was certain they were the most beautiful words I'd ever heard, and I longed to hear them over and over again.

'And I love you, Hayden.'

Chapter Twenty – Frustration
GRACE

'. . . I think we should have enough ammo to hold them off for a bit but I'm worried about our food supply.'

I stood back from the table Hayden, Kit, Dax and Docc were gathered around to try and observe, but I really ended up just thinking about all that had to be said between Hayden and me yet. Yes, he said he was in love with me, but I still had so many questions and confusing things we needed to discuss. I wanted answers, and I wanted to be able to tell him I'd lost my father. I wanted to feel his arms around me and soothe me in a way no one else could, because the pain of losing him was starting to eat me alive.

My eyes slid over Hayden's back as he hunched over the table, propping himself up with his arms with a heavy frown on his face. He was very focused, while all I could remember was the way his arms had held me close all night long last night.

Without hesitation, he'd pulled me firmly against him the moment we'd laid down. His chest had pressed to my back and his arms had wound tightly around my waist, my fingers tangling with his as I let him hold me. The heat of his body and the rhythms of his heart had lulled me to sleep quickly – it felt like the first time in ages that I could really, truly sleep. To be so close to him once again had started to heal the cracks in my heart, but deep rifts remained, cleaving through here and there while they waited to be healed.

'*Sleep, love*,' he'd whispered before pressing a light kiss into temple. It was like he knew I was too tired to discuss anything, but that didn't stop me from wishing we had now as I stood and watched him prepare for war. I tried not to feel frustrated with both him and myself for the lack of communication, but it was hard.

All in good time, Grace.

I was irritated with myself for thinking only of these things when they were clearly not the priority in the looming threat of war, but I couldn't help it.

'All right, I think that's good for now,' Hayden announced, pulling me from my thoughts. He stood from the table and stretched by twisting his shoulders to each side before pushing his hand through his hair. His gaze flitted to mine and he shot me a soft, apologetic smile that I returned.

'What do you want us to do?' Kit asked.

'Keep up with the patrols. Maybe try to train anyone who's around,' Hayden suggested, glancing back at Kit and Dax as they started to file out.

'Dibs on training,' Dax said with a wide grin. Kit rolled his eyes and shook his head lightly.

'Guess I'll do patrols, then,' he muttered before shoving Dax lightly with his shoulder. Dax grinned triumphantly as they pulled out the door. 'See you guys.'

'Bye,' I called. I waved once as Docc came into my line of vision.

'How's your head?' he asked gently. Hayden shuffled around behind him, gathering the papers they'd been studying.

'Fine,' I answered honestly. Aside from a slight headache, I felt as good as I had in a long time.

'And your ribs?'

'Better than ever.' With the impending war, I needed to get back into my peak physical condition so I would be ready; I had a lot of work to do after weeks of inactivity thanks to my broken rib.

'Are you sure?' Docc asked sceptically, raising an eyebrow.

'Yes, seriously this time,' I laughed. 'I can't even feel it anymore.'

'All right, girl. Happy to hear that.'

I smiled softly up at him. I'd missed him calling me 'girl.'

'So I can start training again, right?'

'Yes, I think that would be a good idea,' he said, nodding.

'Good.' I shifted my focus to Hayden, who had just finished cleaning up the table. 'Hayden, can we start now? Or do you have something else to do?'

'You want to start again right now?' he asked, concern clear on his features as he joined Docc and me.

'Yes, the sooner the better.'

'If you're sure . . .' he trailed off. He glanced at Docc, raising an eyebrow as he silently asked for reaffirmation.

'She's all right,' Docc told him. My grin widened even more.

'Okay. Yeah, we can start, then. Docc, will you lock these up for next time?' He handed Docc the papers he'd gathered, which he accepted easily.

'Sure thing. Happy training.'

With that, Docc nodded once at each of us before retreating from the building to leave Hayden and I alone once more.

'Are you sure about this?' Hayden asked gently as he peered down at me. I rolled my eyes.

'Yes, I'm sure. I have to or I'll be useless whenever it starts.'

'You don't have to fight, you know. I know it'll be hard for you.'

Hayden's words were soft and understanding as he spoke, and they were accented by his hand reaching up to lightly tuck a strand of my hair behind my ear. He looked almost hopeful that I'd take him up on the offer.

'You're crazy if you think I'm sitting it out. You protect me, I protect you, remember?'

He sighed, but his lips quirked to the side in a small smile. 'It was worth a shot.'

'Sure it was. Now can we go?' I was ready to get started, and I hoped that the exercise would distract me from all the hurt and confusion I was still feeling until we finally got the chance to address it all.

'Yeah. What do you want to do?'

'Let's go for a run,' I suggested. I knew it would be very painfully obvious how out of shape I was, but it was the best thing to start with. He nodded.

'All right. Let's go, then. Tell me if you need a break, okay?'

I'd have liked to say I wouldn't need one, but I knew odds were good that I would. 'Okay.'

It surprised me to see that it was already late afternoon; we'd been in that building for hours without even realising. Hayden pulled his ankle up behind his thigh, stretching his muscles while I did the same. The white T-shirt and black athletic shorts he wore almost made him look like a normal guy getting ready to go to practise for some sports team, though we weren't training for sports; we were training for war.

After a bit of stretching, we started off at a light jog. Hayden led us through the camp, keeping our pace even and relatively slow to get warmed up. I knew he would be reluctant to push me, his lingering belief that I was hurt holding him back. My feet moved a bit faster, determined to get all that I could out of this.

Soon we reached the edge of the camp and I was pleased to see I still felt decent. After sprinting all the way from Greystone to Blackwing, I was a bit sore, but the stretch of my muscles as I ran helped soothe a bit of the dull ache. Trees and brush made our run a bit more difficult, but a thin path wove through the trees as if others often ran here for training.

'You all right?' Hayden asked, glancing sideways at me while we ran. While I had already started to sweat, he looked as casual as could be while he glided effortlessly next to me.

'I'm fine,' I told him determinedly. He nodded once and carried on, the path leading us uphill now. Every step I took seemed more difficult than the last as we covered more and more distance, but I pushed on.

We'd been running about a half hour by the time Hayden stopped us, pausing to take a few deep breaths. A very thin sheen of sweat had formed over his brow, but it was nothing compared to the sweat pouring off me.

'Let's take a break,' he said, observing the way I gasped for air while trying to look like I wasn't.

'No,' I said instantly, shaking my head. 'Let's keep going.'

'Grace, you haven't trained in weeks, it's all right—'

'No, Hayden! I said I'm fine,' I said, a little too sharply. I could feel myself getting surly but I couldn't help it. Hayden frowned at me in concern.

'You sure?'

'Yes. Let's run back too, yeah?'

He let out a deep sigh and pushed his hand through his hair once before nodding. 'All right.'

'Good.'

I took in a sharp lungful of air before starting back in the direction we'd come. Hayden chased after me, catching me quickly while I tried to push myself even faster. Air ripped in and out of my lungs, burning with every single breath I took, and my muscles screamed in protest as I pushed them, but still I didn't stop. It was like every negative thought and feeling I had was pushing me faster and faster, though I was never able to leave them behind.

'Grace,' Hayden said beside me, his tone warning and anxious as I ran even faster. No matter how fast I ran, he kept up easily, which frustrated me even more. I ignored him.

We reached the edge of the camp much faster than it had taken us to leave it, and I felt a surge of pride as I sprinted into the border. Sweat dripped down my back and my throat felt like it was on fire, but the knowledge that every step was making me stronger had driven me forward. People jumped back from the path as I sprinted down it with Hayden on my heels, and his hut finally came into view.

My heart pumped blood furiously through my veins as I raced towards it, determined to beat Hayden, even though he was right behind me. I felt like my legs were about to give out as I pushed on, but it was with an elated sense of accomplishment that my hand slapped against the door, marking my arrival first as Hayden followed seconds later. I leaned back against it, placing my hands on my knees and closing my eyes as I tried to catch my breath.

'I win,' I gasped, pleased to have beaten him. My muscles felt like they were on fire but it was a good pain, a productive pain.

'Didn't know we were racing,' Hayden answered, also slightly breathless. He reached behind his neck to grip the nape of his shirt and haul it over his head, sending the dark waves of hair sprawling as he pulled it off and ran it over his forehead. Sweat glistened lightly over his skin, making him look like he was glowing.

'Come on, let's get some water,' he said. I followed him into his hut, where he pulled two water bottles from a small shelf, handing me one. My breathing was still very short and quick as I took a drink, quenching the dryness in my mouth.

'Come on, let's keep training,' I said as I screwed the lid back on and set it down on the little coffee table. He kicked off his shoes and I pulled off my own, casting them the side.

'I think that's enough for today,' Hayden responded, setting down his bottle and shirt before turning to frown at me.

'No, come on, Hayden, I have to train as much as I can before it's too late,' I insisted. I approached him to stand a few feet away where he frowned at me once again but didn't respond.

'Come on,' I urged, punching him lightly with a playful grin. 'I can take you.'

'I know you can,' he agreed. I threw another soft punch into his chest, trying to provoke him more than hurt him.

'Grace . . .'

'Hayden . . .' I said, mimicking his cautious tone. 'Seriously, I'm fine. I swear.'

I leaned forward to nudge him backward with my shoulder before shooting a grin up at him. He let out a deep sigh then raised his hands in front of him.

'You asked for it, remember that,' he warned, his voice playfully dark as he started to move.

'Don't hold back,' I demanded, raising an eyebrow at him. He nodded.

'Yes, ma'am.'

I leered in a competitive smile as we began to circle,

both of our fists raised between us. He held my eye contact tightly, waiting for me to make the first move. I was suddenly reminded of one of my first days here when we'd fought in the woods, only for Hayden to end up pinning me to the trunk of the tree and later, the ground. I shivered now at the memory, remembering the way his body had felt pressed into mine even before I really knew anything about him.

'Focus, Grace,' he said deeply, smirking while he glided smoothly across the floor. I scoffed once before jabbing my hand forward, aiming a punch at his side that he deflected with his forearm.

His smirk only deepened when I tried again, striking once with my left hand at his side before aiming another hit at his jaw with my right, both of which he dodged easily.

Hayden's face floated in front of me as I tried again and again to strike, each and every blow deflected, dodged, or too weak to make any sort of impact on him. He continued to circle away from me, yet he made no move to attack.

'Come on, Hayden,' I hissed, angry he wasn't trying. I lunged forward again, aiming a knee at his side this time only to be blocked once more. He seemed to catch the annoyance in my voice but didn't respond as he watched me closely.

'You're not trying,' I accused. My left hand swung to strike before my right followed immediately, finally landing a solid blow to his ribcage. It didn't faze him in the slightest as he continued to move on the defensive.

'I'm not going to hit you, Grace,' he said flatly.

'You should. No one else will think like that,' I said sharply as I threw another punch that he deflected. He shook his head, holding my gaze firmly as we moved in a circle.

'No.'

An angry growl sounded from my throat as I failed yet again to land a solid hit. Every frustration I felt rushed back at once: Hayden not telling me anything. Me being unable to tell Hayden about my father. Hayden refusing to fight me. My inability to fight the way I wanted. The impending war that threatened constantly. All of it rolled into one massive ball of rage as I lurched forward, attempting to tackle him to the ground.

I managed to get us both to the ground as I finally seemed to take him by surprise, but he recovered quickly as he landed on top of me, pinning my hips down with his while I tried to land punches wherever I could. Still, he didn't retaliate.

'Fight me, Hayden, come *on*!'

'No.'

An enraged snarl ripped from my throat as I tried to hold off the emotion I was feeling. Every bit of hurt and anger leaked into my actions as I struggled beneath him, twisting this way and that as he tried to subdue my hands. His fingers closed around my wrists momentarily before I ripped them free, rolling to the side to throw him off me finally. I picked myself off the ground quickly to stand.

'How am I supposed to get better if you won't help me?' I seethed, livid now as he jumped to his feet. I rushed forward, pushing as hard as I could. He moved a few inches back as he watched me. '*Fight me.*'

My chest was heaving as I shoved him angrily, furious at his lack of response.

'You want to fight, Grace?' he hissed, his voice thick with tension.

Even though he wasn't trying very hard, his chest was rising and falling heavily as he studied me.

'*Yes!*'

He shook his head once, a tiny scoff pushing past his lips as I shoved him one last time. I glared up at him, desperate to relieve some of the pain I was feeling in a physical way.

'Fine.'

The word had hardly made it past his clenched jaw when he reacted, easily knocking my hands away to rush forward. Still he didn't try to hit or kick me, but his chest collided heavily with mine as he pushed me backward.

He kept pushing, steering my body easily as I tried to shove at his chest again. It made no impact. I forced a heavy puff of air through my lips as my back struck the wall suddenly, pinned there by the weight of Hayden's body pressing into my own. His hands caught mine, trapping them by my head as his face hovered mere inches from my own.

'This is what you want?' he demanded, his voice a deadly whisper as he glowered down at me. Every inch of his body was pushed hard into mine, causing my nerves to buzz and my heart to pound erratically.

'Hmm?' His tone was dark and laced with frustrations of his own. My breathing came out in uneven pants as I tried to regain control of my thoughts, but his proximity had clouded my mind.

'Yes.'

The word had barely made it past my lips before he smashed forward, kissing me roughly. My body responded immediately, moulding my lips against his own as his tongue pushed into my mouth. His hands finally released their tight grip to allow my own to fall at my sides. He paused briefly to push his hips between my thighs, pressing firmly against me as he continued his heated kiss. Every bit of anger, hurt, and frustration seemed to be leaking out into my actions now as my hands tore at him. They tangled into his hair, yanking on the strands to bring him closer to me, before raking down what I could reach of his back. I needed him closer, so much closer.

His hips rolled up against me again, sending waves of heat through my body as I tried to take an even breath. All I could feel was Hayden as his mouth moved against mine hungrily and his hands squeezed my thighs while he shifted his body between my legs, digging me further into the wall in desperation.

His bare skin was hot beneath my palms as they roamed over his chest and shoulders, unable to keep them in one place for more than a few seconds. There was an animalistic, primal need to what I was feeling, and I knew the only way to relieve it was to be with Hayden. My back arched off the wall as he rocked upward again, sending a low groan rumbling from my throat.

'Hayden,' I gasped as he tore his lips from mine to trail them greedily down my throat. He nipped and sucked lightly before pulling back enough to allow me to grip the hem of my shirt and haul it over my head, flinging it to the floor so he could dive back in to kiss me roughly. My tongue met his as my hips rolled against his, still held up by his grip on my thighs and my back against the wall.

'God, Grace, I missed you,' he mumbled urgently against my lips before tugging my lower lip back with his teeth. His hips rolled over mine again, sending fuzzy tingles through my body as I groaned once again.

'Put me down,' I gasped desperately, needing to eliminate the barriers between us. As soon as my feet were on the ground, I pushed against his chest, steering him backward quickly until his legs collided with the bed.

I continued to kiss him eagerly as I let my hands roam down his body, trailing over his firm chest and stomach muscles before reaching the hem of his shorts. Without hesitation, I plunged my hand beneath the band to grip his length, which was already rock hard and ready for me. A low moan slipped beneath his lips as I touched him, and his hands balled into fists in my hair where they had tangled while we kissed.

My hand moved over the silky skin as he released his hold on my hair to grip beneath the hem of my sports bra to tug it upward, disconnecting our lips as he removed the item. I gasped as his hand touched my breast, kneading it gently before flicking his thumb over my nipple. It was too much, and I was too pent up to bother with wasting any more time. A brief mental check of my birth control shot from two months ago told me I still had another month before I needed another, but that was the only rational thought I had before my body's desperate desires took over once more.

My chest caved in and out quickly as I pulled my hand from him to grip the waistband of his shorts and boxers, pushing down until they fell to the floor to leave him naked. Everything was urgent, needy, and undeniably hot as I pushed again to force him to sit on the edge of the bed. He watched me with burning eyes and panting breaths as I removed my own remaining layers, letting them fall to the floor before stepping out of them.

'Jesus, come here,' he growled, reaching for my hands and yanking me forward onto his lap. My knees landed on either side of his hips and I could feel him pressing at my entrance as he resumed kissing me hungrily. His hands drifted down the length of my back before settling onto my hips, where he put just enough pressure to guide me down onto him.

Our kiss broke as my mouth fell open as he pushed inside me, filling me completely. I'd only been with him once before, but this time was already so different. Last time had been emotional, slow, and sweet, while this was heated desperation built up by so many different factors. This was pure, lust driven desire.

'Oh my god,' I gasped as I rolled my hips forward, feeling every inch of him as he moved in and out of me. My arms locked around his neck to draw him closer as I tried to kiss him, but I gave up when he ripped his lips from mine to trail them down my throat. My neck arched as my head tipped back. My hips swivelled again and again, drawing him in and out of me. Every inch of my skin was attended to by Hayden as his hands caressed my hips, my back, my chest. His lips peppered my neck with wet, heated kisses, and his hips moved to meet mine as he continued to push deeply inside me.

'Shit, Grace,' he breathed against my throat as I raised my hips to fall back onto him repeatedly, letting my body set a natural rhythm that was quickly stoking the fire in the pit of my stomach. Every time, another part of my self-control chipped away. It was like every negative emotion I'd been feeling started to be relieved into something more manageable as we moved together, and I continued to lose myself completely in Hayden.

A loud gasp was forced from my lips as he lifted me suddenly, flinging my body backward onto the bed. We were disconnected for only a few seconds before he drove back into me, his body covering mine now as he reconnected us.

My legs tangled around his waist, locking together over his lower back to draw him closer. His pace was desperate and urgent as he moved, and I found myself shaking beneath him as my end crept closer and closer. My hands tugged at his hair, raked down his back, and kneaded into every bit of him I could find as he moved over me and dragged his lips down my neck.

I could feel every muscle in his body contract as he rolled fluidly over me, building the heat and pushing me closer and closer. My mind felt hazy and I had almost no control over my limbs as I felt every action he made. Darkness overtook me as my eyes clenched shut.

'Hayden, oh my—'

I was cut off by the explosion of heat inside me as he pushed impossibly deep to send me over the edge. My hands shook as they roped around his neck again, and I was certain my body was actually vibrating as my orgasm rocketed through me. He let me ride out my high as he raced towards his own.

He pushed back one more time, stilling as his muscles contracted and he let out a low groan. His lips stilled against mine, too overcome with his high to manage to kiss me as he relaxed against me. His lips moved lazily against my own while my arms remained looped around his neck.

'Oh my god,' he murmured against my lips before kissing me again. I gasped a laugh, still feeling the buzz of my orgasm. I hugged him even closer, positively drunk with love for him. 'I love you, Grace.'

'I love you, Hayden,' I whispered. It felt so odd, the words still kind of terrifying, but there was no denying it was so wonderfully right to say them.

Chapter Twenty-One – Verity

HAYDEN

Grace's skin was warm against mine as I held myself over her. Her lips responded to my kiss automatically, fitting into the gaps created by my own as if they were made for them. I could still feel her heart hammering wildly, like my own, as we both recovered from our climax.

Hearing her say those stunning words and seeing the unparalleled beauty she was exuding now after letting our bodies come together was just about enough to ruin me completely. This time together had been much different than the first, though no less incredible. I could feel the emotion that had driven our actions, and I knew there was a deeper source to her frustration than she had let on earlier.

My lips separated from hers reluctantly as I pulled back to study her. Once again, the exquisite glow had settled over her skin. A soft smile pulled at her lips, which were slightly swollen, as she caught me taking in the tiny details of her face.

'What?' she asked lightly, a hint of a laugh lacing her tone.

'I just can't believe how amazing you are.'

I spoke before I thought to filter my words, but they were true; every moment we spent together caused me to fall even more in love with her. She was incredibly beautiful, unfathomably strong, smart, selfless. She was so many things I admired and needed without even realising until I met her.

'Stop,' she said modestly. She tapped me lightly along the jaw with her thumb as her hands rested along the skin there.

'I mean it, Grace,' I said softly, frowning gently at her. She didn't see what I saw and it seemed crazy to me.

'Thank you, Hayden,' she said. She shook her head as if she were only agreeing to shut me up as she pulled my lips down to hers once more. I held the pressure for a few seconds before pulling back again.

My arms landed on either side of her head as I pushed myself up and eased to the side of the bed, grabbing her hand in mine as I stood up. 'Shower?'

'Good idea,' she laughed, looking determinedly at my face as I stood naked in front of her. She stirred from the bed as she stood next to me. Then she allowed me to lead her towards the bathroom. I resisted letting my eyes travel over her bare form despite my urges.

I pulled us beneath the contraption that served as a shower, but she stopped a few feet away from me.

'You need to come closer,' I whispered.

'Hmm,' she hummed quietly in response, shifting closer so she was only inches away. 'I feel like you've pulled this move before . . .'

'Just once.'

'It's a good move,' she replied, nodding in mock seriousness.

'It worked on you, didn't it?'

'It did,' she agreed.

But then her jaw fell open in shock when I pulled the tab to start the shower, dousing us both in cold water. She

286

jumped forward instantly, pressing her front to mine as a gasp blew between her parted lips. A deep chuckle rumbled from my chest, filling the space around us.

'It's freezing,' she commented, glancing up at me in amusement. I was pleased when she didn't pull away.

'I'll keep you warm,' I said lightly, pulling her even tighter against me. She shot me a soft smile before leaning forward to press her lips lightly against my shoulder. The water streamed over us but neither of us made any move to actually shower, too wrapped up in each other to bother.

My skin warmed despite the cold temperature of the water pouring over us as her hands slid over it, passing over scars before settling just below my shoulder blades to hug me. Her lips lingered against my shoulder, puckering once in a while to press a kiss to the skin. My heart gave a heavy pang as she let out a deep sigh, clearly feeling the shift in the mood just as I was.

I could feel the light-hearted, playful mood shifting to one that seemed to grow heavier by the second. We'd allowed our bodies to communicate when words couldn't, but we couldn't hide from it any longer; it was time to talk.

'Hayden . . .'

I knew what was coming – questions we'd somehow managed to avoid until now. Before hadn't been the right time to answer them, but we couldn't put it off any longer. I stalled, trying to think of how to go about this when she spoke again.

'We need to talk about things.'

Her voice was soft and her words were stifled as her lips murmured against my shoulder, but I could hear the pain leaking into her voice despite her efforts to hide it. My hand raked through her wet hair before trailing over her soft skin on her back.

'I know,' I said quietly. I couldn't see her face because of the way we held each other and I suddenly wished I could.

She took a deep breath before pressing her lips to my shoulder once again. Cool air rushed in to replace the heat of her skin against mine as she pulled back just enough to look up at me and reconnect our gaze. 'Let's finish the shower first, yeah?'

'Yeah, all right,' I agreed gently. I didn't think I'd ever be ready for this conversation but it had to happen. There were too many loose ends to leave untied.

We'd wasted most of our water by simply standing beneath it and holding onto each other. So after a few minutes, our time ran out along with the water supply, ending our shower moments after we'd both finished cleaning ourselves of the grime of the day. We were quiet as we dried off, too wrapped up in our thoughts to make conversation. I caught the flash of the scar that had formed over her ribcage from when she'd been cut the day she'd broken her rib.

She shot me another small smile before padding softly back into the main room, pausing at the dresser to pull out enough clothing. I could feel the tension thickening the air around us as we dressed. I had no idea what to say to her to explain everything we'd been through, and I had no idea how she'd react to the truth once it was finally out.

I ran my towel distractedly over my hair before draping it over the chair of my desk, as she did the same. I sat on the bed and leaned back against the wall to let my legs straighten out.

'Come on,' I said, beckoning her to me. She placed her hand in mine and let me pull her to settle between my legs, allowing her thighs to rest on my own as she crossed them and faced me. She looked nervous, and I could feel her anxiety reflected in my churning stomach.

This could either go very well or very, very badly.

'So,' I said slowly, unable to take the silence any longer. Her gaze flitted back and forth between mine as she took a deep breath. 'I know you probably want to talk about why—'

'My father's dead, Hayden.'

Her words stunned me, forcing my jaw to fall open in surprise. I suspected as much but to hear her confirm it sent a jolt of pain through my heart for her. She'd said it so quickly, as if she'd been holding herself back from admitting it the moment she arrived back at Blackwing.

'I'm so sorry, Grace.'

My hands reached out to collect hers from her lap, holding one in each of my own. It was difficult to read her as she studied me closely. A soft frown creased her features as pain reflected in her eyes.

'He's just . . . he's gone.'

Her voice was hollow and flat as she spoke, the tight tone of it causing my own throat to constrict as if I were feeling her emotions. Her gaze dropped from mine as she glanced down to look at our intertwined hands. She drew a shuddering breath as if she were holding herself back from crying.

'Did you get to say goodbye?'

I shouldn't have asked. It was probably too painful for her to think about, but I had to know if what I'd put us through had been worth it. I had to know if my ultimate goal had been reached and she'd got what I hoped she would – to say goodbye before it was too late.

Her gaze flitted back up to mine where it lingered for a few seconds before her face seemed to collapse in on itself, her eyes squeezing shut tightly as she finally choked out a quiet sob. She nodded shortly, but that was all I saw before I leaned forward, wrapping my arms around her to haul her against me. She twisted in my grip, pressing her back to my chest as I hunched over to completely envelop her.

My arms wound around her shoulders as her hands rose to cling to my forearms, her body fitting perfectly between my legs as I leaned into her to hug her. I couldn't get her close enough as she broke down in my arms, the unrelenting sobs she'd managed to hold off until now completely taking over.

'Shh, it's all right, Grace,' I murmured, my lips fumbling against her ear. Our bodies rocked slowly back and forth instinctively, as if trying to soothe each other.

She didn't respond as she let out another choking sob. I could see her eyes were shut tight from my view over her shoulder, my larger body making it easy to surround her completely. I had no way to soothe her, because I knew the pain of losing her father was far more damaging than anything I could heal with words. All I could do was hold her.

'I'm s-sorry,' she stammered, sniffing harshly as she tried to rein in her tears.

'No, babe, don't be,' I soothed, shaking my head slowly as I hugged her even tighter. My head tilted to the side to press a kiss into her wet cheek while I raised a hand to wipe away a tear that was streaking down her skin. She'd already held in these feelings for too long, and I wanted her to be able to let them out completely.

I held her like that for a long time, tight against me while my fingertips switched between running lightly over her skin and wiping away tears. Her hands never released their grip on my forearms, and I could feel her melting into me as she let me calm her down. Every gasp and cry she let out twisted my stomach and jabbed at my heart, making me feel her pain along with her.

I'd lost my parents years and years ago and it still hurt; I couldn't imagine what this felt like.

Finally, her choking sobs turned into soft sniffles before quieting altogether. Silent tears streaked down her cheeks here and there. My lips pressed automatically into the hinge of her jaw, lingering there as she drew a deep, shaky breath. My arms were still crossed over her chest as I hugged her against me, and I let my fingers tickle lightly over the skin on her arms.

'Are you okay?' I asked softly, knowing full well that she wasn't. My words were stifled slightly by the way my lips had come to rest on her shoulder.

'I will be,' she answered quietly. Her voice was the strongest it had been since she'd broken down, but the tone was still thin as she let out another shuddering breath.

Silence enveloped us once again as I argued with myself internally about whether to tell her or not. Instead of responding, I just let my lips pucker against her neck once again, stalling for time. She turned on the spot, resuming her previous position before she'd broken down so she was facing me again.

'It was incredible timing, really,' she began, watching me closely as she spoke. My gaze held hers for a few seconds before dropping to our laps where my hands fidgeted guiltily.

'To think you sent me home just before he died . . . what are the odds of that?' she pressed gently. My eyes flashed up to hers to find them burning into my own. If she didn't already know, she highly suspected my motivation for sending her home. Again, I remained silent as I dropped her gaze.

'Hayden.'

My lips pressed together as I studied my hands closely, reluctant to admit what I'd done even though it had been for her. To say it out loud would only bring back the pain of losing her all over again despite her presence now.

'Hayden, do you love me?'

'Yes,' I answered instantly, tilting my head up to meet her stare once more. I held it this time, unable to look away thanks to her blazing intensity.

'What would you do for me?' she asked, maintaining the intense scrutiny determinedly.

'Anything,' I replied automatically. My voice was slightly breathless but rang true as the words floated between us. 'I would do anything for you, Grace.'

Her eyes flitted back and forth between mine beneath her deeply furrowed brows, and I could practically see her thoughts flying through her mind. I could see the weight of the truth as it settled on her shoulders, weighing her down like it was doing to me.

She understood.

'You knew, didn't you,' she stated, her voice quiet and disbelieving. 'You knew he was dying.'

My pulse throbbed in my veins as I stalled, my jaw opening to speak only to clamp shut again. A deep sigh forced its way through my teeth as I sagged slightly, holding her gaze while she waited for my reply.

'Grace . . .'

My words trailed off as I reached for her hand, but she pulled it out of my grasp as she stared at me with a burning green glare. My stomach seemed to drop a few inches at the subtle rejection as I tried to ignore the sting.

'Tell me. Tell me you knew he was dying.'

Her words were colder than they had been previously, a hard determination lacing through her tone. My brows pulled lower over my face as I frowned, upset over the way this conversation was going.

'Tell me, Hayden!' she snapped suddenly, impatient with my silence. The sudden outburst caused me to jump before my line of vision fixed back on hers.

'Yes, Grace. I knew.'

'Why didn't you tell me? Why force me to leave and make me think you didn't want me here?' she demanded, the hardness from the moment before completely gone now as hurt replaced it. Any momentary anger she'd felt melted away as pain overtook her features once more. I felt a flash of guilt run through me for making her feel this way, but I reminded myself that it was better for her to be angry with me than angry at herself for choosing one of us over the other.

'I didn't want you to have to choose,' I said softly, reaching forward again for her hand. She didn't retreat, this time, and let me clasp it lightly in my own. A small flicker of relief seared through me.

'That wasn't your choice to make,' she said sternly, frowning deeply at me. I could tell she was on the verge of tears again and I hated myself for that. She was so strong, so for her to be reduced to tears partially because of something I'd done sent a stake through my heart.

'I know,' I admitted. 'But I couldn't make you choose, don't you see that? I didn't want you to feel guilty for picking one of us over the other. I didn't want you to be worrying about me when you only had so much time left with your father . . .'

It all made so much sense in my head that I prayed she would see my logic. I continued on. 'I thought if you thought I didn't want you here, it'd make it easier for you. I thought you'd be able to spend what was left of his time with him without feeling guilty for leaving me.'

Her breathing was coming in shallow gasps now as her chest rose and fell quickly, while she clung to my every word. The air seemed to crackle around us with tension as I waited desperately for her to respond.

'If you knew how much I need you, you never would have left. Please, Grace . . . I did it for you,' I pleaded weakly. I needed her to see that or I would collapse into a heap on the floor. She sucked in a sharp breath at my confession before mulling the words over silently.

'Hayden . . . you broke my heart,' she said softly, her voice cracking on the final word as a tear slipped from her eye. My touch lingered for a few seconds to rub it away before dropping back to cradle hers in my lap.

'I broke mine, too.'

My words were a mere whisper, just barely loud enough to hear, but it was the absolute truth. Sending her away had shredded me from the inside out, damaging me more than anything ever had since the death of my parents.

'You did all that so I could be with my father?' she questioned. She sounded slightly shocked still even though I knew she had worked it out a while ago.

'Yes. And I'm sorry I didn't tell you I just . . . I couldn't do that to you. I couldn't make you choose.'

Did she truly understand my motivation? Would she accept it?

'Did you love me then? When you let me go?' She sounded like she was afraid of my answer but she held my gaze determinedly nonetheless.

'Of course I did,' I answered with no hesitation.

She sucked in a soft breath between her parted lips as her hand tightened around mine, squeezing lightly. 'I loved you then, too.'

'You did?' My voice was quiet and awe-filled as I spoke. I knew she'd been about to say it before I'd cut her off, but I'd figured she'd change her mind after I sent her away. She nodded slowly, never dropping my eye contact.

'Yes.'

One of my hands pulled from hers to reach up to her face slowly. My fingers tickled along the side of her jaw before sliding into her hair as my palm rested beneath her ear. She tilted her head into my touch lightly as her eyes drifted shut momentarily, soaking in the heat of my palm on her skin.

'You understand why I did it, right? I need you to understand,' I begged softly, leaning in closer to her as I spoke. Her eyes opened once again to meet mine as she let out a deep sigh.

'Yes, Hayden. I understand.'

'Good, because I don't want you to think it wasn't because I didn't love you. I think I loved you a long time before I even realised it . . .' I hadn't considered it but I knew it was true as I said it.

'I think I did, too,' she agreed quietly. Both of our voices had hushed as we spoke, as if afraid speaking too loudly would scare the other off.

'So we're okay, right? Please say we're okay.'

She was quiet for a long time as she watched me, her mind racing behind her gaze once more. I waited anxiously for her to respond, my stomach twisting into knots in my abdomen the entire time.

'We're more than okay, Hayden. What you did . . . what you gave me . . . That was the most incredible thing anyone has ever done for me.'

A sigh of relief so large forced its way from my lungs that my chest physically caved in from the impact. I was unable to stop myself from leaning forward to press my lips desperately against hers, holding the kiss for a few lingering seconds before pulling back just a few inches.

'Really?'

'You let me say goodbye to my father, Hayden. That's such a beautiful gift, these days.'

My thumb stroked lightly over the soft skin of her cheek and her hands found their way to either side of my neck as I hovered in front of her. My heart seemed to be caught in my throat, making it difficult to speak.

'I'm just glad you got some time with him before it was too late. That was all I wanted for you, Grace.'

'I know,' she said softly, her voice soothing as her thumbs shifted slowly over my skin. She sighed before she repeated herself. 'I know.'

'I meant what I said earlier . . . There isn't anything I wouldn't do for you.'

A small smile pulled at her lips, softening the intense expression that had settled on her face for so long. 'And there's nothing I wouldn't do for you.'

The space between us disappeared again as I pushed forward, desperate to reconnect our lips. The kiss lingered for a few seconds before she pulled back.

'Thank you for what you've done for me, Hayden.'

It seemed odd for her to thank me for such a thing. 'Don't thank me.'

'But I'm thanking you anyway, so just accept it,' she said lightly, a soft smile playing on her beautiful lips.

'All right, Grace.'

'Is your heart still broken?' she questioned delicately. It thumped heavily, very much alive and warm in my chest.

'My heart could never be broken while I have you.'

She appeared slightly stunned by my confession, but it

was true. She was all I needed to keep me going, keep me alive, keep me happy. She had full command of my heart without even knowing it.

'You'll always have me,' she responded softly. Her gentle gaze made every cell down to my toes seem to vibrate in place.

'Then my heart will never be broken.'

Chapter Twenty-Two – Essential
GRACE

I felt an odd sense of déjà vu as I followed Hayden around camp. I was reminded of some of my first days here when I hadn't been allowed out of his sight as he went through his daily routines. So much had changed since then that I could hardly wrap my head around it; rather than enemies, we were a single force, bound together by an intensely real love that had grown between us. Instead of checking for simple supplies, we were checking for weapons and necessary items for defence. Rather than preparing for daily life, we were preparing for war.

'Raid building next?' he asked, glancing down at me as we moved down the path.

'Yeah, last stop?'

'Yeah, I think so,' he muttered distractedly. I could tell he was trying to keep track of the mental list he was forming of all the supplies we needed to get in order before the impending attack arrived. We'd visited Docc in the infirmary, Maisie in the kitchen, and Dax who was currently presiding over the makeshift garage.

'We need a lot of stuff,' Hayden said as we arrived at the raid building. A frown had creased his face after our second stop and it had only grown deeper as the day went on. I had a suspicion but desperately hoped it wouldn't be necessary.

The door creaked slightly as Hayden pushed his way inside, startling the middle-aged man who had been assigned duty for the moment.

'Hello,' he said quickly, straightening up in his chair as if intimidated by Hayden. It struck me as odd for a moment until I remembered just how intimidated I had been when I'd first arrived, too. Now he affected me in different ways.

'Hey, Frank,' Hayden murmured. 'Give us a second, will you?'

'Sure, all right,' he said, jumping quickly off his stool to slip out the door and close it behind him to leave Hayden and I alone. Hayden let out a deep sigh and crossed to one of the ammo lockers, opening it to inspect its contents.

'Want me to start a list?' I offered. Hayden's shoulders sagged with disappointment as he saw our ammo supplies were not nearly where they should have been for such a time.

'Yeah, that's a good idea.'

I nodded, unseen by him as he rifled through the locker. I retrieved a piece of paper and a pen from the table in the middle of the room and wrote down what I knew we needed from our morning rounds.

Food. Antibiotics. Bandages. Pain relievers. Fuel. Wiring. Batteries.

I frowned at the list. It was quite extensive and full of things that were already hard to find, much less now that the city was quickly running dry.

'Add ammo, will you?' Hayden called as he moved to the second locker.

'What kind?'

'Everything.'

'Awesome,' I muttered sarcastically, adding it to the list. Hayden huffed out a deep breath again before slamming the locker shut and joining me at the table. His palms spread wide on the surface as he supported himself, leaning over to examine the list I'd created.

'You know what that means, don't you?' he said deeply. My gaze flicked upward to see him watching me.

'We have to go on a raid.'

He nodded sullenly, clearly as upset with the news as I was. Of all times, now was the absolute worst to risk being away from camp. I held his gaze for a few seconds, wishing there was some way to avoid this even though I knew there wasn't.

'Any chance I can persuade you to stay here?' he asked, raising his eyebrows hopefully though his tone made it clear he already knew my answer.

'Absolutely not.'

He let out a low, humourless chuckle as he moved around the table to join me on my side before throwing his arm loosely around my shoulders to haul me against him. A light kiss was pressed into my temple where his lips lingered for a few seconds before he moved away as quickly as he'd arrived.

'Thought as much.'

A small smile tugged at my lips at his casually affectionate gesture and his easy acceptance of my refusal to let him go without me.

'When do we leave?' I asked, folding the list I'd created and tucking it into my pocket.

'Now,' he said with resignation.

He moved back to the locker and pulled out two 8mm handguns, handing one to me and keeping the other for himself. He already had, I assumed, a pistol stuck beneath the waistband of his jeans and at least two blades of some kind, all equipping him with lethal weaponry. The switchblade

I'd claimed was tucked into my pocket next to where I stowed my gun, as Hayden did.

'Come on, then,' he said softly, running his hand lightly along my own, as he moved through the building towards the door. Again, the man on guard, Frank, jumped at our appearance.

'Easy, buddy,' Hayden teased flatly.

I chuckled at the man's obviously flustered state as he retreated into the building. Hayden was probably half his age but it was clear the man was beyond intimidated by him.

'Who's coming with us?' I asked, following as Hayden led us back toward the garage.

'Kit and Dax, probably,' he answered.

'Who will be in charge while we're gone?' I asked apprehensively. I didn't like the idea of leaving with so many of the leader figures at once. Hayden, Kit, and Dax all ranked very high around Blackwing, and leaving with all three of them now felt dangerous.

'Docc,' Hayden replied. 'Used to be Barrow . . .'

He frowned, clearly thinking of Barrow and his place at the top of the tower. At least three people guarded him around the clock, making sure he made no attempt to descend and start another revolt against Hayden.

'I'm sorry.'

I felt like I needed to apologise; it was partially my fault one of their own had fallen so quickly from the ranks.

'It's not your fault,' Hayden said, glancing quickly at me as we neared the garage. 'Don't apologise for things you can't control.'

His words were hardened and fierce as he spoke, his gaze returning forward as we moved into the garage. He was truly a man unlike any other I had ever met.

We were greeted by Dax. 'Back so soon? Must have missed

me,' he said lightly. He was bent over the four-wheeler they had acquired on the last raid they'd gone on, messing with the engine. I felt a sting of irrational anger at the inanimate object as I remembered Hayden riding up on it after Kit and Dax's arrival, and my immediate belief that he was dead.

'Right,' Hayden scoffed lightly, unable to hold back a ghost of a smile. 'Where's Kit?'

'Last I saw he was heading to Malin's so not sure if you're going to want to interrupt that,' Dax said with a chortle. He wiped his hand across his brow to dab away the sweat that had formed there but only managed to leave a dark streak of grease across his forehead.

'Jesus Christ,' Hayden muttered, shaking his head. 'Now?'

I couldn't help but feel Hayden was being a bit hypocritical given what we'd done only yesterday, but I chose not to comment.

'Hey, men have needs,' Dax said, shrugging.

'Give him a break, Hayden,' I said. I was unable to hold back my grin as he threw a glare in my direction. 'We have to get ready anyway.'

He huffed in annoyance but didn't reply as he moved to start loading supplies into the truck. Dax shot me a conspiratorial grin as he moved away from the four-wheeler to start filling the truck with petrol. I took it upon myself to help load things we'd need – empty jugs for fuel, bags to carry things, a few water bottles for each of us.

It was still early in the day and only a half hour or so had passed since we'd arrived at the garage to get ready for the raid, but I could tell it irritated Hayden to have to wait on Kit. I knew he wanted to get going and get back as quickly as possible. Finally, just as I was about to suggest someone bite the bullet and go and find Kit, he appeared in the doorway looking more relaxed and happy than I'd ever seen him.

'Well, well, well,' Dax said with a wide grin.

'Hey, guys,' Kit said, ignoring Dax as he waved at Hayden and me. Hayden ignored him while I greeted him in response.

'Hey, Kit.'

'Aren't you looking refreshed and glowy?' Dax continued, undeterred by Kit ignoring him.

'Shut up, Dax,' he shot back, his words negated by the wide grin on his face.

'Hey, man, no shame in getting some,' Dax said. His arms rose by his side in surrender.

'Maybe someday you'll know what it's like,' Kit returned jokingly with an even wider grin. I watched their exchange with a smile, pleased to see Kit appear happy for once even if it was just because he'd apparently got laid. I wondered, once again, if there was more to him and Malin than just a physical relationship.

'Hey, mate, trust me, I know what it's like,' Dax said. I was surprised to hear a serious undertone as he spoke but didn't get to think of it any further.

'Will you two shut the hell up? We have a raid to get going on,' Hayden interrupted, appearing from around the truck with a disapproving frown on his face.

'Jeez, all right!' Dax said reproachfully, casting a wide-eyed look at Kit and I.

Hayden scowled before retreating to the other side of the vehicle. I rounded the corner to see him toss a heavy duffle bag full of ammo into the back of the truck.

'Hey,' I said softly, approaching him slowly. My hand landed lightly on his back where I could feel the tense muscles. When he turned to face me he looked incredibly irritated.

303

'You all right?' I asked gently as I peered up at him cautiously.

'Fine,' he said gruffly, pushing his hand haphazardly through his hair.

'No, you're not,' I observed. I took a step closer to him and lowered my voice. 'What's wrong?'

'They're not even taking this seriously,' Hayden muttered, dropping his feigned indifference. He hadn't been fooling anyone anyway. 'They're acting like everything is just fine when we're just waiting to be slaughtered.'

My brows pulled low at his dark words and my hand reached out automatically to grip his arm lightly. My thumb rolled over the skin covering his bicep. 'Hayden, that's not true. They know it's serious, okay? They're just . . . I dunno, but you know how Dax is. And Kit . . . I mean you can't really blame him when you think about what we were doing yesterday . . .'

A light blush crept up my cheeks as I trailed off, waiting for him to speak. His deep frown softened slightly at my words.

'That's different,' he argued.

'How?' I asked sceptically.

He was quiet for a few moments, then gave a slight shake of his head before speaking. 'It just is.'

I rolled my eyes. At least he was calming down a bit. 'All right.'

'It's different because I love you,' he said simply, as if it explained the difference. My heart fluttered in my chest before I recovered enough to respond.

'And Kit doesn't love Malin?' I pressed, raising an eyebrow at him.

'I don't know,' he admitted.

'Exactly, you don't. I know you're stressed right now but

we don't know how many days left of this we have, you know? Our days of living normally are limited so just . . . try to let it go, okay? Let them spend their days how they like before everything turns to madness.'

Hayden's jaw clenched tightly as he thought over what I'd said before he let out a slow, deep exhale and ran his palm across his face in defeat. 'You're right.'

A soft smile pulled at my lips. 'I know.'

A spark glinted across his eye as he reached forward to grip my chin lightly between his forefinger and thumb, nudging me softly before letting his touch drop. I was pleased to see some of the tension had lifted from his shoulders and a bit of his anger had melted away.

'Oi, lovebirds, thought we had a raid to get to?' Dax called suddenly, interrupting the bubble Hayden and I seemed to have found ourselves in. Hayden's gaze left mine to shift over my shoulder, causing him to roll his eyes. I turned around to see Kit and Dax standing with a clear view of us, both of them smirking as they observed our private moment. It was still strange to me to think that they both knew what was going on between us when the rest of the camp was still relatively unaware.

'Shut up,' Hayden muttered, moving past me to climb into the driver's seat. Dax let out a hearty bellow of laughter before skirting around to the other side of the truck and jumping into the passenger seat.

'Really?' Hayden said flatly, casting a sardonic gaze his way.

'What?' Dax asked obliviously as he buckled himself in. 'Just because she's your girl doesn't mean she automatically gets shotgun.'

Hayden rolled his eyes but didn't argue as Kit and I climbed in. I ended up sitting directly behind Hayden as

I always seemed to, though this time I didn't mind. I liked that I could see his face in the rearview mirror as he drove. It felt like an old routine now, going on raids with these three, and I felt the adrenaline of anticipation starting up in my system.

The familiar roar of the engine filled the space around us as Hayden started the truck, wasting no time in pulling out of the garage and setting off on the path that led away from Blackwing. Trees flashed by the window as he drove, his impatience at our late start showing through in the slightly reckless way he manoeuvred the vehicle.

It seemed like no time at all before we cleared the trees to head across the flat that separated us from the city. Hayden increased the speed of the vehicle even more, and it was clear to see in the way he held his shoulders that he was tense. I reached up to squeeze the muscles softly to try and relax him. His eyes flitted to the rearview mirror to finally connect with mine, where I shot him a soft, reassuring smile. He let out a deep breath and tried to return it but only managed a half-hearted grimace.

'So where are we heading, Bossman?' Dax asked, finally breaking the silence. Hayden was quiet as he thought for a few seconds.

'I don't know,' he admitted. 'I was thinking . . .'

He paused as his gaze flitted to mine once more. Everyone waited anxiously.

'What about the Armoury?'

'What? Mate, are you nuts?' Kit asked incredulously. I'd never heard of an Armoury.

'Yeah, appreciate the enthusiasm and all but . . . that's insane. You know it's always crawling with Brutes,' Dax added. His brown eyes were wide as he stared at Hayden, his mouth slightly agape.

306

'What other choice do we have? All the usual places are out, and the Armoury will have almost everything we need all in one place,' Hayden argued tensely. His shoulders tightened beneath my touch as he spoke.

'Hang on, what's the Armoury?' I interrupted, feeling out of the loop.

'It's not a real armoury, but it's this massive stocked bomb shelter we found a few years ago. We think someone or some group of people started it before the whole world fell apart, but every time we try to go back it's too overrun with Brutes to risk it,' Hayden explained.

'Where is it?' I asked. Buildings started to flash by the windows now as we entered the city. Every once in a while Hayden had to veer off to the side to avoid a piece of fallen rubble or a crater blasted into the concrete.

'Not far from here,' he answered. 'What do you all think? I think we should at least check it out. It may be the only shot we have.'

'You're boss for a reason. It's your call,' Kit said, a fierce determination on his face. Dax murmured his assent quietly.

Hayden's gaze flitted to mine again, burning into me through the rearview mirror as he waited for my response. I couldn't help but agree with Hayden – our usual spots were running low if not completely out by now and if we could get everything in one shot, even better. I remained silent but nodded at him, giving him my opinion.

'That's it, then. We're going to the Armoury.'

Adrenaline spiked in my veins as he spoke, the mystery surrounding this new place and the obvious danger setting my nerves on edge. I hardly had time to mentally prepare myself for what we could be walking into when Hayden started to slow the car down until finally coming to a stop in an alley between two very tall buildings. He killed the engine and sat back, turning to face everyone in the truck.

'All right, here's the plan. It's in the basement, so I'll go first, Kit, you bring up the rear, and Grace and Dax stay in the middle. If it's too much, we'll turn back, but if it's only a few . . . We go for it. Sound good?'

Chills started to creep up my spine as I listened in awe to Hayden speak. Kit and Dax agreed, muttering quietly before they all looked at me expectantly. I realised I hadn't replied.

'Yeah, sounds good,' I said sheepishly. Hayden glanced warily at me as if reconsidering his decision to allow me to come along. 'Really. Let's go.'

With that, we all piled out of the truck, loading ourselves down with as much ammo as we could carry while still remaining nimble. Each of us took an empty backpack with another bag stuffed inside, prepared to carry as much as we could. We lined up, preparing to start the raid, when Hayden hesitated. He glanced quickly at Kit and Dax before crossing the distance between us.

I hardly had time to realise what he was doing before his lips landed on mine, his hands cradling my face as he drew me to him. My pulse, which was already pounding because of the raid, thundered as I felt the desperate tension beneath the kiss. He pulled back before I was ready and slid one of the hands to the nape of my neck, pulling me into him in a quick hug.

'I love you. Be careful,' he murmured just loud enough for me to hear. Kit and Dax, who were surely watching this entire exchange, were completely forgotten as I let myself melt into him for a few moments.

'I will. You be careful as well,' I whispered, squeezing tight. 'I love you.'

I could feel the weight of our promise we'd made beneath

the words. The air was thick with tension and emotion as we pulled back, studying each other with fierce determination to protect the other.

This wasn't intended as a goodbye, but it very well could be.

Hayden held my gaze for only a moment longer before stepping in front of me, nodding at the group. 'Let's go. Everyone be alert.'

We all agreed softly before Hayden turned and moved toward a side door that led from the alley. He pressed his ear to the door to listen, then gripped the knob to open it. The building was, as expected, pitch black inside as we filed in.

Our steps were nearly silent as we moved, eyes constantly scanning what appeared to be some type of auto repair shop. Hayden led us to the back, guiding by the tiny amount of light that managed to filter in through the grime-covered windows. My heart hammered wildly, waiting for a shadowy figure to appear from the darkness, but none came. I hoped that the unnerving silence was actually a good thing, as Brutes were often anything but quiet.

Somehow, Hayden managed to find a narrow door at the back that he nudged open with the butt of his gun, peeking into the darkness to try and see past it. He frowned but ticked his head towards it, indicating we follow him. Dax put himself in front of me, so I was between him and Kit. I focused on keeping my breathing even as we filed through the narrow door, and descended the steps.

It was nearly pitch black now and I could hardly see Dax in front of me, much less Hayden leading the way. The steps seemed to go on much longer than normal stairs should have, and the air started to change to a thick, musty scent that felt like it hadn't got fresh air in decades.

I jumped slightly when I collided with Dax's back as the stairs stopped abruptly, putting everyone on level ground once again.

'I can't see a damn thing,' Dax muttered quietly, his voice nearly lost in the stiflingly musty air.

My body tensed even at the softest of sounds when a quiet 'click' sounded as a thin beam of light appeared, illuminating the space we'd arrived in. I blinked at the sudden light before I recognised the source as a tiny flashlight held in Hayden's hand. He shot it at me, to confirm I was still present and uninjured, before sweeping around us.

We were in a narrow hallway with walls made out of grimy, slightly damp stone blocks that looked like they'd been in place for hundreds of years. There was only one direction to go from the stairs, down a tunnel so long that I couldn't see the end of it even with Hayden's small beam of light.

'How the hell did you find this place?' I whispered incredulously.

'Hayden found it,' Kit shrugged.

'All right, let's keep moving,' Hayden said softly, cutting off our whispered conversation.

I stepped in front of Dax to follow Hayden directly. I didn't like being separated from him even by a few feet at a time like this with so much potential danger.

He clicked off the light again and started moving, taking my hand in his to guide me through the dark. Our feet padded almost soundlessly along the firm ground. I could practically feel Dax behind me and knew Kit was just a few feet further back as we skulked through the tunnel.

The farther we went, the more my nerves seemed to jump in my body. I didn't like not being able to see anything and I especially didn't like that if we were to be attacked, we'd have virtually one way to go, making it all too easy to become trapped.

We'd been walking in the dark for about twenty minutes when Hayden stopped suddenly, causing me to bump into his back just as I had before with Dax.

'See?' he whispered, leaning back into me as he hesitated. I squinted down the passage, just barely able to see over Hayden's shoulder. I didn't see it at first, but after a few seconds of focusing, I detected a soft flicker of light coming from what appeared to be a doorway about twenty yards further down the hall.

'Yeah,' I breathed in response. He squeezed my hand before starting to move again, pulling me along, ensuring I was behind him at all times. I heard soft clicks as Kit and Dax both loaded their guns.

Each step we took closer seemed to make my heart beat one tick faster, increasing more and more until I was sure it was going to beat out of my chest. I could feel my palms sweating as I held both my gun in one hand and Hayden's in the other, but the thrill of the raid was still there. Even though I was terrified, I was completely exhilarated.

We were mere feet away now, and the outline of the doorframe was clear as we approached. There was just enough light coming from inside the room to indicate maybe a few candles lit, nothing more. Without speaking, the four of us flattened out against the wall that housed the door, inching closer and closer while keeping ourselves out of sight from anyone inside the room. Still, no sounds came from within.

The edge of the open door was inches from Hayden's shoulder. I could hardly keep my pulse in check as I felt him squeeze my hand tightly one last time. Putting both hands on his gun, he took a deep breath and leaned to his side, peering around the corner as slowly as possible to see what was inside. Kit, Dax, and I waited anxiously for his response, our bodies tense and ready to respond to anything.

Hayden paused before taking a tentative step forward, aiming his gun through the doorway to scan around the room. His face was focused as he moved stealthily through the door, before he disappeared into the room.

The moment I lost sight of him, I felt like I had to go after him. Slowly, I leaned around the doorframe just as he had, leading with my gun. I only needed to lean in a few more inches before Hayden came into view again, only this time his gun was lowered, hanging by his waist.

I followed quickly and heard Kit and Dax do the same, though the three of us didn't make it more than a few feet into the room before we froze in surprise. My eyes scanned the dim room, taking in the surroundings as my jaw fell open.

I hadn't been exactly sure what I'd been expecting, but it certainly hadn't been this.

Chapter Twenty-Three – Magnitude
GRACE

I could feel my jaw fall open as I looked around in an attempt to take everything in. I stood a few feet inside the room, framed on either side by Kit and Dax, while Hayden was a few feet away. His brows were pulled low and his jaw was clenched tightly as he examined our surroundings, his obvious surprise and unease sending a wave of nerves through me. If Hayden was this surprised, I couldn't think it meant anything good.

'Holy shit,' Kit muttered, expressing something similar to what I was feeling.

'What is this?' Dax asked, finding his voice, too.

Finally, I seemed to recover enough to stumble forward towards Hayden. I hadn't got far when I felt him pushing me backward.

'Hayden, what's going on?' I asked, keeping my voice quiet.

We stood in a giant room dug into the earth in a similar way the tunnel had been.

Tall stacks of boxes filled the room, similar to what I had supposed we'd find, though much larger in number. What I hadn't been expecting, however, were the bundles of cloth scattered around the ground, covering the dirt floor. Nor had I been expecting to see the dishes piled here and there, smaller bags meant for daily travel, half melted candles and dimly glowing lanterns. I had been prepared for Brutes, for weapons, maybe even stashes of food, but I hadn't been prepared for obvious signs of inhabitation.

This wasn't an armoury or a storage area – this was where people lived, and by the looks of the place, a lot of them.

'Hayden,' I repeated, unable to look at him this time as I took in the details surrounding us. My gaze was caught by a large, rusty knife stuck into the dirt next to a bundle of cloth that must have served as a bed, as if someone had stuck it there before going to sleep and forgotten to retrieve it later.

'I don't know,' he finally said, answering my question. 'This isn't what it was like last time we were here.'

There didn't appear to be anyone in here, but the few burning candles and lived in feel made it very clear that it hadn't been long since anyone had been.

'We should go,' Dax murmured from behind us. I couldn't help but agree – there was only one way out as far as I knew and I didn't like the sounds of getting stuck here when whoever inhabited it decided to return. Judging by the countless makeshift beds, we were vastly outnumbered.

We were good, but nobody was that good.

Hayden moved forward, raising his gun as he approached one of the boxes stacked to the side. Tentatively, he reached forward to flip open the lid, leaning back slightly in case it exploded. I blew out a breath I didn't realise I was holding when nothing happened.

I moved forward again, earning a disapproving look from Hayden. He held the lid open as I leaned over the box to see inside, and I sucked in a breath of surprise as I took in its contents. There, in a single box, was more ammunition than we'd been able to bring with us on the raid. Boxes and boxes of bullets were stacked inside, filling it to the brim.

'Oh my god,' I muttered, my eyes widening in surprise. I glanced around to see more and more boxes, presumably filled with bullets just like this. Ten, twenty, thirty, forty – more boxes than I could count lined the wall, and it was only a small fraction of the boxes in the room.

'Keep watch,' Hayden muttered hurriedly as he moved a few feet over, bending to open another box. He did the same for ten other boxes before straightening up to face Kit, Dax and me.

'They're all full,' he said quietly.

'What kind of ammo is it?' Dax asked after peeking inside, his brown eyes wide.

'All kinds,' Hayden answered. 'Check those over there, but be quick and quiet. Who knows how long we have until whoever lives here comes back.'

Dax and Kit nodded before moving to different parts of the room. Room didn't seem to be the right word for it – it was more of a vast bunker, stretching further than I could see in the dim light. From what I could tell, it was about fifty metres wide and much longer, housing more supplies than we could dream of carrying back with us.

I was about to tackle another area when Hayden's hand closed around my arm, tugging me back toward him.

'Stay with me,' he requested firmly. For the first time since arriving here, his eyes locked on mine and truly focused as he seemed to get over the shock of what we'd found.

'I'll be fine, Hayden,' I argued. 'We don't have time to waste.'

I tugged my arm lightly in an attempt to break his grip but he only shook his head, holding me near him. 'No. You stay right with me, okay? There could be people here that we can't see.'

'I think they'd have come out by now,' I reasoned.

'I don't care, I'm not risking it,' he muttered. His hand slid down from where it gripped my bicep to squeeze my hand once before releasing it. 'Please.'

I let out a frustrated huff. I knew he was only trying to protect me but it would be more beneficial to split up. Hayden frowned at me, and I was reminded of how much time we were wasting by even discussing it.

'Fine,' I grumbled. Without a word, he nodded and led me to a different area, skirting around the beds and strange personal items that seemed to belong to each site. Everything looked dirty, as if whoever lived there wasn't too concerned with keeping things clean and orderly.

A quiet buzzing reached my ears as we moved, causing my head to turn in the direction it came from. I jerked my head back as a fly suddenly darted into my vision, and I raised my hand to swat it away. It was then that I noticed a small swarm of flies off to my right, and a thick, putrid scent wafting from the area the flies seemed to be gathered.

Anxiously, I approached, nervous as to what I would find and absolutely certain it wouldn't be good, but I didn't stop.

'Grace!' Hayden hissed as he noticed I was no longer following him. I could hear his hurried steps as he ran back to me to try and stop me, but it was too late.

The source of the acrid scent was obvious now. Behind a small stack of boxes were the remains of several decomposing bodies. I froze, a quiet gasp pulling from my lips as my eyes roamed over the horror. Grey, mottled skin covered stiff limbs as they tangled together, thrown there haphazardly and with no consideration how they fell.

Worse, the bodies were missing something, and next thing I knew, my eyes travelled up the wall to find another gruesome discovery. A wave of nausea swept through me as I saw endless severed hands tacked to the walls. Large hands, hands with obviously broken fingers, hands that looked too impossibly small to belong to adults. Every single one of them was the same pale, ghostly colour of the bodies, and the stumps their arms ended in now made sense as I gaped at the sight before me.

A single word was written in what could only be blood on the grey concrete wall: *thieves*.

My blood ran cold in my veins. The message was clear and unmistakable – this was what happened to those who stole from this place.

'Grace.'

Hayden's voice beside me made me jump as I ripped my eyes from the sight. I could feel the blood draining from my face and the way my lips were parted in shock as I focused on Hayden. His face was set in concern and determination, and he was clearly upset I'd seen such a thing.

'Stay with me,' he repeated softly. His hand reached for mine as he tugged me away, leading me back in the direction we'd come. My stunned mind was swirling with the horrid images, unable to shake them from my train of thought as Hayden led me toward another set of boxes.

'Don't think about it, Bear,' he murmured. He cast a concerned glance in my direction.

Focus, Grace, this is important.

I nodded to myself as I shook my head, determined to carry on with the raid as planned. I'd seen horrific things before, but that was the destruction of humanity, an act rotten to the very core. The nagging sensation that it was only a taste of what was to come sent a wave of nausea through me that I struggled to fight off.

It was with great determination that I managed to refocus my attention to the task at hand. We wasted no time in ripping open the boxes we arrived at now, and I was surprised to find something different. The second collection of boxes we opened held no ammunition, but something just as valuable – canned food. Scores and scores of tins of food, at least thirty in each box.

'Hayden,' I breathed, shocked and pleasantly surprised.

'I know,' he answered. 'Start filling a bag. Fit as much as you can carry. We need to get out of here before anyone comes back.'

'Okay,' I nodded. I ripped one of the bags from my shoulder and immediately started cramming cans into it. Hayden did the same beside me, filling a large duffle bag he had until it was bulging. I was worried he wouldn't be able to carry it before he heaved it up and slung it over his shoulder, the strap cutting into his muscle.

'Kit, Dax,' he called softly, squinting across the dim room.

'Yeah?' Dax replied, emerging from a shadow. He moved a little closer to hear more clearly.

'What'd you find?'

'Medical stuff, but I don't know what it all is,' he replied.

'And batteries and some electrical equipment,' Kit added from a little further back. He had just ripped open a box to find what he described.

'*Yes!*' Dax cheered quietly. As the resident technology expert, this finding excited him.

'Okay, Kit, get as much ammo as you can. Dax, get whatever you think we need for electronics, Grace and I will get the food and medical stuff,' Hayden decided.

Without wasting time to respond, Kit and Dax did as they were told. Hayden filled another giant duffle with food while I resisted the urge to sprint across the room and collect the medical supplies. Finally, he straightened up, heavily weighed down, and nodded. I grunted slightly with the effort of lifting my bag and throwing it over my shoulders. It was heavier than I had anticipated but was determined to carry as much as I possibly could since we'd only get one trip.

Inside the boxes Dax had discovered was everything we needed for Docc – antibiotics, pain killers, bandages, antiseptic, sutures and more. Even a few small bottles of morphine. Without hesitating, I grabbed as much as I could to stuff them into my bag, filling it to near bursting with everything Docc had asked for.

Hayden hovered anxiously behind me, bouncing on the balls of his feet as he silently willed me to move faster. Finally, when I couldn't fit a single thing more into my bag, I straightened up. On impulse, I ducked down to grab one of the boxes that held more medical supplies, determined to take as much as I could physically carry.

'Ready,' I whispered.

'You sure you can carry all that?' Hayden asked. His eyebrow cocked as he studied me, clearly noting how weighed down I was and how it would hinder my ability to move quickly or use a weapon.

'Yes, now let's go,' I replied. The straps of the heavy bags were already digging into my muscles but I refused to acknowledge it.

He hesitated, frowning slightly.

'We're wasting time,' I said, rolling my eyes as I started to move back toward the door. 'Let's go!'

He let out a deep sigh before following me, where we met Kit and Dax at the door. Both of them were equally loaded down with bags of stolen items and each carried a box. Hayden stooped to retrieve one more box of ammunition before flicking his head toward the door. I realised how long we'd been in the room. Too long.

'If anyone comes down that hallway, drop the stuff. It's not worth getting killed over, you hear me?' Hayden said harshly. His eyes travelled between the three of us but landed lastly on me, where he held my gaze fiercely.

Everyone murmured their assent, placating Hayden enough for him to glance cautiously out the door as he had before. He apparently heard nothing, because he shifted through it quickly and disappeared into the darkness of the hallway. I followed him immediately, cutting off Dax as he tried to go first.

Every step we took carried us further and further down the hallway, which was pitch black now as we left the soft light of the room behind. I hated the feeling of walking in total blindness, loaded down with goods that probably exceeded my own body weight, and no solid grip on my weapon, but it was necessary. I grasped the gun lightly between my palm and the box, but at least I was holding it.

My ears pricked nervously at every tiny sound, counting down the seconds until something inevitably went wrong, but all I could hear were the soft, panting breaths of my companions, their quietly padding feet, and the occasional clinking of one of the stolen items against another.

It still hadn't really sunk in yet that we'd not only found an incredible stash of supplies, but the dwelling for far more people than I could have imagined. It was difficult to tell, but based on what we'd seen I would guess at least five hundred people lived in that area. I hoped my mind was playing tricks on me, because five hundred was more than all of Blackwing and definitely not something we'd want to encounter as we ran away with bags and bags of their stuff.

The blood-red word kept flashing before my eyes in the darkness as we continued to move, accompanied by flickers of dismembered bodies and grey corpses.

Thieves.

Thieves like us who had got caught and butchered, left to rot in the very room these mysterious people lived. A shudder ran through me and I picked up my pace despite the burning ache that was quickly settling into my muscles; I had no desire to end up like those poor souls and have my hands removed and nailed to a wall.

I had thought the trip into the tunnel had felt long, but this one felt like an eternity. Every step I took seemed to dig me further into the ground as the bags I carried ripped into my muscles. Sweat poured down my back as I strained to move quickly, and my breath ripped from my chest under the exertion. By the sounds coming from the rest of my crew, it appeared I wasn't alone. Each guy carried even more than I did, and despite being in top physical condition, they were struggling, too.

I began to fear the tunnel would never end and we'd be left to collapse under the weight of our stolen goods, waiting to be found by the violent people who would surely return. Anxiety rumbled in my stomach, spreading through my limbs as my muscles screamed in protest, but still I kept going. The longer we lingered in the tunnel, the better chance we had of being caught.

'Almost there,' Hayden whispered.

'Thank god,' Kit muttered from somewhere behind me. I could hear the strain on his voice as he, like me, struggled to keep moving.

I felt like my legs were about to collapse under me when I bumped into Hayden without warning, colliding with one of the bulging bags he had slung over his shoulders as I bounced backward slightly.

'We're back at the stairs,' he announced. 'Stay alert – we just have to get back to the truck and we'll be good.'

It was hard to see in the darkness but I could feel his gaze burning into me. I knew he was dying to make sure I was okay but I also knew he didn't want to mention what we'd seen to Kit and Dax before he decided how to tell them.

Nerves had taken over my body – nerves because of where we were, nerves because of what I'd seen, and nerves for fear someone was going to get hurt in the home stretch. I had a sudden urge to rush forward and hug Hayden, but the bulk of our loads made that impossible.

'Be careful, Hayden,' I whispered.

He nodded sharply, letting his gaze linger on me for a few more seconds before turning to ascend the stairs. My heart pounded harder than ever as I followed, certain we were going to be either surrounded or shot the moment we emerged from the door. It didn't seem possible that we'd made it all the way through the tunnel with our stolen goods without interruption.

I forced my breathing to be silent as we reached the top of the steps and tried to ignore the stinging of my muscles while I watched Hayden peek out of the door once again. The sweat dripping down my back was now accompanied by a trickle leaking from my brow, my body more than exhausted after the stress and physical exertion I'd just put it through.

'Clear?' I breathed, waiting anxiously for Hayden to move.

'Yeah,' he responded in a hushed voice before moving forward.

Hayden moved deftly through the dark, shifting silently among the shadows to move closer to the door we had come through in the first place. I followed, more anxious than ever to get outside and get back home.

A sudden crash sounded from outside in the alley, causing all four of us to jump in surprise.

'Get down!' Hayden hissed, dropping his bags and gripping my arm to yank me behind a service counter. He had just enough time to drag the bags after us, shielding our bodies from view as Kit and Dax did the same a few feet over behind a tattered couch.

Hayden's arm had just settled over my shoulders, hauling me against him as we crouched on the floor, when a loud thud of the door swinging open sounded in the building.

'. . . I'm just saying, we should have taken those two girls. Been lonely down with all these bastards and I could use a little female company . . .' a gruff voice said as heavy footfalls sounded through the room.

'Like any females would give *you* attention,' a second voice responded darkly.

'Don't need permission, now, do I?' the first shot back, irritation lacing his voice. A shiver ran down my spine as I realised what they were talking about. Hayden's arm tightened around me and I could feel the soft tickle of his breath over my skin as he hovered over me.

The heavy footsteps carried on as they neared, as I waited for them to see us. I held my breath and leaned into Hayden's side and squeezed my eyes shut, certain we were going to get caught. They were just on the other side of our hiding spot now, mere feet away from where Hayden and I remained secluded.

Any second now . . .

But the footsteps didn't stop as they carried on towards the door we'd just emerged from, their gruff voices continuing their filthy conversation as they went. My body sagged with relief against Hayden's as they pulled open the door and started down the stairs. We now knew exactly what type of people we'd just stolen from, and I found myself beyond relieved we'd made it from the tunnel when we had.

If we'd taken only a few seconds longer, who knew what would have happened?

We waited until their voices were a soft murmur before daring to take a full breath.

'Jesus,' Hayden muttered softly. 'You okay?'

'Yeah,' I answered automatically. 'Let's just get out of here.'

Hayden nodded before rising slowly, peeking over the top of our hiding spot to make sure they really were gone before he grabbed my hand and hauled me to my feet. Kit and Dax rose from a few feet over, hefting their bags back up onto their shoulders. After everyone gathered their boxes and bags once more, we were ready. With no further hesitation, Hayden led us toward the door, pausing only briefly to listen for noise even though none came. I just wanted to get out of this place and I knew Hayden did, too.

Light burst through the darkened room as Hayden reopened the door and emerged into the alley, the rest of us close behind him as we picked up the pace as much as we could. The brightness seemed even more extreme than usual after our extended stay in the darkness, and my eyes squinted automatically as they adjusted.

A sigh of relief so big washed through me that I nearly tripped as the truck came into view, looking surprisingly unharmed. Hayden arrived first, throwing open the trunk and tossing his box and bags inside before taking mine unceremoniously without bothering to ask if I needed help. He then tugged me out of the way as Kit and Dax followed and began loading their boxes and bags as well.

I revelled in the lightness that seemed to settle over me after being unburdened by the crushing weight. I sucked in a quick breath as Hayden's hand rested on my face and his thumb drifted gently over my lip.

'Don't think about it,' he murmured softly, his gaze intense as he studied me. I shivered as I thought about exactly what I knew he didn't want me to – the bodies, the hands, the warning on the wall, and now the deranged men who were clearly responsible.

'I'm serious, Grace. Forget it,' he pressed, stepping closer to me. A soft metallic clink sounded as Dax shut the gate to the trunk, signalling it was time to go.

I nodded. Hayden didn't look happy with my lack of response but didn't say anything further before steering me toward the vehicle. He caught the handle and pulled the door open hastily, grabbing my hand to help me inside. I settled into my seat and tried to pull my hand away but couldn't as Hayden brought it quickly to his mouth, pressing his lips gently into my knuckles before releasing me and shutting the door.

His gentle action surprised me and it had happened so fast I couldn't help but wonder if he even realised he'd done it, but it sent a wave of warmth through me that managed to fight off some of the chill that had settled into my bones from what I'd seen. I tried to focus on that feeling that Hayden had given me as he threw himself roughly behind the wheel and started the engine, filling the alley with the familiar roaring.

'Let's go home,' Hayden muttered softly. He glanced behind him before peeling out of the alley, righting the vehicle before starting to retreat down the path we'd come.

'Ah, yes,' Dax agreed, letting out a deep sigh.

Home.

Blackwing was my home.

A small smile tugged at my lips as I reached upward again

to let my hand land lightly on Hayden's shoulder. His gaze flitted to mine in the mirror and he shot me a gently reassuring look as he manoeuvred down the streets. The same flicker of warmth I always felt flared through me.

His expression changed, however, as he turned the corner and his eyes focused on something else. The soft smile left his face and his brows pulled low as his eyes widened in surprise, sending a chill down my spine before I even saw what he was reacting to. My heart rammed painfully against my ribcage as I dropped my gaze to look out of the windshield.

The two men we'd encountered in the building above the armoury had obviously not been alone, but I was nowhere prepared to see them in such numbers. Directly ahead of us, spread so thickly across the road that it would be impossible to go through, were more Brutes than I had ever seen in my entire life. It was an indestructible force of the roughest, most brutal men the city had to offer, and they were all staring right at us.

Chapter Twenty-Four – Infamy
GRACE

'Holy shit.'

I wasn't able to focus on who had spoken as I stared slack-jawed at the overwhelming wall of men glowering in our direction. My body jerked forward as Hayden slammed abruptly on the brakes. I could hardly hear over the pounding of my pulse in my ears as panic rose in my body. A fresh cold sweat pricked at my forehead as I took in the sight before us.

I hardly had time to look, however, before they started charging forward. A low, menacing rumble filled the air as their mouths opened to release barbaric cries, their brutal nature shining through in their enraged faces.

'Oh my god,' I muttered, goosebumps rose on my arms.

'Hold on,' Hayden shouted through gritted teeth. We'd only been paused a few seconds at most when he slammed the truck into reverse, hammering his foot on the accelerator to lurch the vehicle backwards. His head whipped around to look back and his eyes caught mine for a split second.

'Get down, Grace,' he commanded sharply.

'What, no—'

'Kit!' Hayden's shout cut me off. Before I could resist, Kit's hand landed on my shoulders, forcing me to duck down low in the truck.

Not even a full second after I was forced down, the ear-splitting sound of shattering glass rang out as a bullet ricocheted through the vehicle. Judging by the whizzing sound and the soft whoosh of air, its trajectory was directly over where I had just been sitting.

'*Jesus!*' I heard Dax shout in surprise. My heart pounded even harder against my ribs. 'Everyone okay?!'

'Yeah,' Hayden, Kit, and I all responded at once.

A flood of relief washed over me but it didn't last long as Hayden repositioned the vehicle to head away from the rapidly advancing mob. Their shouts grew louder and I could hear more and more bangs echoing through the air as guns were fired. They didn't appear to be fantastic shots, however, because very few of the bullets appeared to hit the target as a lack of impact made evident.

'You guys shoot, I'll get us out of here,' Hayden shouted tightly.

I could feel the vehicle lurching left and right to avoid piles of rubble or craters. Next I heard bangs going off much closer as both Kit and Dax returned fire. Muffled shouts and screams of pain sounded from the crowd as they took down targets. Feeling completely useless, I sat up and brought my gun with me. Kit was leaning out his window while Dax stood up through the sunroof as they fired into the crowd.

'Grace! Get down!' Hayden hissed angrily as he saw me rise.

'Just drive, Hayden,' I growled.

I felt angry that these men were trying to kill us – the man I loved, and two people I had come to call friends, and myself. I couldn't sit by and not help when I was fully capable of it, even if it distressed Hayden.

Without any further hesitation, I leaned out the shattered window with my gun cocked and ready. I hardly had to aim as I fired the first shot, because there were so many following us. My bullet hit one of them square in the chest, causing him to fall and trip several others behind him, just as Kit and Dax were doing in different parts of the line. Instinct took over as I aimed again, the desolation of human life lost on me in the moment.

Even though so we were hitting our targets, there were still too many. Three guns against over the hundred or so I guessed to be chasing us was no match. They had an advantage in being on foot, making it easier to jump over rubble and avoid the things we had to swerve so widely to miss in the truck.

'Grace! *Get down!*' Hayden roared again, anger clear in his voice as I ignored him. My heart pounded almost painfully against my ribs as I aimed, careful to make each bullet count. One by one, the Brutes I aimed at fell, though it hardly made a dent in the crowd.

'Jesus *Christ*, where did they all come from?' Dax shouted, pausing to reload his gun while Kit and I continued to fire.

'No idea,' Kit called back.

He pulled a second gun from his waistband and continued to fire as bangs echoed around us. A loud metallic *clink* sounded as a bullet ricocheted off the back of the truck, inches from where I leaned out of it. My stomach flipped over but I stayed focused, firing one last time before the gun clicked, indicating I was out of bullets.

'Shit,' I muttered, ducking back into the truck to reload. I dug into a bag by my feet for more ammunition.

'Grace, I swear to god—'

'Stop it, Hayden,' I retorted sharply, torn between frustration and adoration for his determination to protect me.

I slammed another magazine of bullets into my gun and shifted once more to lean out of the window as more bullets whizzed past us. Small, jagged holes ripped into the truck as bullets hit, sending the metallic crunching sound ringing out around us as Hayden drove.

The distance between the crowd of Brutes and our truck was farther now and I could feel Hayden speeding up to make it even greater. The continuous bangs of the guns going off melded together, blending into a chaotic blur that invaded all of my senses.

I remained steady, however, as I emptied my clip into the crowd, bringing down more than I could count along with Kit and Dax, yet *still*, it made no indent. They kept coming, firing their weapons at us and charging with no second thoughts to their own lives. A dark fear crept through me as I fought them off. What kind of men were these who gave so little thought to their own lives for such a small cause?

Dangerous men.

'Hang on!' Hayden shouted. I whipped around just in time to see a small side street shoot off the main road. I just managed to slip back inside the truck as Hayden jerked the wheel, whipping the vehicle into the narrow alleyway and cutting us off from the view of the mob.

Sweat trickled down my face and my adrenaline was pumping my blood a hundred miles an hour as I whipped hastily around to watch out the back window. Kit, who had just pulled back inside the truck, did the same beside me.

I jerked to face forward again before my jaw fell open in surprise. Bright red blood streaked out from beneath Dax's hand that was clamped over his skin, a grimace on his face as his eyes squeezed shut. He leaned back in his seat and let out a tight hiss of pain.

'Mother fuc—' he started to swear, cutting himself off with another sharp inhale.

'What happened? Where are you hit?' I demanded

instantly, my training kicking in despite the shock of seeing my friend profusely bleeding.

'I *hate* getting shot,' Dax muttered through tightly gritted teeth. Concern clenched at my heart as he let out a low, guttural groan. 'Aghh!'

'Hey!' I shouted, drawing his attention enough to cause him to open his eyes. 'Where are you hit?'

'My arm,' he answered. He shifted his hand slightly to reveal the deep gash along the outer edge of his bicep, causing a new spurt of blood to leak from his muscle before he covered it once again.

'Hayden, get us home, now.'

My voice was authoritative as I spoke, something that mostly happened whenever I fell into the medical role.

'You have to stop the bleeding, Grace,' Hayden said anxiously. I could feel his gaze on me in the mirror but I didn't return it, already too busy digging through one of the bags we'd packed with medical supplies.

'I know,' I snapped. I finally managed to find a packet of gauze and tore it open.

Hayden continued to rip through the streets, the ever present symphony of brutal cries and echoing bullets accompanying us as we fled. A strange sense of calm settled over me as I reached forward to remove Dax's hand where it was clamped over the wound, causing a fresh trail of blood to streak down his arm.

'Dax, you're going to be fine,' I murmured, reassuring him as well as myself.

Without another second's hesitation, I wadded up the gauze and pressed it into the jagged flesh, attempting to stem the warm flow of blood. Within seconds, the pristine white of the gauze was soaked scarlet, staining my hands along with the fabric. My stomach flipped as I pressed another few gauze squares into the cut, soaking them just as quickly.

All I could see was the deep read of Dax's blood as it poured from his arm; all I could hear was the roaring of the Brutes, still somehow within range despite our attempts to draw further away. The impending sense of doom settled into the pit of my stomach as things seemed to fall apart, making it difficult to focus on the one thing I really needed to at the moment, stopping the bleeding.

'Hayden, you're going to want to drive faster.'

A gentle breeze whispered over my skin as I sat next to Hayden, the calming sensation at odds with the rising anxiety in my stomach. It was the same view we'd seen months ago, but things were so much different now. We'd returned from the raid only an hour ago. Our desolated world spread out before us, shattered and obliterated by the dark havoc men could inflict upon each other when pushed to their limits. It had taken my breath away the first time I'd seen it and it did again, though for different reasons.

We'd been sitting in silence for a while now, resting upon the same log we'd found at the top of the cliff after that first visit. In an attempt to forget everything I'd just seen, I conjured other thoughts.

'How am I going to do this, Grace?'

I turned to look at him to see him studying the view from the cliff. Even though it was dark, his eyes were narrowed in concern and his brows were pulled low.

'What do you mean?' I asked. His tone was quiet and vulnerable, something he seemed to reveal only to me. To the people of Blackwing, he was always strong, brave, courageous, but I knew that at least a small part of him was afraid of what was coming, just as I was.

'How am I supposed to pull this off? There's a *war* coming. Not a raid, a war.'

I was quiet as I thought over his question; for once, I didn't have an answer for him. I had absolutely no idea how we were going to manage this, but I knew one thing for certain: we would handle it together. Hayden had dealt with the burdens of leading those he cared for alone for too long, but as long as I was alive and breathing he would never have to do it alone again.

'You'll find a way, Hayden. I know you will.'

His profile was set in a deep frown, and a dark shadow was cast from his neck down to his tightly clenched jaw. He leaned forward, resting his elbows on his knees. I couldn't help but see the dried blood along his hands – blood that did not belong to him.

'But *how*, Grace? I can't do it. I can't protect them all.'

I heard the obvious discouragement in his voice. His lean muscles were tight with tension as I tried to soothe him.

'Don't do this, Herc, come on,' I said gently. My hand continued its slow course across his back. 'You're doing everything you can for them to keep them alive. You're protecting them better than anyone else could and they trust you enough to believe in you.'

'I can hardly protect you, much less everyone else,' Hayden argued bitterly, still not looking at me even though I knew he could feel me watching him.

'Hayden—'

'What, Grace? How am I supposed to keep you safe if you never listen to me?' he snapped suddenly, anger leaking into his voice. For the first time since arriving here, his gaze jerked towards me to lock on my own. Fire burned there, hinting at more emotions than I could fathom. My hand retreated from his shoulders to drop back into my lap.

'That's not how this works,' I responded. I tried to fight down the frustration I felt because I knew he was coming from a place of love, but it irritated me that he suddenly didn't want me to do *anything*.

'No?' he asked sarcastically, raising an eyebrow.

'No,' I said tightly, trying to control my voice. 'We've been over this – you protect me, I protect you. I can't protect you too if you don't let me do anything.'

'Why do you have to be so damn stubborn?' he muttered bitterly, glaring at me from just a few inches away.

'Why do *you*?' I spat back. I returned his glare with one of my own.

Silence enveloped us; I knew we both believed ourselves to be in the right, which was the problem. The anger was short lived, however, as something else moved in to take its place.

'Don't you get it, Grace?' he started slowly, frowning deeply at me as his brows knit even lower on over his eyes. 'I just . . . I can't do this without you.'

Some of the pride that had chilled my heart melted away at his words as a warm rush flooded through me. I remained silent, holding his intensely burning gaze. Hayden drew a deep breath and a flash of what almost looked like annoyance crossed his features.

'If I lose you, I lose everything.'

'Hayden . . .' I trailed off with a heavy sigh. I leaned forward in resignation as I pressed my lips lightly against his shoulder; my lips lingered there, while I gathered my thoughts. I could feel his tight gaze on me, burning into my skin as he watched me.

'You know how much I love you, right?'

Hayden's vulnerable words surprised me, and my gaze flicked up to meet his as I pressed one last kiss into his shoulder before sitting up once more. If there was one thing I was certain of in these quickly darkening times, it was that; Hayden had made it very clear with his every move how much he truly cared for me.

'Yes,' I answered slowly. 'And you know I feel that for you, too, don't you? You can understand how much I love you?'

I let out a light sigh as I reached across his lap to grab his hand and lace his fingers lightly between my own.

'Hayden, you're everything to me. Can't you see that? You're just . . . you're my lifesaver. My family. You're . . . home.'

Hayden's hand stilled in mine as I squeezed it gently, and I could feel his intense gaze burning through every cell in my body as he hovered in front of me. His eyes flicked back and forth between my own and his parted lips allowed soft wisps of air to pull through as he breathed.

Before I had a chance to draw a full breath, he ducked forward to press his lips firmly against my own. A hand rose to cradle one side of my face, drawing me to him as he held the kiss for a few lingering moments. Time seemed to freeze as he held the kiss, neither moving nor deepening it but somehow managing to set me on fire with the simplest of touches.

I sucked a gasp of air through my lips as he pulled back, stopping only a few inches away as his eyes opened to study me once more.

'I love you, Grace,' he said simply, his voice deeper than usual.

'And I love you, Hayden. If anyone can do this – keep everyone alive and keep people safe – it's you. I truly believe that.'

Again, he remained silent as if deciding whether or not to believe me.

'We should get back,' he whispered, ignoring my

statement. I felt a short whisper of disappointment but decided to let it be for the moment. It was clear that no matter what I said, he wouldn't believe me tonight. I sighed and nodded in agreement.

Hayden's lips pressed together in a kind of attempt at a smile, though it fell flat as he stood from the log and offered a hand to help me up. I followed him silently back to the motorcycle we'd taken up here; this trip had been much less carefree than our first thanks to what we'd just endured. My mind was still having trouble processing it all.

Soon, my chest was pressed against Hayden's back and we were zooming down the hill toward the camp. His stomach muscles were firm against my arms as I held on, not indulging in the free feeling like I had the first time. A darkness had settled over us, weighing us down enough to prevent getting any real enjoyment out of the trip.

I was surprised when we arrived back at the camp so quickly. Hayden killed the engine as he parked the motorcycle right outside the infirmary, where the light of the day was nearly gone as night approached. I climbed out from behind Hayden as he held it still before he propped up the brake and copied me.

'Come on,' he said softly. He allowed himself to reach forward and squeeze my hand once before releasing it altogether.

I followed him into the infirmary, bracing myself for what I knew we were going to find. It was strangely quiet inside, almost unnervingly so, and it was hard to ignore the tension that lingered in the room as we moved further into the building.

A small group was huddled around a bed that included Kit, Docc, and Malin. No one glanced at Hayden and I as we approached, and it wasn't until we were only a few feet away that they sensed our presence and parted to give us a clear view of the bed and its occupant.

'About time you two showed up,' Dax said sarcastically, a wide grin tugging at his admittedly pale lips. 'What could possibly be more important than me, eh?'

'We just needed a moment,' Hayden responded quietly, unable to suppress the ghost of a smile presenting on his features.

A thick white bandage was wrapped around Dax's bicep, hiding the fine stitches Docc had put in after my attempts to stop the profuse bleeding had finally succeeded. I'd needed to hold so much pressure on his gaping laceration that Kit had had to help me. We'd arrived just in time for Docc to step in and take over before Dax passed out from loss of blood.

'Right, sure,' Dax said knowingly, nodding. Even now, he was the most light-hearted of the group. 'Don't mind me, just recovering from getting shot yet *again*.'

I wasn't exactly sure what he was referring to but it didn't shock me that he'd been shot before. Hayden was absolutely riddled with scars so I would only expect Dax and Kit to be in similar shape. Even I had been shot on more than one occasion.

'You get shot in the neck then maybe I'll be impressed,' Kit chuckled, shaking his head amiably. Dax let out a hearty bellow of laughter.

'Grace has done it again,' Docc said gently, casting a small smile in my direction.

'Oh, no, anyone could have done it . . .' I trailed off. I always felt awkward whenever someone complimented me. Light pressure was applied to my back as Hayden's hand settled comfortingly there.

'Always so humble,' Hayden murmured softly.

Light seemed to blaze from behind those green eyes as he watched me, warming me from the inside out. It was like he was looking past my eyes into my very soul, making the rest of the world melt away as he captivated me completely.

Everyone jumped suddenly when the front door to the infirmary was thrown open followed quickly by someone shouting, breaking the moment.

'Hayden!'

We all turned toward the source to see a frantic-looking Maisie standing in the doorframe.

'What is it?' Hayden asked sharply, concern etching across his features instantly.

'It's Barrow – he's losing it on top of the tower and they need help,' she said, slightly winded from her obvious haste to get here.

'Great,' he mumbled, shoving a frustrated hand through his hair; we couldn't get a break. 'Right, thanks, Maisie. I'll take care of it.'

She nodded sharply, glancing nervously around the room before turning around and heading back in the direction of the tower.

'Should have pushed him off from the start,' Kit mused aloud.

'Seriously,' I whispered so quietly no one heard me. A deep anger raged inside me directed completely at Barrow for everything he'd put Hayden and I through.

'All right, Kit come with me. We'll handle this and come right back. Grace, you stay here. You coming with me will only set him off more,' Hayden instructed, his gaze already weary as he waited for my rebuttal.

I was about to open my mouth to argue when I remembered his vulnerability on the cliff and his dejection at my reluctance to listen to him. Despite my every instinct screaming to protest, I needed to show that I trusted him as much as I claimed I did. He needed to believe that I believed in him, because I truly did.

'Okay.'

Hayden didn't look happy, though he did appear relieved when I agreed. He blew out a soft sigh of relief and nodded as Kit started toward the door. Hayden took a step toward me, before his eyes swept around the group, noting Malin's presence. He hesitated, as she was the only one who didn't know about us; I could see he was unsure about revealing our relationship to her.

His eyes locked on mine once more, silently communicating the angst he felt about leaving me. Only about two feet separated us as we held each other's gaze, the river of emotion flowing freely between us despite the several pairs of eyes focused on us. I wanted so badly to reach up and hug him that I was pleased when his hand folded around my forearm and steered me away from the group and behind a cabinet along the wall, blocking us from everyone's view.

'I'll be right back but . . . we promised,' he whispered lowly. Without a moment's hesitation, he ducked his lips down to fold against mine in a gentle kiss. It was far too short for my liking, however, when he pulled back almost instantly. Just a centimetre separated us as he murmured three words softly against my lips.

'I love you.'

'I love you, too,' I breathed, unable to acknowledge much else going on around me other than Hayden.

As quickly as he had pulled me into the corner, he was gone, leaving me leaning forward and gasping slightly at the loss, even if it was only for a little while. Forcing myself not to blush, I emerged from behind the cabinet to rejoin Dax, Docc, and Malin.

Dax was grinning far too wide and very clearly knew what had just happened, but I ignored him and focused on Docc for fear of blushing.

'Anything I can help with, Docc?' I offered. I needed distraction until Hayden returned.

'You've already done so much,' he said slowly. 'But if you and Malin would like to take out those empty boxes, that would be great.'

'Sure,' I nodded. Malin and I silently moved to the corner of the room to start gathering the boxes Docc indicated as he tended to a still smirking Dax. Once we each had several stacked up, we made our way out the door to stack them in the pile where boxes were usually kept.

'So,' Malin started the second we were outside.

'So,' I repeated uncertainly.

'How are you doing? All healed up?'

I didn't realise what she was referring to until I remembered she had been on the raid the day I'd broken my rib. Despite my best efforts to hide it, she'd noticed on the ride home that I was not okay.

'Yeah, loads better,' I answered honestly.

'That's good,' she said sincerely.

'Yeah,' I said, feeling slightly awkward. 'How's, um, Kit?'

'He's fine,' she sighed, sounding as if it were anything but. 'I dunno, sometimes things are great and sometimes they're not.'

'Ahh,' I responded lamely.

'He certainly doesn't look at me the way Hayden looks at you.'

I nearly tripped as I processed her words, beyond surprised she'd noticed such a thing, let alone brought it up. 'Um—'

'You don't have to explain,' she said, shrugging. 'I get it. He's just . . .'

'Hayden,' I finished. Hayden was a lot of incredible things, but choosing one didn't seem to do him justice. Hayden was just Hayden, and that was one of the best compliments I could have given him.

'Yeah,' she agreed. 'What I would have given for him to look at me once the way he looks at you.'

I frowned, confused by her statement. The darkness of the night seemed to slow my thoughts, making things difficult to understand as we moved through camp.

'What do you mean?' I asked slowly.

'After every time we were together, it was nothing like that,' she explained casually. My blood seemed to chill in my veins as the puzzle pieces started to fall into place.

'You two were together?'

I suddenly felt slightly sick to my stomach.

'Yeah, for a while – wait,' she paused, glancing at me suddenly with wide eyes. My stomach clenched painfully. 'You didn't know?'

'No,' I said tightly, shaking my head sharply as I fought off the chill in my bones.

'Oh my god, Grace, I'm sorry, I thought you knew,' she said frantically, truth ringing clearly in her tone.

No matter how I tried to rationalize my thoughts, I couldn't help but feel a sting of something stabbing at my heart.

Hayden had been with Malin?

Why hadn't he told me?

I was about to open my mouth to speak when an ear-splitting bang echoed around the camp, followed quickly by countless screams of terror that dug into my heart. A blaze of fire flared up suddenly, engulfing the darkness of the sky and illuminating the entire side of Blackwing as some type of explosive detonated. Panic ripped through me as I jerked around to face the source of the explosion, taking in the horrific sight that was quickly unfolding before me.

'Hayden,' I muttered quickly without meaning to.

In a split second, I was on my feet moving toward the source of the chaos, where the heat of the fire from the explosion could already be felt on my skin.

'Wait, Grace!' Malin called after me, but I ignored her as I charged forward.

I dodged people running in the opposite direction as they fled the explosion. I heard angry shouts and sudden gunfire as I approached, only increasing the panic inside me. I frantically scanned every face I passed for signs of Hayden, but he was nowhere.

The haunting sounds I already heard were now accompanied by screams of fear, their sounds meshing together in a dissonant tone that reverberated through the air. Panic was everywhere as I darted past crying children, fearful mothers, angry, weapon wielding fathers. Everywhere I looked, chaos was unfolding around me, yet he was still missing.

A flash of someone running toward me caught my eye and my heart leaped in hope that it was Hayden before quickly plummeting to the ground. This person was someone I recognised but did not want to see; this person was not a friend to me, as they were a member of the camp I had betrayed to save another.

This person was from Greystone, and he was part of the attack on Blackwing.

This was it.

This was finally it.

The war had started, and Hayden was nowhere to be found.

Bonus Chapter

HAYDEN'S MOTHER

The faint drone of the television buzzed in the background as I scooped up my particularly exhausted son. I felt my muscles protest as I did so, as if they hadn't quite adjusted to how big he had gotten in his five years of life. It didn't seem possible that at twenty-eight years old I could have a five-year-old son. Sometimes it was as if I expected to go into his room and find a sleeping infant, but was instead surprised by a quickly growing, healthy child.

Not only healthy, but strong in so many ways. He often played with kids several years older and kept up better than most despite being younger. He would frequently delight in playful wrestling matches with his father, who would let him win and encourage his strength. Kindness was yet another strength he held, for he would often stick up for kids who couldn't quite keep up like he could, offering them friendship when no one else would. He was intelligent, too. I remembered how often his teachers had commented on how quickly he learned, how intuitive he seemed to be, how observant he was.

Of course, he hadn't been to any sort of school for a while now.

The soft pattern of his breath heated my shoulder, bringing my mind back to the present. His body was limp with sleep, a dead weight in my arms, as I carried him up the stairs and to his room. The drone of the television faded, but the tension from what I'd been hearing remained. The news had been overwhelmingly negative for the last few years, but there was no denying it had become even worse in the past months.

Hayden slept soundly as I reached his room and lay him gently on his bed. He was quickly outgrowing it, and his toes almost hung off the end when he stretched out. We would have to replace it soon.

Gently, I pulled up the covers to tuck him in. His dark hair sprawled across the pillow and soft breaths panted from beneath his parted lips, his sleep undisturbed despite being moved. A soft smile pulled at my lips as I studied my sleeping child, so grateful and proud that such a brilliant and wonderful young boy was mine.

I bent over and pressed a light kiss to the top of his head, lingering for a few moments to push back the unruly strands from his face before murmuring a few quiet words he would not hear.

'Mum loves you, Hayden.'

With that, I cast him one last smile before retreating from the room, careful not to make any noise and disturb him while he slept so deeply. When I reached the hall, I was greeted with the sight of my husband standing there. He wore a concerned expression, and it was obvious many things were weighing him down.

'What is it?' I asked, suddenly feeling anxious.

'I think you should come and watch the news,' he said solemnly, eyes holding my gaze. I swallowed nervously and nodded before joining him at the end of the hall. He paused when I reached him, taking a second to grasp and squeeze my hand, before we moved into the living room together.

The television was still on, just as I had left it, and the same heavy news was playing.

'. . . *reports coming in that North America has been decimated by bombs from unknown countries. There are no statistics yet as to just how many lives have been lost but estimates are well into the millions. This report comes as tragic news after last week's events in Eastern Asia and Australia, which have also suffered catastrophic losses as a result of mass destruction implemented against them by enemy countries. It is still unclear as to who is behind these attacks, but the suspect list spans half the globe as resources continue to disappear. The War for Life has taken yet another devastating toll, and most of the world is in a state of upheaval. We'll have more as updates come in. This is the London News Network. Stay safe.'*

The station's network symbol flashed up on the screen before changing to something else, ending the segment. Throughout the report, my heart had steadily picked up speed, and now my breath seemed caught in my throat as silence rang in my ears.

'It's getting worse,' I finally said tightly. I was unable to tear my eyes from the screen, even though the news anchor had been replaced by an old advertisement for apples, which were on sale for twenty-eight pounds each. It had been running for months now, despite being out of date.

'I know,' he said, seriously. He stood a few feet away from me, both of us standing in the living room, unable to sit or even move.

'It's never been this bad,' I continued.

He didn't speak right away; the green of his eyes held my attention as I looked at him, so similar to our son's. The simple thought of Hayden sent my nerves into overdrive, the fear of anything happening to him. My husband seemed to sense the shift in my emotions because he stepped toward me, reaching for me until I was enveloped in a hug against his chest. I felt his arms encircle me as my head rested on his shoulder, hugging him around the neck.

'It's going to be okay,' he murmured. I could feel his lips moving against my temple before he pressed a light kiss there. My throat started to tighten but I pushed down the tears threatening to creep up.

'What if it's not?'

'It will be,' he promised, soothingly. His hand ran gently down my back. 'London is a long way away from those places.'

I frowned and pulled back, keeping my arms linked loosely around his neck as his hands settled around my waist.

'But it's happening everywhere,' I said, shaking my head. As much as I wanted to believe him and let him comfort me, I knew he wasn't being completely truthful.

The last few years had been unlike any other in human history. Just as scientists had been predicting for years, the world had started to run out of resources. The few efforts being made to help restore the things that were so essential to life were not even close to enough; slowly but surely, everything had dwindled to nearly nothing. Prices of things like fruit, grains, milk, even water, had skyrocketed to the point that most couldn't afford them. Those who could took everything for themselves.

This didn't just happen in London.

This didn't just happen in the United Kingdom.

This didn't just happen in Europe, the Northern Hemisphere.

It happened worldwide, and it happened all at once.

The human race had neglected the planet, using up everything with little thought as to what would happen

346

when the earth had no more to give. We were now paying dearly for our ancestors' narrow-minded views of the world, and we were paying for it with our lives.

Australia was the first to be bombed. No one knew who had launched the attack, but it was clear why. Countries around the globe were getting desperate for resources, and they would do anything to get them. If one country had to be obliterated to survive, it was considered a sacrifice that many countries were willing to make. The darkest essence of human nature took over as people's selfish desires to carry on overrode the inherent good that had previously kept the world civilized.

That civilization was gone, just as the resources were gone from the earth.

After Australia, it was as if we heard of a new country being destroyed every day. Places from all over the globe were blasted to bits, further demolishing what little we had left to profit from the devastation. It got to the point where no one knew who was attacking who, which countries were at war with which countries. Chaos reigned throughout the globe, and it wasn't long before people stopped caring who the enemy was, because everyone was the enemy.

People lost their trust in others, lost their desire to help. All that remained was an intense desire to survive, no matter what the cost.

These were the things we heard about on the news, each day grimmer than the last. England had, so far, managed to avoid being hit with the bombs, but it was impossible to ignore the growing tension in the nation. It was as if everyone was waiting for the inevitable day when London would be just another city on the news, highlighted with videos of shattered buildings and broken bodies.

People began to form small groups that consisted of the

few they trusted. They'd meet in secret, plan for evacuation, store up what materials they could. Whispers of groups were murmured through the streets of London, but only whispered, for most people could hardly trust their own shadow. After a certain point and a certain number of devastating stories on the news, we began to lose hope that things would ever go back to normal. Too much of the world had been destroyed to dare hope for such a thing.

It was then that we joined a group of our own.

At first, we met once every few months. We'd get together at someone's house, talk about what we'd do if London were ever to be attacked. We'd slowly begin to store what we could to prepare for the worst. Newcomers were few and far between, for only the most trusted were included in our plans. While we knew others were doing the same, there was no trust left that our own countrymen wouldn't turn on us just as the rest of the world had. Desperation had caused the world to destroy itself, and we saw the grim reality that desperation could wreak havoc among our own city as well.

So we were careful. So, so careful.

At that point, society was still functioning, if only just. People still went to work. Children still attended school. Public transportation still existed, if you could afford the outrageously high price of using it. The façade that things were normal carried on for a while. During the day, people carried on their normal lives as best they could, but by night, they slinked off into the dark to meet with those they trusted, planning out their uncertain future with only their own interests in mind.

It was about two months ago when everything shut down. Jobs, transportation, schools, everything. There was no warning, no explanation other than an announcement on the news saying it was no longer safe. People locked themselves away in their homes, idly sitting by as the world continued to implode. Even after everything shut down, still the news came. We were never released from the constant stream of nightmares, which crept closer and closer by the day.

The only time people left their homes were to either meet in secret with their groups, or to attempt to find food and water. After years of horrendous inflation, money had finally lost its value. No one cared for useless money anymore, because money could not keep them alive. Currency now existed in the form of food and water, which were scarcer than ever.

That was our current state of things. Our lives now consisted of spending almost all of our time in our home. Sometimes we'd bring Hayden into the garden and let him ride his plastic tricycle, but it wasn't what I wanted for him. I wanted him to be able to do things like go to the zoo, play sport, eat ice cream on a hot summers day. He'd done those things, thankfully, but not in the last few months. Despite losing things he used to be able to enjoy, he was still happy. Somehow, mercifully, he remained unaware of the current state of the world.

While I feared many things, there was one thing I feared above all: that any harm should ever come to Hayden. It was what kept me awake at night, tossing and turning until eventually the sun rose and I could pull him from his bed to cuddle him to me. Only then could I feel some relief, for he was close, and I knew he was, at least in that moment, safe.

I sucked in a sharp gasp, reorienting myself as I blinked several times. My husband's green eyes came back into focus, both of us still locked in our positions before my mind had drifted down a dark path. I felt so many emotions at once: nerves, determination, fear, fortitude. The recent newscast seemed to demand action.

'When was the last time you saw them?' I asked, my voice steady and strong.

My husband blinked in momentary surprise but recovered quickly. 'I spoke with Docc and Barrow this morning.'

'And?' I prodded.

'And the plan remains the same. Should anything happen, we're to meet beneath the bridge and make our way to the woods. Our supplies should still be hidden there, which would be enough to support us, at least for a little while.'

I nodded, eyes drifting downward in thought. Over the last few months, we'd managed to transport what we'd been able to save up out to the woods outside of the city. There was an old lookout tower and a few old cabins that were abandoned; it was the perfect place to escape should danger come to London. Our group, which consisted of about thirty people, had agreed on that plan of action only a few weeks ago.

'Okay,' I finally said. I was mentally and emotionally exhausted, and I couldn't shake the feeling of impending doom that had settled into my stomach.

'No matter what happens, we'll be together,' he said softly. His hands ran soothingly up and down my arms as he gave me a small smile. 'You, me, and Hayden. We will be okay.'

I sighed and nodded, desperately trying to believe him.

'I love you,' he reminded me. I felt a soft wave of happiness run through me at his words despite the dread that weighed in my stomach. At least I had him.

'And I love you,' I returned easily. My eyes drifted shut as he ducked down to give me a soft kiss, lingering a few moments before pulling back.

350

'How about we grab our son and go to bed?' he offered. My throat automatically tightened as I nodded. He knew how much I worried about Hayden, and how having him in my arms could help ease that just a little.

'That sounds perfect.'

He leaned forward and pressed a kiss to my forehead before linking my hand in his. After clicking off the television, he led me from the room, back up the stairs, and back into Hayden's room. A soft sigh of relief pushed past my lips when I saw him lying exactly where I'd left him. I watched as my husband moved quietly into the room and scooped him up, cradling him easily in his arms. When he carried him back to me, he paused where I leaned against the doorframe to allow me to press a light kiss to our son's cheek.

Silently, we both made our way to our room, where he laid Hayden down in the middle of the bed. After quickly changing, both of us joined him, bordering him on each side like protective pillars. My body curled around his instinctively. I was mirrored by my husband across from me, keeping Hayden safely in the middle. When I reached for him one last time to brush back his hair, he finally stirred.

His eyelids fluttered for a moment and he pulled in a deep breath, shifting as if to stretch in his sleepy state. His nose wrinkled up in a quiet sniffle once before he opened his eyes, blinking blearily as he looked around in confusion.

'What's going on?' he mumbled, still not oriented to his surroundings.

'We're having a sleepover,' I said softly. My fingers couldn't seem to stop petting over his soft, wild hair.

'A sleepover?' he asked. His green eyes darted back and forth between mine and his father's.

'Yes, little man,' his dad lulled. 'Is that okay with you?'

'Yes!' he said excitedly, suddenly losing his sleepiness.

I felt a smile pull at my lips as he moved his head back and waved off my hand clumsily. He would accept my affectionate touches if he was half-asleep, but as soon as he was fully awake, he was determined not to be babied. Every time I told him he would always be my little boy, he would protest in embarrassment.

'But we have to go to sleep,' I continued. 'If you go to sleep, you can play with your tricycle tomorrow.'

His eyes widened in excitement. 'Really?'

I nodded, smiling at him.

'Okay,' he replied, nodding to himself a few times. I heard the soft tones of my husband's laugh as he chuckled across from me. 'Goodnight!'

'Goodnight, Hayden. I love you so much,' my husband murmured to him. He ducked to press a kiss to his forehead, which Hayden squirmed away from with a giggle. His squirming, however, sent him directly into my arms, where I took advantage and squeezed him in a hug before kissing his cheek.

'And I love you, Hayden,' I added.

'Ew!' he said, giggling as he pretended to wipe my kiss off his cheek.

'Be nice,' I murmured softly, still grinning at him. Hayden let out a deeply dramatic sigh before smiling reluctantly.

'Goodnight. I love you, Mum and Dad.'

My heart was the happiest it had felt in a long time as he squeezed my arm gently. After murmuring his words, he closed his eyes again, ready to drift off into peaceful sleep with only the promise of riding his tricycle to worry about. With a heavy sigh, I cast one last look over my son's chest at my husband, who held my gaze lovingly.

'Goodnight,' he mouthed. 'I love you.'

'I love you. Goodnight.'

With that, my eyes shut, comforted by the presence of my son and husband.

I slept well that night despite the terrors we'd heard on the news and the feeling of impending chaos, because I was with the two I loved more than anything in the world. That, and that alone, was what kept me at peace.

The night passed silently, slipping by without our notice as the three of us slept soundly. Hayden lay safely between my husband and I, deeply asleep without a worry in the world. It was a perfect night – the type I cherished whenever I got the chance to have them – and this night was no different.

I was pulled from the peaceful slumber in the morning. Sunlight flooded though the room, and at first, it wasn't completely apparent what had awoken me. My eyes opened slowly, bleary with sleep and reluctant to awake. I felt the comforting warmth of Hayden snuggled into my chest, and the reassuring weight of my husband's arm as it draped over the both of us. A soft smile pulled at my lips, content to lie there forever.

My smile was wiped clean, however, when a distant thunderous boom resonated through the air. The ground quivered, shaking the house enough to wake both my husband and Hayden. My husband's green eyes snapped open suddenly in alarm, darting around to Hayden first then to me before he spoke.

'What was that?' he asked sharply.

My heart started to thud heavily in my chest as I heard a few more distant rumbles. Fear gripped my entire body as if I already knew what was happening before my mind could comprehend it.

'I don't know,' I answered, shaking my head. I swallowed harshly and glanced at our son, who was waking up more slowly and with less panic than we had.

'Morning,' he mumbled, rubbing sleepily at his eyes. He squinted in the bright morning light as he lowered his hands.

'We should—'

My words were cut off by another echoing rumble, this one much louder and closer than the last. Again, our house shook, this time hard enough to make the bedframe rattle against the wall. A gasp of fear left Hayden's lips as his hands automatically tightened around me.

'Mum,' he said fearfully, eyes darting around wildly.

'We have to go,' my husband said quickly. I nodded, jumping out of bed while he pulled Hayden out with him. I ran hurriedly to Hayden's room, grabbing the first pair of shoes I could find before darting back to the bedroom. I knelt in front of him, where he stood in the middle of our room as my husband rushed to tie his own shoes.

'Hayden, sweetheart, I need you to listen to me,' I said quickly, forcing my voice to remain calm. My hands shook as I helped him stuff his feet into his shoes. It took me several tries before I finally managed to tie the strings. He waited for me to continue as I finished tying his shoes and brought my hands to rest on his shoulders.

'We're going to go outside and we're going to run very fast, do you understand?'

'Mum, what's—'

'I'll explain later, okay sweetheart? I just need you to run. Everything is going to be okay,' I continued. My throat started to tighten as fear and emotion crept up, but I forced it down. Hayden couldn't know how truly afraid I was.

'I don't understand,' Hayden said. He frowned, frightened

and confused all at once. Just as my husband appeared beside us, yet another round of booms and earth-shaking shudders hit.

'Hayden, do you remember that bridge I showed you?' he asked, kneeling beside us. I could feel precious time ticking away, but it was important.

'Yes,' Hayden replied shakily.

'That's where we're running. No matter what happens, you have to run to the bridge,' he said firmly. I glanced to see him staring intently into his son's eyes, so like his own. I felt another wave of fear crash over me at the thought that something could happen to either of them.

'Okay,' Hayden said, nodding.

'No matter what happens,' repeated my husband. He spoke slowly, looking Hayden in the eye the entire time to make sure he understood. Hayden nodded, fear clear in his eyes.

'I love you so much, Hayden,' he continued. I heard his voice catch and noticed the wetness around his eyes. Hayden looked kind of confused when he hauled him forward into a quick hug, but returned his sentiments all the same.

'I love you, too, Dad.'

They hugged for a few short moments, for that was all we had. When they separated, I placed my hands on either side of Hayden's face, hovering in front of him. Again, tears threatened to choke me, and this time I wasn't strong enough to fight them down as they spilled over my cheek.

'Hayden, my sweet Hayden,' I started, already struggling to keep my voice even. 'You will always be my strong, brave, boy, right?'

He looked more confused than ever, but he seemed to sense how serious the situation was. Slowly, he nodded, reacting to my tears with an expression of concern.

'Yes, Mum,' he said softly.

'I know you will,' I replied shakily. 'I love you so much. So, so much.'

Hayden's little eyebrows pulled low over his striking green eyes, deepening his frown even more. 'I love you, Mum.'

'We have to go,' my husband said from the doorway. His expression was a mixture of fear, determination, anxiousness, and so many other things that I was feeling, too.

I nodded and stood, stuffing my feet quickly into the shoes my husband had placed near my feet. I took Hayden's hand in one of mine and gave him one last look before pulling him along. My husband led us through the house, taking Hayden's other hand quickly. When we reached the front door, yet another deafening round of booms ripped through the neighborhood, this one closer than ever. Other sounds, too, ricocheted through the space, different than those we'd heard before. There were loud zooming sounds as planes flew overhead, relentless pinging as bullets ripped through anything in their path, echoing bangs as bombs exploded, and perhaps worst of all, blood-curdling screams arising from all around us. It seemed as if hell itself had risen to the surface of the earth, intent on destroying each of us one by one.

A chill ran down my spine as we paused behind the door. Despite what terror waited outside, we had no choice but to run. We knew from experience that when this happened, the city would be destroyed; our only chance to survive was to get out of it and make it to our stores in the woods.

I drew a deep breath and turned to glance at my husband to see him doing the same. His gaze drifted to me. His free hand reached to land lightly on my cheek, pulling me in so we leaned over our frightened son. I sucked in a shaky

356

breath just before his lips pressed to mine, lingering for only a moment, just in case.

'I love you. It'll be okay,' he reminded me. My jaw quivered beneath his touch as I tried to stay strong.

'And I love you.'

My eyes met his blazing green ones one last time before we nodded silently to each other. I squeezed Hayden's hand in mine and reached for the front door, preparing to open it so we could make our attempt at escape. My husband spoke just before I pulled the door open, making my heart pound even harder than before.

'Now we run, little man.'

Gathering all the strength that I possessed, I pushed open the door and stepped outside. My husband followed quickly, keeping Hayden between us as we moved quickly down the walkway. All around us, more chaos and panic than I ever could have imagined was unfolding. Hayden's hand shook in mine as I gripped it impossibly tight.

The rumbles and booms of the bombs going off was almost continuous now, the sounds melding together into one indistinguishable blur that threatened to drown out any other sound. The ground shook beneath our feet, as if a continuous earthquake were striking London. Deafening whooshes of planes as they flew overhead whipped the hair around our faces, causing even more noise as the bombs they dropped exploded. Bullets ripped through the streets, mowing down anything and anyone in their path.

We had hardly made it to the street when I saw the first body, so bloody and battered that I couldn't make out even the largest of identifiers. My stomach churned as I immediately averted my eyes, tightening my grip on Hayden's hand.

'Don't look around, son,' my husband called to Hayden.

'Just focus on your feet and keep running!'

Hayden let out a whimper and nodded, though I could hardly hear him for all the echoing carnage around us. I'd never felt such a terrifying mix of emotions before, and it took all I had to keep my feet moving one after the other. My fierce desire to keep Hayden safe, to keep my family alive, was the only thing pushing me on.

As we ran down the street, it became almost impossible to run in a straight line. The continuous bombs and other weapons of destruction were blowing our neighborhood to bits, causing massive chunks of debris to litter the street. One moment we darted around a broken couch, thrown from its house into our path. The next, we skirted around massive crevasses in the street, caused by bombs that had already exploded.

Most sickening were the bodies that littered our path. Every few feet, we'd come across another. Some were whole, and the people looked completely untouched. Others were mangled beyond recognition, destroyed by whatever it was that had ended their lives. There were pools of blood so large that I found it hard to believe a single body could contain so much. My feet slipped several times as we ran through one we could not avoid, splattering the still warm substance over my legs, but still we carried on.

'Mum, Dad,' Hayden called, clearly terrified.

'It's okay, Hayden,' I returned. My voice was, miraculously, steady as I tried to reassure him. My efforts were weak, however, as more and more destruction carried on around us.

Every few seconds, another bomb would drop. Some felt like they were right behind us, and more than once, I felt the hairs on the back of my neck stand up as a blast of hot air rushed past us. Bullets whizzed through the air from unknown sources, and I saw a pair of fleeing people fall to the ground who had not been running far from us. Fear ripped through me so roughly that I was shaking, though it was hard to tell if it was me or the ground beneath my feet.

'Run, Hayden, run!' I shouted, encouraging him as we moved along. My stomach churned as we stepped over a dismembered leg, ragged on one end as it bled onto the cracked pavement. Hayden slipped in the blood, but our grips on his hand held him up.

'You've got it, Hayden, keep going!' my husband called encouragingly. I saw his eyes dart down to Hayden as we ran, his face strong and determined. We were getting closer to the bridge we were aiming for, and he was just as resolute as I was to get us there.

Suddenly, there was a high-pitched whistling sound that only came from gunfire, followed by a sickening, wet thump as the bullet ripped through my husband's chest. The look of strength and determination was wiped from his face in a split second, and his legs stopped as he crashed to the ground, yanking Hayden's arm back with him.

No.

A shuddering, choking gasp escaped from my lips as I realised what had happened. Agony like I'd never felt before ripped through me as I was jerked backward too, shaking from head to toe as my eyes poured over the now lifeless body of my husband. He lay on his back, blank, once blazing green eyes staring straight up to the sky. Hayden collapsed onto his chest, panic and confusion in his eyes.

'Dad, get up!' he begged. His small hands pushed weakly at the wound on his chest, where blood still poured out despite already being dead. 'Dad, we have to go!'

Tears were now spilling from Hayden's eyes as his shaking hands pushed at his father's chest. No matter what he tried, his father did not respond. My heart completely shattered in my chest, for I had just lost my husband, and I had watched my son lose his father. I knelt beside him and placed my hand on his back, flinching as yet another bomb went off nearby and more bullets ripped through the air. We didn't have long before we had to move again.

'Dad,' he choked out, leaning his small body over him.

'Hayden, sweetheart, we have to leave him,' I said as calmly as I possibly could. My throat felt like it was being torn to shreds, just like my heart. I wrapped my arms around him and brought my lips to his ear. My broken heart seemed to suck up whatever warmth was left in me as I continued, 'He's gone, love.'

'No, he's not,' Hayden argued, weakly. My throat tightened painfully, and I failed to stop the tears from pooling in my eyes. Hayden's body shook beneath my touch as I gently turned him to face me, gripping his face gently between my hands.

'He would want us to run, Hayden,' I said. Of that, I was absolutely certain. I sniffed and struggled to draw a full breath as I studied my son intently. Finally, he nodded.

'That's my boy. My strong, brave boy,' I said quickly, hauling him forward to press a kiss into his forehead. I sniffed once more before standing up and taking his hand in mine once more. 'Come now, love.'

Hayden nodded and looked back over his shoulder one last time, taking in the sight of his father's lifeless body. I could barely manage to bring my eyes to his figure, for when I did, I felt as though the pain would crush me straight into the ground. I'd lost one member of my family, and I refused to lose another. We would get to that bridge.

Together, we started running again. The bridge was in sight now, and there were crowds of people gathered beneath it already that I couldn't quite make out. I hoped those I trusted the most had made it — Docc, Barrow. They were the ones who had promised their lives to take care of Hayden should anything happen to my husband or I.

It looked as if I would need them now that my husband was gone.

Breath ripped through my lungs as I pushed my body forward, making sure to only go as fast as Hayden could run. It was faster for us both to run than for me to try to carry him, so we surged on. We were drawing closer, and now I could see people waving us on, encouraging us to run faster.

'Almost there, Hayden,' I called hopefully. I squeezed his hand tightly as we ran. Never in my life had my heart pounded faster.

'We're going to make it, Mum,' he called back. He was breathless from the sprinting and fear, but I felt a surge of pride for how strong he was, even now. My boy, my brave, sweet boy, deserved to survive this more than anyone, and I was going to make sure he did.

We were so close now, only twenty or so metres. I just started daring to hope we would make it as I saw the faces urging us on, the arms waving us forward. I just started daring to hope it would be okay as I felt the warmth of Hayden's hand in mind. We were close, so close, to making it to safety.

So close, before there was a whistling scream of a bullet in my ear.

A thick ripping of flesh in my chest.

A brief flicker of pain.

And finally, darkness.

After *Loyalty*

COMES A REVOLUTION

THIRTY MILLION READERS WORLDWIDE

Revolution

YOU FIGHT, YOU KILL
YOU STEAL, YOU LIE...
OR YOU DIE.

Megan DeVos

Read on for an extract now.

Chapter One: Genesis
GRACE

The dark night was filled with the gruesome soundtrack of war as the chaos unfolded around me. Gunfire, explosions, and bone – shattering screams of terror and agony ripped through the air. Mesmerising tongues of fire engulfed a building next to me, the heat of the flames searing into my skin and melting my thoughts. War cascaded through the camp, tearing apart buildings and people alike as I tried to figure out my next move.

A mixture of terror, adrenaline, and gut-twisting anxiety coursed through me as a sudden shadow streaking toward me caught my attention. I'd barely turned my head to look before I recognised who it was, and the despair hardly had a chance to sink in before his body collided roughly with my own. The wind was knocked from my lungs. I hadn't seen him for days, and I was certainty not excited to see him now as he wrestled against me on the ground.

My last remaining family member.

My brother.

Jonah.

'You filthy traitor!' he spat angrily as he struggled to pin me down.

His arms fought to secure mine as I shoved at his chest to try and throw him off me. I was at a significant disadvantage beneath his weight, but I never stopped moving for a second. My legs thrashed as I tried to kick him off, but it didn't work.

'Get off me!' I hissed angrily. Frustration ripped through me as he gripped my shoulders and pulled me off the ground only to slam me back into the dirt. Air rushed past my lips as again my breath was knocked from me. I managed to free one of my fists long enough to swing it upward, connecting my knuckles to his jaw. The hit was strong enough only to cause him to pause his attack.

'You betrayed us,' he seethed, glaring down at me with bulging eyes. His actions were strong and urgent, giving no thought to potentially hurting me; on the contrary, that was his goal.

'No, I didn't!' I yelled back.

But that was a lie.

I had betrayed them.

All this flashed through my head in less than a second as I struggled against him. He gripped my wrists tightly, wrenching them to the side as he tried to pin them down. I twisted beneath him, making it difficult for him to control me.

Panic flashed through me as I saw him pull back and rip a knife from his belt. The long, sharp blade glinted in the light of the fire burning next to us as he hovered over me. Heavy pants escaped both of our bodies as I pushed against his chest, trying to create more space between us, but he was too strong.

'Jonah, don't—'

'You chose your side, Grace. Now you can die with the rest of them.'

'No—'

I huffed out in frustration as I exerted all of my strength.

My arms shook with the effort of pushing him off, as his blade inched closer and closer by the second. Sweat dripped from his brow to land on my skin, his teeth gritted in determination just as mine were.

This was it.

My own brother was going to kill me.

I could feel the point of the knife on my chest now, directly over my heart. The sharp edge had just started to break the skin when I remembered being in such a position before, only under much different circumstances. Hayden's face flashed through my mind as he hovered over me, pinning me down in the soft brush of the forest as he taunted me. I remembered the way he'd thrown me off him with his hips. I was in a similarly vulnerable position now.

Without further hesitation, I summoned every ounce of strength I possessed to use my legs as leverage. Jonah had been so focused on guiding his knife that he momentarily forgot about the lower halves of our bodies. In a split second, his body rolled to the side into the dirt, freeing me from his weight long enough to roll away.

'You little—' he seethed, scrambling on the ground.

I jumped to my feet. Without thinking, I took a deep breath and cocked my leg back before swinging it forward with all my strength. The heavy part of my boot collided with his jaw, jerking his entire head to the side before his body followed, going slacken in the dirt – clearly unconscious from the blow to the face. His chest rose and fell still, telling me he was alive.

'Arsehole,' I muttered. I couldn't resist aiming one more kick at his side, swinging my foot just as hard at his ribs.

I should have taken his knife and plunged it into his chest as he'd tried to do to me, but I couldn't. I couldn't kill my own brother.

I did, however, duck to take the knife from his hand as well as the two guns he had stowed in his belt. Air ripped through my lungs as I panted heavily, exhausted but determined to find Hayden. My hands moved quickly to make sure both guns were loaded, slamming the magazines back into the chamber of each. Soft metallic clicks told me they were both ready to use. I kept one in my hand before storing the other behind my waist, keeping the knife in my other hand.

With that, I cast one last derisive look at my brother's prone body before spiriting into the chaos. More than one building was fully engulfed in flames, and more than a few bodies had already fallen to litter the pathway. I didn't pause long enough to see who they were, terrified I'd recognise someone I cared about.

It seemed that everywhere I looked, shadows darted through the night. Friends, foes, it was impossible to tell. Gunshots rang out so frequently that it was hard to determine which direction they came from, much less who was shooting at who.

My feet carried me on, searching for one face amongst the pandemonium: Hayden. Out of the corner of my eye, two shadows collided before fists started to fly. A few punches were struck before a sickening wet *thunk* sounded – the sound of a knife finding its target. One shadow stilled on the ground as the other stood, rising from their position before darting off again.

'Hayden!' I shouted, unable to resist any longer. I needed to find him before my heart hammered its way out of my chest.

'*Hayden!*'

Panic ripped through me as I moved toward the largest fire I could see. If Hayden was anywhere, he'd be in the thick of it all to defend those he cared about. I was about to round the last corner that would lead me into the fray when I saw two more shadows emerge from between some huts.

One was much smaller than the others, and it darted hastily from the gap in the buildings. The reason for the haste became clear as a much larger, more menacing shadow emerged immediately after. The larger shadow gained on the smaller one, closing the distance quickly. The larger person was just about to jump on the smaller one when the fire illuminated their faces, sending a wave of horror through me.

Jett.

The second face was someone I recognised from Greystone but didn't know by name. He was in his early thirties, bloodlust clear in his eyes as he chased after Jett.

The man launched himself into the air, about to tackle him to the ground, at the same time I aimed my gun in his direction. Without pausing, I fired, sending my bullet rocketing their way. As if attached to a rope, the man's body jerked to the side as the bullet sunk into his skull. As he fell, his body had enough momentum to allow it to crash into Jett and trip him.

A shrill scream of panic left Jett's lips as he fell to the ground, beneath the corpse. Jett twisted jerkily beneath him, confusion and terror clear in his eyes as he took in the wide, blank stare that met his.

'Jett!' I shouted, rushing forward. He squirmed fearfully, unable to free himself. As soon as I reached them, I squatted down to shove the man off enough for him to wiggle out. The man's body toppled into the dirt as Jett stood shakily, tears pouring down his cheeks. I hardly had time to straighten up before he launched himself into my chest, hugging me tightly as he sobbed uncontrollably.

'You shouldn't be here,' I managed to say. I had never been in such a frenzied situation before; if it was so unsettling for me, I didn't want to know what effect it would have on naïve, innocent Jett.

He didn't respond as he hugged me tightly. As much as I wanted to be able to comfort him, I couldn't. I could feel time slipping away, every second I wasn't with Hayden adding to my alarm. My eyes scanned the area around us, searching for enemies or allies in need, but for the moment, we were alone.

'Come on, Jett, come with me,' I said quickly. Impatience and anxiety had taken over, hastening my actions. I separated myself from him and stuffed the knife into my pocket before gripping his hand in my own. With one final hasty look around, I turned back from the madness to lead him away.

My eyes landed on a small hut, bordered on either side by a few others of similar size. I practically dragged a still sobbing Jett behind me. My gaze never stopped scanning for danger as we approached, but I still saw nothing as we reached the door. Without hesitating, I threw my shoulder into it to force it open.

A terrified squeak greeted me as I burst through the door, though it was too dark to see anyone.

'Please don't kill us,' a small voice said, from the corner of the room. I squinted into the darkness, my eyes finally adjusting to make out two little girls pressed into the corner. I had never seen them before but it was easy to assume they were members of Blackwing just trying to stay out of the fray.

'I'm not going to kill you,' I said as calmly as I could. 'I'm on your side.'

The smaller of the two, who looked to be around four or

five, peered up at me with wide eyes. The older one, maybe nine or ten, looked up in fear before I saw her gaze shift to Jett in surprise. He'd managed to stop crying now but still had tears streaked down his face as he stood next to me.

'Jett?' the older girl asked.

'Hi, Rainey,' he murmured quietly, as if embarrassed all of a sudden.

'Jett, you know these girls?' I asked hurriedly, desperate to get back outside and find Hayden.

'Yes,' he answered. I hunched down so our eyes were level, locking my gaze on his.

'You're brave, right, Jett?'

'Yes, I— I'm brave,' he stammered.

'I know you are,' I told him. 'Listen to me closely, okay?'

He nodded in determination, his features hardening as he did so.

'I need you to protect them, all right? You stay here with them until this is over and shoot anyone who comes through that door that you don't know.'

His eyes widened as he gulped harshly. I felt jittery and anxious as I wasted time here with him.

'Can you do that?'

'Yes,' he said tightly. He took a deep breath and nodded before speaking again. 'Yes, Grace, I can do that.'

'Good, I know you can,' I said, shooting him a quick, tense smile. 'Here, take this gun. Remember what I said about shooting? Two eyes for moving, one for still?'

'I remember.'

'I have to go, but you can do this. Someone will come find you when this is over. Keep them safe, Jett.'

'I will, Grace, I will!' he said firmly. He puffed his thin chest out as he tried to appear brave. A small sense of pride washed over me as I nodded encouragingly at him. With that, I turned back toward the door. I had just reached it when I heard him speak again.

'Grace, you're going to find Hayden, right?'

'Yes, Jett. I'll find him,' I promised. I'd just slipped outside, the door nearly closed, when I heard Jett speaking softly to the two girls.

'Don't worry, I'll protect you.'

My stomach clenched tightly at his words, desperately hoping they were true. I closed the door behind me and started running again. I had a knife and a gun with a single round. I sprinted back toward the centre of things, kicking the dirt with each step.

All around me, fights had broken out. Fists flew, knives slashed, guns fired, and bodies fell. So many bodies, more than I could count, were piling up as I darted through camp. I ignored the wave of nausea that rolled through me and tried not to think about how many lives were being lost at this exact moment.

Finally I rounded the final corner, and no amount of mental preparation could have prepared me for what I saw. Amongst the brawling people, raging fires, lifeless bodies, and endless carnage, stood a horrifically shocking centrepiece. The eight-storey tower, the pride of Blackwing, was burning from the ground up.

Fear gripped my heart as I remembered exactly where Hayden had gone before he left me: the tower. It was nearly impossible to see through the thick, choking smoke that smothered the night air. Keeping my gun and knife in hand, I darted forward again, both terrified and hopeful that I would find Hayden.

A sudden flash of movement to my left appeared as someone jabbed a knife at me while I ran by, but the blow was stilled as another body tackled the first to the ground.

'Oh no you don't!' shouted a familiar voice. My eyes darted toward the wrestling pair, sending a shock of recognition through me as I saw Kit on top of a man from Greystone. I hardly had time to be afraid for him before he landed two powerful blows across the man's face, followed quickly by a flash of his knife across his throat. Instantly, bright red blood flooded from his neck.

Just like that, Kit had killed him.

'What are you waiting for, help him!' Kit shouted, as I realised I was gaping at him. He threw his hand towards the tower. As quickly as he'd arrived, however, he was gone, leaving the lifeless corpse to sprint off toward another enemy.

From this new position, I could just make out a shadow a few stories up, hunched over as he lugged something behind him. He was about halfway down the tower, above at least two stories of flames. The curve of his back and the small halo of hair was all it took for me to identify him: Hayden.

It was difficult to see what he was doing, but there was no ignoring the fact that the closer he got to the ground, the closer he got to the inferno.

'Hayden!' I shouted. He didn't seem to hear me, however, as he continued to drag whatever he had behind him down the stairs. My heart thumped painfully against my ribs. A scream of agony cut through the air, accenting my fear. This wasn't fear for myself, however: this was fear for him. How was he supposed to get down?

'Hayden!' I shouted again. His head jerked towards me as he caught the sound, and he leaned over the rail to squint down at me. It was then that I saw he had his shirt tugged up over his nose in an attempt to block the choking smoke.

'Grace!' he called back in surprise. 'Get out of here!'

'No!' I yelled back. Every second he wasted was a second the flames grew fiercer.

'You have to jump, now before it gets too high!'

Why hadn't he jumped in the first place? Much to my horror, he retreated over the railing, cutting himself completely from my view.

'I can't,' he grunted. It was difficult to hear him over the roar of the flames and the sounds of war raging on around me. While most of the gunfire seemed to have transitioned to hand-to-hand combat, yells, screams, and the occasional burst of flames continued.

'*Why not?!*' I demanded, actually stamping my foot in the ground in frustration.

He didn't answer, sending a wave of fear washing over me.

'Hayden!'

My eyes scanned the ground, searching for something to act as a cushion. All I could see was dirt, a few patches of grass, and most horrifically, the occasional body. A heavy grunt and a loud thud jerked my attention back up the tower, where I breathed a sigh of relief as I saw Hayden once again.

The reason for his slow descent was suddenly clear as I saw him drag two heavy bundles along after him.

No, not bundles.

Bodies.

I couldn't identify who they were, but I had a strong suspicion about one. But if Hayden was risking his own life to lug that worthless piece of crap down the tower, I was going to be furious. Barrow did not deserve to live.

'Hayden, leave them! You have to jump now or none of you will make it!'

I sounded cold, heartless, but I didn't care. All that mattered was getting Hayden out alive.

'*No*,' he hissed angrily, as if frustrated by the whole situation. He was only one storey above the flames now, three above the ground. I huffed out in angry exasperation as he leaned over the side again to inspect the ground. His skin was streaked with black from the rising smoke all around him, and his T-shirt had fallen away, leaving him exposed. A deep cough rumbled from his chest as he squinted through the smoke.

'Grace, see that hay bale over there?' he called, pointing between two of the nearest huts. I jerked around and squinted through the darkness to see what he was indicating.

'Yes, got it,' I said, reading his mind as I sprinted away. I leaped over a fallen body, without looking. The bale was nearly as tall as I was and incredibly heavy. Luckily, it was round, so I positioned myself behind it and threw my shoulder into it to try and roll it.

My feet dug into the ground as I shoved again, letting out a yell of frustration before I finally managed to dislodge it from where it had settled. Once I got it moving, it was much easier, and I continued to throw my shoulder into it as I rolled it toward the base of the tower.

I met resistance when the bale collided with a lump. I cringed as I realised it was probably a body and tried to wipe the thought from my mind. Sure enough, when the bale finally moved, a body was revealed beneath it. Making sure to avoid stepping on it, I manoeuvred around it before finally reaching the base of the tower.

Burning flames heated the air as I stood mere feet away, whipping my knife from my pocket to slash the ties that held the bale together. Instantly, the hay lost its form and collapsed into a pile of twigs, aided by my fervent pushing and shoving. As soon as I had it spread, I jumped back and looked up at Hayden.

I was relieved to see him watching me, though he disappeared quickly as he ducked down once again. Every second that ticked by seemed like an icepick hammering at my heart despite the overwhelming heat. Finally, a limp arm emerged over the railing as I heard a loud grunt from Hayden. The arm was followed by a torso and a leg. Hayden leaned over, barely managing to lift them over the railing.

'Okay, Grace, move her as soon as she's down,' he called.

'Got it!'

He didn't hesitate any longer before shoving the unconscious body over the side, careful to ensure she cleared the flames below. I watched in awe as her body soared through the air, blonde hair fanning out around her as if she were in slow motion. In a split second, she landed with a thud in the pile of hay. I cringed before rushing forward.

After reaching down to grab her arms and pull, I saw who it was. Her eyes were closed and her skin was covered in black smudges, but her chest rose and fell slowly as she drew life sustaining breath: Maisie.

Without hesitation, I dragged her away from the fire, leaving her to settle in the grass before returning to my position.

'Hayden, hurry,' I urged, bouncing on my feet. A quick glance around told me that everyone was thankfully too busy fighting to notice my work at the base of the tower.

There was no warning as a second body fell, the thud much louder this time. My face contorted in disgust: as I suspected, Barrow lay in the hay, very much alive and very much unworthy of Hayden saving his life. Despite my reluctance, I gripped his ankles and tugged as hard as I could, grunting loudly as I yanked his heavy body out of the

374

way. I managed to set him next to Maisie before I carelessly dropped his legs and darted back to the tower.

'Hayden, come on,' I muttered anxiously under my breath. My hands shook by my sides as he climbed carefully over the railing. Deep coughs ripped from his throat as he spluttered against the choking smoke. I let out a shout of panic as his body swooped forward, his eyes flickering closed for a half a second before he snapped out of it, jerking his body back upright.

It looked like he was seconds away from passing out as the smoke closed in around him.

'Jump, Hayden! Jump!'

But his eyes drifted shut again, the feeble cough he gave causing his chest to cave in as his body leaned dangerously far over the side.

'Hayden!'

My shrill attempt to snap him out of it didn't work. I watched in frozen horror as gravity took over, pulling his body down over the edge. His limbs flew out limply and the breeze pushed his hair back, his body twisting uncontrollably. The space between him and the ground disappeared as he landed with a heavy thud, his back taking most of the fall when he landed in the thinning pile of hay.

'Hayden,' I breathed as I jerked forward, nearly tripping myself as I flung my body down into the hay next to him.

His arms were thrown out by his sides, and his legs were bent somewhat awkwardly. I collapsed beside him and took his face desperately in my hands. A thin line of blood trickled from his lips and trailed down his neck.

'Hayden, wake up, please wake up,' I begged. Tears pricked at the back of my eyes but I fought to fight them off. I felt like I was going to be sick. 'Come on, please . . .'

He didn't respond. I hovered over him, unsure of what

to do. The skin on his throat was dirty and hot as I pressed the pads of two fingers to it, feeling for a pulse. Panic ripped through me as I felt nothing, but was calmed when I shifted them and felt a faint thudding beneath my touch.

He was alive.

It was only then that I noticed the faint, weak breaths escaping his lips. A gasp of relief so loud ripped through me that I nearly collapsed. He was alive. Hayden was alive.

It was as if that realisation brought everything back at once: the blistering heat of the fire, the raging sound of it as it consumed everything in its path. Sound, too, as I heard the endless onslaught of bullets, the dull thuds of bodies beating others, the agonising shouts as people died around me. It all closed in on me as I clung to Hayden's limp body.

Everywhere I looked, I saw people falling. One shadow killed another, sending them sprawling into the dirt. A mysterious bullet connected with a target, wiping away the tension and life as fast as the bullet itself. A few yards away, a body burned before me, fermenting the air with the sick smell of singed flesh.

War was everywhere, invading my senses and taking over my every thought. There was nothing I could do except protect Hayden. Darkness overtook me as I closed my eyes. My arms roped around his neck as I leaned over him, shielding him from the desolation of man and their twisted capabilities.

Suddenly, the loudest sound rocked me to my very bones. There was a flash of light so bright that it burned through my closed eyelids, followed quickly by a bang so loud I thought my eardrums had been shredded. Next came a burst of scalding heat.

That was it.

Light.
Fire.
Heat.
Darkness.

Thirty million readers worldwide.

Don't miss out – *Revolution* is available to order now.